Secrets of the Enemy

by

Debbie G. Brownfield

Acknowledgments

I owe a great deal to those who have believed in me such as my family, colleagues at the schools where I've taught, and friends who have put up with my inquisitive and often too forthright nature (especially here in the South!).

Thank you for patiently listening to me and answering some of the dumbest questions so I could get a grasp of the material and a visual in my brain.

A special thank you to two men in my life who, while they were here, greatly impacted my life, believing in me even when I was a little girl: Henry Vierow and Wes Hamilton.

Thank you, too, to those who have served in high places and were willing to give me enough information to make my scenarios relatively realistic. You know who you are; I won't jeopardize your anonymity!

A special thank you to Skip VanDyke, Chip Googe, and the support personnel at SmartDraw for their work on the covers and help with the family trees.

But most of all, I want to thank those who faithfully serve as the first defenders of our freedoms. Some are janitors, some are firefighters and security guards, and some have jobs that are so dangerous, they don't dare establish any kind of "normal" life. You have this American's heartfelt gratitude.

The Merrill Family

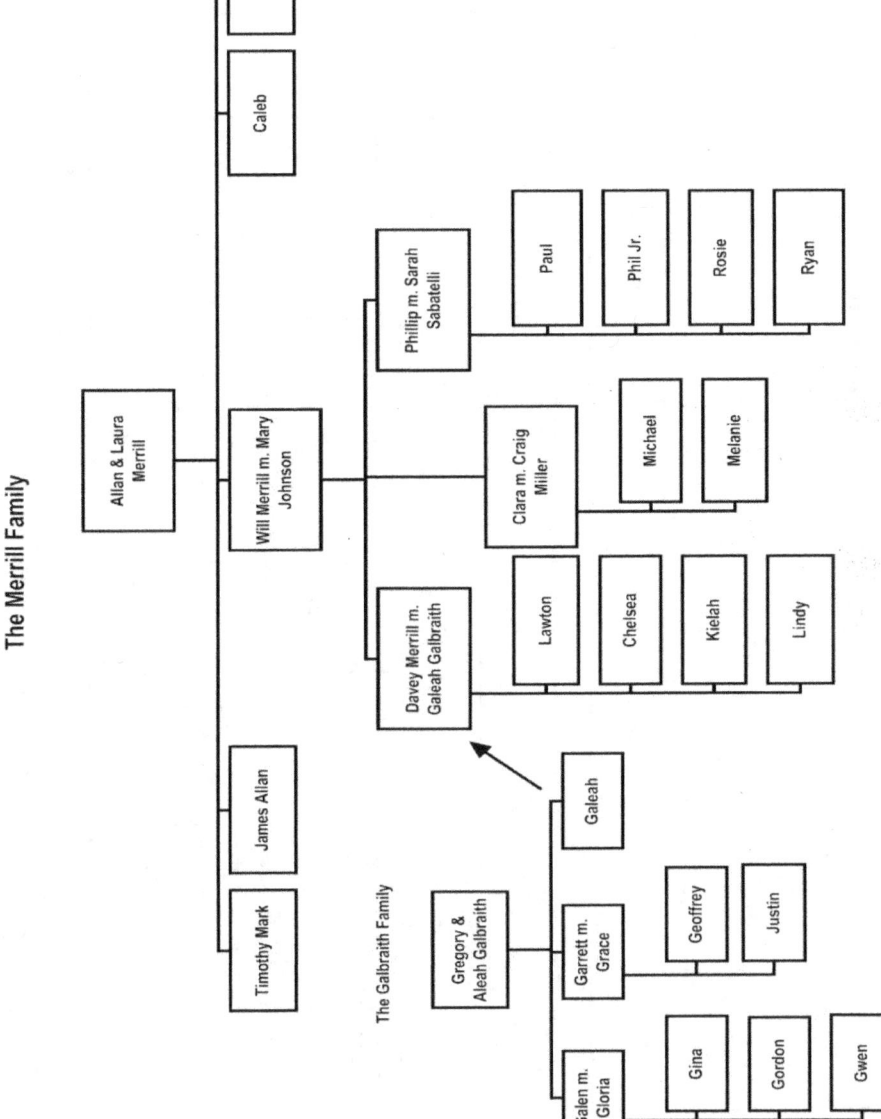

The McKinnon Family, Part 1

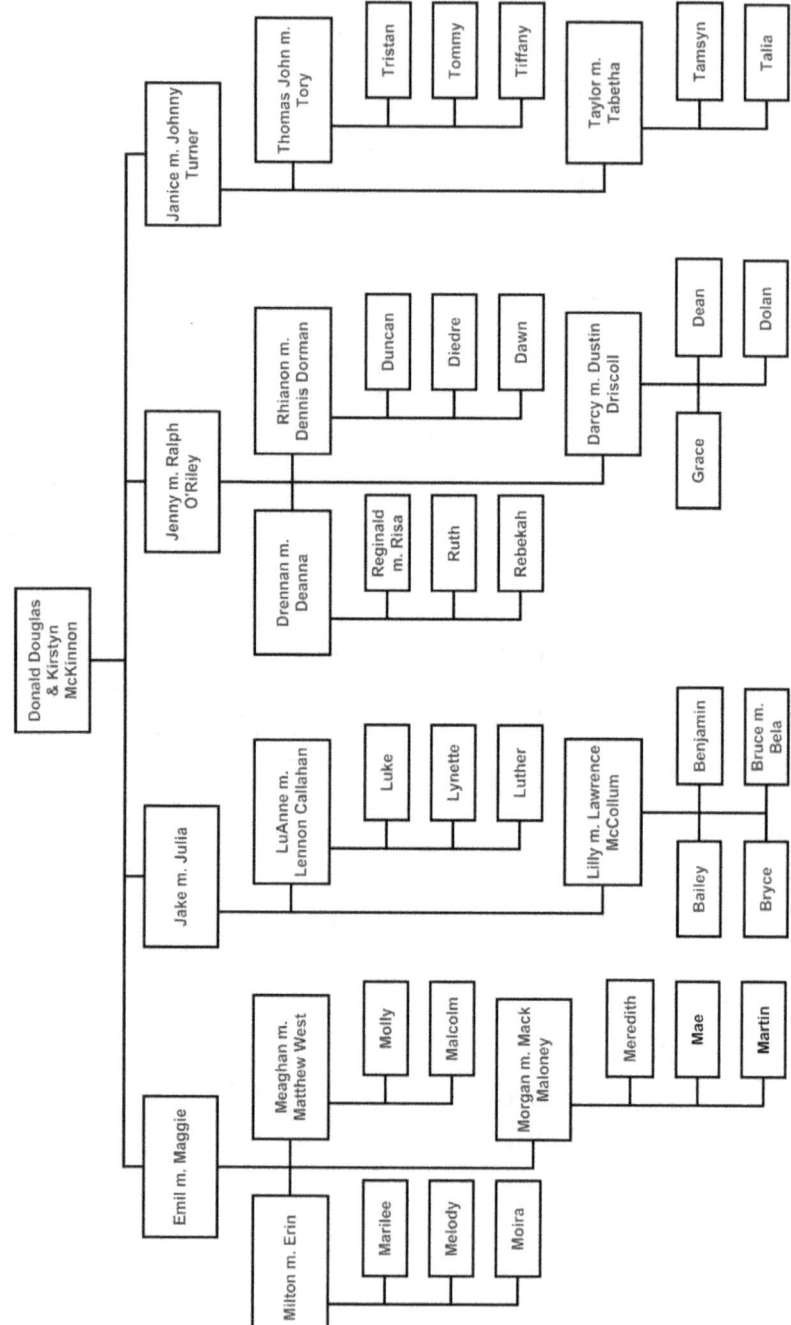

The McKinnon Family, Part 2

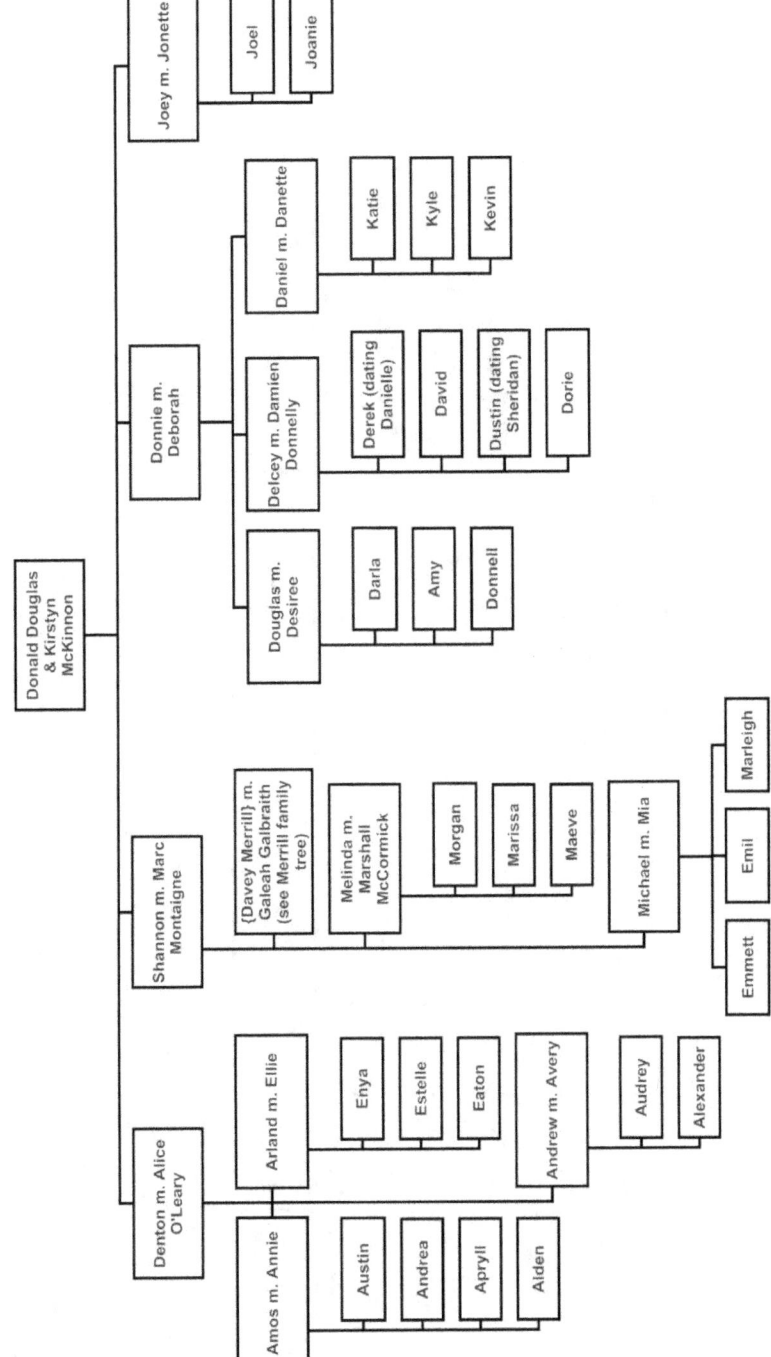

The Peters-Templeton Family

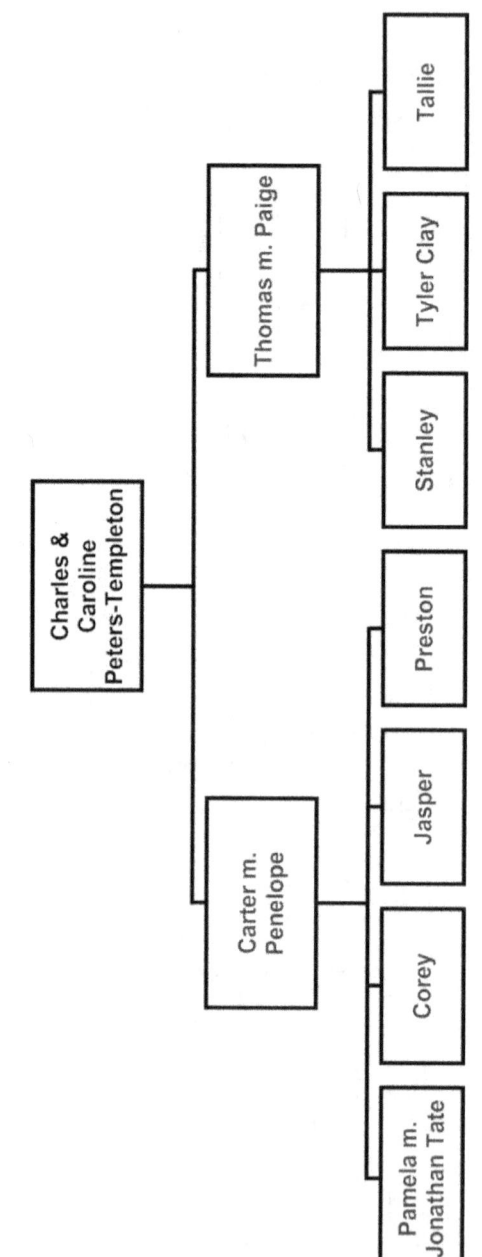

The Montaigne Family

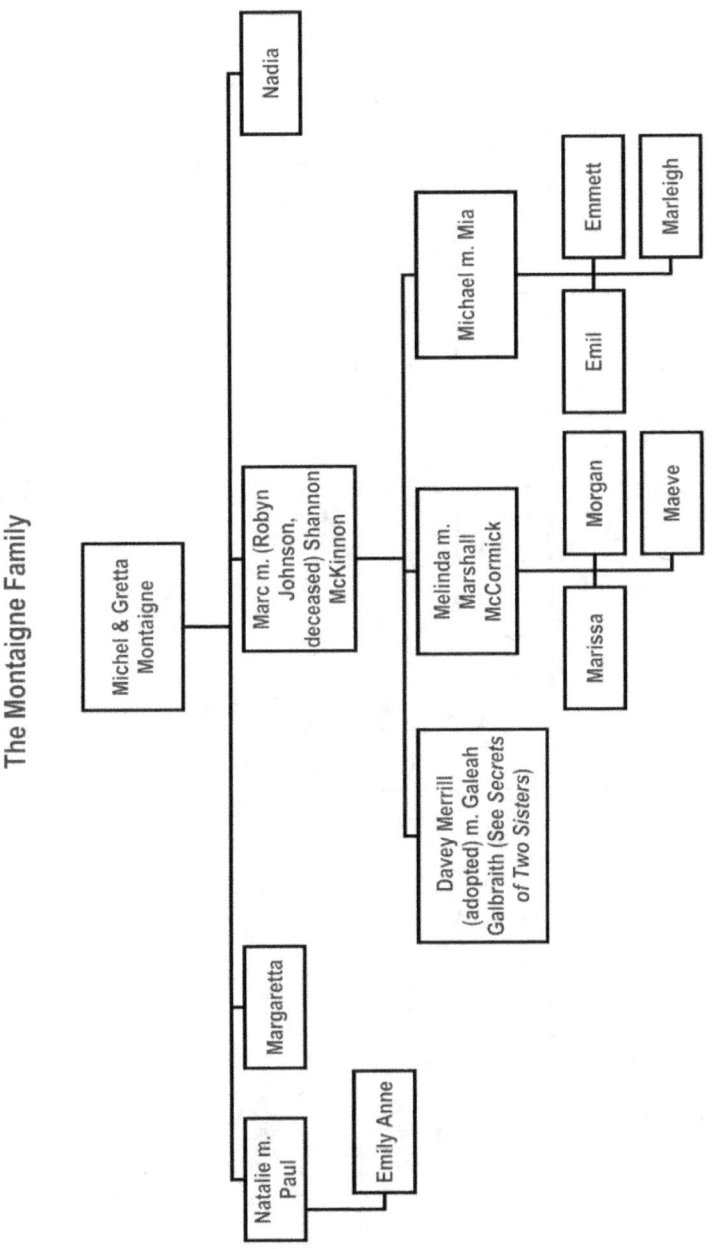

The Dumotte Family

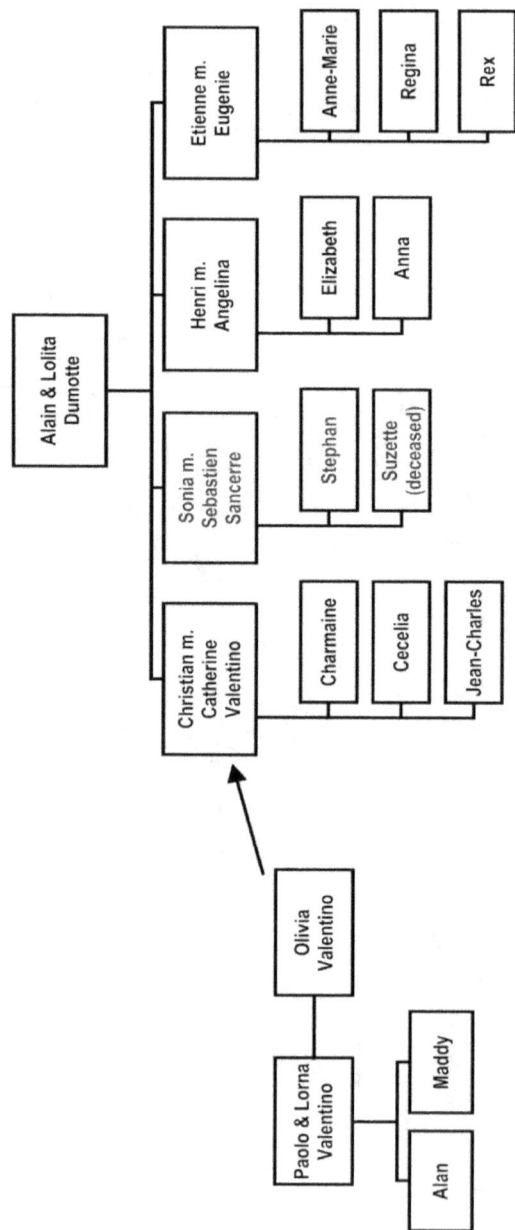

Characters to Remember
(all others are superfluous!)

Chelsea Merrill, first female Presidential aide
        Lanie, good friend of Chelsea's and engaged to
           Chelsea's brother, Lawton

Jasper Peters-Templeton, Secret Service agent
        Tillot Thomason, Jasper's boss
        Frank, older Secret Service agent, semi-retired

Charm Dumotte, pop/rock star
        Guy Brown, Charm's agent
        Colin Criswell, Charm's stage manager
        Sandy Daniels, Charm's dresser and best friend
        Jonette O'Bailey, Charm's makeup/hair artist
        Megan Keenan, Charm's electric guitarist and alto
        Michael Shannon, Charm's keyboardist and tenor
        Kelly Kennedy, Charm's bass guitarist and singer
        Max, Charm's bus driver
        Geveon, Charm's body guard

Donnell McKinnon, Interpol agent assigned to Charm
        Natalie, next in command to Donnell, walking
           encyclopedic brain of the team
        Tiffany, angelic-looking yet lethal karate expert
        Gregor, explosive expert, known for strength and
           endurance
        Seamus, extremely observant of details
        Marcus, computer/electronic expert

See family charts for other characters who are family members of the
four main characters.

Greenville, South Carolina, USA
May 18th

Chapter One

Jasper Templeton's nerves buzzed with excitement. This was his first official assignment as security detail for the President of the United States of America. For three years, he had directed traffic at official functions, checked identification, and memorized information about anyone who would come in contact with the President. For the last twelve months, he had been working at the Greenville, South Carolina field office.

His job today was very simple: make sure the visiting dignitaries had proper seating.

As easy as it sounded, sweeping the chairs for possible bugs, bombs, and other devices had been painstaking and tedious work. The extras were stacked neatly at the side of the stadium field where they had remained under his watchful eye after the sweep had been completed.

He glanced around the field, noting with satisfaction the live video feeds of the crowd on monitors that had been set up where the football team usually sat, the medical team at the far end, the secret service in uniform around the perimeter of the stadium, and those out of uniform in the stands. They even had several amongst the graduates in full regalia!

And he'd had a direct hand in the planning of all the details. The last twelve months had been a whirlwind of activity and preparation, but he'd learned where, how and why to position sharpshooters and other "invisible" personnel, as well as how to strategically place chairs, cameras, and even ferns and flowers.

The band played a rousing medley from *Pirates of the Caribbean* as the crowds in the stadium fanned themselves in the stifling heat of a late May, southern afternoon. The green and gold college banners scintillated in the breeze that occasionally wafted across the appreciative observers with a cooling hand.

*****

Another observer was also grateful for the breeze. He was in the stands with his "step-sister," his blonde hair dyed brown, facial prosthetics around the nose distorting his profile, and bushy, false eyebrows making his eyes recede further into his face. He was dressed to blend with the crowd in a white golf shirt and khaki Dockers. This was simply an observation mission, and behind the darkly tinted glasses, his keen, blue eyes were aware of every detail of security personnel movements.

In a few hours, President Bell would give his final commencement address as President. Next May, another man or woman would have the title of President, and other secret service agents would have the nerve-wracking honor of guarding the President with their lives.

The observer's orders were to find any possible breaches, no matter how small, and report these to headquarters. President Bell still had six months in office with important legislation pending, and an assassination would not only kill the legislation, but it would put the government in disarray, allowing their men to win the coming elections easily.

*****

Chelsea Merrill waited beside the President himself for the helicopter, Marine One, to land. Three landing locations had been "advertised," but who knew for sure where the chopper would really land, she thought wryly.

Her hard work in grad school had given her the polish and panache she'd needed to apply for the job of Presidential aide though sometimes she did little more than secretarial work. Her facile use of words, her research capabilities, and her keen and intuitive grasp of situations, however, had earned her the respect of her colleagues, and she had more than earned her status as the first female to ever have the job of an aide.

Now here she was back in South Carolina nearly two years after receiving her diploma as a graduate student from the prestigious Clemson University.

Pulling a small compact from a pocket, she quickly checked her hair and makeup. She had the golden, blonde hair of her grandpa Will, her father's intelligence, and her mother's merry brown eyes. Although she wasn't overly concerned with her looks, when one traveled with the entourage of the President of the United States, one must keep a tidy appearance.

Marine One landed, and in seconds President Bell and his wife were being placed in the limo with his doctor and nurse while Chelsea took a seat in the second limo with the First Lady's assistant and another secret service agent.

Quickly, she checked the attaché she carried with several bottles of hand sanitizer, pens, pictures, Presidential stationery as well as the morning and noon reports from the Chief of Staff, a copy of the itinerary, and a secured Blackberry with weather and both national and international news playing in a continual live feed. All was in order and ready for use.

Peering at the beautifully manicured garden outside the limo, Chelsea wondered if she should dare roll down the window an inch to inhale the heady, sensual perfume of the jasmine she could see beyond the low hedge. Chelsea grew homesick thinking about the side porch back home in Summerville with the swing that was afforded privacy with a screen of jasmine and honeysuckle.

While she enjoyed her job, she returned home far too seldom, and she was beginning to question her decision to leave her position and Washington D.C. at the end of President Bell's term in office when she could have taken a job with one of the presidential hopefuls.

The signal to roll interrupted her thoughts, and she reviewed the President's speech in her mind. It was an easy one that he had given as a new governor; she would only need to tweak it or to retype it should the necessity arise, and she had already discovered a connection to the university that the President would use to make his speech more personal.

Now the nerves of all security personnel were buzzing, giving them the edge they needed to do a superb job. It would take a very skilled terrorist to even point a gun at the President with all the people assigned to guard him.

*****

The observer in the stands scanned the stadium and surrounding area. The stadium was under such watchful care. Marksmen were stationed in the hills surrounding the area with their high-powered Steyr SSG 69 guns, and he knew the entire stadium, field, and field house had been carefully screened.

His own stolen dossier, he knew, had received much scrutiny. Yet here he was at this gathering, an American graduation to find yet another crack in their security. And he would find it; he knew he would. He continued his survey of the stadium. Security was rather strict.

However, he noted the patch of woods to the right. His keen mind reviewed his arsenal of bombs, and he realized that although a ground bomb might be detected, bombs placed in the trees might not. Tricky, but he enjoyed a challenge. He grinned in silent amusement.

A lady behind him wondered aloud where the President would enter the stadium. She thought he was already there, but hidden under the stands opposite the crowd which had been cleared and remained empty of occupants. He was careful not to betray his sardonic amusement; the public was so gullible.

Her son declared that the President would arrive by helicopter and land right on the field. Enough space existed, but again, the observer thought it would be too easy for an attack to take place.

Minutes later the Presidential helicopter flew overhead, circling the field. Oohs and aahs erupted from the stands. The man behind the observer was disappointed when the chopper didn't land where he had predicted.

*****

Chelsea's limo was stationed before the one the President and his wife occupied. In mere seconds from their arrival by helicopter, they were moving smoothly forward. The secret service agents certainly had their timing down.

The phone beside her buzzed softly. She picked it up.

"Chelsea?" the President inquired.

"Yes, Sir," she answered.

"I just wanted to thank you for the research you did and the changes you made to this speech. You certainly did your homework relating the officer who was killed in the line of duty during World War II to the name of the university. Good job!"

"Thank you, Sir. You know I enjoy that kind of research."

"Don't your parents live around this part of the South?"

"Yes, Sir, they live in Summerville about three hours south of here." When you talked to a President who had traveled around the entire world several times, a three-hour drive was close.

"Why don't I make some arrangements with Tillot to send you home for a few days?"

"That would be great!"

"I'll have him talk to you after the speech is over. Wish me luck on a perfect delivery."

"Good luck, Sir, and thank you!"

Chelsea sat back in the soft, cushioned seat. Tillot Thomason, head of Security detail, would not be happy and would likely fuss like a mother hen, but home! Wouldn't Mom be surprised?! Her homesickness abated, and she sent prayers of thankfulness heavenward.

*****

The observer watched the Presidential limo arrive behind the stadium. The fifteen hundred or so graduates milled in the stands across the field. They had all had to go through security clearance as well.

As he watched, they began lining up behind the fence that clearly separated the participants from the staged area set up on the field. He wished he could use the small, but powerful binoculars he always carried, but he didn't want to attract attention to himself.

Wait. Now he could see the President, surrounded by Secret Service, separating from the rest of the crowd and heading for the building to the left. That made sense. The rooftop of the building was crawling with Secret Service. Two were visible, but he had detected two others all dressed in black, even their faces.

The processional music began, and the faculty filed to their places. He noticed with amusement the faculty members who wore t-shirts in dissent instead of the long, pompous gowns and hoods that declared their status. His accomplices would certainly obtain video footage and check each dissenter thoroughly for a possible foothold of future access to the President.

Now the graduates were moving into place, but his focus was on the building to the left. As the last few graduates straggled to their seats, the president of the college, dressed in a black hood and gown edged with the brilliant emerald and gold colors of the college, emerged from the building followed by President Bell in a black hood and robe lined with royal blue. Several other people followed the President. The crowd erupted in cheers, whistles, and calls although some stood stonily silent.

The observer clapped with not an ounce of genuine sentiment. He was allowed to display approval, even warmth for the enemy. If it resulted in gaining access, he would receive his rewards in another place.

*****

The speaking began, and Jasper breathed out a small sigh of relief. He had seated the governor of the state and his wife, several state senators and their families, the President's wife, a few members of his entourage, the chorale members who had been standing on risers behind the orchestra, and the college president's family and assorted friends. He'd had enough chairs.

His gaze slid to the last member of the President's staff he had seated, wondering who she was. She looked young like him, but she was oblivious enough to the pageantry around her to give him the distinct impression that she had seen much of this before. He liked the simple style of her blond hair and her tailored business skirt and jacket in an exquisite baby blue. She looked business-like yet very feminine at the same time.

*****

Chelsea waited impatiently for the President to begin speaking although she was polite enough to be able to make small talk with First Lady, Anne MacKinsey Bell on one side of her and the First Lady's aide on the other side. She really was happy for the graduates, but, technically speaking, they were rivals of her alma mater, Clemson, and she wanted this last commencement address to go smoothly. Then there was the promised visit home. Oh joy!

She was idly watching the new security detail who had seated her. He was rather cute with his curly, dark blonde hair. He had an indolent air about him, yet she knew he must be sharp and quick-witted or he wouldn't have been hired. Just then she saw him tense slightly.

Jasper was listening to the security frequency that came through the sunglasses he wore. As the sun waned and the heat and glare grew less intense, he had pushed them to the top of his head. Either way, they were programmed to be close enough to the ear for sound to be transmitted, and the lens as well as the other earpiece could pick up speech.

Someone had spotted a known enemy in the stands. Female. Blonde. Another had been spotted as well. Male. Dark hair.

*****

The observer grew uneasy. The President was speaking now, and everything seemed to be fine. Yet every secret service agent had suddenly stiffened, gone on alert. He had already planned a quick exit. He knew how to avoid camera coverage, slip through crowds, change crucial parts of his facial features.

He waited, knowing that any movement during the speech would bring extra scrutiny his way. The attention seemed to be in his section as well as higher up, over his right shoulder. He signaled his companion, his "step-sister," that he would be leaving.

She responded with a slight shrug of her shoulder. She knew she would be on her own. She was merely another operative, and she knew what was expected of her, what to do.

The President's speech was ending. The crowd stood to applaud when a resounding boom behind the stadium occurred. Screams erupted, the observer's companion sagged, and one look at her face told him she was dead.

He ducked behind the person in front of him and disappeared from sight. He was not seen again nor caught on any subsequent video footage to the bafflement of the men who were examining the video tapes less than an hour later.

Two other observers, seated on opposite sides of the stadium, attracted no attention at all until later. One was a small, wiry, dark-haired man. He watched grimly as his double agent slumped in her seat. He could only hope the "package" would get into the proper hands. He would have to send "Madame Orr" on yet another dangerous mission when her strongly worded wish was to retire from the spying business.

The other observer was an elegantly dressed older woman with carefully coiffed blonde hair, and enough white gold and diamonds to finance a small business for the requisite three years.

London, England
May 18th

Chapter Two

Half a world away in London, England, a frisson of awareness ran down Donnell McKinnon's spine, but he straightened casually, noting all the entrances and exits on the top level of the Wembley Stadium where the evening concert was to take place. Although he noted nothing amiss, plenty of places existed where a potential terrorist could hide, he thought with concern.

Actually, he was dawdling. He knew very well that his presence was resented by the performers, and more specifically by Charm Dumotte. At five foot eight with a mane of rich auburn curls, she was an imposing figure on stage, and her energy created a tour de force that was compelling.

At least this assignment would be an enjoyable one. He loved music. His dad's family owned a bed and breakfast in Killarney, Ireland, and, with eight children in the original McKinnon family, they had often entertained guests in the evening with song and dance.

He had fond memories of Christmases spent at his grandparents' home with all of his aunts, uncles, and cousins. Inevitably, the fiddles, flutes, and pipes were brought out, and the music began.

Great Uncles Emil and Jake, who co-owned a large construction business, had deep bass voices and often had contests with their bodhrans. They worked together amicably enough, but place a drum in their hands, and they became fiercely competitive. Even if their beaters were hidden, they were superbly inventive in replacing them, using knives, forks, chicken bones, or even a hairbrush!

Great Uncle Joey, Uncle Thomas and his Dad, Douglas McKinnon, had rich baritone voices that they used to add achingly beautiful and intricate harmonies, giving a multi-layered sound to many of the songs, and, of course, Great Uncle Marc and Aunt Shannon were the international opera stars.

Nineteen of his fifty-three cousins were actively involved in music, either studying at conservatories all over Europe or making music in bands and orchestras. Some were dancing as well as singing. In fact, he couldn't think of one of his cousins who couldn't put some fancy footwork to music, and all of them had learned to play an instrument.

Granda', being a man of vision, had a larger hall built onto the dining area, and even in the winter when the tourists were sparse, the neighbors often dropped by evenings, keeping the place festive with music and cheer. Great Irish ballads, classical pieces such as the *Toreador Song*, and music from U2 could all be heard at the McKinnon's place.

But now he must turn his attention to this investigation. Like his father and grandfather, he had chosen a career as a special operative for Interpol; his work was with the terrorism division. He needed to check the back stage areas before Charm and the rest of the band members arrived.

About ready to move toward the exit, he noticed two things simultaneously: a very faint whiff of smoke reached his nostrils--he subconsciously blessed his ancestors for a keen sense of smell, and he also noticed a tiny glint near the base of the ground floor arena exit stage left.

Whipping a small but powerful pair of binoculars from his pocket, he examined the area stage left, but could discern nothing. He stood stock still, noticing the air currents in the arena. The faint yet acrid smell seemed to be coming from the ground floor dressing area stage right. Was the glint a ruse to throw him off track or was the smoke the real cover?

"Ops Two and Three check all exits. Ops Four and Five check the hallways stage left. Then meet me at the dressing rooms stage right. All other Ops stay on duty," he tersely radioed his assistants.

He was potentially sending them into danger, he thought as he raced down the stairs and toward stage right, but they were trained for such scenarios. He had chosen to check the dressing area himself because he considered the safety of the band, especially Charm, his primary duty.

The acrid smell was stronger now. With his gun drawn, he checked each small and large cubicle along the hall. As he neared the largest, Charm's dressing room, the pungent scent grew stronger. The slightly opened door revealed the mirror, which reflected nothing but a pale gray smoke.

Still, he entered cautiously, checking off the list in his brain of potential hazards. When those cleared, he reached the trash can that contained the fire. He hesitated, thinking that if he moved the can, he could detonate a bomb. Where had he seen that fire extinguisher?

Rushing to the hall, he grabbed the small but powerful device, raced for Charm's dressing room, pulling the pin as he went. The stream of chemicals did their job. Still cautious, he waited for the smoke to subside.

His operatives arrived and spread out, searching the rest of the dressing rooms minutely as they had been trained to do.

Donnell was the bomb expert. The smoke was entirely gone before he allowed himself to look in the can. At the bottom was a small incendiary device. Certain the danger was past, he picked up the can and carefully took it outside.

The pale afternoon sun of the cool, May day tried in vain to warm what it touched. Donnell was glad he was wearing the butter-soft, brown leather jacket his sisters, Darla and Amy, had bought for him this Christmas past.

Turning the waste can on its side, he slid the device onto the handkerchief in his palm. Puzzled, he examined it thoroughly. With the right amount of explosives, it could decimate a small bus, but obviously had been used for a much less explosive service. Was this warning? Mockery?

These devices were a dime a dozen, but perhaps the lab could detect some sort of signature of the creator.

Slipping the now-cool device in a plastic bag, he reentered the dressing area. His colleagues had kept a respectful distance. They had all worked together before and made an excellent team.

"Nothing in the other dressing rooms, Boss," Gregor reported. Seamus, noted for his careful search of crime scenes, nodded his head in corroboration.

Natalie, the walking encyclopedia and second in command of the Ops, and Tiffany, the karate expert, had scavenged for clues around the stage area and stationed security guards at the entrances of the dressing area. He would examine Charm's dressing room, clearing it before any of the performers were allowed there.

Right on cue, he heard Charm's voice in strident derision questioning the security guards.

He decided to confront her himself, sparing the guards grief and giving him a chance to gain some time for uninterrupted investigation of the area. He would have to work fast.

"Yes, Ms. Dumotte?" he questioned. None of his disdain of her supercilious air revealed itself in his calm, authoritative manner.

Charm drew a deep breath. The stupidity of having to be babysat by police because her manager and agent, Guy Brown, feared terrorist activity filled her with an acidic rancor that she knew would ooze from her voice in response to his infuriatingly cool tone. She tried, without much success to keep the scorn from her voice.

"I want to get to my dressing room, and this officious oaf won't let me pass," she accused in an icy voice.

"There's been an incident in your dressing room, and I need to clear the area before you can enter," Donnell replied firmly.

"What incident?" she asked in a testy voice.

"A fire was set in a trash can in your dressing room," he answered carefully.

"How do you know it was set? Someone could have left a cigarette butt burning or something like that. I don't believe anyone would deliberately set a fire in my room."

"An incendiary device was at the bottom of the waste can, powerful enough to detonate a bus and put a rather large hole in the ground, but I suppose you would just consider it a 'happening'?" he asked. He couldn't quite control the sarcasm in his voice. He wondered how Uncle Marc and Aunt Shannon handled the divas with whom they had to work.

"Let me see it," she demanded.

"See what? The hole? It didn't explode, thanks to the quick thinking of my team," he said, carefully quelling any hint of disdain. No need to let her know his major part.

"No, the incendiary device," she said.

He considered her briefly then nodded to the security guards. "Don't allow anyone else back," he said. He would escort her backstage himself.

Chapter Three

Once again, he entered the dressing room, scanning the area carefully and preceding Charm in case any miscreants had decided to make a surprise visit.

"Don't touch anything, please," he commanded. He pulled the plastic bag from a pocket. He hadn't wanted to leave it in the room and have it "magically" disappear, nor had he wanted to show the device to Charm with the curious guards observing. In fact, he got the distinct feeling that whoever had planted the device was still in the vicinity.

Inside the plastic bag was a blasting cap with some wires protruding from one end. Hardly enough to worry over, thought Charm, yet her eyes narrowed before she shrugged her shoulder.

"It looks harmless enough to me," she said icily.

But Donnell had caught the narrowing of her eyes before she spoke. She's lying, he thought. She is worried, belying her air of unconcern, and she may suspect something, as well. He would have to tread carefully, however.

"Charm? Are you alright?" Guy entered, his red hair mussed, his hazel eyes alight with concern over his number one account.

Donnell's jaw tightened. Where had Guy come from? If the guard had let him pass, he would be fired immediately. The lives of his operatives would not be endangered.

"I'm quivering with terror," Charm said, her voice dripping with sarcasm and her deep blue eyes beginning to blaze. "A little, old battery with a few wires didn't do a tad of damage, except to put a little smoke in the air."

"But Dearie, you could have been killed!" Guy looked as if he was about to burst into tears.

"Don't you 'dearie' me," Charm's anger began to bubble. "I don't want to hear another word about this new incident." She rounded on Donnell. "Is my dressing room ready for occupancy yet? In case anyone has forgotten, I have a concert to perform in about six hours."

"Give me ten minutes, Miss Dumotte," he said with a reassuringly authoritative voice as he guided her and Guy toward the front of the stage. If he read her correctly, she was a bit frazzled.

His calm was catching, and he could see her imperceptibly relax.

"Guy, take her to the caterers and get her some water or something to nibble," commanded Donnell.

As soon as they had left, he rounded on the guard. "Why did you let Guy through to the back?" he asked.

"I-I didn't," stammered the guard.

"You mean he didn't come past you at all?" questioned Donnell precisely.

"No. I haven't seen him today until he came through with you just now." The guard swallowed convulsively, but Donnell could tell he was telling the truth.

"All right. Carry on, and don't let anyone back," he instructed.

In the distance, Donnell saw Megan Keenan hurrying toward them. She was Charm's best backup vocalist. Donnell waited patiently for her, considering. She had a touch of Charm's swagger, but whereas Charm had deep, rich auburn hair, Megan had luxurious blonde locks with highlights that were dazzling gold. She sure was something to behold until she opened her mouth. When she did, she often spoke with a petulant whine that revealed her dissatisfaction with life. At least this was Donnell's first impression of her.

"Where's Charm?" she asked breathlessly when she was close enough to be heard over the din of the sound and setup crews.

"Guy took her to catering until I finish clearing the dressing rooms."

"Oh. Did something 'happen' again?" she asked.

"Just a little smoke," he replied carefully, unwilling to give too much information.

Megan frowned. "So how long until we can get into the rooms?"

"Give me ten minutes," Donnell replied.

"Okay. I guess I'll get a bit of something to eat, too." She tossed her golden tresses and followed the route Charm had taken to the other side of the stage.

Donnell gave the guard a pointed look who replied with a salute. Moving quickly along the corridor, Donnell pulled a fingerprint kit from a small pouch he wore around his waist. He dusted the doorknob and a few other key places, looking for prints. He found none. Surely some smudges should exist, but finding none indicated that someone had carefully wiped clean the doorknob and the rest of the places he had checked.

Carefully, he looked around the room. Charm's three trunks had been delivered and placed in the order she required. They were unlocked and opened, revealing the sequined, glittering garments inside, ready for her dresser.

Inside the front of each was a list of the contents. Feeling like a schoolboy looking where he shouldn't, he made sure each garment was accounted for without actually touching much of the material until he came to her final dress.

He loved her final dress. It was white and flowing with a dusting of diamond stones and silver glitter. It swayed with every seductive movement she made as she sang her final song, "To Love You." He allowed himself to barely sense its softness with the back of his left hand. Touching her clothing seemed somehow rather intimate. He couldn't objectively guard Charm and her band if he allowed himself to become emotionally involved with any of them.

Wait a minute. Were any of the other performers' trunks unlocked? Only the dresser and Charm herself possessed the keys. He looked in the other dressing rooms. None of the trunks in the other dressing rooms were opened. That was strange. He was sure he was missing something, but what?

The only other items in the dressing room were her makeup box, unopened on the counter in front of the mirror and a bouquet of flowers: roses and baby's breath. Many glossy green leaves were incorporated into the arrangement. In fact, it contained too many green leaves. He approached the dressing table, and his radio vibrated.

Puzzled, he went to answer it, but the vibrations stopped. He placed it in his pocket, and it vibrated again. Pulling it from his pocket, this time he held it in his hand and approached the dressing table. The vibrations grew stronger as he approached. He waved it nearer to the makeup box; the vibrations diminished. He moved it toward the floral arrangement; the vibrations increased.

He searched the arrangement. Aha! A small camera had been hidden just under a leaf near the top of the arrangement. He enclosed it with his handkerchief-covered palm, carefully placing it, wrapped in the white linen, inside another plastic bag.

Dissatisfied, he looked around again. He was sure he was still missing something. Whoever had placed the camera in the floral arrangement might have done so for a peep show at a famous celebrity, but given the smoke bomb and the open trunks, Donnell felt sure that the camera had been placed to give the viewer a picture of something else.

Even the air smelled strange, but with all the foo-foo stuff women sprayed and pampered themselves, he wasn't sure he could trust his sense of smell in here.

Reluctantly he left the dressing area and headed toward stage right. Charm, Guy, and Megan were waiting for him along with the rest of the band members. Five hours remained until show time, the doors opened in three, and Charm had a private party with supporters and fans an hour before the show.

He gave a nod to the assembled band members, and they dispersed quickly into the dressing rooms. He moved under the balcony and showed Gregor and Tiffany the small wireless camera that would give a feed to at least one computer.

"Have you called it in to Marcus?" asked Tiffany.

Marcus Dellaney was their computer expert, and waited in a private office several blocks away.

"No, not yet. I haven't had time. I'm sure we're still being observed, and I don't want to reveal our operational setup in case whoever planted these items is not working alone."

"Do you have any ideas?" asked Gregor.

"Yes. I'm puzzled by four things. Who opened Charm's dressing cases? Who planted the bomb? And who planted the camera? Also, where did Guy come from? I'm curious, too, about motives." He directed a look at Natalie then continued.

"Charm is Guy Brown's only major account. He could be doing this to raise publicity for her and her concerts. None of the 'incidents' have actually harmed Charm in any way, and he obviously cares for her very deeply.

Also when I talked to Megan today, she was not as whiney as she usually is. Why not? And then there's Charm, herself. She was lying to me today. She knows or suspects something or someone. I'm going to have to get much closer to her so I can discover what it is."

This last was said as much to himself as to the others. Perhaps he was giving himself permission to get more personally involved with her. The others, however, knew that to do so would make him more vulnerable, weakening his abilities to think clearly and act decisively.

They had a plan for this eventuality. Natalie could and would take charge of the operation if the necessity arose.

But right now they needed answers to his questions.

"Natalie, find Guy and question him about his whereabouts today," said Donnell. "And Seamus, can you get this to Marcus?" he asked, indicating the bagged incendiary device. "I can't trust anyone else to do it, and I don't want to leave the premises right now."

Chapter Four

Charm Dumotte sat in her dressing room, alone finally. Her dresser, Sandy Daniels, had helped her into her opening outfit, a sexily short, sequin-studded, emerald dress. Her hairdresser, Jonette O'Bailey had coiffed her hair into carefully arranged locks that gave the appearance of being carefree. Jonette also did her makeup, a bit more heavy than was her normal wont, for the evening performance.

She had fifteen minutes to compose herself before doing a meet and greet with adoring fans. Donnell McKinnon made her angry with his supercilious air, yet she admired his calm. She wished she could be calm.

Frankly, she was terrified, and each new 'incident' made her suspicious of everyone. She didn't like being suspicious of everyone from her hairdresser to her manager. Concerts were supposed to be about the music and her ardent fans, not some maniac threatening to bomb the entire concert hall to kingdom come.

Pulling herself together, she shakily decided to concentrate on one of her favorite views of the Seine River back home in Avon, France. She and her dad, Christian, were avid bicyclists, and Sunday mornings were the best. They would wake early, don their gear, and head out for a two or three hour ride, sometimes through the larger town of Fontainebleau and the gardens around the castle or at other times through Samois-Sur-Seine and other little towns that dotted the Seine River.

One of her favorite views, especially on frosty, October mornings was of the mists rising from the Seine to reveal the beautiful fall landscape on the other side of the river. She and her father tried to time their rides so that the sun would just be dawning, touching the aspen, maple, and chestnut trees with a golden light.

So she sat under the air conditioning vent in her dressing room and visualized herself turning the corner behind her dad and getting that first glimpse of the gentle rays of the dawning sun, turning the aspen leaves to gold and firing the leaves of the maples to brilliant vermillion hues. She could see the glass-like waters, so still in the morning light, could feel the light, frosty breeze that tried to tease tendrils of hair from her ponytail.

Sometimes she missed her childhood so much. She often thought of the two teachers who had so encouraged her to pursue her dream of becoming an international singer. Madame Theallier had begun the process; the next year she was replaced by a teacher from America, Madame Newman. Charm was blown away by the thought of leaving one's country to pursue a dream, but the idea had bloomed under Madame Newman's gentle encouragement.

Her parents had played no small part either. They had provided for tutelage in dance and music, accompanying her on the long train rides into Paris and the even longer train rides home, exhausted and tired, met by the other parent at the train station with the car.

A knock shattered her reverie. Colin, her stage manager, was announcing the five minute warning for the meet and greet. She couldn't recapture the relaxing images, but they had accomplished the task of removing her mind from the latest incident.

She squared her shoulders, checked her lipstick in the mirror, and carrying the ever-present bottle of chilled water, opened her dressing room door only to bump into Donnell.

Her eyes widened in surprise before she could help herself. He had changed into evening clothes, and he looked as handsome as two devils. He extended the crook of his arm.

"Shall we, my lady?" he asked gallantly.

Thrown off stride by this unexpected truce, she placed her small hand on his arm, and they walked quietly down the hall and around a corner to a large reception room. It was filled with fifty admirers who were part of her "Charmed Circle Fan Club."

Along one wall stretched a long table laden with bottles of water and other drinks as well as some of Charm's favorite finger foods: bite-sized brownies, oatmeal raisin cookies, delectable tuna-dill and tuna-cucumber sandwiches and fresh, baby vegetables with a creamy artichoke spinach dip.

The noise in the room instantly quieted at her entrance before her fans erupted into cheers and whistles. For the next forty-five minutes, Charm circulated around the room, talking and chatting with no other apparent concern on her mind than the lives of her fans.

Donnell watched her in admiration. When she was talking with someone, she concentrated fully on that person, making them feel as if they were the most important person in the world. Yet he knew she was aware, not only of his observation, but of others in the room as well.

Colin entered to give her the fifteen minute warning. She took another five minutes to wrap up her time with her fans. Then she headed for the door.

Donnell was right behind her. She would have to get used to his presence, he thought. He intended to stay close until he knew who was making threats, what they were up to and why.

"You don't have to stick to me like a leech," she said voce sotto as she passed by the door he held open for her.

He waited until they were in the hallway out of sight of her fans before replying. "Yes, I do, and I will. No note came with the bomb," he mentioned casually.

She had kept her head of red curls down, listening to him as they walked side stage from where she made her entrance. Now she lifted her blue eyes to look at him warily.

"For now, I'll be escorting you to most of the places you go," Donnell stated calmly.

Charm's thoughts whirled as Colin gave her the five minute warning through the earpiece that one of the stage assistants gave her.

"Can we discuss this after the concert?" she asked icily. "I need to prepare mentally for my first number."

"Certainly." Donnell bowed and moved to a position where he could see the entire stage and most of the audience once Charm was onstage. He had his own instructions to give to his Ops. Actually, he just had to check on them, making sure everyone was in place.

Additional agents, standbys, had arrived to add another layer of protection. Half a dozen were sharp shooters who would be watching the audience with binoculars, their guns poised to bring down anyone who pulled out a gun.

Charm closed her eyes and rubbed her left temple. She didn't need a migraine tonight, and they most often began on the left side of her head. Squaring her shoulders under the sensually glittering green sequins, she visualized the first number and especially how she wanted to make her entrance. That had to be spectacular.

No one believed her, but she usually had nerves in her stomach until she had entered and retrieved her guitar. Once the guitar was in her hands and the first pulsating lines were sung, she was fine.

The first number was fast and rhythmic, included some dance moves that demanded her entire attention, and ended in a crescendo of movement, sound, and color from the lighting director.

Colin cued her in her earpiece, and she walked onstage to thunderous applause. She normally ignored the cameras and large video screens, but a quick glance told her that even under her skillfully applied makeup, she looked rather pale.

Determinedly, she took a deep breath, reached for her guitar, and sang the first few notes. The hot, liquid notes mesmerized the audience, and she was gone, lost in the emotion and pull of the music.

Donnell watched, keenly aware of both the operational aspect of what he was doing and the musical panorama. The first number melded into another high energy number with Charm and Megan doing a duet with intricately switching parts, sometimes right in the middle of lines. His respect for both Charm's and Megan's talents grew.

The third number slowed considerably. A sensuously beautiful Irish ballad of lost love, it stirred Donnell to the gut. But of course it would with his Irish blood and musical roots. Michael Shannon, who also played keyboards, added his gorgeous tenor, and Kelly Kennedy, the bass player, added a low bass whenever the chorus was sung.

After Charm spoke a few words, Megan took center stage for a solo number while Charm whisked past Donnell to her dressing room to change for the next set of numbers. With plenty of security coverage in public areas, he dutifully followed Charm to her dressing room where he respectfully stood guard outside. She was so involved now with the concert that she barely registered his presence.

Charm's second outfit was a pair of black, silk pants topped with a long, gold embroidered, kimono-type jacket. Halfway through the set, she removed the jacket to reveal a gold, sequin-covered tank top.

The second set was a combo of rock and jazz numbers. The middle number had a big band jazz/swing feel to it that the audience greeted with great enthusiasm. In fact, four couples from the audience had been selected before the concert began to display their dancing techniques on the smaller, shorter stage areas erected either side of the main stage. They had been scanned by security with wands as unobtrusively and painlessly as possible.

Donnell was tense during this number. He understood that it pulled the audiences even more deeply into the concert, and everyone certainly enjoyed it. Charm, still singing, moved energetically from one side of the stage to the other, giving each couple her electrifying smile and approval. But still, it was a security nightmare. Besides, his right hand felt strange.

He relaxed some on the last number of the set, enjoying the mesh of saxophones and brass instruments although his right hand was beginning to burn. Michael and Kelly took center stage to sing a duet while Charm again rushed past him for another costume change. He followed her and stood at his post with a keen eye and attentive ear, noting he could hear most of what was said in the dressing room.

This time she chose a deep midnight blue dress. Instead of sequins, the fabric itself was shot through with silver thread, and the dress, gathered under her breasts, fell in a long swath to mid-calf, emphasizing her long legs and swaying sensuously with every movement. Donnell reminded himself that he would need to stay objective in spite of Charm's beauty.

The third set of music consisted of more classic pieces interspersed with numbers from modern movies to keep it lively. Megan, Michael, and Kelly added their voices on several songs, and then Megan and Michael sang a duet while Charm changed into a deep purple outfit consisting of a halter top that hugged her figure and pants that flared slightly past the knees. On this outfit, sequins formed a pattern on the fabric that distorted the light, creating a rather mesmerizing effect.

For the fourth set, Charm chose two rowdy rock numbers with a slightly country flavor. Donnell admired her courage. European crowds were not as hot about country music as Americans were. The songs seemed to be accepted enthusiastically enough, however. Again, she changed tempo as the band behind her swung into a sassy Irish number followed by a slower melancholy number.

Charm headed back stage for her last change with Donnell following. Onstage, Colin was giving an announcement of her upcoming concerts and cds for sale. Colin and the rest of the crew froze onstage as they heard a scream in their earpieces. Colin, bless his heart, reacted with great presence of mind and launched Megan and Michael into a number while Donnell, not caring about impropriety, swung open Charm's dressing room door.

Greenville/Charleston, SC, USA
May 18th/19th

Chapter Five

Chelsea sank back against the cushions in one of the limousines in the Presidential motorcade, well-satisfied with her phone call home. Her mother was more than thrilled to have three guests for the next two days, especially since one of them would be her daughter. The news was already being relayed to others, and the next few days would be filled with food, family, and fun.

Following the shooting of one minor terrorist and the disappearance of someone who was thought to be the brother of an international terrorist, Tillot Thomason went into action. Some agents immediately began scavenging the grounds as well as trash cans for discarded IDs or any other illuminating items, others went to work on the video pictures of the suspected terrorist, searching for a match with computer pictures, and Tillot decided to use the President's idea of sending Chelsea home as a way to create a decoy.

The private driveway of the college vice-president's residence had been debugged as a backup measure, so Tillot had the President, his chief security detail, and his driver switch vehicles with Chelsea and her driver. The First Lady's assistant was to stay with the President's entourage along with the First Lady. Tillot also assigned Jasper and a driver to go home with Chelsea after her assurances that her mother would thoroughly enjoy the company.

Tillot had not wanted them staying in Chelsea's home, but she had finally reassured him that it really would be okay with her family and that they would probably stay in the converted garage, called the bunkhouse, where her older brother, Lawton, had one of the four bedrooms. After a private conversation with Jasper, they were on their way, the entire switch taking less than four minutes.

Chelsea glanced ahead to see that both limousines were heading toward the Spartanburg airport. However, one limousine had already deposited the President and most of his group at the downtown airport which was not that far off the interstate so that group could leave in Marine One.

The second limo was going along with them. Once they had arrived at the airport, the two cars were driven to a secure location where most of the security team flew on to D.C. and only one security member traveled with the driver as the limousine was flown back to Washington.

At last Chelsea, Jasper and their driver, Frank, were on their way. Chelsea was exhausted. It had been a long day. She wondered what she and Jasper would talk of for two and a half hours, but she was pleasantly surprised to find that Jasper was an excellent conversationalist.

He tapped on the window, and Frank rolled it down. "Hey, Frank," said Jasper. "Chelsea and I are going to play twenty questions, and she's going to tell us about her family." He lounged against the seat, his tie loosened and the top buttons undone. His chin showed definite signs of a five o'clock shadow, and he sat directly opposite her so he could stretch his long legs catty-corner beside her.

Frank rolled down the window another two inches so he could hear their conversation. He was in his fifties, and although demoted to the job of chauffeur at his own request, he was still considered a member of the secret service force.

Obediently, Chelsea replied. "Well, my Dad's name is Davey Merrill. He works in computers like my Grandpa Will. Grandpa was one of the pioneers of the computer programming industry. My Mom's name is Galeah, and she's a school librarian. My brother, Lawton, is twenty-six and engaged to one of my friends named Lanie. And I have two younger sisters, Kielah and Lindy. Kielah is a senior this year, Lindy is a sophomore, and they're both cheerleaders."

Chelsea looked at Jasper enquiringly. When he didn't respond, she said, "Your turn."

"I was going to ask you some questions," said Jasper, "but okay. Let's see. My parents' names are Carter and Penelope Peters-Templeton, and don't ask me how we got a hyphenated last name. I think it's just an affectation to make people think we're famous or something." He grinned engagingly while deriding his family name.

He continued. "I have two brothers, one older than me and one younger. Corey is my older brother and a real daredevil, and Preston, my younger brother, we call 'nature boy' because he loves the outdoors so much. Then there's my sister, Pamela. She's the oldest and was married last November to a guy named Jonathan Tate."

"What kind of business does your Dad do?" asked Chelsea.

"That's your first question; you have nineteen more left. Dad's in commercial real estate. And before you ask, Mom is an attorney, but she keeps her caseload light so she can do charity work in Virginia, D. C., and New York."

"What about your brothers?"

"Corey has followed Dad into commercial real estate, but Dad is always complaining that he spends nearly as much as he makes. Preston is still in high school, but he's done scouting since he was a bitty thing. Well, I was in scouting, too, but I dropped out when I got to high school. Preston stayed in it and became an Eagle Scout last year."

"Now it's my turn. You only have eighteen questions left, and I still have twenty. Let's see." Jasper thought about the previous thread of conversation. "You were laughing with your Mom about a family reunion. Who will that include?"

"Just about everyone in Summerville." Chelsea laughed. "No, not really. It will just seem like it. Grandpa Will and Grandma Mary will be there and great-grandma, Laura Merrill."

"My Aunt Clara and Uncle Craig will come," Chelsea continued. "They're the Miller family. They have two children, Michael, who is fifteen, and Melanie, who is thirteen."

"Uncle Phillip Merrill and his wife, Aunt Sarah, have four children. Phil Jr. or PJ is nineteen, Paul is seventeen, and the twins, Rosie and Ryan, both girls, are fourteen. That's just Dad's family. How are you ever going to remember all this?"

"You just wasted a question. And trust me, I will." Remembering names and faces came with the territory when your mom continually used you to round out the numbers at social functions Jasper thought wryly.

"So now tell me about your mother's family. Galeah is an unusual name. How did your mother get that name?"

"Her mother, my grandmother, is nearly full-blooded Cherokee, and her name is a derivative of a family name from the Cherokee side of the family. Grandma married Gregory Galbraith, so when mom came along, they combined their names to create her name. She was Galeah Galbraith until she married Dad."

"What about her family?" asked Jasper.

"Mom has two older brothers. Uncle Galen's wife is named Gloria, and they have three children: Gina who is twenty-one and has a little boy named Caden, Gordon who is nineteen, and Gwen who is sixteen. Mom's other brother, Garret, married Aunt Grace, and they have two boys named Geoffrey who is eighteen and Justin who is seventeen. Are you <u>sure</u> you can remember everyone?"

"Trust me. I've had plenty of practice. And I won't be able to walk into your house and name everyone immediately, of course, but now I'll be able to associate names, faces, and families, and it won't take all that much time to learn everyone."

Jasper addressed Frank. "Hey Frank. Did you get all that? Think you can name everyone?" Jasper asked slyly.

"You know me. Got it all down already. Everyone pegged." Frank laughed. "And now who's wasted a question?"

"Got me, Frank! Okay Chelsea. Now we get personal. Three questions popcorn style. What's your favorite color?"

"Green," answered Chelsea.

"Where did you attend high school and college?"

Summerville High and Clemson, and that's not fair. You sneaked two questions into one," protested Chelsea.

Jasper raised an eyebrow cockily. "Just answer the questions, Ma'am. What's your shoe size?"

"My shoe size is… " Chelsea began obediently. "My shoe size? Why do you need to know my shoe size?"

"You never know. We might have to chase some terrorists, you lose your heels, and I have to buy some sensible flats so we can outrun the enemy."

"No. No," protested Chelsea. "We'll be minding our own business in downtown Charleston when a pickpocket steals your wallet, and I have to ditch my shoes so I can punt a football, knocking the thief down and saving your reputation with the Secret Service."

"Where did you get the football?" asked Jasper.

"Oh. I have many hidden assets," Chelsea retorted.

Jasper thought she probably did, and her comment made him aware of her innocent sensuality, a potent combination. He couldn't let the pause become awkward, however, or she might become aware of the direction of his thoughts.

"So what kind of music do you like?" he asked.

"I like everything. Well, most everything. I was raised on pop rock, Southern gospel, and some country. But lately I've developed a taste for classical when my mind needs a break. I don't pretend to understand classical music, so it requires no thought, and I can mull over whatever problem on which I'm working. How about you?"

"Straight up rock with some Hip Hop flavor, but my mom listens to classical mainly, so I actually like that, too. Depends on my mood," answered Jasper.

"My turn for three questions," said Chelsea. "What is your shoe size?"

"Size thirteen."

"Do you have any pets, and what are they?"

"Three dogs, black labs," answered Jasper.

"What's your favorite dessert?" asked Chelsea.

"Ice cream."

"What flavor?"

"Hey, that's five questions. But vanilla is my favorite," answered Jasper. "Now it's my turn. I have twelve more questions."

"Nice try, Jasper," said Frank. "You wasted two questions on me, so now you're down to ten."

Chelsea looked from Frank to Jasper. "You mean you all are really keeping track of these questions?" she asked.

"Sure," answered Frank. "Playing twenty questions keeps us on our toes and helps us with certain types of interrogation. We learn to read body language as well as other things. Jasper's class started the game, and now his team does variations of the game to while away the hours when nothing is happening."

Chelsea felt rather disconcerted. "You mean you're practicing on me?"

"Don't feel bad," answered Frank. "We do this with each other quite frequently during down time. You have to watch out for Jasper. He may be new, but he's sharp."

Chelsea looked at Jasper with new respect.

Jasper looked rather embarrassed. "It's nothing. I had a great deal of training from my mom. Whenever she had galas or other events, she would expect us to memorize information about the guests so we could speak to them about 'their interests.' After a while, it becomes second nature."

"I guess you won't have any problems with my family," responded Chelsea.

"Nope. And I still have ten more questions," said Jasper gleefully. "What's your favorite dessert?"

"Pecan Pie."

"What's your favorite movie?"

"*A Knight's Tale.*"

"How many boyfriends have you had?"

"What? Is that any of your business?"

"Two more wasted questions. If I'm going to protect you, I need to know about potentially jealous boyfriends."

"Now wait a minute. I didn't ask you to protect me," protested Chelsea.

"Part of my job. But if it's such a touchy subject, don't answer," said Jasper.

"Of course it's not a touchy subject. I've had three boyfriends. Blair was my first boyfriend in high school, and Alan was my second. My only boyfriend in college was Charlie.
Your turn."

Obligingly Jasper answered. "I dated Delcie, Kathleen, Alicia, and Jennifer in high school at Franklin Academy. At Purdue, I had to spend more time in the books, so I only dated two girls, and not at the same time either, Leslie Anne and Allison."

He halted, but swallowed and gamely continued. "Allison and I were engaged for about three months, but she broke it off. She died two months later from a rare form of cancer." Quietly he added, "I loved her, and I wish she had trusted me enough to walk with her to the end. It would have been my privilege."

Chelsea leaned forward and laid her hand on his. "It was her way of showing her love for you," she said simply.

The car lurched suddenly to the right. Chelsea fell on the floor. Jasper immediately ducked and dialed a number on his cell phone.

"Frank, are you all right?" he called.

"Someone in a black Cadillac is trying to run us off the road. Thank God I have good reflexes."

Chelsea sat up and took note of the mile marker. "Frank, take the exit coming up, but do it at the last minute so they can't follow us quickly. I know a back way home." She ducked down, sitting on the floor again.

Jasper was talking on the phone. "What exit is it?" he asked Chelsea.

"Exit 186 to Jedburg."

"You already have the address?" Chelsea heard him ask.

The Cadillac hit them again, and Frank struggled to keep the car on the highway. When the exit appeared almost immediately, he veered off sharply, barreling through the stop sign and continuing to the right.

Jasper put a protective arm around Chelsea, helping her to the seat. "Frank, are you okay to drive, or do you want to switch?"

"I'm fine. Just shaken."

"Who was it?"

"I'm not sure. I couldn't see but one person, so I'm pretty sure that was a single perp. If more people had been in that Cadillac, we would have received gunshots, I think, but none were fired. And they lagged behind so I couldn't get a read on the license plate." He hit the switch for the GPS system.

Blue lights appeared in front of them and then behind them. Ignoring all traffic signals and signs, they wound their way toward Chelsea's house. The officers turned off their lights when they reached the outskirts of Summerville.

Only then did Jasper relax although only slightly.

With his arm still around Chelsea's shoulder he asked, "So which boyfriend was that? Blair, Allan, or Charlie?"

Chapter Six

Chelsea stared at Jasper. "What?" she asked.

He gave her a wicked grin. "Which boyfriend just tried to run us off the road?"

"None," Chelsea sputtered. She suddenly became aware that Jasper, sitting beside her now, still had his arm around her shoulder. He was leaning back against the seat, appearing relaxed again, with the ankle of one leg on the knee of the other leg.

Her focus shifted as she recognized they were turning onto Sumter Avenue. "We're almost home!" she announced. The limo turned onto Charleston Street, and there on the left was her childhood home with the black iron fence, the wide porches, and the lights left burning by her mom.

She instructed Frank to turn into the driveway, and then she was out of the car, not waiting for any help.

Jasper's immediate concern was to get them out of sight. But he paused a moment to inhale the scent of jasmine and honeysuckle, to enjoy what he could see of the massive oak trees above them, and to watch the warm welcome between Chelsea and her parents.

Davey Merrill, Chelsea's father, came forward and grasped Jasper's hand, giving him a searching glance.

"Welcome to Summerville and to our home, Son," he said.

"Thank you, Sir," said Jasper.

"Chelsea says you've had some excitement today. Is there anything I can do to help?"

"Yes, actually. I'd like to get our vehicle out of sight as quickly as possible, and, with your permission, I'd like to scout around the premises." Jasper was all business now, yet Mr. Merrill respected the fact that he asked for both help and permission.

"We have room in the garage for your vehicle." Mr. Merrill pulled a remote from his pocket and indicated where the limo should park. Frank, who had waited in the driver seat, pulled forward smoothly, and Jasper breathed a sigh of relief, especially when he noted that Chelsea and her mother were in the house already.

He and Mr. Merrill entered the garage, and this time Jasper was impressed that he helped by taking Chelsea's bag from Frank instead of treating the older, black man as a lackey. Mr. Merrill led them toward the back of the garage. They passed through a door into a spacious living area.

"This is the bunkhouse, adjacent to the garage. Upstairs are the bedrooms. You'll be able to tell which is Lawton's." He chuckled. "You and Frank are welcome to use any of the other three."

He led them through another door next to the first they had entered and onto a covered walkway to the house. It was much more private than the courtyard, and Jasper, although still on alert, relaxed somewhat.

They entered the mud room and kitchen area. Mr. Merrill pointed toward the family room. "I know you won't feel right until you check everything outside, so I'll let you two do what you need to do. You can meet us all in the family room when you're finished."

"Thank you, Sir," said Jasper.

"Just call me Dad," Mr. Merrill responded. "Everyone else around here does." He chuckled again.

After a brief consultation, Frank and Jasper decided to split up. Jasper searched the perimeter of the house, stepping softly and barely making a sound, especially on the areas of well-manicured, lush lawn.

He noted that the wrought iron fence circled the perimeter of the property of well over an acre. Beyond the fence behind the bunk house and to the east of the house were the woodsy lots of neighbors. The windows of the kitchen, the library bay, and the front room were located on the east side. Hydrangea bushes graced the flower beds interspersed by plots of iris, lilies, and other flowers Jasper couldn't quite identify. Honeysuckle and jasmine had been trained along the porch railing, creating a partial screen of privacy for the swing that was positioned just off the library.

The house actually had two "front" yards since it was located on a corner. A porch wrapped around from the front room and all along the south facing front yard. Several magnolia trees dotted the side and this front lawn, as well as high, arching angel oak trees with their strands of Spanish moss swaying gently in the evening breeze. Along the front of this porch was a row of azalea bushes; king segos grew on either side of the sidewalk that led to the elaborately ornate, wrought-iron gate. Along the four-foot fence was a full border of jasmine, trimmed in box style.

Jasper stopped in the shadow of one of the magnolia trees for a moment to enjoy the night sounds of crickets and the occasional tweet of a sleepy bird. He noted the broad windows on either side of the front door. Lamps glowed dimly behind the closed curtains, giving the home a welcoming aura.

He now understood why southern cities were often referred to as bewitching females. The warmth of the hospitality he had already felt along with the sensuous scents and sights of the landscape, even the weight of the humidity in the air gave a languorous, female feel to this area.

An owl hooted in the distance, and a church bell chimed twice when he finally heard the underlying growl of a car engine about fifty yards down the street that extended to the west. Quietly he crept past the water fountain in the middle of the west facing front yard to the shadow of another oak. Another time he would enjoy the heady scent of the varieties of roses that surrounded the fountain.

He noticed that the porch wrapped around to the west side of the house, turning into a screened porch that emptied into a gathering and dining room along the back of the house. But he had no time for a more thorough inspection.

He tapped the sunglasses in his pocket to signal Frank. When he noted Frank's quiet shadow slip around the perimeter of the courtyard, he moved forward to the equally ornate gate in this section of fencing. Fortunately, the gate did not squeak as he opened it, and he silently thanked Mr. Merrill for excellent upkeep of his property.

Moving quickly across Charleston Street, Jasper took cover beside a tall pine and waited several minutes. The black car certainly was a Cadillac! Pulling a small pair of binoculars from his pocket, he tried to get the license plate number, but not enough light was available on the very dimly lit street.

He bent low and moved forward slowly, cautiously. Finally, he was able to get the number and note that the tags were issued in South Carolina from a rental agency. He could vaguely see the shadow of someone in the driver's seat, back lighted by the glow of what appeared to be a screen. Was it a small computer screen or a GPS?

Simultaneously almost, Frank stepped on a twig, and a dog across the street from the car began barking. The car moved forward, the taillights giving twin demonic grins at him as it slipped around the corner and out of sight.

When they had quickly and quietly gained access to the bunkhouse, Jasper and Frank compared notes. Frank mentioned the rather excellent security system Mr. Merrill used and noted that the bunkhouse had three windows on the ground floor; the garage had two. Jasper called in the info on the vehicle, and, with a quick conference call, they both informed Tillot of the evening escapades.

Tillot sounded alert in spite of the fact that the time was half past two. "You're doing well as a team down there. I'm glad I put you two together. We should obtain some valuable information. You may have more nocturnal activity, so I'll alert the chief of police to drive by several times tonight for added precaution. Get some sleep, men, but stay on the alert."

Jasper and Frank made their way to the kitchen. Mr. Merrill appeared, asking for a report. They told him what had happened.

"Let me turn on the security system now. Do you need to see how it works? No, of course you don't," he said, noting Frank's smile. "The one in the bunkhouse is similar. Come with me, and I'll show you something no one else knows except Galeah, of course."

He led them to the library. Only a small lamp glowed, but it highlighted the polished gleam of hardwood floors, the muted golds and reds in a huge oriental rug, the brass work on a lovely, old roll top desk. The blinds and curtains were closed for the evening, giving the room a cozy feel.

Mr. Merrill tugged on a section of the floor to ceiling bookcases that lined two of the walls. The whole bookcase came away from the wall, revealing a console with screens, a computer, and a keyboard.

Frank gave a low whistle, and his eyes glowed with eagerness to see how this prime piece of security equipment ran.

"I had this installed when we had a rash of burglaries in this neighborhood six months ago. The burglaries have stopped, so I turned it off, but I think it will serve us well to have it on tonight." He pressed several buttons and, one by one, the computer screens came to life, showing various angles of the property outside as well as the access to outside doors and windows. The larger rooms also had video input.

"May I?" Frank requested.

"Sure," responded Mr. Merrill.

Frank sat down at the computer, hitting buttons until the windows on the ground level of the bunkhouse and garage were shown in greater clarity. He did the same with several other screens. "All ready, sir," said Frank.

Mr. Merrill shook his head in amazement. "At least we'll all get some much needed sleep tonight. Chelsea and her mother have already gone up to their rooms. I'll bid you goodnight as well. The fridge in the bunkhouse is well-stocked, but Galeah wanted me to tell you that brunch will be served at ten, considering how late the time is already."

He shook hands with them, thanking them for their protection of his daughter. He addressed both of them, but his eyes held Jasper's.

Jasper felt a twinge of disappointment that he couldn't see Chelsea. Then he reprimanded himself. The excitement of the day was catching up to him. He was here to do a job for the government. But he remembered the sun highlighting the gold in her hair, the green flecks in her brown eyes when she had laughed at his crazy questions as he wearily drifted to sleep. He did not think of Allison as he was falling asleep, nor did he dream of her for the first time in many months.

London, England
May 18th/19th

Chapter Seven

The sight that Donnell saw as he entered Charm's dressing room was of Sandy stripping the final costume of gauzy white from Charm's body. Her back was to him, but he could see, both in front of him and in the mirror, the red blistering from where the fabric had touched her body.

The man in him wanted to enjoy the lusciousness of her body, particularly her exposed breasts, but she was in obvious pain, and he was invading her privacy terribly. If his older sisters, Amy and Darla had been there, they would have boxed his ears.

Both women turned to him. Sandy, holding the dress, clearly did not know what to do, and the agony, shock, and disbelief in Charm's eyes superseded any modesty she would have normally felt.

Donnell sprang into action. "Sandy, put that dress in the corner, and don't let anyone, not even security personnel, touch it. Charm, there's a shower behind this screen. Strip off everything and run cold water on your body. Make sure it's cold. Sandy, help her in there, and make sure you run your hands under cold water as well."

Sandy disposed of the dress and turned to help Charm with her slip, panties, and shoes.

Donnell turned his back and began issuing orders. "Ops Two and Four, I need you in Charm's dressing room, pronto. Op Five, establish procedures to secure all trash can contents, beginning with those backstage.

Op Three, establish procedures with security guards to keep all personnel away from backstage area except for band members. No managers other than Sandy Daniels and Colin Criswell are allowed backstage per the orders of Interpol. Oh, and escort the doctor on call for emergency care backstage immediately."

Natalie and Tiffany arrived seconds later. "Natalie, I need this dressing case dusted for prints. Tiffany, darling, your talents are wasted here. But I do need a chemical analysis of the dress done immediately. Get it to Marcus, tell him it probably has a chemical agent that has given Miss Dumotte burns, and ask him to get me the results within the hour. If anyone tries to stop you, well, you can work your karate magic!"

Tiffany grinned, tossing her short blond curls and knowing she could take down a man three times her size.

"Here, let me put the dress in this plastic bag. I've already been burned." Nevertheless, he put on some gloves.

Sandy appeared. "Charm wants to perform the last number. What can I put on her skin? My hands are starting to blister, too."

Donnell stared in disbelief. His respect for Charm rose yet again. Quickly in his mind he ran through chemical burns and solutions for non-invasive yet immediate relief. "Talcum powder. I think talcum powder will help, but it needs to be a very light dusting. Emphasis on the light. Her wounds need to be kept moist. What will she wear?"

"She has another white street dress, nothing fancy, but it's in her own suitcase on the bus. Can I get it?"

Sandy was clearly intimidated by him, but Donnell knew she adored Charm and would do anything to help her or protect her.

"I'd rather you not leave right now. She really shouldn't be performing; she needs medical attention."

"I'm finished here, Boss. I can get it," said Natalie.

She and Sandy conferred, Natalie headed for the bus, and Sandy went to put powder on Charm. Donnell alerted the operators stationed at the bus side of the building. Just then he heard a discreet knock on the door. It was Colin.

"Is she okay? Will she be able to perform the last number?" he asked.

"Yes and yes, but definitely against my best judgment. She needs medical attention immediately. How much time until whatever you're doing out there wraps up?"

"Michael and Megan will be finishing their number in about one minute. The band is standing by for my instructions. We all heard the scream."

"One of my agents went to get a new dress. Charm should be out in about three minutes." Donnell, hearing enough talk about performances from Uncle Marc and Aunt Shannon, the international opera stars, knew that timing was always critical.

"Okay. I'm on it. I'll find out the details later." Colin rushed back toward the stage area.

Donnell checked his watch. It was hard to believe that only four minutes had passed since Charm had screamed.

Natalie returned with the replacement dress just as the emergency doctor arrived, breathless. "Sorry. We had a pregnant woman faint in one of the bathrooms."

Donnell waved aside his excuse and quickly outlined Charm's injuries. The doctor approved the emergency measures but cautioned that Charm should be examined thoroughly after the performance.

"Watch her breathing in case she may have breathed in the fumes. She may also have temporary vision problems, especially if she looked down when she put on the garment to see why it was causing the burning."

"I'll see to it. Gregor, escort the doctor out of this area, please. Then secure the dressing room as a crime scene and finish processing it. And if you can arrange an unmarked vehicle for transport to the hospital, I'll make sure she gets immediate medical attention after the concert."

Gregor gave his typical salute, and Donnell knew his requests would be accomplished quickly and efficiently.

Charm emerged from the dressing room. The simple white dress fell from her shoulders to mid-calf. Puffy, short, white sleeves and a scoop neck completed the garment. The strappy, silver sandals and diamond-encrusted hair ornament set in silver completed the outfit. Even with her extreme makeup for stage, Donnell thought she was breathtakingly beautiful.

She nodded to him and held out her hand. Donnell felt the coldness of it and realized she needed some reassurance, unusual in someone who was usually so self-possessed.

"You look stunning," he assured her. "We'll talk this all out after your performance or tomorrow when you've rested. You'll be okay. Go out there and wow them, Darling."

She gave him a shaky smile that turned to confident radiance when the spotlight picked up her entrance. The band played the opening chords of her final song.

Donnell took his station, mentally willing her through the performance. It was a song she had written herself.

> *Love kept going wrong for me,*
> *Leaving me depressed and empty.*
> *I thought that I would live my life alone;*
> *My heart was slowly turning into stone.*
> *But then you came along as just a friend,*
> *Wiped my tears and gently held my hand.*
>
> *Now I have found that I can truly see*
> *All the beauty in the world around me;*
> *I am finally free,*
> *For I have learned to love you.*
>
> *To love you is to wake and greet a new day in*
> *your arms.*
> *To love you is to learn that simple things are*
> *filled with charm.*
> *To love you is to trust and know that life is*
> *good again.*
> *My heart is on the mend, I'm standing strong*
> *again,*
> *And just to think it all began, when I learned*
> *To love you.*

She repeated the chorus again a capella and ended by repeating the last two lines with the simplest of accompaniment.

The crowd erupted in cheers. Charm flashed her famous smile. Only Donnell could see the effort it cost her to maintain her stage presence. As she joined him, he noticed the wheezing as she breathed.

He tucked her hand under his arm and started to lead her straight past the dressing room to the waiting car. Sandy, however, caught his sleeve and asked permission to go with them to help Charm.

"Oh yes, Sandy's coming. She's one of my best friends from home. She'll know what to tell the doctor if I don't. Besides, she's injured, too."

Donnell had observed the close bond between them. Now he knew why they were so close. Actually, he had been going to suggest that Sandy come as well since she was also injured. He nodded assent, and they exited through a side door into an unmarked car. On the way to the hospital, he called Marcus to get the identity of the chemical agent used.

"You're not going to like this boss. It's pepper spray mixed with bleach, which can be purchased at nearly any store. But at least it's easily treated. And more bad news. We've lifted no prints off of the dressing cases or the dress from anyone but you, Charm, and Sandy. But we've just begun. I'm still checking the video camera feed and the download site. We're hitting some snags there, as well. But we'll nail this bastard, boss."

Yes, they would nail him. Or them. But now, no one could call the happenings accidental. Donnell had a feeling they were working against one man in particular. The man might hire others to do his bidding, but he had made a personal attack against Charm. Furthermore, he had installed a video device so he could watch the results of his deviltry. That made it very personal, indeed.

"Donnell?" Beside him, Charm plucked plaintively at his sleeve. "I feel really funny like I'm going to pass out, and I can't see too well, either."

"We're pulling up at the hospital now. Hold on." But his admonition came too late. Charm sagged against him in a dead faint.

As the car came to a halt, he pushed her toward Sandy, and, running into the emergency entrance, began barking orders.

"I need a gurney, stat."

He knew some hospital lingo, and combined with his authoritative confidence, people usually jumped to do what he asked. Now was no exception.

In no time at all, Charm had been placed on the gurney and was being wheeled into emergency where she was immediately hooked up to IVs. Carefully, Donnell helped Sandy from the car as well. Her injuries also needed tending.

He looked ruefully at the back of his hands. The skin was very red, but no blistering had occurred. His injuries would get treated eventually.

Charleston, SC, USA
May 19th

Chapter Eight

Chelsea lazily stretched her arms above her head. She loved coming home. Her mother had not changed much in her room in spite of threatening to do so. The maple furniture was complemented by the blue carpeting and the blue and white bedspread with plenty of pillows and a fuzzy white blanket at the foot of the bed.

She had two days to spend with her family, and, thinking about Jasper, she wondered how he would like a taste of Southern life compared to the glitzy life his family seemed to live in Virginia. Or was it New York? She knew Jasper had mentioned both. Oh well. She shrugged mentally. She didn't care how pompously families in those states thought of themselves; she would take Southern hospitality over their East Coast elitism any day.

Moses, her cat, jumped purring onto her pillow. He had been an alley cat, tormented by neighborhood children and dogs alike. He was solid black with beautiful green eyes, and Chelsea had made sure he was rescued well before Halloween.

The bathroom was filled with her favorite scented body washes. After a quick shower, she pulled on some comfortable jeans and a Henley top left in one of the dresser drawers, quickly applied a minimum of makeup, and ran down the stairs to the kitchen to help her mom.

"There's our sunshine," her dad greeted her. He stood, and with the newspaper in one hand, kissed her warmly on the cheek.

"Top of the morning to you, Dad." Chelsea returned his kiss with a half hug, and then turned to her mom who was placing a huge platter of scrambled eggs on the table.

"Did you sleep well, Honey?" asked her mother.

"Sure did. Like a top, although why and how tops sleep is a puzzle to me."

Lindy and Kielah followed their mother with platters of bacon, fried potatoes, biscuits, and Valencia orange and kiwi slices. Lindy and Kielah squealed as cheerleaders will, giving her hugs from each side, nearly squishing her and spilling the food. Galeah rescued the platters of food, freeing the girls to jump up and down with Chelsea in the middle.

Just then they heard a cheery whistle and a polite knock on the door. Chelsea crossed the kitchen to open the door for Jasper and Frank.

"You all don't have to knock at our house," Chelsea reproved mildly. "The only people who knock come to the front door and want to sell us something."

"I'll remember that," said Jasper.

After introductions were made and everyone was seated, Mr. Merrill said the blessing and the food was passed. Seeing the coffee service on the buffet table, Jasper poured for whoever wanted some.

"Quick. Here comes Lawton, our first born. He's also our late bloomer, and he won't be coherent until we get some coffee in him. One cup, black, please, Jasper," said Mrs. Merrill.

Lawton entered, yawning hugely, one eye closed, dark hair standing high on the right side of his head, his garish red and purple satin robe loosely belted. Jasper handed him the coffee. He took an appreciative sniff followed by a gulp. The other eye popped open, and he finally realized the presence of those other than family in the room. Immediately the teasing began.

"Late night with Lanie, huh Lawton?" asked Kielah.

"No. I had to work, and then I went with the guys somewhere, and where is none of your business," he retorted.

Just then he spied Chelsea. He jumped up and danced around the table. She met him halfway, and he twirled her in a spin before giving her a huge hug and returning her to her seat with a plop.

"Chelsea, girl. You must have come in late, too." This was said in the hopes of deflecting some of the teasing.

"Before you, bro. This is Jasper, and this is Frank," she said in introduction, but she stopped, not knowing whether to identify them as secret service or not. But Jasper immediately filled the gap. He stood and grasped Lawton's hand.

"A pleasure," he said. "There was a little snafu with the President yesterday, so Chelsea graciously invited us here to provide a decoy. I'm sure you'll be able to read all about it in the morning paper."

"It's all here," said Mr. Merrill, thumping the paper that now sat folded neatly beside his plate.

"Oh, good," said Lawton. "Any blood and gore?" he asked hopefully.

"Gross!" "Yuck!" said Lindy and Kielah at the same time.

"Lawton," said Mrs. Merrill. "Not at the table."

Lawton subsided, filling his plate and his mouth with food, a great way to avoid verbal trouble.

"So did you have a quiet evening, men?" asked Mr. Merrill of Jasper and Frank.

"Absolutely," responded Jasper.

"How about you, Sir?" asked Frank.

"Call me Davey, and nothing I could see or hear. But I'll let you form your own judgment later."

Once those cryptic messages had been given and received, the conversation flowed brightly around the table. Following breakfast, the girls helped their mom clean the kitchen and prepare for the afternoon cookout, but Galeah had begun cooking the previous evening, fixing macaroni salad, the kind with fresh cucumber and peppers that Chelsea liked most, as well as her favorite pecan pie.

Aunt Clara and Uncle Craig came first with Michael and Melanie. Aunt Clara liked to help Galeah in the kitchen while Uncle Craig talked "computerese" with Davey. He had a job at the retired navy base in Homeland Security. With permission from Frank, Davey led Craig to the library, and they checked out the bells and whistles on his new video security.

Chelsea noticed that Jasper took pity on Michael and kept him talking until Uncle Phil and Aunt Sarah arrived with Paul and PJ. Lawton had disappeared to shower and change into something presentable after dire threats from Galeah.

Rosie and Ryan, both athletic, joined her and Melanie outside on the front lawn to watch Kielah and Lindy show some new dance moves they had seen at a recent cheerleading competition. They all learned the new moves until by mutual consent they went upstairs to Lindy and Kielah's room to do pedicures before the late afternoon barbeque. Gwen joined them when her family arrived, making excuses for her sister, Gina, who had to work.

When the girls retired upstairs, the boys took over the front lawn, starting a desultory game of soccer. All of the cousins had played at some point in their lives, but Gordon, who had come with Gwen, Geoffrey and Justin who had just arrived with their parents, and Michael, Paul, and PJ had all played on their schools' soccer teams. In fact, Geoffrey and Justin occasionally played against the others since they attended Stratford High and the others attended Summerville High.

The day was growing warmer, so the boys decided to move to the bunkhouse. As they were moving in that direction across the courtyard, Grandpa Will and Grandma Mary arrived with Great Grandma Laura. The boys gave dutiful hugs, and Galeah called Chelsea and the rest of the girls down for hugs and kisses, too. Jasper stood quietly in the background.

Grandpa Will tugged a strand of Chelsea's hair that was blowing in the breeze. "So how's the famous President's aide today? Were you near the action yesterday?"

"No, Grandpa. All the action took place in the stands yesterday."

"That's interesting. So the President's life wasn't directly in danger. That's good. We want to keep him and, more importantly, you safe."

"That's the job of the Secret Service. Grandpa, Grandma, I want you to meet Jasper. He works for the President, too," said Chelsea, tugging on Jaspers arm to pull him forward.

"It's a pleasure to meet you, Sir, Ma'am," said Jasper. Chelsea's explanation was very neatly executed, Jasper thought. She hadn't given away much information about his specific duties. But Grandpa Will wanted more information.

"What is your job, Jasper?" he asked.

Jasper could see no reason to lie. "I'm employed by the Secret Service."

"Oh. So you're here to guard our Chelsea."

Chelsea was sending him murderous looks, so Jasper quickly rectified this erroneous assumption.

"No. We needed a decoy, and the President had promised Chelsea a day or two off. So we used the Presidential limo to drive down here. And since I'm the new kid on the block, I drew decoy duty, I guess. Does Chelsea need guarding?" he asked innocently.

For the last comment, he received a sharp dig in his side.

"I can take care of myself," Chelsea said sweetly. "Grandma, it's so good to see you!"

Grandma Merrill hugged Chelsea. Then she turned to Jasper.

"All young ladies need guarding," Grandpa Will was saying.

Grandma Merrill just patted Jasper's cheek. "Grandpa will have his fun. Don't mind him. He's just 'old school' in some ways. Isn't that how you young people say it?"

Jasper showed his surprise at her knowledge.

"I have plenty of help with all these teenagers around." She chuckled. "It's very nice to meet you, Jasper. Enjoy your time with us." She moved slowly toward the kitchen with Galeah amid a chorus of greetings from the men who had been pulled away from their new toy in the library.

"I'll talk to you later," Chelsea said menacingly to Jasper. She went back upstairs with the rest of the girls who were now looking at him with much more interest in their eyes.

When he turned to go with the guys to the bunkhouse, they were also eyeing him with new respect as well. Oh yeah. Frank had warned him. It was the 'Secret Service' thing.

"Have you ever shot anyone?" Michael wanted to know as they entered the bunkhouse.

"No." Jasper laughed. "Only at the shooting range. Remember, I'm new at this."

"Are you carrying a gun right now?" PJ wanted to know.

"Yep." Jasper lifted the hem of the longish, white, knit, collared shirt to reveal a slim belt with a gun in a holster, two extra magazines, handcuffs, plastic gloves, a small but powerful flashlight, OC spray and his cell phone. The belt was part of his 'civilian' clothing, specially made so that he could fit these items in loops and pockets for ease of movement and concealment.

"Cool!" said PJ and Justin.

"I had to train to be able to carry these items. For instance, to carry a tazer, regular policemen have to be tazed. Trust me, it's not fun. The OC or pepper spray is even worse. That stuff will stay with you for a while."

Since Gordon, Geoffrey, Paul, and Lawton were now deep in a two versus two battle of Mario Kart, Jasper challenged the remaining three to foosball.

Meanwhile, Chelsea was being barraged with questions about Jasper.

"How long have you known him?" asked Gwen.

"Only since yesterday. He's new on the force."

"He's so cute," sighed Melanie. "I just love the natural curls he has. Have you kissed him yet?"

The others laughed as Chelsea began to sputter. "No, Mel. You don't kiss a boy you barely know. And for your information, we are NOT dating. He's just here on business, basically."

"Me thinks the lady doth protest too much" said Lindy. Her drama class was studying *Hamlet*.

"I don't have time to get involved with anyone right now," said Chelsea.

"Well, when and if you decide to date him, let us know. We promise not to say a word," said Kielah. She glanced around the room, catching eyes with each cousin present, getting their nodded consent. Chelsea was getting perturbed, and Kielah was the peacemaker. Besides, if they wanted more juicy details later, they needed to give Chelsea some space.

"There you go, Chels. None of us will say a word, especially in front of Jasper. If something develops between you two, great! But if not, no problem."

Chelsea sniffed, somewhat mollified. "It's not easy being the oldest cousin. Y'all will find yourself in the same position some day."

"Girls. It's time to eat," called Aunt Sarah up the stairs.

The men had placed a long board across two sawhorses. Aunt Gloria had placed a tablecloth over it. Aunt Grace, who worked at a nursing home, made sure that Great Grandma Laura was comfortably seated in a cushioned chair at one of the patio tables. Two more patio tables, a long, rectangular table, and their chairs had been pulled from the garage.

Soon the makeshift buffet table was laden with all of their favorites: fried chicken, several varieties of baked beans, homemade mac and cheese, potato salad, Chelsea's favorite macaroni salad, green beans sautéed in rosemary-garlic butter, baby carrots in a honey-mint glaze, a huge green salad, rolls and gallons of southern sweet tea.

Once the boys had reluctantly left their game, whooping and hollering about Lawton's defeat by Gordon and had joined the group, Grandpa Will led them in a short prayer of thankfulness for the food and Chelsea's safety.

The sun shone gladly on the group, and a cooling breeze made the outdoors bearable. No one, not even the keenly observant Frank, noticed the small silver Cobalt slide down the street and pause, just briefly by the courtyard entrance. Nor did anyone observe the jogger who passed by twice around five o'clock.

The evening news stunned them all, however. Katie Couric reported that the blonde-headed woman who had been killed at the graduation the previous day had not been hit by a bullet from a Secret Service gun. The bullet had come from a high powered rifle, a type often linked to al-Qaeda, and once the woman's wig and nose prosthetic had been removed, she was recognized as being linked to Iran's government.

Frank's fork paused over the excellent coconut cake Grandma Mary had made. Jasper was drooling over the creamy chocolate cappuccino pie brought by Aunt Grace, but the next news item gave him pause as well. Another visitor to the graduation had actually been the recipient of the bullet that had killed the woman. It had caught him in his left shoulder, fortunately coming to rest above his heart.

In addition, the huge explosion that had occurred was nothing more than gunpowder often used in pyrotechnic displays for the Fourth, but without the glamour of the sparkles. It had been detonated by remote control.

Chapter Nine

Frank worked at the computer in the library, Jasper beside him. They were watching the video for the day. Frank had left it running as a precaution.

Jasper watched Chelsea walk away from the camera. As he admired the little wiggle in her butt, he realized her feminine assets were often hidden by dress clothes. At home, dressed casually in jeans, she was much more alluring.

And instantly he felt guilty. He really had loved Allison. But it was time to move on. No false guilt, he ordered himself. He knew in his head Allison would agree. His heart, however, didn't always cooperate.

"Wait a minute." Frank paused the screen, making a still of a woman jogging by the house. He enlarged the face and saved the image. Then he rewound the tape to the driver of a silver car that had passed while they had been eating. He enlarged the frame and placed the pictures side by side on the computer screen. It was the same woman!

Frank immediately downloaded the pictures to the office in Washington with a quick email of explanation. Then he placed a call to Tillot.

Tillot had news for them, too. The black Cadillac was a rental car, loaned to Mariann Fenton.

We've run the social security number connected to the driver's license, and it's of someone deceased. You two are needed back here. Plan on leaving tomorrow afternoon. We've had new developments on this case."

"So the news has reported. Iran, huh?"

"It's much worse than that," Tillot said dryly. "But I'll clue you in person on Monday morning. Jasper, too."

Speculation had run rampant in the Merrill living room following the six o'clock news.

"If the woman was from Iran and Secret Service didn't shoot her, who did?" asked Uncle Phil.

"Only two possibilities exist," said Uncle Craig. "Either a member of another terrorist group shot her, or a member of her own party shot her. My question is how did she get into the arena? And for that matter, how did the person who shot her get close enough to shoot her? He or she had to be within shooting range, surely another security breach."

"Did she have any weapons on her?" asked Uncle Phil. Everyone looked at Frank and Jasper.

Frank spread his hands and arms and gave a shrug. "We're not in the information loop right now," he said. "Jasper and I won't get the all of the known facts until we return to Washington."

"Actually, the news report stated that nothing was on her body to identify her. I imagine though, that she was videotaped entering the facilities if she entered by legal means," said Uncle Galen quietly. "That's probably how they discovered that she is with the Iranian government. But it also means that she disposed of her identification once she was in the arena. She probably had a fake id." He was a professor at the College of Charleston and the deep thinker in the group.

"I wish we could see the ballistic report from the autopsy," stated Uncle Garret. He worked on the police force for North Charleston. Aunt Grace was in forensics, so they often discussed cases together.

"Why?" asked Uncle Phil.

"You answer that one, Dear," said Uncle Garret. Most of the aunts were also in the room with the exception of Clara and Galeah who were finishing with the wipedown of the kitchen.

"Well, for one thing, the entrance and exit wounds will reveal the distance the shooter was from his target. In addition, if they've recovered the bullet which almost certainly they did,
they can determine what kind of weapon it was fired from," explained Aunt Grace.

"One more thing," added Uncle Garret. "With the bullet becoming lodged in the shoulder of the man who was hit, investigators can trace the trajectory, determining where the suspect stood when he or she fired the shot."

"What was she doing here in the first place?" The question popped out of Chelsea's mouth before she could stop it. Everyone looked inquiringly at her.

"Was she working for the Iranian government? Was she here to do evil? She obviously wasn't a suicide bomber; she didn't have any explosives on her. Could she have been working as a spy?"

"Given the way women are treated in most Muslim countries, maybe she was here in America seeking asylum, or maybe just getting away from mistreatment," said Aunt Sarah.

"If that's true, maybe others were afraid of information she could give to the United States," said Chelsea slowly.

"We need to look at the larger picture here, too," said Uncle Craig. "How is this going to affect our relationship with Iran which is already strained? We suspect they have nuclear capabilities."

"In my opinion, they already have nuclear warheads. And I'm not the only one who believes so," interrupted Uncle Galen. "Ahmadinejad has already threatened to wipe Israel off the map. He needs to be taken seriously. Iran calls Israel Little Satan and the United States Great Satan. We'll be next if they attack Israel, but wait," he said sarcastically. "They've already attacked us on our own soil once. Who's to say they won't attack us first and then go after Israel just to make sure we can't come to Israel's aid?"

"That's true," said Uncle Craig. "Over half of the U.S. population lives within a three-hour drive of the coast. We know this. Iran knows this. In my opinion, an attack on major U.S. ports will be their next dirty deed. And if Iran doesn't perpetrate an attack, Al-Qaeda will."

"We all may believe this to be true, but it makes me sick that many in our country still don't," said Uncle Phil heatedly.

Chelsea looked sympathetically at Paul, PJ, and the twins. Their dad was starting to get wound up now.

"It's the fatal flaw of many Americans," said Uncle Galen soberly. "Americans have been raised in such an unparalleled atmosphere of tolerance, they refuse to believe that true evil really exists, that there are those who hate them without cause. Or to look at it from another perspective, our very existence causes such a blinding fury to rise in the hearts of our enemies that they want to totally annihilate us."

"In addition," he continued, "those who refuse to believe in such unmitigating hatred usually refuse to believe in exceptional goodness, in morality, in absolutes. Because if they believed in good and evil, then they would also have to believe in a standard of right living, and then they would have to question their own actions in the light of such a standard. It is much easier to believe in neither extreme hatred nor extreme goodness. That allows such thinkers off the hook morally, but it also tends to totally blindside them when they are confronted with unprovoked hatred and evil."

Wow, thought Chelsea. Uncle Galen might not express himself in verbal excess like Uncle Phil, but he was no less impassioned in his beliefs.

"You're absolutely right, Galen," said Davey, speaking for the first time. "Look at how many times America has been warned of impending enemy threats that she did not take seriously."

"The Iraqi invasion of Kuwait is an example of that," said Uncle Craig. "No one believed Saddam would really invade Kuwait, that he could really be so evil in threatening chemical warfare, but he did and he was."

"Another example is the September 11 attack," said Davey. "From the papers I've read, our enemy continually tells us what they are going to do, but we underestimate them, then we are surprised and stunned when they do exactly what they say they will do."

Galeah appeared in the doorway. "Have we solved the world's problems yet?" she asked, adding some cheer to the somber atmosphere.

"Don't mind them," she said to Jasper and Frank. "Every time we get together, they try to analyze world events and develop solutions. Of course, they have their own opinionated viewpoints about everything."

"We have to do what we can to protect our Chelsea-girl," protested Uncle Craig.

Aunt Clara appeared in the door. "Anyone want more dessert?" she enquired. The cousins made a concerted move for the dining room.

Chelsea joined Jasper at the table as he put a small slice of pecan pie on his plate.

He shook his fork at her mockingly. "I just have to try some of your favorite dessert," he said. "No chasing villains until we've been fortified with more sugar and caffeine."

"I've eaten twice as much as I normally do when I'm on the job back in D.C." Chelsea admitted. "I'll just have to put in some more time at the gym when I get back, or go for longer walks."

"Maybe we can go for a walk later when everyone has left, and you can show me Summerville," responded Jasper.

But the cousins stayed, Gina and three-year-old Caden joining them in time to get plenty of leftovers, although most of the aunts and uncles left, some having work the next day. Chelsea wanted to catch up on the news with Gina, whose fiancée had romantically proposed at Christmas. Jasper became involved in a major foosball challenge, and they never did take a walk.

Considering the images of the woman caught on the video surveillance screens, that was probably a good thing, thought Jasper.

The next morning, Frank encouraged Jasper to attend church with Chelsea's family. He said he would stay and watch more surveillance video and generally keep an eye on things. But the morning was quiet, and Frank had nothing new to report when Jasper, Chelsea, and her family returned.

Following Sunday dinner with the rest of the family, Chelsea was finally able to take Jasper on a walk around Summerville. She showed him the Mary Arden house on Sumter Avenue, the bronze sculptures of children playing and reading in Magnolia Park, the stained glass at the back of Guerin's Pharmacy, and the name of Saul Alexander also done in stained glass and discovered when the awning had blown off of the Single Smile Cafe, a wonderful little tea shop next to the train tracks, which had been an important link to Charleston in the golden age of railroading.

As they walked, quite a few people greeted Chelsea by name, asking after her family, her grandparents, and her job in Washington. Jasper realized that they were all proud of her accomplishments both in graduating from Clemson and in becoming an aide to the President. Many gave her pieces of advice, reminiscent of her relatives' sentiments from the previous day, to give to the President.

Mrs. Dunning opened Guerin's just for Chelsea so that Jasper could buy her an orangeade—made on the spot with real oranges, and they companionably ambled back toward Chelsea's house.

"So how do you like my quaint little town?" asked Chelsea.

"It's certainly different from my home town, but I like it. I like the feeling of connectedness you seem to have with so many others in town. They are certainly proud of you. And they seem to be rather opinionated about politics."

"Oh? And people in Virginia aren't opinionated as well?" asked Chelsea.

"I didn't mean that in a negative way. I just think it's interesting."

As they entered the courtyard, Galeah met them. "Uncle Craig is closeted with Frank and your dad, and your orders are to leave immediately."

"Has anything happened?" asked Jasper, at once on the alert.

"You'll have to talk to Frank about that, once you get on the road, I suppose."

They left within the next fifteen minutes. Galeah had packed some of the homemade foods Chelsea liked. She had come with very little, so packing to leave took very little time.

Jasper rode in the front with Frank, listening to the new developments and then keeping the phone lines to the office busy.

At the Air Force Base in Charleston, The Beast, as the Presidential limo was affectionately called, was loaded onto a plane. Chelsea, Frank and Jasper were shown to seats near the cockpit.

Chelsea was somewhat peeved when Jasper and Frank huddled close to talk shop, but the drone of the plane lulled her to sleep. She didn't even realize when Jasper took the seat next to her, stretched his long frame as best he could, and slept beside her.

London, England
May 19th

Chapter Ten

As the car left the hospital, Charm, still weak and recovering, breathed a sigh of relief. She was anxious to take a break, and she was tired of people hovering over her, especially Guy.

Sandy and Donnell, on the other hand, had been wonderful. In spite of Sandy's own injuries, she had taken care of all the paperwork at the hospital, giving her full name of Charmaine (pronounced with an 'sh' instead of 'ch') Marie Dumotte from Samois sur Seine, France.

Donnell stored the information about her name in his brain. He would ask her about it at a later date. Right now he needed to stay near Charm and make sure the doctors had pertinent information so she would receive immediate help for her specific injury.

He gave the lead nurse, whose name was Maria, the information, watching with satisfaction as they gave Charm oxygen and prepared to flush her body with solution to remove the oily residue of the compound.

"You actually have two more patients," he told her. "Sandy helped Charm with her dress, and she has some injuries on her hands."

Sandy looked at him gratefully. Her hands, arms, and neck were burning with even more intensity now, and the pain was nearly more than she could bear. She was hustled to the curtained cubicle next to Charm.

Who's the third patient?" asked Maria.

Donnell held up his hands. Another young nurse, who had been not so covertly ogling him, flushed with pleasure when the head nurse assigned him as her patient. He was relieved when he was placed on the other side of Charm. He didn't want to make a huge disturbance about it, but his primary responsibility was still Charm's protection.

Once his burns were flushed, Donnell had a private talk with Maria, and showing his badge, he arranged a private room for Charm and Sandy with an extra cot for himself. He also asked that the nurses obtain ID on anyone asking for information about Charm, especially anyone who came to the hospital asking about her.

Since his wounds were the least serious, he was shown to the room first, and he made a quick inspection but found nothing strange or out of place. A reclining chair was hidden by a wall that jutted out about five feet from the window, giving him privacy and an idea.

Donnell had a suspicion that the perpetrator would be frustrated at being thwarted from seeing the damage of his or her handiwork. He or she just might come to the hospital. Donnell intended to watch all visitors closely. However, he knew sleep deprivation could interfere. Not only would he have Natalie spell him occasionally, he would place an unobtrusive camera somewhere in the room.

Immediately he placed a call to Marcus. Within thirty minutes, Natalie appeared with the equipment, and working quickly and efficiently, they had it operating mere minutes before Charm was wheeled into the room followed by Sandy in a wheel chair. She had opted to keep Charm company once she had been treated, giving Donnell the time he needed to do his work.

"Here we are." Sandy spoke cheerfully despite the exhaustion evident in her face.

"I just want to go home," said Charm petulantly.

The nurse wheeling Charm's bed into the room gave Sandy, Donnell and Natalie a wink. "We'll have you all situated within the next ten minutes, Sweetie," she said soothingly. "If you go outside again, it will aggravate your injuries, and we don't want that." Deftly she situated the bed beside the one already in the room, locking the brakes and adjusting the IV poles. Another nurse entered with a computer board and medication.

A hasty signature was scrawled, and quickly the medication was injected into the IV bag. Donnell noticed an immediate change in Charm. He rubbed, in small circles, the only place on the back of Charm's hand that was not red.

Charm knew she was being petulant, but she felt powerless to act any other way. When Donnell began to rub the back of her hand in slow circles, she felt herself melting. It was an oddly intimate and caring gesture, and even in her medicated stupor, she felt cherished. Cherished and vulnerable. But before she could dwell on her vulnerability and garner some defense in the form of anger, she was sucked into sleep.

As Maria helped Sandy into bed, Donnell glanced at Natalie. They had already discussed their next step.

"We need your help, Sandy," Donnell said. "But first, let me introduce you to Natalie. She's my assistant, and should I be absent or incapacitated, she takes my place."

Natalie perched on the end of Sandy's bed and continued with their request. "Obviously, someone is trying to get to Charm. Donnell, here, is the first line of defense, and I form a second line. But we need someone else, just in case. Would you be willing to help us guard Charm?"

"Oh, yes! She's my best friend from high school. She let me come on tour with her and do her costuming, giving me a chance to work on my dream of designing. I'd do anything to protect her."

"I know you're exhausted," continued Natalie. "But if you happen to see anyone or anything that strikes you as odd, call me immediately. I'm going to give you this cell phone with a protected frequency. Just hit the green button, and it will access me immediately."

"I can do that," said Sandy stoutly.

"One more thing. Donnell and I will be switching back and forth on guard duty while you are here in the hospital, so we believe we have the situation covered. Tonight's attack, however, is a very personal attack against Charm, and the perpetrator will most likely try to garner information about the result of his handiwork in the next few hours. We intend to be ready for him."

"I just wish we knew his motivation," stated Donnell wearily, rubbing a hand over his face. "Why is Charm being targeted?"

Two pairs of keenly observant eyes watched Sandy's reaction, and Natalie thought she detected the slight shock of recognition of a thought, but she couldn't be sure. That would bear some watching.

Sandy yawned once then twice, and Natalie laughed, saying she had work to do at the office. "I'll leave you all to chase some dreams for a while."

Once Natalie had closed the door behind her, Donnell explained that he would be out of sight behind the partition wall should he be needed but that he was going to get a few hours of sleep as well.

Late the following morning, Maria finally allowed visitors. Guy was the first person to enter. Charm was still sleeping.

"Sandy! How are you feeling?" he asked.

"I still have some minor burns, but I feel much better. Probably because I'm getting some rest, you slave driver," she teased.

"I feel so guilty," responded Guy.

Sandy knew better than to let this opportunity slip past her. "Why do you feel guilty?" she asked with as much umbrage as she could manage in her voice.

"I slipped into the dressing rooms and unlocked Charm's cases. I was just trying to help before the concert."

"You know I always do that. Where did you get the keys?" asked Sandy.

"I'm the one who bought the trunks. Of course I have the second set of keys."

"Why do you have them? What if you're not present at the concert and the keys are needed?"

Donnell didn't feel the need to intrude. Sandy was doing fine without his assistance.

"I'm usually at all of Charm's concerts," Guy said dryly. "She's my only account right now."

Sandy relaxed slightly and sat back against the pillows. "When did you arrive? I didn't see you at all. Of course, I wasn't really looking for you."

"Actually, the trunks arrived at eight o'clock yesterday morning, and I unlocked them then."

"Ooh. They were unlocked all that time then. Anyone could have accessed them."

Guy shrugged, slightly embarrassed.

Donnell would have to check with his operatives about the times they had arrived. He had come at six a.m., but, of course, he had been over every inch of the concert venue and probably not even close to the vicinity of the trunks and Guy when they had arrived. He would double check on the whereabouts of the rest of the crew at that time.

In the bed beside Sandy, Charm stirred. "Is that you, Guy?" Her eyes felt leaden, her head woolly, and her mouth extremely dry.

"Yes, Babe, I'm here. Would you like a drink of water?"

Charm opened her eyes to slits and reached both hands toward the cup and straw Guy held toward her. Sipping greedily, she drank the entire cup of water then leaned back with a sigh of satisfaction.

Donnell, watching from the shadows of the partition, noticed her tousled curls and her pale skin. His gut clenched, and he realized this woman stirred him on a physical level more than he liked to admit.

"Where is she? Where is our petite fille?" The voice preceded the entrance of a tall, well-muscled man with a full head of dark red hair. He was followed by a nurse, a small woman with gray eyes, her blonde hair pinned into a chignon, a younger version of Charm, and a boy of about twelve.

"Papa! Maman!" Charm's eyes filled with tears. She had been having a silent pity party for herself, wishing she could go home to recuperate, and now her parents were here!

Sandy watched with satisfaction, knowing her quick phone call, late as the evening had been, was very appreciated by Charm and her parents.

During the confusion of greetings, gentle hugs, and explanations, Donnell stepped from behind the wall and blended into the background, watching the warmth of the reunion and Guy's reaction. He seemed none too pleased that Charm's parents had appeared. Donnell wondered why.

Charm's family knew Sandy very well, and Guy they had met. As Charm looked around, she realized they had not yet met

Donnell. Although he had spent the night behind the partition, she had, in moments of wakefulness, been conscious of his presence.

"Papa, Maman, this is Donnell," said Charm, motioning him forward. "He does security work for my concerts."

Her words minimalized his position, but Donnell was loathe to have his real position and purpose known, and perhaps Charm did not want to alarm her parents.

"A pleasure, Monsieur," said Donnell extending his hand in greeting to Mr. Dumotte. He took Mrs. Dumotte's hand and kissed it in an old-fashioned gesture of civility and homage. "Madame," he said simply.

"Please call me Christian," requested Mr. Dumotte, "and I know my wife would prefer to be called Catherine."

"Indeed, I would," she added to her husband's words with merriment in her eyes over Donnell's greeting.

"Now tell us what happened to you," Cecelia, Charm's sister, demanded.

Explanations were made by Charm, who was still hoarse, and Sandy about the dress for her final song being sprayed with some sort of caustic material that had burned her skin severely, even choking her breathing.

"But I don't understand. Why would someone want to harm you?" asked Catherine. "Not everyone has loved you, you are a strong personality, Cherie, but I've never sensed that anyone has hated you to the point that they would inflict such damage."

Charm just shrugged, keeping her eyes downcast as she played with the edge of the blanket. Donnell, watching closely, was struck again with the sense that she was not revealing everything she knew. He would need to get close enough to her to discover what secrets she had. He just hoped his heart was strong enough to withstand the attraction he felt.

"Why can't she come home to recuperate?" asked Christian.

Guy, who had been so still he appeared comatose, came alive at this point. "No, no. She has concerts to perform in America. She has built an interest in her music, and we must capitalize on this interest overseas."

Behind his back, Charm's brother, Charlie, made a gamin face, causing Sandy to giggle.

"I'm not talking about a long time. A week at most; maybe just three or four days. We can keep our petite fille safe at home," responded Christian.

Donnell's mind raced. He would need to accompany Charm, but this might provide him with the time he needed to discover what information Charm was withholding. Moving to the back of the group, he tapped a code into his cell phone to place his operatives on the alert.

Marie entered, and Christian questioned her about getting the doctor to possibly release Charm for recuperation at home. She looked at Donnell who nodded almost imperceptibly.

"I think that can be arranged," she said cheerfully, "although the doctor will probably want her to stay one or two more nights for observation, just to make sure her lungs are clear. We don't want her to develop pneumonia or asthma."

"But what about the concerts?" protested Guy.

"Oh, stop, Guy," commanded Charm hoarsely. "The next concert is not for more than a week. Surely I can spend a few days with my family. I trust you and Colin will make the appropriate arrangements." She gratefully sipped the orange juice Marie had thoughtfully placed on her bed table.

"Well, that's settled," said Catherine. "We will plan to take Charm with us then. Meantime, we need to get accommodations, and let Charm rest for awhile. We'll come by again this evening to visit."

Donnell wanted to follow Charm's parents from the room, but he also wanted to hear what Guy had to say to Charm in private. Quickly he stepped to Marie's side and asked her to waylay the Dumotte's at the nurse's station until he could escort them to their vehicle.

Guy watched their departure morosely. "Charm, you can't be late arriving in America to prepare for this concert."

"I won't be late. Surely I've made enough money to warrant the trip in a private jet. I would think you had work to do. Don't hover, Guy, I can't tolerate it. And again, I won't be late. I didn't get to where I am by being a slouch, but I can and will be a diva if it suits my purposes."

In spite of her confinement to a hospital bed, Charm was every inch a commanding queen. Donnell couldn't help but watch the scene in admiration.

"I'll tell Colin, Sean, and the other band members. But I'm your concerned agent, not your bloody messenger boy. Remember that," Guy said with a glower.

He stalked from the room, and Donnell followed with a mock salute to the girls.

With the room emptied, both sighed, looked at each other, and then laughed.

"Why did you sigh?" asked Charm of Sandy.

"I think Donnell is very handsome, don't you? With someone like him around, a girl would always feel protected and cherished." When Charm didn't respond, she asked, "Why did you sigh?"

"I'm tired," was all Charm would say. She lowered the bed, and, pulling the covers over her, sank into a sound sleep.

London, England/Samois-Sur-Seine, France
May 21ˢᵗ

Chapter Eleven

Donnell spent a half hour with Charm's parents at a quaint, mostly empty pub around the corner from the hospital where he briefly related the attacks made against Charm and the need to keep her well-protected. Charm's trip home was made with relative ease. The doctor had made her spend an extra day as a precaution "to protect her lungs." No one, least of all Charm, could argue with his reasoning.

Donnell procured a vehicle from the department. He chose to ride in the back of the bullet-proof car with Sandy, Charm, and her family so he could get to know them better.

The vehicle looked small from the outside, but inside, an extra seat in the back gave Charm room to lie down should she need it. Tiffany, the only other operative he thought wise to bring, rode in the front with the driver. He had arbitrarily left the rest of his ops in London, working the few leads they had or taking time off so they would be fresh for the trip to the United States. He hoped this would be a wise call.

"Charlie, stop bouncing from window to window," complained Cecelia, or CeCe, as she was called by her family.

Charlie wanted to see all the sights he could from the windows of the vehicle, especially the great Wembley Arena. The last time he had been in England, he had been too young to appreciate what he was seeing.

"Do you know when you're scheduled for a concert in the southern part of the United States?" Christian asked Charm.

"Actually, I think we have a concert in Charleston, Papa," said Charm. She understood why he asked.

Christian turned to Donnell to explain. "We have a bungalow in the Beaufort area of South Carolina. Some of my ancestors were French Huguenots who escaped to the Charleston area in the 1600s. When I did some genealogical research, I found some of my relatives, the Laurens, and bought some land from one of them."

"Ooh! We can go shopping in Charleston, Maman." CeCe was thrilled at the thought.

"We'll see." Catherine smiled. "I'll look forward to some time in the hammock or the swing or lolling on the beach—nothing too strenuous. I need a break from temperamental chefs. But Beaufort has some quaint stores, too," she added to prevent the pout she could sense was soon to come from CeCe.

"What exactly do you do, Catherine?" asked Donnell.

"My formal title is executive director of *Cuisine Monde*, but in reality, I contact guest chefs and arrange for them to appear on the show, and coordinate set requirements, shopping lists, lighting, sound and camera needs with the various teams and departments."

She continued. "My secretary, Jean-Anne, is superbly organized, but she has interns working for her. Some are good, but others can cause complications, especially when they buy wrong items on the grocery list. And then there are the chefs themselves. Some of them are naturals in front of the cameras and make working with them a joy, but others are demanding, nervous, and temperamental."

"What do you enjoy doing, Donnell, that is, when you are not guarding our daughter?" she asked, her eyes twinkling.

Donnell was at a loss. He rarely did much outside of his work. "I'm a very boring person. I enjoy a good hike in the quiet of the woods. When I'm home in Ireland, my family often has musical sessions in the evenings, and my grandparents can always use help with their tourist lodging. When I'm in London, I go to the gun range regularly to hone my skills, and I run several miles a day whenever I can."

"You should try riding a bike with Charm and me sometime. Nothing like wind in your face to blow the cobwebs off of the brain," said Christian.

"I would probably enjoy that," responded Donnell.

At Gatwick, they took a private plane, also arranged for them by Interpol, to Orly Airport south of Paris but very close to the Dumotte's hometown of Samois-Sur-Seine. Once again, they were all placed in a bullet-proof, specially equipped vehicle for the trip home.

By this time, Charm was very tired. While the others had enjoyed a light lunch and cocktails on the fifty minute flight, she had said nothing during the drive and little during the flight across the Channel. She wasn't feeling well, and she kept thinking about what Sandy had said the day before in the hospital.

Watching Donnell furtively as he talked to her family, she had to agree with Sandy—he was very attractive. And she did feel safer with him around. But she knew better than to talk about emotional things when she felt so poorly. In fact, who had her medication? The pain meds were wearing off, and she felt rather nauseous lying in the back of the car.

She sat up, slowly so she wouldn't faint, and poked Sandy, who was sitting in front of her, in the shoulder.

Sandy's face brightened. "Are you feeling better?" Her face fell. "Obviously not."

"Do you have my medication?" Charm's voice was still raspy, and she felt hot and achy.

"No. I didn't get any meds for you." She turned to face the rest of the group. "Did anyone get Charm's meds?"

"I have them," Donnell and Catherine said simultaneously.

Donnell gave Catherine a long look, and her eyes widened when she realized someone could have mixed up her daughter's medications.

"Where were the ones you packed, and when did you pack them?" asked Donnell.

"They were sitting on the nightstand with the rest of her things," responded Catherine. "I packed them while Sandy was helping Charm change into street clothes."

"And I saw these sitting on the little table that can swing over the bed that was pushed into the corner. I thought they had been overlooked. But we're taking no chances." After asking the driver to pull to the side of the road, he quickly pulled out his phone and speed dialed.

"Marcus," he said to his operative, "Connect me with the nurses' station at the hospital." After a brief wait, he asked for Marie.

"Marie, this is Donnell McKinnon. Can you tell me the name of Charmaine's medication and what the pills typically look like?" While he was talking, he exited the vehicle and after putting some distance between himself and the car, carefully opened the vial.

The bottle had not been booby-trapped. Good. "They're supposed to be pink? Are you sure? Okay. Yes, Charmaine is fine. She is nearly home. I'll tell her. Thank you."

"Do you have the number of your pharmacien, someone you trust?" he asked Christian and Catherine.

They nodded mutely.

"Call him or her and get a prescription filled for this." He showed them the name of the medication on the bottle he held. "And ask him or her if you can pick it up in fifteen minutes. We'll be there by then won't we?"

They nodded, and Catherine placed the call.

When she was finished, Donnell requested the bottle Catherine had. He would have them both inspected that night.

As soon as they arrived at the Dumotte home, Charm was given her medication and put to bed. Sandy was only too glad to lie down on the extra bed in Charm's room as she had often done when they were teens.

Meantime, Donnell drove into Paris to an Interpol office and submitted the bottles of pills for testing. They would have the results for him the next afternoon. Then he placed a call to Natalie on one of the office's secured lines.

She reported that Marcus had found a feed from the video camera to a computer in a nearby hotel. The room had been searched, but the occupant had left, and no clues of the person's identity had been unearthed. They were processing the name under which the occupant, a male, had registered.

In addition, Marcus and Seamus were looking through the video from the hospital room to discover who had placed the bottles of medication in the room. So far it looked like someone in hospital scrubs had entered Charm's room at about four in the morning, definitely a male with dark hair, but with a surgical mask and hat, positive id would probably not occur.

"Get forensics in to measure facial features and see if they can match measurements and bone structure with pictures of known terrorists," Donnell ordered. "However,   I'm still extremely suspicious of Guy. He's like a bad gas leak—he shows up everywhere."

"I think you need to concentrate on the lady herself," said Natalie. "She will provide the key to the motivation for these attacks, I'm sure of it. Just don't get emotionally involved. You know that's against ethics."

"Right. I'll try to contain that McKinnon 'charm,'" Donnell said dryly. "This isn't going to be easy. She really resents me intruding into her personal domain."

"Be a friend. Instead of trying to fit all the puzzle pieces together right now, get more puzzle pieces."

And that was the crux of the problem. He was attracted to Charm in spite of her apparent disdain of him. He wanted to drool over her silky red hair and the tight, trim package of her body that still had all the right curves, but he curbed his thoughts. He had a job to do. If he really cared for her, he would contain himself and find the person or persons threatening her.

But what was the reason for the attack and the threats? All three threatening notes had been found at the end of previous concerts. Guy, who had called Interpol, had given them to him. Now, she had been attacked personally.

He opened a folder and pulled a brochure of Charm's concerts. She had begun with a concert in Paris at the Opera Bastille, and for her first nine concerts in Dublin, Edinburgh, Copenhagen, Finland, Germany, Belgium, and Austria, she'd had no problems. Her tenth concert had been in Athens to a sold out crowd. Rome was also packed with no adverse problems. But following her twelfth concert in Florence, she had received the first note.

It read, "Return what's mine. Leave in dressing room." She had sworn to Guy that she had no idea what she had taken that belonged to someone else.

Following an open-air concert in Verona, she had discovered a second note in her hotel room: "Give it back. Or else." Again, Charm had shown bewilderment at the meaning of the note. Aix-en-Provence, was the site of the next concert. This time, the note portrayed a picture, in red ink, of a female's head with a knife slicing the throat and dripping with blood.

The first two could be dismissed as pranks, but the picture was frightening and ghoulish. Guy had found it but had kept it from Charm. Donnell and his team had been formed immediately and their assignment was twofold: to protect Charm and to discover who was making the threats and why.

But the point was that she had to have something that the perpetrator wanted. She had insisted that she had nothing, but Donnell wanted to examine every single item she carried while on tour. Her costumes, makeup, and other luggage and equipment were all going through scanners before the transfer to America.

He pushed his hand through his dark curly hair and sighed deeply. He was tired tonight, and he still had to drive back to Samois-Sur-Seine. Also, he didn't want to be away from Charm any longer than he had to be although Tiffany was more than capable of handling any crisis that occurred.

Tomorrow he would need to work on his relationship with Charm. He rather thought Sandy would be helpful in ascertaining both the way into Charm's confidence and the item the perpetrator wanted returned.

Samois-Sur-Seine, France
May 22nd

Chapter Twelve

Charm stretched carefully. Good. No pain. She was amazed yet grateful that she was, once again, in her own bed. She had been gone for nearly three months, promoting her new album on tour. Tours were a marathon of endurance and stamina. Fortunately, the bicycle rides had toughened her. A side product was the increased breath support she gained.

Across the still room, in the deep quiet and shadows of early morning, she could hear Sandy's even breathing. Sandy had been her friend since sixth grade when they had discussed shaving their legs in the girls' bathroom at school.

Charm stretched again and sat up. She really did feel good. Her mother must have slipped her a sedative last night because she felt completely rested and refreshed. What she would really like to do is to go for a bicycle ride. Her watch said six ten, and she knew that Sandy would sleep at least two more hours.

When they were on tour, early rising was at nine since they often didn't get to sleep until after three a.m. But she had been sleeping for the last three days or so, and being home, she knew her parents would be stirring soon. Her mom usually arose at six thirty to start the coffee that they all sucked like the English did their tea.

She wanted to try to ride her bike, even if it was just down to the park by the river. That was only half a mile. If her lungs felt the least bit impacted, she would stop and slowly walk her bike back home.

Pulling on some old navy sweats, a long-sleeved tee and a navy Speedo jacket with white trim, she sat back on the bed to slip on her tennis shoes. So far so good. Sandy hadn't moved, and she was still feeling marvelous.

Her own bicycle was in the storage shed, and she didn't want to either be stopped or disturb anyone, so she decided to take her father's bike that he kept in the garage. She let off the brakes and coasted down the winding drive to the road. It would have been faster to go down the trail behind her house to the road along the river, but the driveway was much smoother.

The breeze lifted her hair, and she felt the exhilaration of movement, the nearest she could come to flying. At the bottom of the hill, she turned left onto the boulevard that followed the path of the river. A small park sat one block down and went right to the edge of the quietly lapping water of the Seine.

Charm sat on one of the benches and turned her face toward the east, waiting for the sun to send a single beam signaling the beginning of the day. The grass was covered with dew, and the leaves of the tall maples seemed to be holding their breaths as well for the first gleam of light.

Light footsteps behind her didn't break her concentration.

"Charm! There you are!" came Donnell's voice.

"Shh." Charm ignored him until the sun broke over the horizon. Then she turned her head to him.

Donnell saw her face change from glowing and peaceful to sharp and imperious in an instant.

"Yes?" she questioned impatiently.

"I'm sure I don't need to point out to you that not only will you aggravate your medical condition, but that you make an excellent target for, say, an assassin."

"First, I feel marvelous this morning. I've only come for a short ride to the park with plans to do no more until I regain my strength," Charm said reasonably in spite of the annoyance she felt at his intrusion into her peaceful morning.

"Secondly, I've had time to accustom myself to the idea these last few days that someone is, indeed, threatening me. But I also think that killing me would make the news, and I question the judgment of even a terrorist to make even more of a scene, especially when they believe I have something of theirs."

"That may be true, but what if you continue to ignore their warnings, and they begin killing fans at your concerts?" Donnell stopped to let her digest this thought.

A haunted look came into Charm's eyes, and Donnell knew his question had elicited the response he wanted.

He continued. "What I'd like to do today, after you've had breakfast and in between any naps you may need, is look at, piece by piece, every single personal item you take with you on your tour."

At her sputter of indignation, he held up his hand. "I know it is an intrusion, but unless we discover exactly what they think you've stolen, the lives of not just you, but many are in danger. I have two sisters, Darla and Amy, and I've seen all their girl-stuff. Sandy can help us because, Charm, we simply have to get to the bottom of this. Are you game?" He held out his hand, palm up.

The sincerity in Donnell's voice, his concern for her fans, his respect for her as a woman all compelled Charm to place her hand in his. He brought it to his lips and, still holding her gaze, kissed it.

Charm had difficulty quelling the tingle that shivered down her spine. She wanted to pull back, knowing that she would not be able to ignore or merely tolerate him any longer. Could she simply remain friends with him without any emotional entanglements? She surely hoped so. She didn't need complications. She wanted to concentrate solely on her music, avoiding sappy love scenes.

She knew from experience that emotion clouded clear-headed, objective judgment. Her relationship with Davi'd had cost her a year of her music career, and she would not let that happen again.

But she also could not have the deaths of fans on her conscience. Could she work with Donnell and avoid emotional conflict? She must for the sake of her career and her fans.

She deliberately broke eye contact and rose to get on her bike.

"Wait. I have a better idea, if it will work." Donnell gave her a sheepish grin. "I haven't done this for a long time, but let me pedal and you can ride on the handle bars."

Charm gave him an incredulous look. "You can't be serious."

"It will ensure that we both get back at the same time, and it will save you all the work of getting up the hill again. I'm the one who will have to prove I'm still in shape. Imagine my embarrassment if I can't pedal all the way to the top."

"That might be worth seeing," Charm said with a straight face. Then she spoiled the moment by giggling. "You're on," she challenged him.

It took a few moments, but Charm positioned herself on the handlebars while Donnell balanced the bicycle. Then they were off. Donnell was proud that the bike only wobbled once before he had it moving smoothly forward.

If her fans could see her now, thought Charm. She was, however, enjoying the moment hugely. The sun was just touching the tops of the trees where the valleys were, but her family's house, made of white stucco, sat on the top of the hill, shining in the early morning sun. The small breeze that had brought a slight chill to the air was warming, and she could hear birds twittering in the high branches of the trees.

They nearly made the top without Donnell breaking his rhythmic pedaling. But Charm saw a beautiful blue butterfly land on the fragrant white blossoms of a small bush, and without hesitation, she jumped from the bike and landed at the side of the driveway. She felt giddy with happiness. She put her nose to the fragrant blossoms and watched as the butterfly circled around her head once and then flew away.

What a picture she made with her richly red hair curling in tendrils around her carelessly pulled back hair, thought Donnell. The creamy white blossoms nearly matched the creaminess of her skin, driving him mad to touch that skin, and the contrast of the blue butterfly heightened his appreciation for the picture she made. If only he could capture this moment on film. But film wouldn't catch the quiet of the morning with the sun's fingers burnishing the fiery red of her curls to a halo of gold.

Donnell could sense her joy. Was she always this happy when she wasn't being the professional singer? She seemed to have a way of embracing the moments of life and enjoying them. Was she also running away from the close proximity they shared as she rode the handlebars of the bicycle?

"Race you to the garage," called Charm. She dashed toward the garage at the side of the house. Donnell, always one to enjoy a challenge, was only a few feet behind her.

"There you two are," called Tiffany. She had stayed in one of the downstairs guest bedrooms but only after securing the premises while Donnell was gone to the city. She had made sure he was safely ensconced in the room over the garage before she had slept herself. It was her job.

She had enjoyed watching the tableau unfolding before her. An early riser herself, she had seen Charm steal quietly from the house with Donnell, also an early riser, watching. She gave him kudos for watching without panic as Charm had circled the hill and landed in the tiny park she had discovered herself the evening before. He had been smart enough to cut across the large yard on the back side of the house that sloped down to the street.

She sighed. She had also noted their encounter in the park and the ensuing bicycle ride. They were falling in love. It was so sweet. One day it would happen for her, but right now was Donnell's turn.

She, Natalie, Donnell and Gregor had been together since they had graduated from the academy, and she and Natalie had often discussed how intense Donnell was. He would need someone as passionate about life as himself. Charm sure seemed to fit the bill. She couldn't wait to tell Natalie. But now he would need just as much protection as Charm.

So far he hadn't lost his edge, but operatives, especially men, always seemed to lose their edge when they were blinded by love.

"Breakfast is served, and we have a message from headquarters," Tiffany informed the two. "Your parents were concerned until I told them you were with Donnell," she said to Charm.

"Oops. I'd better scoot." Charm made a face and disappeared into the house.

"What's the news?" asked Donnell.

"We have the results of the med switch. It was a lethal cocktail of phenyl and versed. Even if Charm had survived, she would not have remembered much as versed is an amnesiac. Marcus and Seamus reviewed all the video footage. The fake meds were brought into the room by the nurse, not by Charm's mysterious visitor, so the switch was made in the hall or elsewhere in the hospital. And honestly, anyone dressed in scrubs would not look out of place in a hospital."

So much for Charm's theory that her attacker wouldn't really kill her thought Donnell. He knew just how fatal phenyl was. They simply must find whatever her attacker wanted so badly.

Chapter Thirteen

An hour later after a quick breakfast of toast with an assortment of jams, fresh yogurt from a farm on the outskirts of town, and a yummy and filling seven-grain cereal that Catherine favored, Donnell, Sandy, and Charm were opening her luggage.

Catherine and Christian had decided to travel to work together after being reassured several times that Tiffany and Donnell would be able to protect the girls. CeCe had already left with a friend to travel into the city to school. Tiffany took up patrol outside while Donnell hauled the girls' luggage and bags into the living room where they would have ample room to work.

They began with her large suitcase. Nothing had been unpacked except for the clothes she had worn home and the simple white dress Charm had worn while singing her final number after her show dress had been contaminated.

Sandy unpacked each item, handing it to Donnell who inspected it closely. When not performing, Charm wore sweats and other athletic type clothing. They quickly went through her clothing, her socks, her shoes. When they came to her undergarments, Charm protested.

"Do you have to touch each one?" she asked, her face growing red in spite of her best intentions.

Donnell looked at the large, see-through plastic bag in which they were packed. "I've seen my sisters' unmentionables when Ma is doing laundry. But no, I'll let Sandy examine each one. Who packs your clothing?"

"I used to do it at first, but Sandy does a lot of that now," replied Charm.

Sandy took up the explanation. "Even though Charm has twice as many costumes now as she did when we first began touring three years ago for her first album, I became more efficient at packing those, so now I pack her regular street clothes, too."

"Does anyone guard the bus while you are in the concert hall?" asked Donnell.

Sandy glanced at Charm. "You might as well tell him," she said.

"Tell me what?"

"During my first tour, I was dating a guy named Davi'd. When we broke up toward the end of the tour, he threatened to blow up my bus, so Dad hired a security guard to assist the bus driver. He doubled as a body guard when the bus driver was on duty. Now Geveon is a full-time member of my tour, and when I'm not on tour, Dad or Mom use him as a bodyguard/driver at the studio."

Donnell had met Geveon, a tall, well-muscled black man and knew he was a security guard, but he hadn't known he also doubled as Charm's bodyguard nor why he'd been hired. Sometimes, some of the smallest details could crack a case, and this information gave him another suspect, Davi'd. Perhaps their suspect wasn't a terrorist after all.

Finishing with the suitcase, they began on another case, this one filled only with shoes. Each shoe had to be examined both visually and tactilely as well as with the small x-ray machine with him.

"Just when I was going to compliment you on being a light packer, Darling," he said to Charm, using his fingers on the inside of sneakers to check for anything unusual, and eyeballing the heel on the outside to check for any discrepancies that would indicate room for an explosive.

"Oh, a girl can't have too many shoes," she replied, the wicked gleam in her eyes belying the sugar in her voice.

"She rarely uses these," said Sandy in Charm's defense. "That's why she keeps two or three pairs in her main suitcase."

"It keeps me from wasting my hard-earned money shopping for shoes in every country I visit," teased Charm.

Donnell laughed, but his mind was busy on another track, and he asked another question. "What does Davi'd do for a living?"

"He's a med student at Universite de Paris. This should be his third year. But I haven't talked to him for about two years now. I've just heard things through the grapevine."

"I've heard plenty," said Sandy with a scowl on her face. My brother graduated from the same class and is also at the Universite. That Davi´d is a scumbag player. Thinks he's God's gift to women and all that."

Hmm. Donnell didn't say anything, but his suspicions of Davi´d grew. As a third year medical student, Davi´d would have access to meds, and phenyl and versed were rather common drugs.

They finished checking the shoes and moved to a carryon bag of makeup, perfumes, and other female paraphernalia. Charm watched in fascination as Donnell lined up the bottles, numbering them. Then he numbered sections of his arms and laid a test patch of the contents of every container on his arms.

Donnell looked up and saw how intently Charm was watching. "This is the old-fashioned way to do this. If anything comes up suspicious, we'll run it in the lab. But this way, I can test every bottle right now and rule out tampering."

"We should put the makeup on you, too," said Charm teasingly. "Remember how we used to do that with Charlie?" she asked Sandy.

"Your poor little brother," said Donnell with feeling.

"Actually, you don't need to test the makeup. I've already used it this morning."

"When?" asked Donnell, clearly worried.

"Right after breakfast. I didn't know you meant you wanted to check *everything* of mine."

"Yes. Everything." Donnell continued to look worried.

"It's okay," Charm said exasperated. "I haven't had any adverse reactions yet, and it's nearly lunch time."

"Speaking of lunch, let's take a break," said Donnell. He could tell Charm and Sandy, though intrigued by his examination procedures, were growing rather weary. And he was still concerned that Charm would overdo it, thinking she could bounce back from a hospital stay with very few repercussions.

"Actually Mom and Dad will be expecting a visit from me soon," said Sandy. She looked uncertainly from Donnell to Charm, not wanting to desert her friend.

"Charm should probably take a nap after lunch anyway, and I need to check in with my operatives," said Donnell smoothly.

Charm's face grew haughty again. "I'm not a bloody child," she said tersely. "I don't need babysitting."

"You're absolutely right, Darling. You certainly don't look like a child to me," he said, letting his eyes rove deliberately over the curves of her body.

"I'll stay if you want," Sandy said to Charm.

"No. Go ahead and go home. You certainly deserve some time off. Give your parents my love, and I'll come over later. Besides, I can handle this oaf myself if I have to," she said flicking a disdainful look in Donnell's direction.

"Is your bike still in storage?" asked Sandy.

"No. Dad pulled it out as well as your old bicycle before he left this morning," answered Charm as they stood and headed for the kitchen.

"Oh good. I can use some fresh Samois-Sur-Seine air." She gave Charm a long hug. "I still think he's handsome and worth getting to know," she whispered in Charm's ear. "If you don't want to pursue a fling with this guy, I'm willing to give it a go."

"Silly," said Charm and made a face.

Sandy turned to Donnell as he entered the kitchen. Stepping smoothly beside her to prevent her from speaking first, Charm asked, "What would you like for lunch? Mom left some chicken salad and some nectarines." These were some more of her favorites.

"Sounds good to me," answered Donnell. "Let me go talk to Tiffany. She's probably in need of sustenance as well." He had noticed the little by-play between Sandy and Charm but thought better of saying anything.

When he had left the room, Charm whispered to Sandy, "I'll think about it."

"Well, don't take too much time thinking or you'll miss your chance," responded Sandy. She closed the door where she'd been standing, then opened it again. "Find out first if he's attached." And she was gone.

Charm's mind was whirling. She knew a provocative look when she saw one, and Donnell's eyes had been smoldering. With Sandy's advice still in her ears, it was as if she had been given permission to pursue a relationship that she normally would have shunned. And probably should shun. She had a concert tour to finish. Davi´d had been a bounder anyway, but being on tour had wrecked whatever promise had existed in their relationship.

The war continued to wage in her mind as Donnell returned. Her desires were so ambivalent at this point. But a small step in getting to know Donnell wouldn't hurt, she told herself. Sandy was right. She could at least discover if any other girl was in the picture. One smoldering look did not a relationship create.

The chicken salad, on a bed of lettuce, lay temptingly beside the thinly sliced, juicy nectarines. They needed a light wine to add the right note to the meal. A chardonnay would do. She considered sending Donnell to the small but well-stocked cellar her father kept, but he'd probably get lost.

"C'mon," she said to him. "Let me show you where the wine cellar is. You'll need to know. And don't tell me you don't drink while on duty," she said frowning. "I don't intend being considered a duty by anyone."

"Wouldn't dream of it," Donnell said blandly.

The cellar was located in the basement. A large game room with a pool table and comfortable leather seating was on the north side of the house. A sliding glass door led out to a restful garden with shrubs, flowers, and several fountains. On the far side of the game room, a doorway opened to reveal a short hall with four more doors. One led to a small guest bedroom, one to a laundry room and another to a storage room. It was the last door that led to the wine cellar.

Many people kept wine on hand, but the Dumotte cellar contained a rather extensive selection. Donnell nearly whistled in admiration.

Charm moved on ahead, her light footfalls echoing lightly on the stone floor. She went on tiptoe to read a label. "Yes, a light chardonnay will do." She reached for it, but when she turned with the bottle, she nearly slipped on the slick, stone floor.

Donnell caught her quickly, his reflexes well-honed with training. Her face inches away from his, he engaged in an intense study of her face beginning with her eyes, their blue deepening to nearly midnight, and ending with her mouth, tantalizingly open and moist. He lowered his head and held his lips a mere inch from hers, knowing that a kiss would change the dynamics of their relationship, and at the same time wanting to prolong the agony of anticipation.

Briefly he questioned the wisdom of kissing her, but her indrawn breath clouded his better judgment, and he responded to the involuntary invitation. Lowering his lips to hers, he brushed his lips against hers, slowly, gently. Still holding the bottle of wine between them with one hand, Charm moved her other to the back of his neck, unconsciously bringing him closer.

This time when their lips met, he tasted, he explored, layering sensation upon sensation until he felt he was drowning in her fragrance, her essence. But the passion was building, and he wouldn't cross that line, not yet.

Slowly he pulled away from her lips, still nuzzling against her neck to give both of them time to slow their shuddering breathing.

"We were both aching for that, Darling," he murmured. "But you've made me ravenous. Let's go pop the cork and feast on some food." He smacked her on the cheek and, grabbing the bottle of wine, led her through the game room toward the stairs.

Charm was still bemused by the kiss, but she was glad that his last smacking kiss had put their relationship firmly back on a more platonic level.

Tiffany joined them, and as they munched on the chicken salad and sipped the Chardonnay, Donnell told them stories about his seven aunts and uncles, their lives helping his grandparents with their bed and breakfast in Killarney, Ireland, and their love of music.

Charm was amazed at Donnell's rich musical heritage. When she heard the names Marc Montaigne and Shannon McKinnon, she realized that she had seen his aunt and uncle perform several times when she had gone to the opera or charity concerts in Paris.

Following lunch, Charm refused to sleep. "I'll only stay up half the night if I sleep now," she complained.

Instead, they decided to go through Charm's personal bag. Knowing about his background and his intense love of music made it easier for Charm to show Donnell her notebook filled with scraps of papers with ideas for songs, lines to use in songs, and songs in all stages of being written.

"Sorry, but I need to go through each piece of paper," he said, and they began. "Why do you write on scraps of paper and napkins even?" he asked, holding up a napkin from the Horse's Tavern in Odeon.

"I never seem to have a notebook with me when an idea for a song pops into my head. So I write on anything that's close at hand. I wish I could be more organized," she said, handing Donnell a small selection of the papers.

"Wait a minute! What's that?" demanded Donnell.

"It's some scrap paper from a restaurant where we ate following the concert in Rome. The sound techs were telling a story, and I didn't want to interrupt them, so I began doodling and working on a song in my head." She reluctantly showed Donnell the paper with her words.

But he turned it over and looked at the words written on the back in Arabic. "I think we've found it," he said.

Silver Spring, MD/Chantilly, VA USA
May 28ᵗʰ

Chapter Fourteen

Chelsea Merrill walked briskly down the sidewalk from the subway toward the small apartment in Silver Spring, Maryland that she rented with two other girls, Angie and Brianya. Angie was from upstate New York and worked as a tour guide for Atlantis Tours in the D.C. area.

Brianya was from Georgia. She had graduated from Georgia State University, so she and Chelsea often discussed Tiger and Bulldog football in the fall. She was interning as a page in the Capitol building with the hopes of getting a full-time job for one of the senators in the fall.

It was a relief to leave the sweltering heat of the city behind. Her own neighborhood boasted a wooded area in the back where she usually entered her apartment complex, along with a small park with a pond and rustic benches, yet the convenience of a subway station close by and an apartment building that housed many other young people, some who were single and some who were recently married, who also worked on Capitol Hill.

A curly, blond-headed young man was feeding their resident duck, Josey and her family of ducklings. The back of his head reminded her of Jasper. She hadn't seen him for just over a week now, and she wondered how he was doing.

Actually, she had expected him to call. When you shared a somewhat scary adventure with someone, it bound you together in a unique way. She had really enjoyed getting to know him, and he had seemed to adapt well enough to her family and their Southern ways. The game of twenty questions had begun their relationship, and their Sunday afternoon walk holding hands had seemed somehow intimate and bonding.

Well, she would probably never see him again she reminded herself for the umpteenth time in over a week. No problem. She had plenty to do. But really, she didn't, at least not at work. Her duties were gradually lessening. She needed to find some other job possibilities as she would be unemployed by the end of the year. The bottom line was that she felt rather restless these days. Maybe she should take some of her leave time now and just go home for several weeks.

A tap on her shoulder as she was unlocking her door brought her hurtling out of her reverie. She turned, and couldn't help the gasp of surprise.

Jasper stood with his hands in his pockets, looking entirely too self-assured. Given her state of ambivalence, his confidence annoyed her, and she spoke more sharply than she felt.

"Well, look who's here! You dropped out of sight for a while."

"I was sent out of town for a while," he replied, deliberately repeating her time frame. Actually, he had been sent down to Greenville, South Carolina to finish reports at the field office there and fill in his replacement.

With the pending case, he was being reassigned to the Washington office. But he was learning to give replies that revealed very little, especially in this case when he was waiting to be briefed. That would occur tomorrow when he met with Tillot Thomason.

Chelsea wanted to ask where he had gone, but she guessed from the brevity of his reply that he wouldn't be able to tell her anyway.

"I have the next several days off, and I was wondering if I could spend some of my time with you, beginning with dinner tonight. My car is at your service, ma'am."

"I would like that," Chelsea replied, wanting to ameliorate her tartness and relieved not to have to spend the evening by herself. Angie was out of town, and Brianya's family was visiting, so she was showing them around the city during the evenings. "Make yourself comfortable while I change," she added as the door finally opened.

Jasper took her at her word. He raided the frig, and, noticing the pitcher of sweet tea, he poured himself a glass. He had grown fond of it during his stay at Chelsea's home where it was often made four or five times a day.

He liked the Oriental rug in gold and red hues that covered most of the carpet in the living room. The drapes were also in gold. The huge sofa in burnished cinnamon invited visions of him and Chelsea sitting closely or of him kissing her senseless against the cushions. He had missed her, thought of her often, couldn't get her out of his mind. But he had no idea of how she felt about him, so he admonished himself to derail his current train of thought.

Crossing to the west window that faced the street to get his mind on a different track, he gazed down at the parking lot, idly noticing the flow of traffic and the pedestrians, many returning home or to their evening activities. Two men carrying cello cases were headed toward the metro entrance two blocks away. They were dressed in white shirts and carried black suit coats—obviously headed for a performance.

A red-headed woman in garish lime green shorts and t-shirt was walking her poodle. A dark-haired young man in his twenties was standing across the street, looking at a newspaper. Hmm. Actually, he was looking over his newspaper at the front of Chelsea's apartment. Curious, Jasper glanced down at the awning covered entrance but could see nothing.

Just then Chelsea entered the room dressed in white slacks and a turquoise blue silk blouse. She was placing tiny silver hoops in her earlobes to match the three hoops on a silver chain nestled in the hollow below her throat. To Jasper's eyes, she looked stunningly beautiful, and the street scene below left his mind entirely.

"I didn't know what to wear since I didn't know where we were going. Is this okay?" she asked anxiously.

"You look beautiful and quite coolly elegant on this warm summer evening," Jasper responded.

Chelsea was pleased by his reply, but her brain, usually so quick with words was turning to mush with the appreciative look in Jasper's eyes. "Thank you, kind sir," she managed. She led the way to the door.

Jasper's car was a sporty, silver Saturn Skye with a convertible top and gray leather upholstery that did the typical thigh-hugging as Chelsea settled into the seat. He had parked by Josey's domicile in the back, and once they were both buckled into their seats, he turned the key and they left the back parking area, turning right down Chelsea's street behind her apartment building. She was surprised that he knew the back roads, turning right and then left.

But she relaxed and enjoyed the ride. The air conditioner softly circulated the new car smell, and some artist was making love with a tenor sax on the cd that played softly.

"I'm surprised you know your way around so well," she finally said. "I thought your family lives in Virginia."

"They do." He hit a button on the console, and Google Earth zoomed in on the Silver Spring area. A red blip showed where they were traveling. "I drove the streets this afternoon to get my bearings while I was waiting for you," he confessed. "I like to get a feel for areas by using maps and gadgets to explore."

"Dad has been wanting one of these. He has an older model. Uncle Craig has a GPS system very close to this one. Of course, with his job in port security, he needs it."

"You didn't tell me he was the head of operations in Charleston," Jasper said.

"Oh? You've been checking?"

"Everyone I know or spend time with goes through a check," Jasper replied. "Don't worry, you passed, too," he said teasingly.

"Well, I hope so since I work with the President," Chelsea replied.

Just then Jasper pulled up to the curb of a recently remodeled part of downtown. "Have you been here before?" he asked indicating the little Lebanese restaurant across the street.

"No. It looks interesting."

"My sister says it's awesome. She and her new husband have come here with friends."

They entered, and Chelsea was impressed with the spaciousness of the table arrangements. She hated being in restaurants where she could hear the conversation from the next table. The white tablecloths contrasted with the dark, modern wood décor, and the lighting gleamed from golden sconces on the walls and single, cylindrical lights that hung from the high ceiling.

After they were seated, a waiter in his crisp, white apron filled their water glasses and took their order.

Chelsea chose chicken and shrimp served over angel hair pasta, chestnuts, mushrooms, and crunchy bean sprouts with cilantro and lime adding a burst of flavor. Jasper chose sesame encrusted chicken with raspberry soy sauce.

Once they had been served, Chelsea commanded, "So tell me more about your sister."

"Pamela? She's a whirlwind of activity and best taken in small doses."

Chelsea laughed. "Really. You make her sound difficult."

"Well, she is very active. She's pretty bossy, too, and tries to rope all of us into helping her with her current projects. Between her and Mom, something was always happening at our house. Now that she's married, Mom is still very active, but we have more peace than we did when Pammy was there."

"How did she meet her husband?"

"Jonathan is the grandson of one of my Grandpa Charles's friends. The Tate family helped to found Virginia, one of the Virginia blue-bloods, I guess. Jonathan is being groomed for Congress. Members of his family often come to Mom's galas and charity events, and that's where they met, ages ago it seems."

"What kind of charity events and galas does your Mom spearhead?"

"Her favorite is the Midsummer's Eve Ball for Kidsave, but she also works with My Sister's Place in Virginia and Mary House in the D.C. area, and Habitat for Humanity as well as several other charities for the homeless. She's just really good at organizing events to raise money for these causes about which she's so passionate."

"Sounds like your sister is not the only one who is a dynamo." Chelsea shook her head in admiration. "Life tends to go a bit slower in the South, I think."

"What do you hear from your family?" asked Jasper.

"Dad is busy with a new computer program for Uncle Craig and the ports. Actually, it's a government contract, but since it's for Homeland Security, he and Uncle Craig are working closely together on it. Mom is thankful that school is out for the summer and is enjoying her gardens and socializing with family and friends."

"How is Lawton? I really enjoyed meeting him and the rest of your family, too."

"He's saving for an apartment or even for a house for when he and Lanie get married, but right now, Mom and Dad don't mind him staying in the bunkhouse. Meantime, Kielah just graduated from high school and she and Mom are getting ready for her big move to Clemson, and Lindy is at cheerleading camp."

The waiter removed their empty plates. Chelsea was surprised. She had enjoyed their conversation so much that she had barely noticed that they had finished. Declining dessert, they headed for Jasper's Skye.

"Do you mind if we take a little drive out in the country?" asked Jasper.

"Sounds great to me," replied Chelsea. She was enjoying the evening immensely.

Jasper headed for the Capital Beltway, crossing into Virginia.

"Now that we're private, have you heard anything new about the explosion, or the woman who was shot, or the woman who was trying to run us off the road?" asked Chelsea. "Or can you not tell me anything?"

Jasper considered a moment. "I'll tell you one thing. I don't know if it's hit the news or not, so if it hasn't, keep this to yourself. The woman who was shot was wearing a suit jacket, and in the lining of the jacket was sewn a single piece of paper. It contained a list of names in Arabic, and the CIA is trying to interpret the meaning of the names."

"Wow!" said Chelsea excitedly. "No, that hasn't hit the news yet. Is there any chance I could see the list?"

"I haven't even seen it," replied Jasper. He turned onto Highway 66. He glanced in the back mirror. "Hold on a minute. I think we're being followed."

He slowed down and the second car back slowed down, too, while the Jeep directly behind them moved into the left lane and passed them. He sped up, and the car sped up, too. When he depressed the brakes to slow down, the pedal slid smoothly to the floor without response from the car.

Quickly, Jasper hit another button beside the GPS system. A voice came over the Skye's radio. "Headquarters. How can I help you?"

"Ring me to Thomason immediately," Jasper said.

"What's the problem, Templeton?"

"I'm being followed and my brakes are out," Jasper said.

"Downshift to second."

"Yes. I've done that, and I'm slowing down."

"Good. When you're down to forty, shift down to first. Meantime, I've got your position. Go two more exits to Woodbridge. The off-ramp inclines which will slow you down some more. Take a right at the top. Police are on the way to block traffic for you. Go about forty yards, and you'll see a gravel site on your right. It's entirely enclosed with chain-link fencing which should hold you if you can purposely spin out on the gravel and bring the car to rest with the side of your vehicle along the fence. Do you have a passenger?"

"Yes. Chelsea Merrill."

"Chelsea?" came the voice again.

"Yes?"

"Bend over to brace yourself and place your arms around your head for protection. The police have Woodbridge blocked, Jasper. Fortunately, a patrol car was in the vicinity. You're nearly there."

The seconds seemed to drag. Who in the world was following them, and why were the brakes gone? Suddenly Chelsea felt the car spin. With a sickening scraping sound, the Skye slid to a stop.

Chapter Fifteen

"Chelsea! Are you alright?" asked Jasper in a shaking voice.

Chelsea raised a dazed face. Blue lights flashed in her eyes, and a police radio squawked. Were Jasper's hands shaking or were hers?

"Yes, I think so." She looked at the fencing against her door. "But I can't get out. The passenger door of the car is pinned against the fence."

"Here. Climb over this if you can." He indicated the console between the two seats. "Do you have your purse?"

Jasper's hands guided her into his seat and then out of the car. She breathed in lungfuls of fresh air.

"Don't hyperventilate on me now." Jasper peered at her anxiously. When Chelsea nodded, he pulled her into a long embrace. She leaned into him as he wrapped his long arms around her, holding her tightly.

Jasper's cell phone buzzed. His boss's voice came over the line, asking if he and Chelsea were okay.

"Yes. Just shaken. Maybe a little shock."

"We need to bring your car in and see what it tells us. We lost your tail. Did you see who was in it?"

"It looked like two men in the front seat, but that's all I saw."

You're close to your home in Chantilly aren't you?"

"Yes."

"Take Chelsea there, and let your mother take care of her for the night. You'll be safe there with all the security your parents have," he said with a hint of amusement.

"What about work tomorrow?"

"Tell Chelsea that I'll clear it with her boss to be absent from work, but neither of you are to leave until I tell you. Is that clear?"

"Yes, sir."

"I'm going to send a team doctor to check on both of you, and I'll want to meet with both of you in the morning. I'll be there around ten. The lady is a special package, and we need to take care of her."

"I won't argue with you, sir," said Jasper with feeling.

"I had a feeling you wouldn't." Thomason chuckled.

The connection ended, but Jasper's mind was in a whirl. What information had been withheld from him about this case? He hoped that although he was still considered junior security detail having been on the job just over three years, they would give him a clearer picture of what was really happening.

Ruefully he glanced at his Skye. It had been his pride and joy, the first car he had bought himself. He glanced down at Chelsea, still securely held with one arm. Surely she had heard most of the conversation and would realize his growing attraction for her. They would have to talk soon.

The policeman was on his phone, a sure sign that he was talking to Tillot Thomason who wouldn't talk on the police frequency lest the wrong parties overhear. A tow truck arrived, and one of the operators began loading Jasper's vehicle while the other kept him occupied with paperwork.

When Jasper was finished and was watching his Skye leave, the older policeman respectfully approached Jasper and offered him a ride. "I'll have to put you both in the back, but I'll get you home safely."

As they entered the back seat, Jasper couldn't help turning to the officer and quipping, "Aren't you going to push down on my head?"

"If you had been joyriding, I would, but apparently your car was injured, so to speak, in the line of duty," the officer responded jokingly.

Chelsea gave a short laugh at this, but she was still very quiet, scaring Jasper. He held her close to him, willing her to accept his solace. "Are you alright?" he asked.

When she glanced up at him, her eyes were huge, her pupils dilated. She was shaking slightly. "I'll be fine in a bit. After all I'm a G.R.I.T.S."

Jasper looked confused.

"A Girl Raised In The South," she explained. "I'm still shaky, and this whole scenario doesn't make sense, but we'll talk later." She leaned her head against him, accepting his embrace, and by the time they reached his parents' home of Rosemont, her shaking had stopped.

A black iron fence decorated with spear heads and fleur de lis surrounded the property, meeting at the gated entrance. A gracefully winding drive ended in a circle, with a double set of steps on the north and south sides of the front, meeting at a circular, pineapple-shaped fountain. Chelsea got a glimpse of the diamond droplets sparkling in the rose-hued lights before Jasper directed the officer to a side entrance where Penelope, his mother, waited anxiously.

"Your Dad is on his way," she said to Jasper. "Hi, Chelsea. I'm so glad to meet you. Just call me Nell; everybody does."

Chelsea was led up the stairs and to her right into a large, airy kitchen done in sunny yellow with accents of royal blue. The breakfast nook beyond the kitchen was large enough to make a table with seating for eight seem small. Roll-down blinds and cheerful café curtains on the huge bay window were closed for the night, giving privacy and making the area seem cozy rather than ostentatiously chic.

Three black labs had risen from cushions in the corner, crowding around Jasper as if to console him. Jasper introduced them as Mozart or Mo for short, Schubert or Bert, and Liszt or Liz. Each solemnly offered Chelsea a paw in greeting. She longed to give each of them a hug, they looked so anxious, but she was feeling rather light-headed.

Nell led them through a doorway to a family room, and here Chelsea was implored to sit on a comfortable sofa in rich cocoa and golden paisley swirls on tapestry-like fabric. It matched the other darker pieces of wood and furniture, giving the room a more masculine air. Jasper sat beside her. Nell served the sandwiches she had made with chips and bottled water. She also brought in a tray with mugs of coffee and hot cocoa.

"So tell me what happened," Nell commanded.

Jasper told her of their dinner and the drive after, how he had noticed someone following them and his almost simultaneous realization that his brakes weren't working.

"Do you think someone tampered with them?" asked his mother.

"I don't know what to think. I just had the car serviced two weeks ago. It only has twenty thousand miles on it, so if the brakes failed, it's a major manufacturing error."

Chelsea had merely nibbled at the chips and sandwich offered her, but she was on her second cup of coffee, and it was beginning to make her feel human again.

"Do you think if the brakes were deliberately damaged that this could have something to do with what happened while you were down in South Carolina?" asked Nell again.

"I don't see how. The target was the President, not me," answered Jasper.

"What about me? Could I possibly be the target?" Chelsea asked suddenly.

"Why would you be a target?" asked Jasper.

"I don't know," Chelsea admitted and fell silent.

They heard the kitchen door open and close and two masculine voices. Jasper's father, Carter Peters-Templeton, entered with another man who was holding a small satchel.

Jasper stood, somewhat slowly Chelsea noted, and met his father halfway across the room. He held out his hand to his father, and grasping it, his father pulled him into a bear hug. Jasper's height, topping six feet, and his broad-shouldered build were identical to his father's.

Watching them nearly made Chelsea emotional.

"I'm so glad you're okay, Son," said Carter with feeling.

"Me, too, Dad. Thomason talked me through it, and the training I received at Rowley returned to me when I really needed it."

"I talked to Tillot on the way here. He's proud of the way you handled the situation. He said he has some news for us, but he wants to wait until he sweeps your Skye." Between Carter's commercial real estate business and Penelope or Nell's social activism, they knew many people in the Virginia, D.C., New York, and Maryland areas, and Tillot Thomason was one of them.

"This is Doctor Ted Grainger," Carter continued while Jasper shook hands with the doctor. "He's come to make sure you two haven't any major injuries." He looked at his wife. "How about if we make the library the examining room. You can go in with Chelsea first."

Nell led Chelsea and the doctor to the library, chattering all the way. When Chelsea saw the foyer with its grand staircase done in marble and highly polished oak, she was glad she had seen the hominess of the kitchen first. Opposite the foyer was a large meeting room with groupings of sofas and chairs.

The library, along the hall and past the foyer on one side and the meeting room on the other, was paneled in golden oak. Green velvet drapes lined in gold hung at the immense windows that faced the backyard, and a desk sat in front of them. An inviting leather couch was positioned on the plush Aubusson carpet that covered all but a foot of the hardwood floor around the perimeter of the room.

All three remaining walls were covered with bookcases containing hundreds of books with the exception of the south wall where the fireplace was. Here, tall bookcases flanked the mantel from the floor to the fourteen foot ceilings.

Chelsea sat on the couch while Nell took a comfortable, matching leather chair grouped near it. The doctor prodded, poked and examined. Her pupils were nearly back to normal size, and she felt less loopy, but she was beginning to feel stiff and sore.

She was dismissed, and Jasper took her place in the library. Nell wanted to ply her with questions about her family in Summerville, but sensing Chelsea's fatigue, she told some stories about the dogs instead. Nell was finishing a tale about Mo, Bert, and Liz when Jasper and the doctor entered.

"No broken bones tonight, but they'll feel sore for a few days. Fortunately, they were only going between ten and fifteen miles per hour when the impact occurred. I'm going to leave some pain medication and a mild sedative if they can't sleep. Be sure to take the pain meds no matter what. They're non-hallucinogenic, but they will mask most of the tenderness your muscles will feel," he said, addressing first Nell and Carter and then Jasper and Chelsea.

"Thank you, Doctor," said Nell. Carter escorted him out, and Nell led Chelsea up the back stairs by the kitchen to the second floor bedrooms.

Both Chelsea and Jasper were disappointed. Chelsea wanted to talk to Jasper. She had some ideas about the connection of the Summerville incident and the latest one, but now she would have to wait. Jasper wanted to reassure himself that Chelsea would be alright. Since Allison's death, no girl had intrigued him as Chelsea did.

But Nell was showing Chelsea to her room above the kitchen. The walls were painted a restful green, and the white carpeting had a border of rose. The spread on the white, canopied double bed, was white with rosebuds, some larger, some smaller, trailing a pattern among leaves in various shades of green.

Chelsea peered into the bathroom and knew immediately that she would be taking a long soak in the morning. The gold fixtures gleamed and the side of the white marble tub boasted an array of salts, body washes and sprays, as well as candles, and the towels in rose and white looked luxuriously thick.

"Now don't hesitate to call me on the intercom," Nell was saying. "Just press this button right here, and I'll be wide awake. I'll be disappointed if I find out in the morning that you had a restless night but didn't call me. We keep extra clothes in the dresser here, so help yourself."

Looking from Jasper to Chelsea, she said, I'll let you two say goodnight." She gave Chelsea a hug and another to Jasper before returning downstairs.

Chelsea sank onto the bench at the foot of the bed. Jasper sat beside her.

"I've been wanting to talk to you. I think there is a connection between the two incidents, and maybe someone is trying to get to the President through me. I don't know. I'm so tired and my mind can't seem to focus. But we definitely should talk about it tomorrow." She frowned and shook her head.

"And I want to talk to you, too, but about a different matter altogether," said Jasper. "But I know you're tired. My bedroom is down at the other end of the hall facing the back of the house like this one. Preston's faces the front of the house. Just in case you want to come visit me," he teased.

"For shame," said Chelsea, but only half-heartedly. She yawned.

"Just kidding," said Jasper. Then his look became more intense. "But do think of me tonight." He bent his head and kissed her lightly on the forehead. Then he stood, and with one last look at Chelsea, he exited the room.

When Jasper had bent his head, Chelsea had expected a real kiss. She found herself disappointed, but she was so exhausted. She pulled open a drawer and found a sweatshirt. She pulled it on, and leaving her clothes in a puddle on the floor, she slipped between the sheets and was sound asleep within minutes.

Chapter Sixteen

Chelsea awakened abruptly the next morning, and every muscle in her body seemed to be screaming with pain. She was rather exasperated that even with such a low speed on impact she had so many aches.

Adding the rose scented salts to the steaming hot water and luxuriating in the jet-fortified tub had loosened the knots, and she felt much better when she descended the back stairs to the kitchen dressed in her clothes of the evening before.

"Good morning," said Nell cheerfully. She pressed a steaming cup of coffee into Chelsea's hands. "Help yourself to whatever you want." She indicated several covered dishes on the sideboard.

Before she could inquire about how Chelsea felt, Jasper entered. The stubble on his chin and the circles under his eyes showed his sleeplessness during the night, yet, to Chelsea, they made him appear both sensual and appealing. Silently she chided herself. He was obviously in more discomfort than she, so she'd better get a handle on these feelings she didn't yet want to name.

Since he was quiet and subdued, she helped herself to scrambled eggs and orange slices. Then she sat at the table, noting the beautiful gardens and arbors in the back of the house. The main floor was built over a full basement, so she could actually look down on the graceful butterfly bushes surrounded by banks of lavender, rose, and white flowers, with occasional splashes of yellow.

Jasper's mother, also attuned to his moods, handed him a coffee mug fixed the way he liked it and two pills for pain. Once he had gulped down the pills with half the coffee, he turned and gave his mother a hug.

"Thanks, Mom. I really needed that coffee."

"I should know what you like after feeding you all these years. Those pills will start helping in ten minutes. Now get some eggs and toast, and sit down by Chelsea. The sun shining in the window should warm you right up and help with those aches and pains."

He didn't tell her that his sleeplessness was due more to the emotions racing through him. Dating Chelsea sometimes seemed like a betrayal of Allison. He thought he had gotten over that, but obviously he hadn't. He also found himself terrified that Chelsea might be taken from him like Allison had. Then, too, his feelings for her were blossoming so fast. Calm down, chum, he admonished himself. You don't know how the girl feels.

Just as Jasper sat beside Chelsea, his dad breezed into the kitchen. He plunked a file folder full of papers down on the table in front of Jasper. "I downloaded all the news articles on the shooting at the commencement and the woman who was shot. They just discovered that the woman, Malea Gamarov, was born in Russia although she has lived in Iran for the past fifteen years."

"With Iran soliciting Russia's help for nuclear capabilities and threatening an imminent attack on Israel, that's an interesting twist," said Chelsea. She idly looked through the news articles which included a picture of the woman who had been shot. She looked somewhat familiar, but then, Chelsea saw so many people.

"Makes you wonder which government she was working for," stated Jasper.

"Perhaps she was working as a spy for some other country," said Nell. "Or maybe even as a counter-spy."

"Hopefully Thomason will shed some more light on this incident," said Jasper.

"I'm sure he will," said Carter.

And he did. An hour later, with Jasper freshly shaved and clothed in jeans and a white dress shirt, Tillot Thomason entered with his own folder of information. They all sat at the kitchen table.

"No one can overhear us?" asked Tillot soberly.

"No," answered Carter. I sent Rose and John to run some errands for us. They'll be gone at least an hour. Clinton and Marshall, their boys, are grooming the horses.

"Good," answered Tillot. "What I need to tell you all is classified information, to say the least. Fortunately, all of you have been cleared."

Jasper looked at his mom and dad. They had been cleared?

"Nell you've done some excellent work for us with your activities, and Carter, the information you garner for us in the real estate arena has been invaluable."

Jasper's head reeled. His parents had helped the Secret Service? Were they spies?

"Anything we can do to help our country," said Carter firmly with a tighter jaw than Jasper had ever seen. He usually presented a rather indolent, phlegmatic demeanor--until he was closing a deal, that is. Men and women both had learned not to underestimate Carter Peters-Templeton.

Beside him, Nell nodded solemnly. "We're just ordinary citizens," she explained to Chelsea. "But we see and hear so much. So we decided long ago to pass on any pertinent information to the right sources. Carter and I are both passionate about the ideals of republicanism, democracy, and free enterprise on which our country was founded."

"We have discovered some interesting information about Malea Gamarov since her death," continued Tillot. "Not only did she live in Iran, but she had dual citizenship in Russia and England. She worked in Iran for the Russian government, but what most people don't know is that she also reported to the former Prime Minister of England who has been part of an elite group of freedom fighters and policy makers around the world."

Carter and Nell shared a glance. To Jasper's watchful eyes, they knew more about this group than he did.

Tillot spoke again. "We also discovered that she made contact with a member of the Russian mob right before her flight to the United States. We believe that somehow she has relatives in this mob, and she was trying to get some protection from them while here in the U.S."

"Of course, we examined every inch of her body and clothing in our lab. We uncovered a single piece of paper sewn into the lining of her jacket. It had six words written in Arabic and the letters MC in very tiny print on the bottom right."

"That's where you come in, Chelsea."

"Me?"

"That's right. Our experts believe she was going to try to contact you to get some information to the President."

"What kind of information?" asked Jasper keenly, his ennui disappearing.

Tillot pulled out a copy of the paper found on Malea's body. The words ÒéÈèäèæ, ÑèÈæ, êèÓá, êÓÇäÑ, Óêåèæ, and ÏÇæ were printed in Arabic in legible but faint handwriting. Underneath each word was penciled the English translation of each word: Zebulun, Reuben, Joseph, Issachar, Simeon, and Dan. Scrawled across the bottom and slanting upward as if added as an afterthought was another Arabic word translated as Rahab.

Each of them studied it.

"I know what these are," said Chelsea suddenly. "They're some of the names of Jacob's sons."

Tillot smiled, but everyone else looked puzzled.

"You know, the sons of Jacob who became the twelve tribes of Israel."

"Very good, Chelsea," said Tillot.

"Listening in Sunday School pays off once again," she quipped. "Rahab is the name of a woman who lived in Jericho when the Israelites conquered the land of Canaan. She was a prostitute who was, nevertheless, saved from destruction because of her faith."

"But what do these names mean? What do they symbolize?" asked Jasper.

"We think they are part of a hit list for different sites in the United States by terrorists, but our experts haven't been able to determine what these sites are or who, exactly, is responsible."

"Wait a minute," said Chelsea. "You said this is part of a list?"

"A tear line was at the bottom of the list. We believe more names were on the bottom half of the paper."

"Well, assuming these are the names of the twelve sons of Jacob, wouldn't it be logical to suppose that they used all twelve names? Even if they didn't use all of the names, wouldn't it be safer to assume that they did?"

Impressed with her intelligence, Nell and Carter exchanged glances which Jasper caught, but Chelsea did not.

"Our only problem is if they had more than twelve names on the list, more than twelve sites to hit," said Tillot soberly.

"There has to be some symbolism to the number of sites on the hit list," added Chelsea. "That will, in turn, point to the group who is responsible, but how will you determine the date of the attack?"

"We have personnel working round the clock on it, but we haven't cracked the code yet," said Tillot.

"Do you mind if I work on it?" asked Chelsea.

"Not at all, young lady, as long as you don't discuss it with anyone outside of this room. And by the way, if you ever need a job, submit a resume to me. I like how your mind works," said Tillot. "Actually, we believe Ms. Gamarov was trying to contact you, Chelsea."

"How do you know that?" asked Jasper.

"See these letters at the bottom that read MC?" asked Tillot.

"Ohhh," said Chelsea. "Those are my initials but in Arabic which is written right to left rather than left to right as we do in English."

"Bingo," said Tillot.

"But what is this little flower in the corner?"

"That's not a flower, it's a Maltese Cross," said Tillot.

Carter and Nell exchanged glances. Tillot was watching them like a hawk.

"I see you know the meaning of the Maltese Cross," he said.

"Did Malea have any unusual, uh, markings on her body?" asked Nell.

"She did."

"Oh. Then she was one of ours."

"Whatever are you talking about?" Jasper finally asked in a burst of emotion.

"The Maltese Cross was a symbol of the Protestant Huguenots who endured terrible persecution. If she had a one-quarter inch Maltese Cross tattooed on her foot, then Malea was probably a double agent, one the elite freedom fighters," said Nell.

She continued. "Today, more than ever, we see a form of reverse prejudice against the very principles of freedom on which our country was founded. In an effort to grant freedom to all, some are taking this to the extreme and showing prejudice against the very ideology that gives them the right to dissent. But don't let me get started."

"Can I change the subject then and ask about my car?" Jasper requested looking apologetically at his mom.

"That's the other bit of news I have for you," said Tillot. "Your brake line was sliced, not quite in half, but enough so that they would fail at the appropriate time. My guess is that the people following you were going to finish the job if an accident didn't kill you."

"These people are serious about killing Chelsea, aren't they?" asked Carter. "And since she was with Jasper who is Secret Service, they'll eliminate him, too," he added.

"I'm afraid so," said Tillot.

"But why kill me if the message didn't reach me?" Chelsea protested.

"Because they suspect you'll find out about it from me, and they don't know that you don't know what the names mean," answered Jasper.

"Oh."

"The enemy doesn't want you to tell us the meaning of the names. However, once we determine what the meanings are, and security is tightened around the impacted areas, they will probably leave you alone," said Tillot. "Or not. Right now you are a direct link to the President as one of his top aides. He's going to have to get along without you for a few days. We can't let you return to work until this threat is eliminated."

"Oh, goody," said Nell. "You can stay here with us. Our house is as secure as the Capitol and has fewer visitors," she observed dryly.

Chelsea's mind whirled, and she didn't like the implications of what she was hearing at all. People were trying to kill her, she couldn't return to work, she would go crazy with boredom if she was without work for long, but she did have several weeks of leave coming, and wouldn't this be a good time to get to know Jasper better, provided he didn't have to work crazy hours? Maybe she should just go home. But wouldn't that put her entire family in jeopardy?

When she looked up, four pairs of eyes were regarding her, Nell's with excitement at having company, Carter's with sympathy,

Tillot's carefully, and Jasper's with what? His expression was inscrutable. What was he thinking?

Jasper was excited that he would have Chelsea to himself for a few days, but he was worried, very worried about her safety. He didn't want to show his eagerness to spend time with her just yet, and he didn't want to scare her with his concern over those who were trying to kill her.

Tillot's phone vibrated, and, excusing himself, he stepped into the next room.

"Jasper or Carter and I can take you back to your place to pack a suitcase, and then maybe we can catch lunch somewhere," said Nell. Correctly interpreting her son's frustrated look, she added, "Or you can raid Pammy's room. She left a closet full of clothes here, and you two are about the same size. We have plenty to do here."

"You're very welcome, Chelsea," added Carter. "My wife has missed having our daughter underfoot and doing all those female things. Not enough estrogen in the house these days," he teased.

Tillot re-entered the room. "We got one of them," he said with satisfaction. "Your roommate is very astute," he said to Chelsea. "She saw someone skulking across the street from your apartment building and early this morning saw the doorknob turn, so she made a huge racket and then called the police."

"That must have been the man I saw," Jasper said. Everyone looked at him questioningly. He described the man he had seen, and Tillot nodded.

"I need to call Brianya right away," said Chelsea, pulling out her cell phone.

"No," said Tillot. "Not on that phone. It's probably bugged already." He pulled another phone from his briefcase. "Here's one of ours. It has about twenty-five encryption codes securing it, so I don't think they'll crack that for awhile. Jasper can show you all the little extras on it."

Chelsea accepted the phone, but she was beginning to feel overwhelmed. "Can I go back to my apartment?" she asked rather testily.

"Sure. Neither the police nor your roommate saw anything amiss. I'll send a car for you around three or four. But I'd appreciate it if you'd accept Nell's invitation to stay here for the week. We're assigning an operative to you, but if you're here, her job will be much easier, and, hopefully, you'll never even see her."

"Who is it?" asked Jasper.

"Julie Ann. She just came off another job, so she's sleeping right now, but she'll meet you this afternoon."

"Great," said Jasper. "I graduated with Julie Ann. She's good."

"I've got to go," said Tillot. "Any other questions?"

"I have two more, actually," said Chelsea. "What about my job, and do you think this is related to what happened down in Greenville, South Carolina and Charleston?"

"I'll clear your absence with the President. I've already checked your schedule next week, and it's light. You have no duties someone else can't perform. Of course, he has the final say, but I think he will see the need to keep both you and him safe. The link to South Carolina is another aspect we're looking at. We don't know yet," said Tillot while packing up his briefcase. He left a copy of the coded message on the table.

Carter escorted Tillot to his vehicle. Meanwhile, Nell suggested a horseback ride to Jasper and Chelsea. "There's nothing like a ride to get the cobwebs out of your brain. Let's go raid Pammy's closet."

Paris & Samois-Sur-Seine, France
May 23rd

Chapter Seventeen

Donnell stared at the sheet of paper in his hand. He had made two copies of the paper he and Charm had discovered, faxing one to headquarters in Lyon, France for translation. Handling the original with gloved hands just in case anything could be discovered by forensics after all the handling it had already received, he had put it in an envelope and sent it via courier.

The other copy he had kept for himself. Two hours later, he had another copy of the document with the translation written underneath each Arabic word: ÇÔêÑ was translated Asher, ÌÇÏ was translated as Gad, äêáê was translated as Levi, êçèÐÇ was Judah, æáÊÇäê was Naphtali, and ÈæêÇåêæ was translated Benjamin.

With the copy of the document was a note stating that these were six of the names of the twelve tribes of Israel from the Old Testament in the Bible. The operative felt certain they were dealing with either Hamas or al-Qaeda; his guess was al-Qaeda since Hamas did not usually operate in or against European countries in the same way al-Qaeda did and since the original had been inadvertently picked up in Rome.

In addition, by using a magnifying glass, the operative had found a tiny Maltese Cross in the bottom right hand side of the paper. To the unaided eye, it looked like a tiny flower. However, the operative was fairly certain that the Maltese Cross had been added recently since the color of the ink was younger, more recent than the list of names.

Again, the hour was late. He had waited until everyone was asleep before he had felt free to leave with Tiffany in charge. Charm had visited Sandy's family that afternoon, simply introducing him as her new body guard. She had retired immediately after dinner. The blue circles under her eyes belied her mantra that she was feeling much better.

Similar to the offices in London, the office here in Paris boasted underground tunnels which ended in plain-looking, nondescript houses, helpful in escaping detection of following parties. Donnell availed himself of both a different vehicle than the one in which he had arrived and one of the "safe" houses from which to leave.

He was approaching the exit from the freeway for Samois when his phone began to buzz. "Yes?"

"Donnell?" It was Charm. She was crying softly.

"What's happened?" he asked tersely.

"It's Tiffany. She has blood all over her hands and face, she's unconscious, and she's barely breathing. I called an ambulance. My parents want to call the police, but I thought you would want to make that decision."

"I'll be there in less than ten minutes. Tell the paramedics to treat her, but don't let them take her to the hospital until I get there."

Never had Donnell wanted to drive more recklessly, but he knew that Tiffany's life was probably dependent on him at this point. He cursed himself in fine, fluent Gaelic for not having the foresight to bring more operatives with him. If she was covered in blood, that meant she had put up a fight.

At last he had negotiated the final roundabout and was heading up the driveway. The lights were only on in the kitchen and the living room, and those were low. Was the enemy still lurking in the shadows?

On the alert and with his gun pulled, he made his way from the car to the door. Charm made it easier when she opened the door and turned on the outside light. The ambulance had not arrived yet.

Charm led him into the living room where Tiffany lay covered with a blanket. Charm had changed into black sweats and a long-sleeved black tee before Donnell could have a chance to catch her in the ratty old sweatshirt in which she liked to sleep. She looked more rested than she had when he had left.

"I know a victim shouldn't be moved, but we had to get her inside. Dad is making sure the doors and windows are all locked, and that no one else is in the house. Mom has been carefully wiping away the blood with warm cloths. CeCe and Charles are still asleep," Charm reported in a low voice.

Donnell took Tiffany's pulse and temperature with a thermometer Catherine produced. Her pulse was weak and her body temperature was lower than normal. He felt the top of her head and discovered not one but two huge lumps on opposite sides. Had there been two or more attackers? Probably. A single person couldn't take out the Tiffany he knew.

She probably had a severe concussion. Noticing the dried blood on her hands, he estimated that the attack had occurred about an hour or two ago, around ten or eleven thirty. He began probing for broken bones. Nothing seemed out of place. If the attackers knew any karate at all, they may have bruised her internal organs. She definitely needed an ambulance.

And here they were. He showed his badge, indicating that Tiffany was also with Interpol, and gave them the information he knew. While they prepared her for transportation, placing her on a board and starting an IV on her, he made phone calls.

His supervisors would meet the ambulance and provide the information the hospital would need. Natalie, Gregor, and Seamus would be on their way by helicopter within minutes. He asked Natalie to pick two more from the team to accompany them. His job was to make sure no further assaults occurred, keeping Charm and her family safe.

Just as the ambulance left, Charm received a phone call. It was Sandy's mom, and she was nearly hysterical. Sandy had disappeared, and Mrs. Daniels was certain that she had been kidnapped and that Charm was somehow involved. Her voice was strident enough for Donnell to hear every word.

Without asking, Donnell took the phone from Charm. "This is Donnell McKinnon, Charm's bodyguard. Calm down and tell me what happened."

"Sandy's gone. She's disappeared," moaned Bea Daniels.

"What time did she disappear?" asked Donnell.

"About midnight. She had just said goodnight to her father and me when she suddenly bolted out of the door."

That was certainly irrational behavior, thought Donnell, puzzled.

"Why do you think Charm is involved?" he asked.

"Why she went over to talk to Charm around ten. It's still light outside at that time, you know. She tried to call Charm, but couldn't get an answer. And she didn't stay long, but when she returned, she didn't feel very well. She was pale, but when I suggested taking her temperature, she said she just had a headache and would feel better in the morning."

Donnell's mind clicked into overdrive. Could Sandy possibly have seen Tiffany being attacked? It fit the time frame. And of course Charm wouldn't have answered her phone. She had gone to bed early.

"I'm on my way over," he told Bea. "We'll find your daughter, don't worry," he said with confidence, but inwardly he was hoping they were not too late. If the thugs had realized that Sandy had seen them, they may have decided to attack her as well. But why had she bolted out of the front door?

"I'm going with you," announced Charm beside him.

"No. I want to know you're safe here."

Charm lifted her chin. "If you don't let me come with you, I'll just sneak out later. Besides, I think I know where Sandy is. We used to play in the woods in back of her house, and I know where she would hide."

Donnell raised questioning eyes to Christian and Catherine. She was their daughter.

Slowly Christian nodded his head. "Charm will be able to find Sandy faster than you will on your own. If she's hurt, too, you don't want to be looking by yourself. I'll stay and make sure no one else comes even close to us. Just make sure you keep a good eye on my daughter. And Charm, don't you go on ahead of Donnell. You two stay together," he admonished his daughter in a tone that brooked no argument.

Charm shook her head mutely in agreement. Her eyes were large and the shadows had returned, but Donnell could see her determination to go to the rescue of her dearest friend.

While Charm put on her sneakers and located a light jacket, Donnell ran upstairs to the room given him and opened a satchel filled with equipment he used often in his line of work. He pulled out some infrared goggles and a pair of binoculars on which he slipped an infrared lens. If he had to walk from the house to the car with Charm in tow, he wanted to be sure the enemy was nowhere on the premises.

Turning off the light in the room, he opened the shutters and quickly scanned the fields behind and to the north of the house as well as the gardens with the binoculars. No one. Good.

He knocked lightly on Charm's door; she was already downstairs, no doubt waiting impatiently for him. Again turning off the light, he scanned the area to the south, but again, all was clear.

Descending the stairs, he stopped Charm before she exited the door.

"Wait. I want to make sure everything's clear. We don't want to be stopped by our enemy before we get there to help Sandy."

Reluctantly, Charm stayed inside while Donnell quickly scanned the rest of the property. He reentered the house and told Christian, "Your premises are clear of intruders which makes me feel better and will alleviate your concern some. If you hear anything, call the police then beep me. My own operatives should be here within three hours." Turning to Charm, he said simply, "Let's go."

On the short drive to Sandy's house, Donnell complimented her on her choice of a black jacket with a hood to hide the flame of her hair, hair he would love to fill his hands with, but now was not the time. He asked Charm to describe the woods, giving landmarks and boundaries and possible hiding spots.

"We used to play Swiss Family Robinson in those woods. We had a tree house, but I don't think Sandy would hide there even though it's probably still in good condition. Her younger twin brothers, Gavin and Kevin play back there now. They're nine years old."

Charm continued. "The woods are back to back with the Fontainebleau Forest. The government challenged Mr. Daniels on the boundaries about fifteen years ago, so he had his acreage fenced. We'll have to be careful of the Tiger Pit."

"The Tiger Pit?"

"Don't you remember in the book, Swiss Family Robinson, how Francis dug a pit, hoping to catch a tiger? Well, we dug a hole, too. We never did catch a tiger, but that's beside the point."

"Is that where you think Sandy is hiding?" asked Donnell.

"Oh no. If someone else fell in there, she'd be trapped with them," answered Charm.

"Well, where do you think she's hiding?"

"Where I think she is hiding is in the cave. Two stones lean together, and if you aren't looking for it, you would never see the opening. But once you squeeze in, there's enough room for three or four people to stand. It has a back exit as well. You have to stoop way down to get out, and bushes cover it, so again, I don't think anyone else will know about it. I don't know if Gavin and Kevin even know it exists."

"Is there a way we can approach the forest from the road? I don't want to talk to Sandy's parents yet, and I don't want the enemy to have the advantage of seeing us first."

"Yes, actually. I know a place to stop the car. Right past the end of their property is a parking area for hikers. We can park there and climb over the fence, coming in the back way."

Donnell turned off his lights before they reached the Daniels' property. Riding in the dark was eerie. Charm was glad Donnell was with her.

"Let me scope things out first," Donnell said before they exited the car. "And let me close your car door. Sound carries farther at night. If we encounter immediate gunfire, get back in the car and lie as close to the floor as possible. If we encounter gunfire once we are in the woods and if we're close to the cave, get in there as quickly as possible and stay there until I come get you. Now where is the tiger pit in relation to the cave from the back of the property here?"

It's about thirty feet past the rocks and to the right, maybe six feet to the right if it was adjacent to the cave."

Donnell closed Charm's door, making sure the car was closed to intruders yet quickly available should they need to escape quickly. Then they made their way to the edge of Mr. Daniels property. They found a place where the fence sagged. Donnell held it down for Charm, and slowly, without speaking, they entered the forest.

The evening air in the forest was cool, but aside from an occasional rustle, the animals were quiet, as if subdued by a malignant presence. Donnell used the infrared binoculars hanging around his neck, but could detect nothing except the heat emitted by small animals.

They moved slowly, their footsteps hushed by the pine needles on the forest floor. Minutes passed. Charm felt as if her heart was pounding so loudly, every living thing could hear it.

The rock formation loomed directly to their left. Charm would have to go around to the front to enter the cave. They began to move in that direction when a twig about twenty yards in front of them cracked.

Donnell immediately crouched low pulling Charm with him. He scanned the area with his goggles. Nothing. Wait. More to the right he found a figure bent low. He heard a muffled gasp. The figure straightened to the height of a man, and began zigzagging erratically further right toward the road.

Beside him, Charm began to move, but Donnell pulled her close and would not let her go. He waited until he heard the very faint whir of bicycle tires on pavement and engagement of the chain.

Well that answered the question of mode of travel. Donnell certainly hadn't seen a vehicle. He wondered why the gasp and the hasty exit. He was about to move toward the cave with Charm when they heard a low moan.

Charm immediately froze, but Donnell pushed her toward the front of the rock formation. "Find Sandy," he whispered in her ear.

Chapter Eighteen

Cautiously, Charm made her way to the entrance of the cave. Expelling the breath she seemed to be perpetually holding, she squeezed between the two rocks. At first she could see nothing, but as her eyes grew accustomed to the blackness, she thought she saw a whitish blob crouched at the far end near the exit.

Very softly, she whispered, "Sandy? Is that you?"

The whitish blob moved slightly. Garnering all the courage she had, Charm lowered herself on her hands and knees and made her way toward the blob. She reached out a hand to touch what she thought would be an arm. It was an arm and ice cold. Had she gotten there too late? She so wished she had a light, but that could be dangerous.

"Sandy?" she whispered again.

The figure moved and suddenly she was enveloped in a bear hug.

"Charm. I'm so glad it's you. I knew you would find me. Is it safe to go out?"

"No, not yet. Donnell's outside. He'll let us know. You're so cold. Take my jacket," she whispered in Sandy's ear, removing the soft, warm velour fabric and placing it around Sandy's shoulders. Remembering that most of the body's heat escaped from the head, she pulled the hood up over her friend's head.

Then leaning back against the solid rock, with hands clasped together, they waited.

Meanwhile, outside, Donnell leaned against the rock and waited. He scanned the woods, but other than small animals could discern nothing. He waited about fifteen minutes and was finally rewarded with the rustlings of night predators. If the animals were moving around, the danger was probably gone.

Just as he was about to move, another soft moan sent the wildlife scurrying for cover and quieted them. Someone or something sounded like they were dying, and he needed to discover the truth.

Carefully creeping forward and testing each footstep before he placed full weight on the ground, he inched forward. He wasn't about to fall into the tiger pit.

He was nearly jolted out of his skin when another soft moan erupted just to the left of his foot. Taking a step back, he crouched down. It could be a booby trap, but then again, perhaps they had caught one of the enemy. Gauging the distance to the nearest group of bushes in case he needed to dash to them for cover, he decided to take the risk of using his pencil flashlight.

When he turned it on, the sight that met his eyes was horrific. A young man dressed in black was flat on his back in the tiger pit, impaled on two wooden spikes that were sticking up through his abdomen and one of his legs.

No volley of bullets confronted the light, so Donnell pulled out his phone to call for an ambulance. Just then the man opened his eyes and glared at him, letting out a volley of what sounded like curses in an Indian or Arabic dialect. He struggled to get to what Donnell guessed was a gun from his pocket. Donnell stepped back, not anxious to make certain.

Well, the man wasn't going anywhere. He'd better check on Charm and Sandy. He didn't want them to go to the house by themselves, and he certainly didn't want them to have to see what he'd seen at the bottom of the tiger pit. He'd have to mark the pit, however, to avoid stumbling into it himself. Pushing his pencil-slim flashlight into the ground with the beam pointing up would work.

He made his way to the cave.

"Charm? Sandy?" he called softly.

"We're both here, Donnell," came Charm's voice. Then he saw both girls emerge from the cave.

He was so relieved that they were both safe that he wanted to give Charm a hug and kiss her senseless, but he refrained and simply took her hand instead. "Can you two lead me back to the house? I want to make sure you're safely inside."

"Sure," said Charm. Sandy still wasn't talking, and when he reached for her hand, too, it was as cold as an ice cube. The poor girl was in shock.

"Let's go as quietly as possible. I'm fairly certain no one is around who can hurt us, but let's not take too many chances."

Single file and silently, but with hands still linked, they made their way to the house. At the edge of the woods, Donnell stopped them, and once again scanned the area both in front of them and behind them with his infrared goggles, but could see nothing menacing.

He motioned them forward. When they entered the house, Bea and Sandy began crying and hugging, and Charm soon joined them. Donnell turned to Sandy's father, Ben, and shook his hand. The moisture in Ben's eyes nearly undid Donnell, but he still had a job to finish. Pulling Ben aside, he explained the situation about the man in the tiger pit and the ambulance on its way.

Just then, the ambulance pulled in the driveway with no lights flashing and no siren as Donnell had requested. He didn't want the man in the pit to escape before they had a chance to question him, provided he lived long enough. Donnell was certain he would be dead by morning.

The three attendants were the same ones who had come to the Dumotte residence.

"You're sure keeping us busy tonight," the driver joked.

Donnell merely smiled grimly.

Keeping four burly men quiet as they tramped through the woods was impossible, Donnell decided. He was fairly certain now that their enemy numbered only two, and he could only hope that the first one had been so spooked he wouldn't be returning.

What had seemed like a fifteen-minute walk was accomplished in less than five minutes thanks to the lanterns and lights the medical technicians were carrying. He had to stop them and have them turn off their lights so he could discern the single ray of his flashlight.

He prepared himself once again for the grisly sight, but when they shone their lights down into the pit, the man was gone! Donnell hadn't counted on the determination of a man who would not be caught by infidels. The blood-stained, wooden spikes gave testament to the veracity of Donnell's insistence that someone had, indeed, been gored, but toe- and hand-holds dug into the sides of the pit showed the method of exit.

The men circled the pit and began walking outward. When a shout went out, they all gathered around the corpse. Removing himself from the pike without medical assistance had been a death sentence for the man.

Donnell stayed long enough to confirm a lack of identification on the body. He also pulled up the bloodied stakes with gloved hands and bagged them. Then excusing himself, he joined the Daniels family and Charm at the house.

Charm had already called her parents to relieve them of anxiety. Sandy had, as Donnell guessed, seen Tiffany being attacked. They had followed her to her home, probably saving Tiffany's life, thought Donnell wryly.

"Why did you bolt out of the house?" Donnell asked of Sandy.

"I didn't want my family to be attacked. It was the only thing I could think of to do. I knew that if I could make it to the cave, I probably would not be found by those men. And I know those woods like the back of my hand. Those men didn't."

"How many attacked Tiffany?" asked Donnell.

"Three. So what do we do now? Are they still after us?" asked Sandy biting her lip. She would stay with Charm to the bitter end, but the cold-bloodedness of these terrorists frightened her.

"One of them was killed tonight," said Donnell. "The other one escaped, and I don't know about a third one."

"Tiffany was putting up a great fight. Maybe she injured the third one," suggested Sandy.

"How did one get killed? I didn't hear any gunshots," said Charm.

Donnell was reluctant to give details, but he didn't want an innocent person to stumble into the tiger pit and meet the same end. "Someone buried two wooden spikes halfway into the bottom of the pit. One of the men fell into the pit and was impaled on the spikes."

The girls' mouths dropped in amazement and horror, but Ben slapped the side of his leg. "So that's what those boys were making," he exclaimed. "I saw the twins whispering and whittling on some wood," he explained to them, "but I never saw the finished product. I'll put a stop to that."

"Well I don't care that one got killed that way," said Sandy, the words bursting from her lips. "I saw their eyes when they looked at me. They didn't care about me or my family. All they wanted to do was kill me."

"You are so brave, Sandy," said Charm, giving her friend another hug.

Sandy shook her head. "I wasn't brave; I was terrified."

"Actually," said Donnell, "you probably saved not only the lives of your family, but Tiffany's life as well. If you hadn't left Charm's house when you did, I'm sure they would have killed her."

"You two need to stay here tonight," said Bea. "We don't want any more scary situations."

"Charm is welcome to stay here," said Donnell, "but I need to get back to the Dumotte residence. My operatives should be nearly here by now."

"I'll drive you to your vehicle," volunteered Ben.

An hour later he had returned to the Dumotte home. Charm had called to report that Ben had returned, and they were all safe and sound. He met the helicopter in which Natalie, Gregor, Seamus, William, and Tommy had flown at the local football field on the other side of the river. Now everyone was seated in the Dumotte living room, Catherine had made some scrambled eggs, pancakes, and, more importantly, coffee, and Donnell was briefing them all on the evening's events.

When he had finished, Natalie asked, "So where do we go from here?"

Before Donnell could reply, Catherine stated firmly, "From here we go to bed. Tonight...," she checked her watch, "No, tomorrow night, Paolo and Lorna, Olivia, Etienne and Eugenie, Henri and Angelina, and Sonia and Sebastien are all coming with the cousins. Christian has arranged for a state of the art security system to be installed, and we've hired extra security to help Geveon for the evening as well."

"I'll have to agree with Catherine," said Donnell. "I need to get some sleep. Seamus and Tommy can take first watch here, and Gregor and William can stand guard at the Daniels' residence. At six, I'd like Natalie to accompany me to the hospital to see Tiffany."

"Consider it done, boss," said Seamus.

Christian volunteered to take Gregor and William to their post.

Catherine escorted Natalie to the extra bed in Tiffany's room, and Christian showed Gregor, Seamus, Tommy, and William where to put their gear downstairs.

Five hours later, Natalie and Donnell walked into Tiffany's room at the hospital. His eyes widened when he saw that the nurse on duty was his Aunt Shannon's sister-in-law, Margaretta Montaigne. Her calm demeanor exuded peace and confidence, and Donnell knew that Tiffany would be in excellent hands.

He gave her a quick kiss on either cheek.

"It's very good to see you, Donnell," said Margaretta. Does Tiffany work with you?"

At Donnell's nod, she replied, "Then I'll make sure she is very well watched and cared for."

Tiffany, herself, looked pale and ethereal lying against the white hospital sheets. Donnell saw her wince as she turned her head toward them. She tried to sit up, but that produced such a nauseous feeling that she had to sink back into the pillow.

"Don't try to move," said Donnell. "Just rest. Margaretta here is someone you can trust implicitly, and Natalie, Gregor, William, Tommy, and Seamus are on the job. We want you well enough to fly to the United States with us in a few days."

Chapter Nineteen

Charm and Sandy slept soundly and with no nightmares from their ordeal. At noon, Bea tiptoed into the bedroom, but they were still sleeping deeply. At three o'clock, Sandy began to stir. When Bea came in at four, the girls had just awakened and begun to rehash the events of the night. As Bea heard more of the details, she shivered and was very thankful for the security Donnell had stationed outside though they had unnerved her at first.

"I don't want to think any more about it," finally announced Charm. "Besides, I have something else to tell you." She smiled secretively and then blushed, engaging the immediate and intense attention of Bea and Sandy.

"Donnell and I kissed yesterday right before lunch," she said.

"No-o-o," breathed Sandy. "Tell us all about it. Is he good?" she asked.

"Very good," responded Charm, giggling.

"How did it happen? Details, woman. We want details, don't we, Ma?" Sandy demanded, threatening Charm with a yellow throw pillow from her bed.

Bea nodded her assent with a twinkle in her eye.

"I was showing him the wine cellar and picking out a nice white to go with our lunch when I slipped and nearly dropped the bottle. Donnell caught me."

"Of course he would," interrupted Sandy.

"And that's when he kissed me," finished Charm.

"Was it a quick kiss or a slow one?" asked Sandy.

"Slow," said Charm. Now that she had started, she was reluctant to share every single detail, even with Sandy. She was saved by Bea's announcement.

"Your mother called to check on you and remind you that your whole family is coming for dinner tomorrow night at seven. Ben, the boys, Sandy, and I have been invited, too," said Bea. "You can spend the night here with us if you want, and we'll all go back to your house tomorrow together. Donnell just needs to know your plans."

"Stay here," pleaded Sandy. "I'll feel so much safer with security around."

"Okay, but let me call Mom and Donnell, first."

"Great," said Sandy when the phone calls had been made. "Now let's raid my closet to decide what to wear and then do facials and our nails."

With the extra security at the Dumotte house, Natalie and Tommy arrived several hours later to give Gregor and William a break.

They slept late again the next day, precisely what both Charm and Sandy needed.

When they arrived at Charm's house the next evening, the evening sun was slanting through the trees, edging the green leaves with gold. A light breeze wound across the field and up to the house from the Seine River, relieving the summer heat and sending the leaves into a graceful, nymph-like dance across the scent-drenched garden flowers.

Donnell and Seamus had been asked to mingle with the guests who included relatives and a small circle of intimate friends. Donnell was rolling up the sleeves of a blue shirt with a stand up collar, open at the throat that contrasted with his white linen slacks and coat when the girls arrived.

Sandy wore a mint colored sundress, bringing out the green in her hazel eyes. Charm had chosen a simple baby blue sundress with a dusting of silver sparkles that enhanced the fiery impact of her curls. Both girls looked beautiful, thought Donnell, but Charm took his breath away. He simply must protect her from the terrorists.

Charm had never seen Donnell wearing anything except dark colored clothing, so when she caught sight of him in his linen suit that contrasted so effectively with his dark hair and eyes, she was equally blown away but wisely schooled her face to reveal nothing of her thoughts.

Donnell came forward and gallantly kissed the hand of each girl. "Obviously no residual effects from your adventures; you two look lovely," he said. He linked arms with them and, with one on each arm, escorted them to the house.

The white railing along the terrace that ran along the front of the house and curved around to set the boundary of the garden as well had been decorated with twinkling mini lights, adding a festive air to the evening. Donnell led the girls across the smooth stones of the terrace and into the foyer.

Stairs curved up to the second story and down to the basement. The short separating wall was topped with a golden oak handrail. But Donnell led the girls past the stairs and into the spacious living room on the left. The high ceiling and walls were painted white, and French doors led to the gardens.

Caterers had placed some of their delicacies on an antique sideboard at the far end of the room while others circulated among the guests offering delicate pastries filled with a delicious pate or spinach and creamy cheese or some seafood concoction while even others offered thin flutes of champagne.

Charm stopped at the buffet and loaded her plate. Sandy did likewise, and Donnell was not reluctant to do the same. He was starved, and he appreciated a girl who could actually eat instead of merely pick at her food.

CeCe joined them along with three more girls Charm introduced as her cousins, Suzette, Anne-Marie, and Regina. The girls began chattering about Charm's tour, and Donnell finally picked up on the fact that Anne-Marie and Regina were sisters. When they began discussing the latest fashions and movie stars, he was relieved to have Regina's twin, Rex, join them.

Rex introduced him to Stephan who was eighteen, a year younger than Rex and Regina.
They wanted to talk about the strange events surrounding Charm's concerts. Stephan's father, Sebastien Sancerre, worked as a body guard for the American Embassy, and he had heard some mutterings about terrorists and the Americans not wanting the terrorists to accompany Charm to their country.

Donnell could understand their concern, and he knew all too well that the tide of public opinion could easily be swayed against Charm, killing her chances for success in the United States.

Another young man, about seventeen, joined them. He kept his hands in his pockets and had a very gloomy disposition about him, making Donnell wonder what was wrong.

"Hello, Alan," said Stephan. "How are your studies?"

"About the same," muttered Alan.

"We were just talking about Charm's concerts and the people who are threatening her," said Rex.

"It's probably Davi'd," said Alan.

"No-o-o," said Stephan slowly. "I don't think so. Davi'd hasn't had access to all of Charm's concerts. He's a Universite student and can't go gallivanting all over Europe. Besides, I've heard he's been dating someone else rather seriously."

"I've heard that, too," said Rex. "Someone named Genevieve who also attends Universite."

Just then the two youngest of Charm's cousins, Elizabeth, ten, and Anna, nine, ran toward the woman who had entered the door. She could have stepped from the pages of a fashion magazine with her elegant if somewhat exotic black and silver ensemble, accented by her glamorous makeup and upswept black curls.

"Charm's Aunt Olivia Valentino, the famous Italian fashion designer," explained Stephan to Donnell. "She really does have a heart of gold, but most people don't realize it. She's never married, probably because when she's in the public eye, she acts haughty and insolent. It's only around family that she shows her sweet side."

As Stephan monologued, Olivia gave the two younger girls hugs while fishing in her oversized bag, finally retrieving two wrapped gifts. They squealed in delight. The noise attracted the attention of the older girls who ran to give kisses on either cheek of the older woman.

Alan wandered off, apparently bored with the conversation, and then Stephan explained his odd behavior, saying, "Alan's younger sister, Maddy, was killed in a freak accident last year. The whole family is still recovering, but Alan was especially close to Maddy, and he continues to mourn her death."

Later, when Donnell was introduced to Catherine's older brother, Paolo Valentino, and his wife, Lorna, he could see the pain still in their eyes. Paolo obviously had inherited the Italian genes in the family, but Donnell could see the similarity between him and his sister, Catherine, especially in the eyes.

Paolo, he discovered, was a pilot for FedEx, and Lorna was a graphic designer. Paolo had experienced tightened security and had heard rumors about the attacks on Charm. He also knew of Donnell's connection with Interpol, had flown some covert operations for them.

"If Charm ever has problems with flights or if you ever need help at the airport, just give me a call," he said, handing Donnell a business card.

Donnell assured Paolo he would. He continued to circulate among Charm's relatives, meeting Elizabeth and Anna's parents, Henri and Angelina. Christian was asking Angelina, who was a travel agent, to book tickets for the family to fly to Charleston around the time of Charm's concert. He also wanted a rental car at his disposal. Angelina promised to make the arrangements the next day at her office.

Etienne joined the group. His charming and urbane manner bespoke his association as an art dealer who often worked with his wife, Eugenie, an assessor for Christie's. In fact, he had a few pieces he thought Christian would find interesting.

"Hey, Dad," said Rex, entering the conversation, "tell Uncle Christian about the pair of candlesticks Mom appraised for the estate sale." Anne-Marie, Rex, and Regina often helped in the store or went with their mom when she traveled to prepare an estate for auction.

"The candlesticks are from an attic of a manor house and date back to the eighteenth century. We're still analyzing some of the pieces, but proving the authenticity of some of the paintings may land the owners a windfall." Etienne's eyes shone at the thought.

Donnell had been keeping his eye on Charm, but somehow she and Sandy had disappeared. He found them with full plates, still animatedly talking to Aunt Olivia in the garden. Aunt Lorna had joined them. In the far corner stood Geveon, watching. He grinned widely and saluted when he saw Donnell.

Donnell returned his salute, noting with satisfaction the security personnel down by the fence that bordered the river road and even more to the north past the garden and in the small wooded area beyond it. Two more were guarding the cars and others were stationed at the entrance of the driveway.

The small estate was a well-protected fortress tonight. Perhaps he could relax some on this rare summer evening as the sky deepened slowly to twilight and stars began to shine in the cobalt heavens. A light breeze ruffled his dark hair, bringing with it the scent of the Seine.

He stood by Geveon who told him that all was well. "I know every one of the guards personally, hand-picked every one myself. The Dumottes are like family to me. We'll not be having trouble tonight," he assured Donnell.

Donnell wondered what kind of connections Geveon had, but thought it wiser not to ask. He was just grateful for the ample protection. It gave him time to dwell, finally, on Charm herself.

He watched her talking animatedly with her aunt. Her face was alight with laughter as she and Sandy described a dress. She drew her face into an imperious mask and acted as if she was strutting a runway, her movements exaggerated. Her cousin, Suzette, began to giggle and Charm instantly dissolved into laughter.

CeCe took up the thread of conversation, giving Charm a chance to glance casually around. When she saw Donnell watching her, her eyes darkened with awareness, and even with the twenty yards or so between them, the sexual tension and energy arced. Charm had to sternly forbid herself to keep from blushing, turning to respond to her sister and to deliberately block her view of him.

The kiss they had shared had rocked him more than he'd wanted to admit. Apparently it had affected her, too. Even when they were engaged in fighting her assailants, the tension had been an underlying layer of knowledge. Now he had the time and freedom to consider it.

He could and probably should ignore it for his emotional well-being and her security's sakes. But the Irish in him wanted to revel in it, explore it, enjoy the ache of it.

Geveon had been watching the byplay. He chuckled. "You have an evening relatively free of responsibility, Monsieur," he said. "It would be a pity to waste such an opportunity."

"Thanks, friend. We'll see what the evening has in store for us once the lady's guests leave," said Donnell noncommittally.

He continued to stand by Geveon, enjoying the building layers of emotion like the skillful building of a pint of Guinness.

The breeze lightly touched Charm's face, playfully touching tendrils of her hair then slowly sinking to the flowers, gently stroking them to elicit the sweet scents of roses, gardenias, lavender, and buttercups. Donnell's fingers ached to do their own exploring of Charm's face, neck, shoulders, and down. What secret scents could he educe other than the clean, sporty scent of her fragrance of choice?

Charm's eyes were drawn to his as if she could sense his very thoughts. Her own darkened under his regard. She shivered lightly, intuitively knowing that the kiss they had shared--was it only yesterday?—was only a foretaste of what would happen tonight when their relationship was taken to a deeper level.

She frowned. Did she want it taken to a deeper level? Oh, yes, her body responded. Shaking off the seduction of his gaze, she laughed again at the antics of CeCe and Suzette.

She was saved staying in the garden when Anne-Marie and Regina returned from their family's vehicle with a notebook.

Chapter Twenty

Anne-Marie arrived in the garden with Regina in tow. "Regina's written a poem that would make an awesome song," Anne-Marie said. "We even put it to some music. But you're the guru," she continued with embarrassment. "Could you look at it?" This was asked anxiously.

"Sure," said Charm. Normally, she used only her own music, but Anne-Marie had trained at a conservatory in Switzerland and was planning to become a music teacher. The group made their way to the white Kawai piano in one corner of the living room. Anne-Marie sat at the piano and played the tune while Charm hummed along. Then she began singing, and everyone stopped to listen.

When she finished the ballad, everyone applauded. Charm bowed, but then she explained that the real stars were Regina who had written the words and Anne-Marie who had composed the music. Everyone applauded again then began talking all at once.

Donnell had entered the open French doors, but instead of watching Charm, he watched Etienne and Eugenie who were seated with several other aunts and uncles, talking to Christian and Catherine and catching up on the news. He was impressed with the warmth in the group as they congratulated, not Christian and Catherine, but Etienne and Eugenie.

"The conservatory training was worth it even though you missed Anne-Marie terribly," said Catherine.

"I'm so proud of her," said Eugenie. "Regina, too."

"Regina has always had a sentimental, romantic side to her, and she's very gifted with words," Sonia said. She was an English professor and had taught several of her nieces and nephews, including Regina and Rex. Fortunately, she had not had to teach her own children, Stephan and Suzette.

"She types the assessments for me, and her descriptions are very well-written," affirmed Eugenie.

As Donnell watched, Aunt Olivia joined the girls at the piano, and he was struck by the fact that she nearly always joined the younger set of cousins rather than the older aunts. Of course, as a fashion designer, her clientele would be the younger, more modern groups.

The boys joined the girls around the piano. Stephan suggested a change in the word order of one line. Regina liked the change, and Charm said it flowed more smoothly when she sang it that way.

"Do you have any other poems?" Charm asked Regina.

"I have several I'm working on right now."

"She won't let anyone see them until she thinks they're perfect," jeered Rex.

"That's a good thing," said Charm reprovingly. "I don't like it when people think their first draft is so inspired that they won't try to make it better. That's just so snobbish. Most writing needs a great deal of revision."

Anne-Marie began playing softly then louder, and soon they were all singing tune after tune. The aunts and uncles were persuaded to join their voices, and Donnell grew somewhat homesick remembering his extended family with their impromptu ceilis back in Killarney, Ireland at his grandparents' bed and breakfast inn.

This time was Charm's turn to seduce Donnell with long looks. She stood in the curve of the piano, her hair a dark, rich auburn in the lamplight Catherine had turned on in the fading evening light. The frosting of glitter on pale blue moved seductively with her every indrawn breath and movement. She blended her voice easily with those of her family with no need to project or to impress anyone.

The golden moment rubbed salt in the too-fresh wound, and the Valentino family made their adieus and bonsoirs. Their relatives ached for them in their loss but didn't know how to lighten their grief. Christian and Catherine returned to the room from personally escorting them to their vehicle.

Their exit effectively broke up the party with the Daniels next to leave. Under cover of the adult conversation, Sandy urged Charm to make the most of the rest of the evening with Donnell. This time Charm did blush, and Donnell looked at her speculatively, especially as both girls turned to look at him.

Donnell was giving instructions to Seamus to escort the Daniels home and stay there since Geveon and his crew would be on-duty at the Dumotte's home.

"Perhaps you could flirt with Seamus," Charm suggested to Sandy in a quiet voice.

But Sandy shook her head. "The more I travel with you, the more I want to date someone from home. Isn't that strange with all those gorgeous Irish and English males assigned to guard us? But it's true. My turn will come. You just enjoy your Irish guy."

Henri and Angelina left with their two little girls, and then Aunt Olivia wrapped her arms around Charm. "You are such a lovely child. They'll get those terrorists yet. You know, I was there at your concert in Rome."

"You were?"

"Of course. Whenever I'm in town, and one of my nieces or nephews is there, I check on them. When Anne-Marie was at that marvelous conservatory in Switzerland, I visited her often—checking out Swiss styles, you know." She winked.

"I didn't know that."

Of course, in Rome, you had grown so popular that I couldn't even get close to let you know I was there. I tracked you down to the little bistro where you ate after the concert, but you had just left."

Overhearing this conversation made Donnell's mind whirl. Aunt Olivia had been there when Charm had written on that paper? Was she an innocent observer to the deviltry that was transpiring, or was she a part of it? Exactly what was common street knowledge about this case, and what was privileged information?

"Just keep your chin up, Child, and enjoy your time in the United States," said Aunt Olivia, and then she was gone, leaving only the scent of her expensive perfume and questions in Donnell's mind.

Charm, seeming to notice nothing amiss, turned to Donnell and grabbed his hand. While her parents were out front seeing the rest of the family away, she intended to make the most of it. She led

Donnell to the garden. In the dark, the fragrances of the flowers seemed to heighten every other sense.

He could smell their scents of floral blended with more earthy notes, feel the light breeze travel sensuous fingers up his arms, hear the leaves rustle, the occasional twitter of a bird, and water falling softly against rock, see the twinkle of the stars overhead.

Linking her arm in his, Charm strolled with him not saying a word. She led him to a sheltered nook that featured a fountain with water splashing gently from the stucco wall. A high arbor with climbing vines sheltered a cushioned bench and beside it, wedged between the lip of the pool the water fell into and the end of the bench, a small table. Charm had often sat here as a teen, lost in her dreams or writing her music.

One moment they were looking at the fountain, and the next Charm was in his arms, taking him by surprise and initiating a kiss filled with the fire and passion of her ardent nature.

Stunned, all thought fled Donnell's brain, and his control snapped. He ravaged her mouth, unable to resist her probing tongue.

After long moments she pulled back, breaking the kiss and resting her head against his chest, still shuddering for breath.

Those shudders nearly undid Donnell again, but he could hardly take Charm's innocence in her father's garden. He was sure they were protected from prying eyes by the arbor, but he was well aware that the security detail on guard knew where they were and probably what they were doing.

"We've both been wanting that, but let's try it this way, Darling," he murmured in her ear. Using his tongue and his lips, he laved a trail around her ear and down the side of her face to her mouth where he sent delicious tremors through her small frame, teasing her by licking her lips with feather lightness.

Changing the angle slightly and gathering her closer, he deepened the kiss again, taking time to tease and tantalize.

Charm nearly groaned aloud as his kiss set her whole body on fire. Her head felt light, her nerves hummed and tingled everywhere his hands touched her, and the golden pulls in her stomach made her long for more.

An image of her on his lap against the cushions of the bench unbuttoning his shirt shimmered in his brain, but with a superhuman effort of will, he released Charm's lips and simply held her in his arms until his ragged breathing slowed.

"This doesn't change our relationship, does it?" asked Charm.

Careful, Donnell, an inner voice warned him. "Of course it does, Darling. You can't kiss someone as we've done and not care about them. Or can you, Charm?"

"No, Donnell." It was spoken softly and rather shyly.

"And now I have even more reason to make sure you are protected from these bullies who want to kill you."

Charm withdrew from the shelter of his arms. "As long as I'm part of the decision-making, Donnell," she said firmly.

"Absolutely," said Donnell.

"Do you really mean that?" asked Charm.

"Of course," responded Donnell.

"Then no going over my head to make 'arrangements,' and you will show me the last note received from the terrorists that Guy thought was too graphic to show me, as well as the translation of the list from the bistro in Rome. Oh, and I expect to be told what was in the medicine bottle, and discuss with you all the finer points of this case."

"Now Charm," said Donnell, his fine Irish temper beginning to rise.

"Don't 'Now Charm' me," she said with some heat. "I'm the one being threatened along with my fans, and I demand to know the entire truth so I can prepare myself mentally and physically for what lies ahead. I've already talked to Tiff about taking self-defense lessons from her."

Donnell realized too late that Charm hadn't missed a single scrap of evidence or withheld information.

"And for that matter, I find it rather peculiar that my aunt was in Rome and didn't call when she has my personal cell phone number. What happened there is too important to be coincidence. Do you think I was meant to get that note, that list all along? Maybe she left it on the table for me. Or maybe she knew about the list but didn't know I would be there to write on the back of it and take it. And maybe one of the terrorists is really a woman."

Donnell sat suddenly on the bench, his former image of Charm doing something to the buttons on his shirt completely erased from his mind. And here he thought he'd been protecting her. If nothing else, he knew when to swallow his temper and give in graciously.

"Is there anything else?" he asked.

"No, I don't think so," Charm said, sweetly submissive again. "At least not until tomorrow morning. I can't wait to see the translation of the note."

She stood in front of Donnell and once again surprised him by bending forward so that her hair hung in silky softness around his face, placing a chaste kiss on his forehead.

"Bonsoir, Donnell," she said quietly.

He nearly called her back, but like everything else she had done and said this evening, she had taken him by surprise. Was she playing a game, using her passionate kisses to discover more information about the case, or did she genuinely care for him?

Charm left Donnell in the garden thoroughly satisfied both with the information she had discovered and Donnell's promise to include her, and with his response to her kisses. She knew she had taken him by storm so to speak, but he was right; they had both been wanting to see where a second kiss would take them. She was beginning to hope that perhaps she would finally find love.

After the fiasco with Davi'd, she realized she had closed herself off emotionally. With fame came people who wanted to use her for the stroking of their own vanity. It had taken her a long time to realize that Davi'd was more in love with himself than with her.

Only later as she was lying alone in bed did she realize that Donnell had not said anything about loving her; he'd said, what was it? People didn't share passionate kisses unless they cared for one another. That wasn't true. Passion and love or even just caring were not the same. And passion without love, she knew from experience, would leave her colder than before.

At least he had intimated that he cared. She held onto that crumb of hope as she fell asleep.

An hour later, Donnell received a phone call. His mother was crying softly on one line. His father was clearing his throat on another. His granddad, the great Donald Douglas McKinnon had gone to meet his Maker. Could he come home?

With only the slightest hesitation, Donnell agreed. He contacted Natalie to take charge of the case with specific instructions about Tiffany and Charm. In less than thirty minutes, he was driving to the small airport outside of Fontainebleau to catch a flight with another operative to Cork, Ireland.

Chantilly, VA USA
May 29th

Chapter Twenty-One

Jasper and Chelsea reined in their horses. They had changed into riding clothes following the meeting with Tillot, and Jasper had led her to the barn to meet the half dozen horses stabled there. Chelsea's mare, a beautiful, chestnut Thoroughbred named Lady, was Nell's horse, and Jasper rode his own Thoroughbred horse, this one nearly black with mahogany tints named Tristan.

Jasper was an excellent rider, a fact that should not have surprised Chelsea in the least. He excelled at many things, but he was so laid back that his talents were often unsuspected. She would just love to see his resume sometime.

Meantime, it was a glorious summer morning, she didn't have to work, and she was riding with a handsome, intelligent, interesting man. They had raced the Thoroughbreds along a relatively smooth track. Now they were at the crest of a hill, looking back down on Jasper's home. The dogs had been in the stable when the horses were being saddled. Now they ran in circles around the horses or darted into the underbrush along the side of the track.

The sun shone warmly on her shoulders, and she was glad for the white baseball hat Nell had insisted she wear. At least it didn't clash with the white shirt and khaki pants they'd found when they had raided Pammy's closet, who was nearly the same size. Nell had also pulled out an orange tankini—"for later when you'll want to swim in the pool," explained Nell.

"How long has your family owned this house?" asked Chelsea.

"Since I was about five years old," answered Jasper. "But the land has been in my Dad's family for over a hundred and fifty years. My grandfather has a farmhouse about ten miles that way;" he pointed to the east. "He and Grams will probably be at the house tonight for dinner, and you'll meet them then. Grams has Alzheimer's, and Gramps doesn't cook, so they eat at our place most nights."

They watched as Nell entered her gardens, wearing a wide-brimmed straw hat and laden with a large basket, gloves and pruning shears. "This must be Mom's day off; she loves working in her gardens, says it gives her time and space to plan her next event in a relaxed atmosphere," explained Jasper.

"Don't you have an older and a younger brother?" asked Chelsea. "I haven't met them yet."

"Sure. Corey, my older brother, is on a business trip in Europe right now, and Preston is at camp in the Adirondacks. He goes for three weeks every summer."

Just then a helicopter droned high overhead. Jasper cocked his head. "That's odd. We don't get much overhead traffic out this way." He shrugged it off. "Would you like to explore the woods with me? We'll have to go single file, but it will give you a break from the sun," he said, indicating Chelsea's arms which were already reddening.

"Sure," Chelsea agreed.

They entered the woods to their right with Jasper leading the way along a faint trail normally used only by forest animals. The temperature dropped ten degrees almost immediately. Chelsea could hear a breeze stirring the tops of the tall pines, creating a murmuring sound and spreading their aromatic scent. Birds twittered high in the trees; squirrels chattered and chased each other from branch to tree, tree to branch; and occasionally she saw the blue flash of a jay's wing.

The carpet of pine needles made a quiet passage possible with only an occasional snort from the horses stilling, for brief seconds, the sounds of the birds and squirrels. The sun filtered gently through the leaves of the high pines, but also through the oak, dogwood, and maple foliage.

Eventually, they came to a small stream tumbling over rocks and boulders and lichen-covered logs. Jasper slid from his horse and

Chelsea was only too glad to do the same. She hadn't ridden for a while, and following their accident of yesterday, she didn't want to overdo it.

Jasper led the horses to a place where the water pooled to let the horses and the dogs drink. Catching Chelsea's uncertain glance, he asked, "What is it?"

"Are you sure the water's safe for them to drink?"

"Of course. This is a spring-fed stream, and we own the property on which it originates. Dad has it tested periodically. The horses wouldn't drink it if it was severely polluted anyway. Horses are creatures of impeccable taste," he said with a slightly raised eyebrow.

This made Chelsea giggle. "Horses with impeccable taste, my foot," she said.

Jasper drew nearer. "Yes. Your foot, your eyes, your lips, Chelsea," he said huskily, and lowering his lips to hers, he kissed her, teasing her lips, parted in surprise, open even wider.

Chelsea had wondered when he would finally kiss her, and what it would be like. His lips were firm and slightly moist, he smelled of horse and of a crisp, clean aftershave mingled with the soap he had obviously used that morning. His long arms gathering her to him felt strong and secure.

Changing the tempo, he deepened the kiss, going from gentle to passionate in mere seconds. But Chelsea's own passion was mounting. She wound her arms around his neck, pulling him closer until she could feel his entire length against her. They used their tongues to tease and tantalize and wage assault until their senses were totally engaged.

Chelsea felt rather than heard a buzzing vibration that had nothing to do with their kiss, and finally realized it was from the helicopter they had seen earlier. Jasper must have sensed it too, because he broke the kiss and cocked his head to one side, listening. The horses were also quivering, looking ready to gallop away, but Jasper's quiet but authoritative tone calmed them.

The buzzing abruptly faded. They faced each other again, and Jasper leaned his forehead against Chelsea's. "I wanted to kiss you last night, but not with my mom there. And there's a strict rule in our house—no opposite sex visitation in bedrooms. Probably wise," he said ruefully, rubbing the back of his neck.

"Yes, very wise" said Chelsea huskily.

"Look, I know I'm not quite over Allison, but a relationship with you feels right to me."

"Shhh. Don't think too deeply, and don't compare our relationship to the one you had with Allison," said Chelsea, placing a finger over Jasper's lips.

When he started to say something, she said, "Uh, uh. I know Allison was special, and you'll always hold a place in your heart for her. But she's gone, and we're here in this moment in this time. Let's give it a chance to see how we work out without any ghosts intruding."

"Yes, Ma'am," said Jasper with a smile, and he lowered his lips to hers once again. This time they kept it gentle and light, exploring the fit of lips, the angles, the pressure that elicited the most response.

Once again, however, the drone of the helicopter intruded, and Jasper abruptly broke off the kiss.

"I don't think this is good," said Chelsea, a shiver of foreboding running down her spine.

"No, it's not." Jasper responded tersely. He helped her mount her horse, and quickly mounted his. They wound their way through the woods as fast as they dared. Before they exited the safety of the trees, Jasper halted.

He pulled out his binoculars. The helicopter was pulling away, but he noted the number. He also saw that someone else was looking at him through binoculars as well, and they looked like infrared ones. Quickly he repeated the number to Chelsea. Then he slapped both their horses and they raced down the track toward the house, the dogs following.

Jasper spotted his mother and father standing on the terrace as the helicopter swooped in again over the woods. His father was holding a Stinger, an FIM-92 in his hands aimed directly at the helicopter.

Nearly simultaneously the helicopter exploded in the air and another fireball rose from the woods. The horses and the dogs were running for their lives now, as if chased by a thousand demons. They overshot the stable, so Jasper and Chelsea pulled up in the back yard near the terrace.

"What was that, Dad?"

"Some more people trying to kill you and Chelsea, Son," his father answered grimly. "I got them first."

His mother was already on the phone, apparently talking to Tillot. In the distance, the faint wail of a siren could be heard.

"I saw the number of the chopper, Mom," called Jasper.

She nodded.

"Let me give you to Jasper. He got the number," she said into the phone.

She tossed the phone down to him, and sure enough, it was Tillot. Jasper repeated the number and then described what he and Chelsea had seen and heard.

Meanwhile, Chelsea was calming the horses, grabbing their bridles, stroking their faces, and talking to them in soft tones.

Jasper finished his conversation and closed the phone. It was then he noticed Chelsea's firm hand and calming manner with the horses.

"You have ridden before," he said admiringly, still astride Tristan.

"One of my many talents," she said. "Grandpa Merrill has a small farm in Walterboro, and we kids often spent part of our summers there, working the farm, which, of course, included the horses."

"Let's get them back to the stables before we have to go through the police grilling again," Jasper said with a sigh.

"Tillot's taking care of that. You two get the horses to the stables and then high tail it back to the house here. Stay either upstairs or downstairs and as the property owner, I'll answer any questions that are asked," said his dad.

Clinton and Marshall saw them coming and came from the stables to secure the horses, still spooked by the smoke billowing from the fire that blazed in the woods.

Chelsea felt a moment of sadness that the peaceful woods and its occupants should be incinerated by the hatred of people who didn't even personally know their target.

The caretaker's sons wanted to talk, but Jasper used Chelsea's well-being, who cooperatively kept silent, to excuse them as they hurried back to the house. Her mouth, however, had turned mutinous.

As soon as they entered the house, she rounded on him. "Hiding behind my skirts?" she asked. "For shame Jasper."

"No, not your skirts, your very appealing legs, or what I've seen of them," he said with a mock lecherous grin.

"You, you—" she sputtered.

He held up his hand. "How about if we hit the pool downstairs in the basement and then watch a movie."

"But what about the people in the helicopter?"

"They're dead," Jasper said gently. "You and I can't do anything for them. Besides, they were trying to kill us. Their deaths are regrettable, but to try to kill us was the choice they made. We could just as easily be the ones feeling like marshmallows on the end of a stick right now," he added trying to lighten her mood. Her eyes were huge with concern and worry.

Chelsea swallowed. "Okay. So what did you want to do?"

"Let's try a swim and then a movie. Do you know how to get to the basement without being seen?" They were upstairs by now, standing next to Chelsea's bedroom door.

Chelsea shook her head.

"Okay, we'll sneak down together. Just give me ten minutes to find my swim trunks, and bring a change of clothes so we don't have to come back up here for a while."

Ten minutes later they had skirted the rise and fall of voices in the kitchen and were in the pool that was in the basement directly under Jasper's bedroom. Tall windows on the back wall overlooked the garden in the back and French doors led to the patio that ran the full length of the back of the house. Chelsea could barely see the smoke to the right in the distance. Another set of tall windows looked over the garden to the north of the house, a wide swath of velvet green lawn and then the trees behind.

Jasper swam a full three lengths back and forth at full throttle. Chelsea joined him but at a slower pace. Finally Jasper turned over and floated on his back. Chelsea came up beside him.

"Don't you dare," he said, eyes shut, suspended in the water, a slight grin on his face.

"Dare what?" asked Chelsea.

"My muscles feel so relaxed right now. Don't try to take me under, at least, not just yet." He opened one eye and trained it on her.

She shrugged and also turned over on her back. "Wow. This is awesome."

For a few minutes they floated side by side in companionable silence.

"Why?" "How?" they both asked simultaneously.

"Ladies first," said Jasper.

"Why didn't they just bomb the house? Oh." Chelsea said as the realization that they were the targets dawned on her. She frowned. "If they had tracked us to the woods, they should have been able to figure that we were heading back to the house."

"Maybe he missed us as the helicopter was turning, and when he realized his mistake, it was too late to notify the pilot to turn the chopper. Then Dad's Stinger got him."

"Which leads to my question: How in the world did my dad get hold of a Stinger? This has been a day of so many surprises. I guess if he really is giving information to the CIA and the Secret Service, they can help him procure any hardware he need."

Suddenly pulling her under, he moved to kiss her wrapping his arms around her. But Chelsea hadn't had a chance to get a full breath.

"You jerk," she sputtered when they reached the top. She splashed water in his face, but he retaliated, and for a full ten minutes they battled playfully in the water.

Finally, Chelsea had enough. "I'm starved," she said.

"Me, too," said Jasper. But the way he said it made Chelsea well aware he wasn't talking about food.

Jasper showed Chelsea to the girls changing room, an area that looked like a dorm bathroom with several toilet stalls, shower stalls and a huge mirror over several sinks. After changing into dry clothes, they attacked lunch. Nell had taken the time to bring down a tray of delectable grilled chicken salads for them with toasted pecans, mandarin oranges, cucumbers, crumbled bleu cheese, and croutons.

"Please don't tell me we have to watch *A Knight's Tale*," moaned Jasper in mock dismay.

"No. We can watch something else as long as it's not something gory and bloody."

They settled on a movie, but Chelsea could never afterward give the name. After all the excitement of the last two days and with a full stomach, she fell asleep, content in Jasper's arms.

Chapter Twenty-Two

Chelsea awoke as the movie was ending. She was wedged at Jasper's side, between him and the back of the sofa. The side of her face was pressed against his chest, her arm flung across him, and his left arm was around her shoulders. He had his eyes closed, but when she moved, he opened them immediately.

"I'm so sorry," she said, intensely embarrassed.

"For what?" asked Jasper.

"For falling asleep all over you like that."

He chuckled. "I'm just glad you felt comfortable enough with me to fall asleep." He stood and helped her to a standing position. When he made a big production out of looking under the pillows, under the sofa, behind the sofa, Chelsea asked what he was doing.

"I'm just checking. No ghosts. Not even a spirit."

"Very funny, Jasper," said Chelsea.

When he said, "I think you should add exorcist to your list of accomplishments," she picked up a pillow and began beating him with it. He responded in kind, and for several minutes, they pummeled each other mercilessly. Chelsea spoiled it by collapsing back onto the couch and giggling.

Jason checked his watch. "We have half an hour to dress for dinner," he said. "I don't hear any voices, so I think we can safely sneak upstairs. I'm curious to discover what really happened this morning."

Chelsea found a cute, white sundress with yellow polka dots in Pammy's closet to wear to dinner. The color set off the golden brown of her tan and put flecks of gold in her brown eyes. She looked in the mirror critically, noting the smudges of blue underneath her eyes before she used the cover up from her makeup bag to dispel them.

Grams and Gramps arrived shortly after six. Everyone was gathered in the upstairs family room with their eyes glued to the TV, wondering how much truth had been leaked to the media. Neither Jasper nor Chelsea were mentioned; Clinton and Marshall were not named but were called grooms in the story, and Carter was the only one of the family said to be home during the "accident." The crash had killed the pilot and his passenger, and cause of the accident was still "under investigation."

"Well, that covered the essentials without giving away any pertinent information," commented Carter. "Tillot did his job."

Just then they heard noises at the side door. "Where is everyone?" a voice called.

"Pammy and Jonathan!" exclaimed Nell.

"Might as well give all the details to the Mouth of the South," muttered Jasper under his breath.

He received a light punch on his arm from Chelsea who was the only one to hear him.

Then they were being hugged by an excited Pammy and given a handshake by a calmer Jonathan.

In the instant she was hugged, Chelsea realized just how relaxed Nell had been on her days off. Here was the dynamism Nell possessed contained in another body as well. No wonder they were called the dynamic duo when they worked together. Pammy's blonde hair and blue eyes were nearly an exact duplicate of her mother's as well.

Dressed impeccably in khaki Dockers and a white and orange striped, logoed shirt, Jonathan stood a head taller than Pammy. His blond hair was cropped short, and he wore an unwaveringly pleasant smile on his composed face that Chelsea came to understand was genuine. Pammy had found her anchor, thought Chelsea.

As they adjourned from the family room to the dining area, Pammy began asking questions about the helicopter crash.

"Let's discuss the **details** later," said Carter with an emphasis his daughter could not ignore.

But once the prayer had been said and the green beans, garden tomatoes, and grilled teriyaki chicken had been passed, Gramps commented on it.

"It's a miracle it didn't blow up the house," he said. "That patch of woods is only a mile and a half away."

"The pilot was trying to turn toward the house, but I, uh, it, blew up before that happened."

"It was probably trying to land and get help," said Grams.

Her son and daughter-in-law didn't correct her nor did Jasper or Chelsea.

The talk drifted to fire insurance and the effectiveness of the fire department in putting out the fire. Chelsea realized that the elder Peters-Templetons had no idea of the additional moonlighting activities of the family or even the responsibilities of Jasper's job in protecting the President.

In fact, Chelsea thought, she was glad she hadn't gone to work today. Mercy, she could have placed the President in direct danger.

"You never did get to go back to your apartment," commented Jasper.

"That's okay," said Nell. "Tillot didn't even send a car. He wasn't taking any chances on adding to the press coverage by having you two spirited off in a government vehicle. I came downstairs to tell you, but you two were sound asleep." She chuckled and her eyes twinkled.

Chelsea blushed and wondered if Nell was trying to send her a message, but was saved further embarrassment by Pammy's comment.

"I thought I recognized that sundress. You're welcome to it; take it home with you. I'll probably never wear half the clothes in my room again, anyway."

Jasper had to tease Pammy about a girl's need for so many clothes while Jonathan smiled indulgently.

Chelsea questioned Jonathan about his line of work and discovered that he was a real estate attorney. The law firm where he was a junior partner closed many of the commercial deals Carter generated, and that's how he and Pammy had met.

Gramps was still concerned about the effects of the fire. "At least we'll still have some good hunting areas," he said to Jasper. Then he leaned across the table to ask Chelsea, "Did you know that Jasper can hit his target every time and from the back of a galloping horse, too?"

Chelsea assured him she hadn't known that, and it was Jasper's turn to look embarrassed.

"Gramps just likes to brag," he said. "He's a fine hunter himself."

"I guess I know a thing or two about it," said Gramps. "I can't go back to England to visit the Templeton family like I used to do, but those were the days. They had huge hunting parties for both men and women with plenty of acreage, and excellent food was provided." His eyes gleamed with fond memories.

"Now, Charles." His wife patted his hand, unable to articulate anything more.

Nell rose, signaling that the meal was concluded.

"Let's help Mom load the dishwasher, then come upstairs with me," suggested Pammy to Chelsea. With everyone helping, the kitchen was put to rights in short order, and while Jasper walked out to the garden with everyone else, Pammy led Chelsea upstairs.

"I hope you don't mind me delving into your closet," began Chelsea, but Pammy waved her hand.

"Mom shops the back racks at her favorite stores when things are fifty to seventy-five percent off. She puts them in here, and it's first come, first served. We always keep extra clothes on hand for the odd situation that arises with our guests. Your situation sure is one of them." She opened the closet door and began searching for something then continued.

"We've heard whispers about what's happening, but Mom and Dad are pretty close-mouthed, so what can you tell me?"

"Whenever you work for the President, you become a target, and right now, your brother and I are both targets," responded Chelsea. She sure hoped she hadn't said too much and that Pammy wouldn't grill her for all the particulars.

But Pammy burst out laughing. "Well done," she said. "You should be a diplomat. My brother really likes you, you know. He hasn't brought a girl home for Mom and Dad to meet since Allison passed away."

"I'm not exactly here by choice," Chelsea protested.

Pammy gave her a shrewd glance. "Jasper planned this, you know. Oh, not the accident, but he had already planned to bring you here last night to meet Mom and Dad. He likes to have his dates meet Mom and Dad casually before they really know who Mom and Dad are so they don't get all tongue-tied and awkward."

"Goodness," said Chelsea. "I'm more rattled by all these 'accidents' that keep happening. Your parents have been very kind."

"Well, of course," said Pammy. "They like you. We all do. So if you and Jasper get serious, you won't find any objections from us. I just thought you should know that," she said, irrepressible and unrepentant of any embarrassment she was causing Chelsea. "Have you seen that pale green tea length dress with the black polka dots and bow? Mom's doing the Midsummer's Eve gala for Habitat for Humanity and I want to wear that one."

"I think I saw it in the closet in my room." They went next door to Chelsea's room before she had enough courage to voice her doubts.

"Thanks for your vote of confidence," began Chelsea, "but are you sure? About your parents' approval, I mean? I fell asleep this afternoon right beside Jasper while the movie was playing, and I'm sure your mother saw."

"Oh, she saw. She thought it was cute."

"But I thought your parents had a 'No opposite sex sleeping together rule,'" said Chelsea.

"That's just for bedrooms," explained Pammy. "Corey started dating even before I did even though I'm the oldest. They had to make a rule since his girlfriends always wanted to come to our house. Believe me, they had many other rules for him, but that's the one that stuck for all of us."

"So tell me more about Allison."

"Allison was very sweet. We all loved her, and what she did to Jasper hurt all of us. I know they were engaged, but if you ask me, she didn't understand him very well."

"Why do you say that?" asked Chelsea.

"My brother is as loyal as they come. And if he says he's going to make the commitment to love, honor, and cherish, it's as good as done. Although he hadn't actually said the marriage vows yet, he wouldn't have become engaged unless he intended to do so, and it follows that it would have been 'til death do us part' for him."

"She underestimated him," said Chelsea soberly. "I'm just beginning to see that he keeps many of his talents hidden, such as the facts that he hunts, rides horses, swims like a demon, and drives like a maniac." They both giggled.

"Ah-hah!" said Pammy as she found the dress. "Did you know that he also earned his black belt in karate and almost earned his badge as an Eagle Scout? He wanted to play basketball at least one season in high school, and he thought he could do both, but he got really sick, and it put him behind in everything, including scouting."

"He only told me that he dropped out of scouting," said Chelsea, somewhat miffed.

"Now don't tell him I told you all of this. He's still my little brother, and a royal pain you-know-where. But if you need to know anything about him like some information to blackmail him with, just ask me!"

"Thanks," said Chelsea. "I'll do that." She gave Pammy a hug, and they walked down the stairs together, Pammy carrying the dress on a padded hanger and covered with a clear, plastic garment bag.

Nell had left to take Grams and Gramps home. Leaving the dress lying over a chair in the kitchen, Pammy and Chelsea followed the murmur of voices and found the three men playing pool down in the basement.

The girls curled their legs under them and sat on the sofa that Jasper and Chelsea had slept on earlier, continuing their get-acquainted chat. Chelsea learned that Pammy had earned a dual degree in early childhood education and business management. She currently taught half-day Kindergarten, but planned, eventually, to begin a group of her own private schools.

"The public education system is in a shambles, and if we can give these children the tools they need to succeed in Pre-Kindergarten through third grade, they will be equipped even if they are placed back in the public school system. Besides, I love little kids. They are just so cute!"

Nell returned. She fixed iced coffee for everyone in the downstairs kitchen area, keeping an ear tuned to conversations occurring. Jonathan and Carter had a standing Wednesday morning squash game planned in the basement court. Since Jasper had a few days free, they wanted him to join them. Carter was telling both of them they wouldn't be able to keep up with him.

The phone rang next to Nell's elbow nearly making her spill the sugar she was pouring into a serving bowl.

It was Corey, and he was ordering tickets for Saturday evening to the American debut concert of Charm Dumotte.

"I heard her concert in Rome, Mom. It was outstanding! You'll like it. I want you and Dad to come and Pammy and Jon, too. Do you think Jasper can come?"

"Let me ask him. He's right here."

Nell dutifully reported what Corey had said. Jasper's eyes swung to Chelsea. "Would you like to go?" he asked.

When she nodded, he said, "Tell him two tickets for me."

Pammy and Jonathan gave their assent. "Jasper's bringing Chelsea, and the rest of us can come, too. Make that six for us altogether," said Nell.

"Tell Jasper that this chick's concerts are being threatened by terrorists. That should pique his interest even more."

Cork, Ireland
May 26th

Chapter Twenty-Three

The Irish called it a soft day, meaning the rain was falling gently. Donnell felt as if God, in sympathy for the sadness his whole family felt, was crying, too.

His dad had met him at the airport in Cork as the women were busy clucking around Mother McKinnon and keeping her occupied. Of course, funerals required food and lots of it. Most of them, from the queens of practical joking, great Aunt Jenny and great Aunt Janice, to the newlyweds, Bela who had just married his cousin Bruce and Risa who had recently married Reggie, were gathered in the large kitchen of the McKinnon Bed and Breakfast to prepare enormous bowls of food and bake quantities of soda bread and sweets.

He wanted to stay outside with the men folk who were stacking peat, smoking pipes, and generally staying out of the way of the women.

"Better get it done, Son," his father advised. "Besides, your mother has been pining for a view of you."

Donnell walked into the heart of the house and into a flood of warm memories. The smell of peat hung in the air, reminiscent of cold, winter evenings spent nursing a Guinness or dancing and singing with his cousins for the pleasure of their guests in front of a roaring fire. The air was redolent with the scent of yeasty bread and biscuits, savory stews and meat dishes, pungent spices for the cookies—his favorite were the ginger snaps—pies and cakes.

For the space of one instant, everyone was silent, but then the greetings and hugs and tears began. His sisters were the first to greet him with fervent bear hugs. The rest of his aunts and female cousins kept a respectful distance as he was held close to the heart of his mother, Desiree. Her eyes were misted, but her smile was a rainbow of welcome.

She led him to Mother McKinnon who was seated in the old rocking chair as if on a throne. He laid his face next to hers.

She, in turn, placed her hands on either side of his face, peering into his eyes. She didn't hear very well these days, but her eyesight was keen, and her insight was keener.

"Ye're a good lad, Donnell. Don't be too cautious in following your heart's desire. Your lady needs to know she's most important with ye with no secrets between the two. Mind that, now."

"Donnell has a girl, now, does he?" asked his sister, Amy. She clearly couldn't see her younger brother, who she had always seen as quiet and intense, with a girl.

"Ay, he does. And she's strong and full of passions, but she needs the man who captures her heart to see past the strength to the vulnerability and the longing," replied Mother McKinnon.

His mother gave him a quizzical glance, but kept her own counsel. She would bide her time and her tongue for now. She sent a warning glance to Amy who subsided with her needling questions.

Donnell spent the rest of the afternoon helping prepare the few empty cottages and the dormitory in back of the main house for the influx of relatives from near and far who were planning to spend the night.

Granda', a visionary man many said, had Emil and Jake and their construction crew build an addition with extra sleeping quarters. He and his cousins had often utilized the facilities, deeming the side with the sleeping porch suitable for the boys. The girls had the other side with the luxury of more bathroom space. Everyone was happy with the arrangement, especially Granda' who liked to keep his family close, if possible.

The evening meal was not really a morbid affair, for The Great McKinnon had lived a long life, making friends of many with his stories and his generosity.

The next day, the clock struck noon, and a general flurry of activity followed as preparations for the two o'clock funeral began in earnest. Most of the womenfolk had brought their black dresses with them, and upstairs and downstairs the bathrooms were inundated with the very feminine scents of perfume, hairspray, fingernail polish, and deodorant.

Guests of the main house had been moved to one of the ten cottages. Seven of the cottages were filled with guests; five guest families who had stayed at the McKinnon B&B before, had graciously requested that their laundry and all other services be suspended for the weekend while the family mourned their great loss.

The Montaigne family had all come from Paris and was housed in cottage eight. Davey and Galeah Merrill and their girls, Kielah and Lindy, had arrived the evening before and were staying in cottage nine although since they were all family, some of the Montaignes were also staying in cottage nine.

By common agreement to let the women have the house and the dormitory, many of the men were changing in cottage ten, and Donnell's steps followed the familiar path to the charming cottage that stood with the other two at the foot of MacGillicuddy's Reek. His father, Douglas, fell into step beside him.

"How are things going on this new assignment, son?"

"How much do you know about it?" responded Donnell with a grin. Although his dad was retired from the force, he could still elicit information about his son's cases and had even helped him a few times by using his considerable expertise and knowledge to connect the dots and match puzzle pieces for Donnell.

"I know the lady is difficult but beautiful, and since she is flying to America tomorrow, I'm guessing she is feeling better and that you've possibly discovered the reason for the attacks."

"I don't know about the feeling better part. We ran into some trouble several days ago. I think she'll find the transcontinental flight more restful than her family's home, at this point." He chuckled softly. "Let's find a quiet spot after the funeral, and I'll give you the details."

"Aye, son, including the details about the lady herself." He'd never known his son to be so reticent, especially in immediately denying involvement. Therefore, the girl must have gotten herself into Donnell's heart somehow.

And Donnell was not one to give his heart lightly. His was a loyal heart with deep founts of passion. But he would ask for equal amounts of trust, respect, and love in return.

Douglas sighed. He had heard the girl was beautiful but imperious. He and his Desiree were concerned that the girl would break their Donnell's heart.

As Douglas and Donnell entered cottage ten, they were greeted by Davey Merrill, Marc and Shannon's stepson, as well as the great tenor, Marc Montaigne himself and Marc's father, Michel.

Michel, the absent-minded professor, had a full head of white hair, and he obviously needed the cane that accompanied him, but his eyes still sparkled engagingly as he listened to the rest of the men, including the McKinnons, discuss how the upcoming American elections would affect European politics.

Most of Donnell's cousins, the younger set, were in the two bedrooms. Uncle Milton, Uncle Matthew and Uncle Mack were standing by the fireplace, looking handsome in their funeral blacks. They were ready to go along with his uncles from Cork: Arland, Amos, and Andrew. The rest were nearly ready with only socks and shoes, cummerbunds or ties to put in place.

By common consent, all had agreed to wear rented or owned tuxedos instead of simple suits. Nothing was too good for paying respects to the great patriarch of the family.

Donnell's great uncles Emil, Jake, Joey, Johnny, Ralph, and Denton were already at the house, ready to lift the casket into the hearse. Even as he was thinking these things, ticking off everyone in his mind as he usually did on the job, his own grandfather, Donnie, entered the door to summon Marc. These eight, his great uncles, were to escort The Donald Douglas McKinnon on his final trip to church.

By decree from Mother McKinnon, the twenty uncles would split pall-bearing duty after the funeral, and Donnell and his twenty-four male cousins would have graveside duties. It was a way, he supposed, to show the perpetuity of the McKinnons.

The church sat more than half way up the hill, firmly attached to the same gray, granite rock from which it was quarried and built, and exuded both a sense of permanency and purpose. Tall stained glass windows told stories of biblical times as well as of local history. Fortunately, the church seated well over two hundred and fifty, for nearly every seat was filled when Donnell entered and sat at the front in the roped section reserved for family.

In church, Donnell sat with his immediate cousins, Derek, David, Dustin, Kyle and Kevin. Though the occasion was formal, enough quiet commotion with hugs and greetings from friends far and wide occurred for him to discover that Derek was dating Danielle and completing his degree in computer science. David was single-mindedly pursuing his degree in pre-law, and Dustin was dating Sheridan and had started a band with Kyle and Kevin. Dustin's twin sister, Dorie, shared the vocals with Sheridan because she was finishing clinicals in physical therapy. Kyle and Kevin's older sister, Katie, was working toward her degree in nursing.

Donnell sat lost in contemplation for a few minutes. How would Charm like his large and complicated family? Would she fit in if he had brought her here, or would she have put on her supercilious façade?

Derek poked him in the ribs. "Did you see who just walked in?"

Donnell turned his head slightly to the right but then nearly pulled a muscle, he turned his head so fast.

It was Charm, dressed in the sweetest black dress he had ever seen. Something to do with the simple, modest cut that still fit like a glove, his sister said later, but it emphasized her curves, leaving a man longing to see more. And he couldn't believe his mind was thinking these things, but he had never expected to see her here of all places.

She kept her eyes downcast under the tiny hat with net veil and appeared very sweet, but Donnell could tell she was furious about something. Following behind her was Tiffany who met his gaze with an apologetic look as well as Natalie, Gregor, Seamus and Marcus, too?

All of his closest friends from the force had come.

"Would you look at that?" Dustin poked him on the other side.

Behind Marcus came some of the top brass from Interpol, at least twenty men and women, and Donnell realized they had come not only to guard Charm, but also in deference to their friendships with his father and grandfather.

These twenty elected to stand at the back of the church, their white-gloved hands folded together in front of them. Their presence subdued the more talkative present. It was then Donnell realized the enormity of the job guarding Charm had become. The terrorists they were fighting must be very well-known, indeed.

Superbly conscious of the woman seated somewhere behind him, Donnell barely heard the words describing the well-lived life of The Great Donald Douglas McKinnon. But many years later he could, with great clarity, describe the scent of the wax-laden air and the sweet flowers wreathed in bouquets and other arrangements, the afternoon light filtering through the prisms of the great stained glass windows, the sonorous sound of the priest's voice, the echo of voices raised in majestic song as the choir sang one last song for their community's great friend.

Charm enjoyed the choir's music, too, but she was furious with Donnell for kissing her and agreeing that they would communicate about everything, and then discovering that not two hours later, Donnell had decided to go to Ireland without her. Of course, a funeral was a personal, family matter, but the kisses they'd shared were personal, too. So she'd allowed the anger to build.

Natalie hadn't been happy about the change in Charm's plans, but Tiffany later confided to Charm that they had all wanted to come anyway to support Donnell, so the extra work in arranging accommodations and transport was really worth it to their small team. The rest of the ops had been left in Samois-Sur-Seine to guard Sandy and her family.

The entrance of the top brass from Interpol gave Charm pause. Were they in Ireland on her account? But as she listened to the service, she saw the respect and esteem these men and women had for Donnell and his family, and her anger was somewhat mitigated. But only partially. She decided she'd still let Donnell know of her displeasure.

When the service ended, Donnell filed out the side door with the rest of his family, but he circled around the church, catching Charm just as she was exiting. She stared at him yet said nothing. Donnell held out his arm formally, and she placed her small, elegant hand in the crook by his elbow.

"What's the matter?" he asked warily.

"Later," was all Charm would say.

He guided her around toward the back of the church where his family was congregated by the side entrance.

Finding his mother, he guided Charm toward her.

"Charm, I'd like you to meet my mother, Desiree. Mom, this is Charm Dumotte."

"I'm very pleased to meet you," said Charm. "And I'm sorry for your loss. He must have been a wonderful man. I wish I had met him."

"He was a great man," replied Desiree. "But he is here; actually he is all around us, present in some way or another in all his family you see around you."

"That's a very unique way of seeing him," said Charm.

Desiree patted Charm's arm. "The past is always intertwined with the present. And we Irish seem to sense it more than others, I think. But you see it, too, and you express it in your music."

At Charm's look of surprise, Desiree chuckled. "Of course we looked up your music on the internet as soon as we heard Donnell's case involved you."

Just then the remaining ten uncles began moving the casket to the back of the hearse for the short drive up the hill and to The McKinnon's final resting place. Charm looked around for Donnell. He and his cousins were getting ready to follow on foot as they would be the ones to retrieve the casket from the hearse. Charm and the rest of the McKinnons and friends followed more slowly.

Charm wanted to know what Desiree and the rest of the family felt about her music, but Douglas, Donnell's father, and Amy and Darla, his two sisters, joined them, and the conversation became more introductory again. She shook hands with Douglas, answered Amy's question about her identity, and met the Merrills who invited her to visit them in their home in Summerville, South Carolina when they discovered she had a concert in Charleston.

"It's very kind of you, but we'll be getting in very late," she began, but Kielah interrupted.

"No problem. Mom and Dad are used to a houseful of teens and college kids who come and go at all hours, right Mom?"

Galeah nodded. "We have a bunk house out back. You might as well bring your whole crew. You and the girls in your group can stay in the bedrooms upstairs."

Natalie, who was following unobtrusively was enjoying the scene hugely. Not only did the Merrills not quite understand Charm's tenuous connection to the McKinnons, but they seemed to not hold Charm in too much awe. They probably didn't really know how popular Charm was in Europe.

Then, too, they could park the bus at the hotel, and use private cars to transport Charm and the crew, thus providing a unique and helpful decoy. Oh, yes, this was going to be fun!

Donnell, his duties performed for his great-granda, returned to Charm's side. He slipped his hand around hers, an action that was not lost on over a hundred pairs of interested eyes, including some that viewed the tableau through a pair of high-powered binoculars.

Chapter Twenty-Four

Donnell rode with Charm back to the family home in one of Interpol's vehicles with Tiffany as the driver and Natalie as the front seat passenger. It was later, but he didn't think now was the time for a discussion with Charm.

The conversation drifted instead to speculation on whether the presence of their superiors could mean anything other than a keen desire to show honor to Donnell's family. Natalie thought so, but Tiffany disagreed, revealing only the differences in their personalities, thought Donnell wryly, rather than astute observation or even gut instinct. Natalie was the cool analyst and Tiffany the eternal optimist.

Most of the aunts had returned by the time Donnell and Charm arrived. The large dining room with a huge, carved table built especially to accommodate their large family also contained at least twelve additional smaller tables for guests and friends who stopped in for musical evenings. The aunts were plying the large table with containers of all shapes and sizes with enough food for the entire community.

At the end where the kitchen doors swung in and out was a fireplace large enough for two small men to stand in with an oval braided rug in front of it as well as scattered armchairs, recliners and settees. Mother McKinnon sat here in the old rocker once again, receiving old and new friends graciously.

At the other end of the room was the bar manned today by Uncles TJ, Taylor, and Drennan who would be careful to notice who'd had enough spirits. This was not a day to disgrace oneself by over-imbibing. Besides, they had often replaced Great Uncles Ralph or Johnny of late, pulling pints for both locals and visitors, and they knew the limits of the locals at least.

Donnell led Charm to the long, family table to get some food, and then they sat at one of the smaller tables in the corner with some of his cousins. By common consent and knowledge of his job, his cousins allowed him to sit with his back to the wall. Donnell never sat with his back to a room, nor did his father or his grandfather. That was considered occupational suicide.

He seated Charm to his right by Risa and Reggie. Risa would put Charm at ease and engage her in easy conversation. To his left were some of his cousins from Cork: Enya, Eaton, Austin, and Alden, as well as the other newlyweds, Bruce and Bela. His American cousins, Kielah, and Lindy, rounded out the numbers.

Donnell blessed Risa for not asking Charm what she did. Instead, she asked Charm if she had ever seen such a large gathering of family.

"No. My family is rather small compared to yours," said Charm.

"It can really overwhelm you. When I was first introduced to Reggie's family here, I thought I would die of nervousness. But I concentrated on two or three people at a time, and now I think I can name them all and put them all together in their proper families."

"That's a good idea," said Charm although Donnell could tell that being overwhelmed had never even crossed Charm's mind.

Risa kept chattering about her work with disabled children and her plans for her new home while Enya captured Donnell's attention.

"I like her, Donnell," she said, her quiet voice easily covered by the livelier chatter around them. "And she's fast falling for you, too, if I don't miss my guess. Does she know how you feel?"

"I'm not sure she's the one yet," began Donnell but stopped at Enya's knowing glance.

"I don't think that's true, nor does Granny," replied Enya.

Donnell cursed the insight that some of his relatives seemed to have. "Regardless of what others may think they know, if I don't know it meself yet, it does me no good," he said rather crossly.

"Oh, I think you'll know soon enough," said Enya with a twinkle in her dark eyes. "Do you think we could convince her to sing for us tonight if we finish the evening with the traditional yet unplanned session? Most of us have brought our instruments." Enya and her sister, Estelle, were studying music education at the university in Dublin.

"Probably," replied Donnell.

"Oh, goody," said Enya. "I'll spread the word, then." She stood and gave him a quick smack on the cheek.

Charm could not hear what Enya said, but she accurately interpreted his disgruntled response. The fact that he felt the freedom to be cross and the quick kiss from his cousin showed that they were close. This both intrigued and piqued her.

Reggie and Risa also left and were replaced by Morgan, Marissa, and Maeve. They were part of the Montaigne branch of the family tree from Paris, and Donnell had stayed at their home several times when his travels for Interpol had placed him in their vicinity.

The girls began plying Charm with questions, knowing that sooner or later, they would have mutual friends. Sure enough, Marissa knew Sandy, and Morgan had a friend who had dated Davi'd. They all agreed that he was a heartless bounder. Then it was discovered that Marissa and Maeve had both met Madame Newman through another mutual acquaintance, and the friendship was sealed.

Emmett, Emil and Marleigh, also from Paris, wandered over to their table and stood talking to Charm about their musical endeavors in writing music, and suddenly, Charm knew she could be accepted as part of this incredible family if she wanted to be. Did she want to be? Oh yes!

Donnell, watching her interaction with his cousins, swelled with pride over her intelligence, her enthusiasm, and her melting reserve. Just then he caught Enya's knowing glance across the room. He scowled and nearly stuck out his tongue at her, but one look at Charm's glowing face as she talked shop, pulled him irresistibly into following the conversation.

Kielah and Lindy from America were also following the conversation intently, and Donnell remembered that accents often confused Americans. He watched as Charm carefully brought them into the circle, addressing them as part of the group and making them feel at home. Lindy reminded her of their invitation to stay at their house in South Carolina, and Charm promised she would come.

Alden, sitting between Lindy and Charm, was clearly enamored with his American cousin. Watching him awkwardly claim Lindy's attention made Donnell all too aware again of watching eyes. Yet Charm seemed to take it in stride. He was more used to observing than being observed, and the attention made him acutely uncomfortable.

Alden, in the spirit of The Great McKinnon, who had once been a *jarvey*, a tour guide, offered to give Kielah and Lindy a short tour of the bed & breakfast with MacGillicuddy's Reeks on one side and the lake across the road.

When his Paris cousins also left and were replaced by Uncle TJ's and Uncle Taylor's children, his cousins who lived in the town of Killarney, he realized that all of the cousins intended to come to their table to meet Charm. Resignedly, he sat back and watched them display the famous McKinnon charm.

Tristan and Tommy began to ply her with outrageous compliments. Charm enjoyed their nonsense immensely, and even Donnell had to laugh outright when they most sincerely praised her "Irish flame of hair." Tiffany, Tamsyn, and Talia wanted to know if she wrote her own music, and when she nodded "yes," they asked if she had written any songs with three-part harmony.

Charm asked them why they wanted to know and discovered that the sisters often entertained visitors to the area with their Celtic airs, sung in tight harmony.

"What instruments do you play?" asked Talia. By now Charm was thoroughly enjoying herself.

"I started taking piano lessons when I was five." The trio nodded wisely. "But when I turned nine, my Aunt Olivia bought me a guitar for my birthday. I played the flute in high school, and I've also tried my hand at the fiddle, but I'm not very good at it," she concluded modestly.

"Then you need to talk to Luke and Luther. They live, breathe, and even sleep with their fiddles and they love to teach others," said Tamsyn. She beckoned across the room, and soon two of the most gorgeous Irish men Charm had ever seen appeared at the table.

They both had striking green eyes, but while Luke had dark, nearly black hair, Luther had golden hair that Charm would have sworn came from a bottle of peroxide if it had been on the head of a woman. They asked her how she held her bow, and the conversation shifted to techniques of fiddle playing.

Most of the guests had cycled through by now, and the aunts were beginning to tidy the eating areas and the kitchen. Uncle Matthew sat at the piano and struck the opening chords of The McKinnon's favorite hymn. Everyone joined hands and sang, "A Mighty Fortress Is Our God." When the majestic notes died, the entire clan knew that "Amazing Grace" would follow.

Magically, it seemed to Charm, Luther and Luke's fiddles appeared, and they played an intricate interlude before the final triumphant verse, "When we've been there ten thousand years."

With not much of a pause for breath, Luke began a breathtaking number with hot, fast licks. As Luther picked up the thread of the melody, Luke held out his hand to Enya and they began a quick step dance, making the line of aunts seated against the wall behind the table tap their feet. Six more cousins joined them, and Charm found just watching them perform the quick, intricate steps was as pleasurable as listening to the lively music.

How and when the small harps made their way into the room, Charm never did discover. But there they were by the piano, and as the eight dancers took their bows to the enthusiastic applause, the mood changed as Marilee and Melody accompanied Moira in the achingly poignant "Oh Danny Boy." Tears streamed down Mother McKinnon's face, but as Charm looked around the room, not many others had dry eyes either.

Tiffany, Tamsyn and Talia joined Moira for the next song sung in rich, female, four-part harmony. Great Uncle Joey, Uncle TJ, and his father proved their title of "The Three Tenors" was not a misnomer, and then Marc and Shannon sang the love duet from *Aida.*

The mood shifted as a rock beat was added and everyone added their voices to the more modern tunes of U2 and Van Morrison and then some rebel songs.

Charm listened and absorbed, her heart and soul coming alive with this feast to the senses. She barely noticed when Donnell left and returned with a Guinness for each of them. When a slow, dreamy number commenced, many of the aunts, uncles and cousins stood and danced. Charm found herself in Donnell's arms. Still under the spell of the music, she danced as on air.

The tune changed once again, and she was about to sit down.

"No, don't sit. Come try this dance with me," demanded Donnell.

So she did and found she didn't do too poorly. Derek and then David cut in, and they didn't complain of bruised toes. Charm figured she could relax and just enjoy. Even when Enya placed a guitar in her hands and asked her if she would sing one of her songs, she surprised herself by acquiescing.

"What number will you sing?" asked Donnell.

"I was thinking of 'To Love You.' It seems to fit," she replied as she automatically began tuning.

"Let me sing it with you," said Donnell.

"Are you sure?" Charm looked at him in surprise.

"Yes, if you have no objections. Remember you were angry with me during the funeral."

"That's because you agreed to include me, and then you disappeared not more than two hours later."

"But this was personal. My granda's funeral has nothing to do with the case."

"Perhaps. But then we shared those kisses in the garden, and you can't deny that those were personal and also have nothing to do with the case." Charm held his eyes with challenge.
"Or were the kisses a means of trying elicit God-knows-what-kind-of-information from me?" she demanded.

"Of course not." Donnell was aghast that she would think such a thing, but then he remembered his earlier intent before her hospitalization to discover just what she knew. Had he really intended to use any means to get his information?

"Of course not," he said again with less heat. He was a gentleman as well as an operative.

Charm began the number with some slow strokes on the guitar strings. She hoped she had made her point. She knew Enya had heard the entire exchange, but few others had. There was something about Enya. She just knew things, and somehow, Charm didn't mind her overhearing their private conversation.

On the chorus, Donnell joined her with a beautiful harmony that was just perfect for the song. Charm was amazed. Her deep blue eyes flew to his and she found his glued on hers.

Enya watched with satisfaction. Donnell was going to fall during this song and fall very hard. It was about time someone claimed his heart.

When they got to the second chorus, Donnell knew. He could sense Enya's knowing behind him, but like Charm, he didn't mind. He and Charm repeated the chorus sans the guitar. With instinct more than plan, he ended the song with a brief touching of his lips to Charm's, and the entire room erupted in cheers.

Chapter Twenty-Five

Later, much later, Donnell wondered how his heart could learn to love a woman so fast and so deeply.

They had made their way back to their table with knowing glances and winks and slaps on the back for Donnell. The music swirled around them, but Donnell was nervous. He wanted to sweep Charm in his arms and assure her of his undying love, but perhaps she didn't feel the same, and besides, he had terrorists to catch, terrorists who wanted Charm dead.

Charm kept a smile on her face. Was the kiss given for effect or did Donnell really mean it? She couldn't, wouldn't presume. It meant too much. And so her anger stirred again, but now she was tired, and she desperately needed to sleep. She had a plane to catch the next morning.

With relief she saw Tiffany enter. She had forgotten that the ops were still guarding her. Tiffany signaled to Donnell with a glance, and Charm knew something was happening. Donnell rose with Charm following, and they stood in the half dark of the deep front porch where Natalie waited for them.

"Marcus and Gregor spotted someone in the woods behind the far cabins. We know they have binoculars and they are presumed armed. We don't want to alarm your relatives, but we don't want them to be attacked tonight either."

Donnell considered. "Let me have my dad call the constable. We can at least get dogs out here to sniff for bombs, and we can make sure cottages eight, nine, and ten as well as the others are scoured for incendiary materials."

Donnell turned and saw Charm for the first time.

"I'm so sorry for exposing your family to danger," she began, but Donnell cut her off.

"No. Don't apologize. It's part of the job."

Charm stiffened. She was just the job to him. Okay. She could handle it.

When Donnell asked Natalie to see her to a bedroom upstairs and stay with her, Charm didn't even have the spirit to resist.

They entered the main room. Donnell first glanced at his dad who casually extricated himself from conversation at his table. By the time Donnell had pulled Charm and Natalie before his mother and explained that the two girls needed a room upstairs for the evening, Douglas was beside him and primed for action.

Most of the Uncles had interpreted the glances correctly, and they gathered around Donnell, as well. He briefed them on the information he had and then began assignments.

"Uncle Taylor, Uncle TJ, and Uncle Drennan, I need you to stay here with the rest of our guests. One of you needs to guard the front door. Don't let anyone leave. Station some of the cousins at the back doors if you must so no one leaves or enters that way."

"Uncle Lawrence and Uncle Lennon, you know the vehicles, right?"

They nodded.

"Check each one, and make sure no unwanted characters or items are hiding in, under, or around the cars."

"Uncle Matthew and Uncle Milton, you check out cottage eight; Uncle Mack and Uncle Dennis, you check out cottage nine. Uncle Dustin and Uncle Damien, if you'll check cottage ten. You all are looking for anything out of the ordinary—something that can catch fire easily, produce a lot of smoke or even a bomb. Check every room, every suitcase, and even outside each cabin."

They all nodded.

"No one works alone. You must have someone with you at all times. Gregor, Tiffany, Seamus and I are going to use night goggles to scan the woods behind the cabins."

"Dad? Can you get a couple of bomb sniffers out here? You, Marcus, and Uncle Danny wait for the constable and generally keep your eyes and ears open to the different groups.

"Can I offer a suggestion, Son?" asked Douglas.

"Sure, Dad." Donnell gave his father a brief grin. He was in charge of the operation, but he didn't mind having the expertise of grayer heads than his, especially his father's.

"They just took possession of a brand new police helicopter in Cork. Let me call the office there and see if we can get some help from the air in scouring the area. It will make your job in the mountains that much easier and give them a chance to show off their new equipment."

"Excellent, Dad. Give them a call. My team will just do a preliminary search of our property. Do you have an extra earpiece?" he asked of Tiffany. When she mutely handed one to him, he gave the tiny plug, which acted as both a receiver and a sender, to his dad who promptly put it in his ear.

Donnell continued, talking to the entire group. "If anyone gets in trouble, do the McKinnon war cry. Everyone except my team report back to the main house in twenty minutes to Uncle TJ. Got it?"

They all nodded solemnly.

"Uncle TJ, if anyone discovers something or gets in trouble, report it to Marcus or Dad, so one of them can get the info to me."

Uncle TJ nodded.

"Okay, let's go."

Upstairs in the main house, Desiree knew hurt when she saw it. Oh dear. She had experienced her own share of miscommunication when she and Douglas had first been married. First, he had demanded that she live with his parents since hers lived in the English countryside. Then, he would leave in the middle of the night with no explanation or word to her. It drove her crazy.

Finally, they had talked, and she learned that he had been given an assignment that involved a clever murderer who performed gruesome and inhumane acts on his prisoners before finally killing them.

She, in turn, had been totally honest about the hurt he caused her when he put his job above her, when he shut her so completely out of his job, and he had explained that the only way he could do his job effectively was to know that she was completely safe. They had finally developed communication skills that worked for both of them.

"Here, a ghra, let me help you." Desiree took a light flannel white nightgown trimmed in lace and ribbon from a drawer laden with lavender. As Charm undressed, she slipped the gown over Charm's head and adjusted it around her shoulders.

"The lavender and rosemary will give you sweet and pleasant dreams tonight, and the sage will bring you wisdom." She shook her head. "Once my husband and my son sight a criminal, they become so focused on catching him or her that they forget the rest of us don't necessarily share their passion for justice, nor do they understand our need for communication."

Charm, tired as she was, knew Desiree was trying to give her a key to understanding Donnell. She smiled rather tremulously, then impulsively threw her arms around Desiree's neck.

"Thank you," she whispered.

"You are most welcome, dear. Feel free to talk to me anytime. I'm not one to carry tales, not even to my son."

Charm crept into a bed with a goose down mattress pad and comforter that smelled of lavender, heather, rosemary, sage, and cinnamon, clinging to the small wedge of hope Desiree had given her. Natalie slipped in and reported that nothing had been found yet.

"I'll just sit in this comfortable chair, if you don't mind," she added.

But Charm was already asleep, worn by the swirling seesaw emotions of the day.

Outside, Donnell wondered if he should have brought some of his cousins along who knew the terrain, but he hadn't wanted to imperil them, too. MacGillicuddy's Reeks rose behind his family's property, and one familiar with the area could hide for days if they so chose.

Scouring the rest of the family property had been easy. They had checked behind boulders and bushes but had found nothing. Now they were on the lower slopes of MacGillicuddy's where the footage was more treacherous and the enemy could hide above them and pick them off with a gun if they weren't careful.

Fortunately, the night was dark, and they could slip from shadow to shadow virtually undetected. Tiffany and Gregor wore masks that covered both their faces and their revealing blond hair. They were fanned out to his left, and Seamus was on his right.

Overhead, a helicopter droned. Wow, that was fast. He watched it become a speck over the sea. Seamus caught his arm and pointed up the pass.

"I think I saw something, boss," came his words quietly through the earpiece. "Fifty yards ahead by the yew tree that has split that big boulder."

He crouched low at the base of a large rock. "Tell your dad to warn off the copter until Gregor and I can circle around behind him. Then they can swoop in and sight the guy for us with lights," said Tiffany.

"I heard, Son. I'm on it."

After a few moments his father quietly reported, "They saw three bodies down there, Donnell. They are waiting out to sea for your instructions."

"Did you copy that, Tiff?" asked Donnell quietly.

"Gregor is almost there. He's faster than me. I swear he has animal vision at night."

"I've got two here," came Gregor's ethereal whisper. "Where's the third?"

"Dad?"

Donnell knew his dad was communicating with the copter, but knowing they needed quiet on the mountain, he had put a hand over his ear, and Donnell was extremely grateful that his father had also been in some covert operations.

"He's on the other side of the path. Looks like they're expecting you. They may have night vision, too. The copter is our ace right now."

"Okay. Have them pass over once more and try to pinpoint if they're all facing downhill or if they've spotted Tiff and Gregor behind them."

"Seamus. Go back a ways and take the path around to the right. It should put you down wind of them, so they might spot you with infrared, but it may be the distraction we need to divert their attention from Tiff and Gregor. They'll also wonder if the copter is part of our operation. That may cover you, as well."

Seamus slipped away, and Donnell waited for the helicopter, making sure that he was not totally concealed all the time. In fact, how could he make it seem as if someone was on the other side of the trail from him?

He spied a stick about five feet long leaning against the rock some ten feet below him. Probably a walking stick someone had ditched. He carefully and quietly retrieved it. Then slipping off his jacket, he tied it loosely to the stick. He hated to ruin a perfectly great jacket, but if this worked, it would be worth it. All the jackets he wore on the job were fire retardant, but they would hold heat.

Carefully holding the jacket to cover the flame, he struck a match. When he thought the jacket was warm enough to show sustained heat for about thirty seconds, he put out the match and, lowering the jacket to a crouch height, he bobbed the stick to make it look like someone was dashing across the path to the boulder on the other side.

With great control, he lowered the stick gently, quietly until it lay in the path. Hopefully it wouldn't trip any of the team going down the mountain.

Now he could hear the drone of the helicopter. As it passed overhead, he heard his dad repeating what the (guy with night vision goggles) was saying. "All three are looking uphill toward their left; that would be toward Tiffany and Gregor. Be careful, Donnell and everyone else. He thinks at least two of them may be holding detonators. If that's true, they are just waiting for you to get close enough. That's all they'll need."

"Seamus, can you site the one closest to them?"

"Got him, boss."

"I've got the one closest to the trail. Tiff and Gregor, both of you go for the second one. On my mark, set, go."

Three shots sounded simultaneously.

"Gregor, Tiff, Seamus?" Donnell called softly.

"Here," croaked Seamus.

"Tiff and I are here, but Tiff's down and not moving," said Gregor anxiously.

"Did we get them all? Nobody move. I don't need a half-dead terrorist detonating themselves and blowing us sky high."

After a few minutes that seemed like a few lifetimes, Donnell said, "Seamus, make sure the two on the right of the trail are dead. Dad, I need an ambulance and a few stretchers up here."

"They're on their way. The helicopter lost a tail rotor, and we've discovered a bomb here in cottage nine, so the bomb squad is on its way from Cork as well."

Donnell ran up the trail, zigzagging from boulder to boulder until he got word on the terrorists. He was the bomb expert, and he longed to be back at cottage nine, the cottage of the Merrills, from Charleston, South Carolina. That was interesting.

"I just checked the one on the trail's left," reported Gregor. "He's dead. I'm back with Tiff. She was hit in the hea...my word. No wonder she couldn't move as fast."

"Boss, there's only one man over here...." began Seamus.

Gregor knew instinctively to scoop up Tiffany and move as fast as possible behind some rocks. Donnell began racing back down the mountain as it was his quickest way of escape, taking cover where he had originally stationed himself behind the huge rock. He could only hope that Seamus would get away in time.

The thunderous blast was deafening, but as soon as it was over, Donnell raced back uphill, looking and calling for Seamus. The chopper helped by turning on its spotlight.

Just as he arrived at the pit on his right where the terrorist had detonated himself, charring the yew tree to a blackened, smoking stick, Seamus emerged from the inky blackness beyond the circle of light. His clothing was torn, and blood was beginning to ooze through the fabric of his shirt from the lacerations he had received from flying rocks, sticks, and other debris. He was alive! But he was also deaf and dizzy.

After ascertaining that Seamus' vital signs were good, Donnell received word from Gregor that he had met the paramedics and was getting help for Tiffany, so he began a search of the blast site. Carefully, beginning at the center and walking in ever-widening, concentric circles, he looked for any evidence of the two terrorists who had been crouched there.

A partially burned and decapitated skull was his first grisly discovery. Hm. Middle East descent or Russian he would guess. Near the edge of the pit, a detached hand was still clutching the detonator that had caused the blast. He looked at the bits of clothing without touching anything. Cheap fabric, probably hired mercenaries.

He turned as he heard the heavy tromp of the ambulance crew on the trail. The police were on their heels. Good. He directed the paramedics to Seamus who was sitting in dazed silence and toward the dead terrorists.

The police began putting a perimeter in place. Donnell vowed to return at first light of day and examine twenty feet around their perimeter. Had these mercenaries been trying to ambush him, put him out of commission? Why? That was not the ordinary MO of terrorists. The suicide bombing was more their style, but detracted from their mission if it was to ambush him. And why try to bomb cottage nine? Why not bomb the whole place?

Donnell had more questions than answers, but as long as he knew Charm was safe, he would get his answers.

Much later, when he tiptoed into her room in stocking feet, he met Natalie with her gun drawn.

"Just checking," he grumbled quietly.

"She's been dead to the world in spite of all the commotion around here," said Natalie wryly. "I suggest you get three hours of sleep before the world awakes and wants answers."

The only room unoccupied in the house was a small cupboard bedroom under the stairs on the second story, but Donnell gratefully wrapped a blanket around his shoulders and fell on the cot after setting his alarm.

"Your lady needs to know she's most important with ye with no secrets between the two. ... She needs the man who captures her heart to see past the strength to the vulnerability and the longing." Mother McKinnon's words echoed in his head just before he tumbled into sleep.

Chapter Twenty-Six

Guy was furious. "Her first American concert is Thursday night in New York City."

"And we'll all be there in New York City by ten o'clock tomorrow morning, ready for a sound check if you like. You fly on with the band in the special charter we've arranged for you, and make sure everything is set up and ready," said Donnell smoothly.

"But…" sputtered Guy.

"No 'buts,' Guy. My job is to protect Charm and discover the perpetrators who are determined to attack her and kill her as well as about ten thousand of her fans. I promise, you don't want my job," said Donnell with cutting sarcasm.

He was getting tired of Guy. "I must go so we aren't late for our flight. I suggest you do the same for the band," said Donnell, and he hung up.

Five o'clock had arrived far too early, especially with the bodhrán drums being played in his head from lack of sleep. But his vigilance had paid. He had found a knapsack filled with money, three passports, and instructions written in painstaking Russian.

The knapsack had been stowed in a hollow under a rock beneath another smaller yew tree located another fifty yards above the charred crater. If it hadn't been a dark green color, he might have missed it.

Clearly, these men had been paid mercenaries. He understood some Russian, and their assignment had been to make sure that he and the Merrills were dead by the time the funeral was over.

He knew The McKinnon had passed from natural causes, so he could conclude that this had been a hastily assembled mission, a major mistake of the mastermind. Obviously, the planner couldn't have foreseen that the nucleus of his team would be here with him; mercenaries were no match for Interpol Intelligence.

But to continue along their line of thinking, if he was taken out, that would leave Charm vulnerable in the United States. Given the partial list he had discovered, wouldn't that mean that one of the intended sites was one of her concerts?

Suddenly, he knew he wasn't alone. He turned casually, but he slipped the note of instructions in an inside pocket as he did so; then he bent down suddenly, grabbing the passports and a few of the bills, and contacting Natalie for help. She was his backup this morning as she'd had the most sleep the evening before.

"Have my dad and as many of my uncles as are awake run up the path, giving the McKinnon war cry. I need cover NOW!" he commanded.

Almost immediately he heard the whoops from the camp below. He could discern his father's voice first, but it was quickly joined by other uncles. Bless his dad! He must have had the earpiece still in place.

Using the diversionary tactic as cover, he slipped between two large boulders that would give him the best coverage. They also led to a small canyon with overhang on one side. A barely discernable path under the overhang circled back to another trail below the bomb pit that led to the road. He would come in the front way to the bed and breakfast if he needed to do so.

He reached the cover of the overhang, and with gun drawn, he peered back through the cover of a shrub. A man in black was bending down and retrieving the knapsack. Was he enemy or local police? The sun had not yet risen, so he couldn't clearly discern, and he sure didn't need to get the locals riled up with the murder of one of their own by one of their own.

Quickly he made his way along the path, calling off his dad and uncles. He didn't want them used as target practice.

His next job was to have Natalie arrange for their transportation to the Shannon airport and a private jet waiting to take them to New York by two o'clock. But he still had to talk to his father, get a report about the bomb under cottage nine, and darn, he desperately wanted to take Charm for a nice quiet walk by the lake.

Back home, he found most of his relatives who had stayed for the night enjoying their first cup of coffee or tea. Even those not directly emitting the war cry had been awakened by it and wanted to know what was happening, especially after the exciting events of the previous evening. About ten years back, a dormitory house with a girls' side and a boys' side had been erected in back of the big house for family occasions. This certainly qualified, and many of his relatives had stayed there the evening before.

"What happened this morning up on the mountain?" asked his dad.

"Someone was spying on me," replied Donnell.

"Well, why didn't you shoot them?" demanded Bryce, Aunt Lilly and Uncle Lawrence's irrepressible and blood-thirsty thirteen-year-old.

"Because I didn't know if it was Bobbie Jo's dad," retorted Donnell. Bobbie Jo was Bryce's current girlfriend, and her father was on the local police force.

Aunt Lilly had just entered with a platter of pancakes. She twisted Bryce's ear as she went by him.

"Ow! What was that for?"

"Because you need to let Donnell do his job. He knows what he's doing. And because I'm your mother" she replied firmly.

Aunt Rhianon, Aunt Darla, and Aunt Deanna followed her with more platters of smoked salmon, scrambled eggs, fried trout cakes, local cheese, and fresh fruit.

Donnell knew that everyone wanted to know what was happening, and after their unquestioning help last night, he felt they deserved to know more, but he also knew that he had to be very careful how much information he allowed to leak even to family. Everyone talked to everyone else in town. The tales would be tall by evening.

He loaded a plate, Seamus joining him. His hearing was beginning to recover from the blast. Marcus also entered, looking surprisingly alert. They took seats at the same large table where Donnell and Charm had sat the evening before.

His father and several of his uncles who had stayed over to patrol the place were also seated at the table. The rest who lived locally would be by later for their breakfasts and more news. So far, none of the guests of the bed and breakfast had come to the main house for breakfast.

"So what can you tell us, Son?" asked his father.

"We are on the trail of some terrorists who have been threatening Charm and her concerts." He had learned to strictly tell only the bare bones of a case if necessary to do so. "Last night's attack was rather poorly planned, so either it was thrown together hastily or we are dealing with novices. Because of several incidents, I don't feel we're dealing with novices, so I can only conclude poor and hasty planning."

His father and several of his uncles nodded their heads, sagely.

"What I need to know is more about the discovery of the bomb." He looked around the group questioningly. "Who found it?"

"I found it," said Uncle Dennis, Aunt Rhianon's husband.

"Where was it, and what did it look like?"

"It was under the cottage in the back. I squatted down and saw what looked like a black briefcase, and I started to pull it out, but Marcus, who was right behind me, yelled at me not to touch it, so I left it where it was."

Marcus took up the tale. "I've learned enough from watching you handle bombs, Boss, to know not to touch it. We let the Cork bomb squad determine that it could be moved. A remote control detonator would have blown all three of the cottages to bits."

He continued. "Fortunately, the perpetrators were killed before they could hit their detonator, or some of the bomb team members would have lost their lives. They had just pulled it out and placed it out on the road where they could look at it properly when we heard the gunshots and saw the explosion up the mountain."

Everyone nodded their heads in remembrance.

"So what kind of explosives were in it?" asked Donnell. Bombs were his specialty, and he wanted every minute detail, but he also realized he couldn't get sidetracked.

"It was filled with dynamite," said his dad, "proving it was quickly assembled. I think the more important question is why the Merrill's cabin, and Davey here has some ideas you're going to find very interesting."

Uncle Davey took up the storytelling. "You probably don't know this, Donnell, but your cousin and our daughter, Chelsea, is an aide for the President of the United States. Ever since she and Jasper, a Secret Service agent, were used as decoys for the President and his wife, she has been targeted by terrorists."

"The story gets sketchy at this point since I'm not privy to all of the details," he continued, "but apparently a beautiful Russian counterspy was trying to get a message to the President via Chelsea before she, the spy that is, was assassinated."

The room was totally quiet as everyone present listened with captivated attention to this new twist to the unfolding events.

Donnell wished Uncle Davey hadn't revealed the last part to the entire group. Tongues would wag tonight, but by then, Charm would be in the United States. He only hoped the Merrills and their family would be safe. Actually, if he could speak to Charm, maybe he could make some things happen that would ensure their safety.

Uncle Davey had a question himself. "Where did this 'McKinnon war cry' originate?" I've never heard it even though, as you all know, I spent a great deal of my childhood right here at this bed and breakfast and attending the grammar school in town."

Douglas cleared his throat and said, "It goes back to the time when Cromwell was trying to purge Ireland of Catholicism. The Killarney area was one of the last strongholds against Cromwell and his soldiers, and one of the reasons it remained impervious to Cromwell is because the McKinnon clan set up watches in the peaks of MacGillicuddy's, the Purple Mountains and over at Torc Falls."

"When they spied the coming soldiers," he continued, "they gave the McKinnon war cry which would reverberate across the valleys and over the waters, warning people to hide their valuables, especially the scrolls and books. The cry has been passed from generation to generation, and, as demonstrated this morning, it is still very useful."

"I'm not surprised you don't remember it, Davey," said Great Uncle Marc to the man who had once been the babe he had first called a son. "While we lived here, you lost both your baby sister and the only mother you had known up to that point."

Everyone listened with respect as he continued, saying, "Robyn was the love of my life, and if it hadn't been for your father, Donnie," here he glanced at Douglas, "I wouldn't have been able to get through that difficult time. Then I realized that Robyn had already picked my next wife which was Donnie's sister, Shannon, and we found Davey's biological parents, Will and Mary Merrill."

"So really, Uncle Davey," said Donnell, "you've had three mothers and two fathers."

"I have been truly blessed in life," said Davey. "And Galeah and I would love to return the hospitality anytime any of you are in America in the Charleston area. The McKinnons took us in when we needed it most, and we are most willing to return the kindness." He glanced around at the McKinnons present, and they all nodded solemnly, raising their glasses of coffee or tea as if in toast.

Donnell rose to refill his coffee cup, and each man began speaking to his neighbor. As he reached the table, he saw Charm enter followed by Natalie.

"Good morning, Sunshine," he greeted them. Charm assumed he meant her, and Natalie merely smiled at him since she had been up since five o'clock like he had.

Uncle Davey approached while Charm was busy loading her plate with food. "I just wanted to tell you privately that the message the Russian was trying to get to Chelsea was actually a list of bomb sites in the United States."

Donnell stopped stock still. Bomb sites in the United States? Maybe Charm's list was a list of bomb sites, too. Could it be that the two cases were connected? That would sure bear more investigation. Thanking Uncle Davey for the information and his discretion in relating it privately, he conferred quietly with Natalie for a minute, and then turned his attention to Charm.

"I'm ravenous," she confessed. "I feel as if I'd biked a marathon: full of energy and exhilaration but starving at the same time."

"Can you be ready to leave by one this afternoon?" asked Donnell.

"Oh, yes. I have very little to pack."

"Good. We'll be leaving at one for the airport, and I want to talk to you before then, but I have a favor to ask you--once you've eaten your fill," he said eyeing her waving fork.

"I thought I was going to have to become the diva again," said Charm grinning mischievously at him.

Oh, I'm learning to never come between you and your food," Donnell retorted.

"Smart man."

They made their way to a smaller table by the fireplace where they were joined by Natalie and Marcus.

"While I eat, why don't you give me the details of what happened last night," commanded Charm, her mouth already working on her food.

How in the world did she eat like she did without gaining weight? wondered Donnell, but he didn't dare voice his question aloud. Instead, he obediently began reciting the events of the evening before but not in too much detail because of all the listening ears.

As Charm finished her breakfast, Donnell asked her to take a walk with him.

"Taking her to Stick Point?" asked his father with a grin.

"That's right," said Donnell with a little twinkle in his eye.

"Very good, Son," replied Douglas. And with that, Donnell knew that his parents approved of Charm, for Stick Point across the street from the bed and breakfast had been used for generations by the McKinnons to get their intendeds to the sticking point in a relationship.

They crossed the road and followed a small path that meandered through the trees toward the lake. To their right, the sun was just touching the tips of the trees with gold, and Donnell found it hard to believe that the time was only slightly after seven a.m.

The water was still with barely a ripple to disturb the profound yet silent beauty of the morning. Charm was as quiet as the scenery although moments before she had been chattering to Natalie. She knew she should say something to let Donnell know that she understood she was just part of the job. But the heart must hope, so the words refused to form.

Donnell knew he needed to tell Charm about his changing feelings. He had meant the words he had sung and the kiss that followed as well. But that meant becoming vulnerable. Could he do it? He didn't know. It might change things too much so that guarding her would become awkward.

They stopped by mutual and unspoken consent under an elm tree, fingers intertwined. Donnell, in tune with her thought processes, knew she would want to welcome the day and the rising sun quietly. So he absorbed the nuances of thought on her face as she watched the sun rise further, sending sunbeams shimmering through the leaves. When the first rays danced across the waters, she clapped her hands and turned to him, her face alight with radiance and joy.

Reverently, Donnell bent his lips to hers and nuzzled gently then sipped, tasting the sweetness lingering on her lips from the tea she had sipped then smelling the sporty scent with the very light floral overtones that, for him, had become the essence of Charm.

He deepened the kiss until he felt like he would explode with the longing to take her completely.

Charm wound her arms around Donnell's neck and pressed her lithe body closer to his. So he wouldn't say the words. Well, she loved him anyway. There. She had admitted it to herself at least. And until he said the words to her, she would make him want her until his eyes clouded and crossed with longing and need.

Donnell desperately wanted to tell her of his love for her. But he wouldn't jeopardize the investigation, and he couldn't quite bring himself to say the words. Why? Did he have such a need for control over situations? He was in an agony of indecision. Would he one day regret not telling Charm how much he cared?

A beep on his cell effectively ended the moment. Duty called.

Charm withdrew, hurt anew that the case was more important than their relationship yet confident that somehow, someway she would get him to love her back. A good night's sleep had given her at least a little more objectivity.

The trip to the airport was uneventful although they had to treat Tiffany like exquisite Waterford crystal because of the injury to her head and the resulting headache. Once on the private jet, Donnell finally got the full story from Gregor.

One of the terrorists had been able to squeeze out a single shot before going down. The bullet had grazed Tiffany above her right temple, but amazingly, she had been spared. When Gregor pulled off her mask, he discovered why. A Kevlar-type fabric had been painstakingly stitched into her face mask, granting her extra protection without impairing her vision or breathing.

Tiffany explained that her mother had hand-stitched all of her face masks for her. She'd tried to tell her mom that the impact of a bullet to her head would still probably addle her brains, but her mom had been insistent. This time, her mom's pugnacity had saved Tiffany's life.

Donnell put back his head and laughed. It was more a relief from all the tension, but it sure felt good. The rest of the ops and the Merrills, who had accompanied them, all laughed, too. But as he looked out the window at the sea rolling beneath, Donnell wondered what new challenges he would face in the United States. He would love to sit and watch Charm; however, he knew that he had at least five hours of uninterrupted sleep at his disposal.

Charm smiled at him, and he wondered if she would smile if he knew he had just chosen sleep over her. Probably not, but he was, after all, a mere man.

Afghanistan
May 30th

Chapter Twenty-Seven

Each cell was nearly in place. Youssef bounced down a dirt road in a nondescript white truck covered with dust, heading for a nearby town where he could hook into a circuitous wireless connection before the final lap of his journey began.

He would soon join his brother in the United States for their final act of jihad before they entered Paradise together. Often now, he thought of the virgins awaiting his pleasure; it helped while away his time when waiting for interminable truck or plane rides to end.

His education at Pacific PolyTech had given him numerous tools with which to manipulate the enemy. The college had been carefully chosen, not only for the expertise he would receive, but also because it was in the same area as a major U.S. naval base. Because he was naturally gregarious, few saw the meticulously disciplined side of his personality.

Amazing his professors with his proclivity for all things technical was his weekday job. Weekends he had spent cultivating friendships with men who had been stationed all over the world, casually eliciting information and worming his way into the confidence of men with increasingly more brass.

The dust-covered truck entered town with a stupid infidel waving them through the checkpoint. More than sixty houses made of the same type of wood occupied the neighborhood where his equipment was stored.

Seating himself before the screen, he began typing numbers and symbols in rapid keystrokes, breaking encryptions and virtually circumnavigating the globe several times until he felt his messages would reach their intended destinations without detection.

When he finished several hours later, he was jubilant. Twelve sites were keyed for destruction with a thirteenth thrown in for personal revenge. He would celebrate with a whipped cream-topped triple espresso from a Starbucks at the airport, one of the small, American idiosyncrasies he truly enjoyed.

*****

Washington, D.C. USA
May 30th

Tillot Thomason cleared his throat, about to commence the special assignment meeting. Jasper looked around the room. Not only was Frank sitting beside him, but Forrest Cummings, Gary Livingston and Kyle Callaway were seated across the table from them, with Trinity DuPriest and Samantha, aka Sam Crenshaw, toward the far end of the table.

Seated at the very end was Martha Miller, one of the oldest female secret service agents. She posed as everyone's mother or a solid secretary type, but she was a crack shot and had nerves of steel in an emergency. Beside her was a young man Jasper had never seen before as well as a stunning brunette with a calm, intelligent face.

"The situation involving Chelsea Merrill and, therefore, Jasper here, will probably be handed over to the CIA. But right now, it's still our case, and I want everyone working at the top of their game since it involves one of our own and since the President is still endangered." Tillot looked directly at Jasper and then continued, summing up the case.

"Malea Gamarov was the woman who was shot at the President's last commencement address. What the press thankfully did not discover is that she was trying to get a list of hit sites in the United States to Chelsea, hoping Chelsea could get them to the President. We have the list as does the CIA, and everyone has been working on linking the coded words to sites in our country."

"But a new twist has developed. We have suspected that the list was only a partial one since it had a tear line at the bottom. A day or two ago, we received notice from Interpol that they have recovered what appears to be the bottom of that note with another six hit sites listed. Since the words are in Arabic like our list and since they contain the remaining sons of Jacob, we believe we are now looking at a total of thirteen hit sites in the United States."

Tillot looked around the room. He certainly had everyone's attention. "That's where our guests enter. I'd like to introduce Donnell McKinnon and Natalie Pelletier of Interpol."

Donnell stood and cleared his throat. He was so glad he had been able to sleep on the plane. Their plane had arrived late, but even so, he and most of his crew had checked the site of Charm's first American concert before they had joined the rest of the ops and Charm's crew who were staying at The Raphael. Since the second concert, the debut concert at Madison Square Garden, followed close on the heels of the first, they had begun security checks on the second venue the very next day before the first concert had even taken place.

Before landing, he and Natalie had conferred quietly. She reported that the Secret Service was still handling the case in the United States. He had placed a call to his father who was personal friends with Tillot Thomason. Now he was here to present their part and to garner help.

He began. "My job the last few weeks has been to guard Charm Dumotte, the famous pop rock star from Europe and to discover why she and her concerts are being threatened by terrorists."

"When we found the bottom half of the note, we discovered the why. They believe she somehow stole it from them. I believe she is the 'Rahab' on your half of the note and that one of her concerts is slated to be bombed."

Everyone stirred, including Tillot. It made sense, thought Jasper.

Donnell continued. "But we still don't know a date or the sites of the other twelve bombings, although, we can't even assume we're talking about a bomb in each case. We may be looking for other subversive action, maybe even bioterrorism, such as poison in the water system or a release of food contaminants."

"I have a team that will be guarding the concerts, but I will need help, so I've come to ask for it, and to offer our services, as well. Normally, I would be talking to the CIA, but after discreet inquiries, we discovered they don't have all of the information, and, as Tillot has said, it's not their case yet, especially since my understanding is that the President will be attending the debut concert, so the situation is still directly under the jurisdiction of the Secret Service."

What Donnell didn't mention was that his father and Tillot had become personal friends some fifteen years back when Tillot was still learning the ropes and Douglas was prime investigator of a group of subversives. Tillot had gone out on a limb so to speak, trusting his instincts, and Douglas had backed him, realizing that Tillot was right.

"My colleague, Natalie, is the brains in our group, and she has some ideas about linking the dates and the events."

Donnell sat as Natalie stood. "I've examined the word 'Rahab' on your list, and the ink is fresher, indicating that it was added later, as all of your experts well know. That would make sense if Charm tore off the bottom and took it with her. Retaliation against her has become the personal vendetta of the mastermind behind this operation."

Natalie pressed a button as she spoke, and a screen popped up on the wall with a list of dates. "But that has been his or her major downfall if my calculations are correct."

"These are the dates of Charm's U.S. concerts. If we can determine one or two more of the attack sites, and if they are events, not just places, and we can link the dates, it will give all of us a time frame since the bombings or subversive acts will likely occur very close together in time. After that, we just have to determine the meaning of the rest of the sites."

Jasper couldn't wait to discuss this with Chelsea. But wait. Tillot was speaking again.

"Charm's first concert is tomorrow night. It's a 'small' affair at Radio City Music Hall but still requires security. Her debut concert is Saturday evening at Madison Square Garden, and because the President and his wife will be attending, our security needs to be outstanding, especially in light of this new information."

"In addition, you are to observe the first concert before the debut, watching with the European team for possible loopholes in our already tight security. You are also to assist them in any way possible. I've pulled Frank out of retirement to head this team since he's worked in anti-terrorism before."

This was news to Jasper. In an instant, the older man rose even higher in his esteem. He hoped the other team members felt the same way. Kyle could sometimes act as if he was a one-man show.

"Any questions before we dismiss?" asked Tillot. "No? Then I'll leave you in Frank's capable hands. I believe he has assignments for everyone."

Tillot left, and everyone looked at Frank. Forrest and Gary seemed merely curious, but Kyle sat with his arms across his chest. Was he hostile or just resting? Jasper couldn't tell. Sam and Trinity seemed eager to begin, and Martha sat watching the entire group with something like a twinkle in her eyes.

Donnell and Natalie were also assessing the undercurrents in the room. The only person who appeared to be oblivious to them was Frank.

"I was briefed with your request last evening," began Frank, addressing Donnell. "Since we haven't had much time to talk and since what has happened on your case will directly impact us, I'd like you and Natalie to tell us everything that has happened on your case. Everyone here needs to take notes and be prepared to ask questions."

Frank sat back relaxed and composed, and, once again, Jasper was impressed with his quiet assumption of leadership. He supposed he'd been duped by his own occupational stereotyping, classifying Frank as a mere chauffeur although he did know that Frank had gone into semi-retirement for personal reasons, something about the death of a family member.

Donnell recited the whole story interspersed with comments from Natalie.

*****

Chantilly, VA USA
May 30th

By Wednesday afternoon, Chelsea was bored. She was beginning to second-guess her decision to stay with Jasper's parents--if she really had had any say in the decision at all. At first she had seen it as an opportunity to learn more about Jasper's family as well as Jasper himself. But now she wondered if spending so much time with him and his family was wise.

Well, she thought philosophically, the enforced confinement would draw them close or push them apart. Her ennui was probably caused by idleness. She needed something to do to occupy her attention during the day while Jasper was at work. He was to be followed to work each morning, but at least he could still go in to work. It wasn't fair!

But then her mother called, brimming with news about their time in Ireland at the funeral of the patriarch of the McKinnon family who had taken in her father and his surrogate parents years ago. When she told of the bomb planted under their cottage, Chelsea was horrified and filled with guilt over the danger in which she was putting her family.

"Oh no, Dear," her mother reassured her. "They were really after one of Europe's music stars, a girl named Charm Dumotte. And if I don't miss my guess, she's fallen in love with one of the McKinnon cousins. He's with Interpol and is guarding her against terrorists."

Her mother continued with her news, but Chelsea's mind had suddenly switched into overdrive, putting pieces of information together. She couldn't wait to talk to Jasper when he returned from work.

She wandered around the house filled with more restlessness than ever. Nell came to the rescue by asking Chelsea to help her prepare for the upcoming Midsummer's Eve Charity Ball she was hostessing.

"My secretary, Cheryl, and her staff are seeing to the decorations, catering, music and such. But I need someone to go over the guest list and type up a blurb about each guest, their family, interests, occupation. Could you do that for me?"

"Sure," said Chelsea, grateful for something to occupy her mind beside Jasper and the case that was preventing her from returning to work.

Nell showed her the color-coded sheets she kept: pink for decorations, green for music, yellow for food, lavender for miscellaneous items, and blue for the guest list.

Chelsea looked at the pages of blue. The entire guest list of five hundred was handwritten. "My goodness! You must have at least thirty pages here," she said.

"I know," said Nell, smiling rather sheepishly. "That's why I keep putting it off. I hate typing, and Cheryl is so busy already."

Chelsea flipped through the pages. "What about the names with nothing written beside them?" she asked.

"I don't know those people very well, so I usually Google them on the internet to find something about them for at least polite small talk," said Nell, waving her hand.

"Well, I'm very good at typing and digging for information," said Chelsea. "Let me work on this for you."

"You're sure you don't mind?"

"No, of course not. I'd like to keep busy, and I'm really grateful that you're letting me stay here."

"Nonsense. I love having company, and if we're going to have a house this large, I'd rather fill it with people."

Nell showed Chelsea the computer in the library. "I'm going to spread out all my papers on this table and fine tune some details and make some phone calls, so if you have any questions, just ask."

They spent the next three hours working companionably together. Chelsea couldn't help but be amused at Nell's ability to get exactly what she wanted out of the vendors she contacted with just the right amounts of courtesy, charm, enthusiasm, and praise.

When Jasper and Carter came home, they found the two women laughing over the outrageous compliments of one Italian caterer. Jasper was pleased. Some girls were so awed by his parents that they never moved past the polite phase.

Carter enfolded Nell in a huge hug that ended with a smacking kiss. Jasper went to do the same, but Chelsea drew back. Then seeing that Nell and Carter were totally absorbed in each other, she relented, allowing Jasper the same privilege. But when he danced her into a low dip, she laughingly challenged him to a pre-dinner game of squash.

Chelsea let Jasper think she was totally ignorant, but once she caught on to the differences between squash and tennis, she made him sweat for the points he won.

"I thought you'd never played squash before," he said panting.

"I haven't. But I was on the tennis team in high school, and I played two years in college," Chelsea replied, mischievousness in her voice.

"You've been holding out on me, have you? We'll have to play twenty questions after dinner," Jasper said with both a frown and a laugh. Here came his suspicious nature, he thought, angry with himself.

He felt stupid for feeling suspicious, but Allison had withheld information from him, too, effectively eliminating his choices and leaving him with, not an overwhelming sense of loss or love, but of betrayal and the accompanying anger. He had to learn how to keep his past relationship from interfering with this new one. He had to learn to trust again.

"Well, yes, we can play twenty questions, but I also want to find out more about what's happening on the case. Remember, Tillot said I could know," Chelsea said, wagging her finger at him.

Over an after-dinner game of chess, Jasper told Chelsea of the meeting with the Interpol team. "I worked with Donnell and Natalie all afternoon, and they are top-notch operatives."

"Are they guarding a singer named Charm Dumotte?" asked Chelsea.

"Yes," said Jasper.

"Then I've got some information, too," said Chelsea, and she related the news from her mother's phone call.

Jasper whistled. "Donnell told us about the bomb and the terrorists on the mountain, but I didn't realize your parents were there."

So Chelsea related the story of how her father had been sent to France as an infant, living with his Aunt, Robyn Montaigne, to escape a sexually abusive grandfather. How Robyn had died and her husband, Marc, had married Shannon McKinnon, both of them now famous opera stars. And how her father had finally been reunited with his real mom and dad, Will and Mary Merrill.

"This concert we're going to on Saturday is going to be a very interesting event if I don't miss my guess," said Jasper.

"I can't wait to meet Charm," said Chelsea. "Apparently she's going to be visiting my family in Charleston when her concerts take her down South."

Jasper's nerves began to buzz. The two women being targeted by terrorists were going to be in the same town together? Did the terrorists know of this? What would they do next? Target Nell's charity ball? He grew very sober as he considered that it was a very real possibility. Should he tell Chelsea?

No. All he had was speculation. He needed facts and evidence.

Manhattan, New York, USA
May 29th

Chapter Twenty-Eight

Guy had done a superb job of finding a top-floor, penthouse suite at the Raphael Hotel with three bedrooms and two sitting rooms for Charm and her entourage. Charm and Sandy shared one room, Jonette, her hairdresser, and Megan shared another, and Natalie and Tiffany the last. Donnell, Gregor, and Seamus rotated their watches, sleeping on the several sofas in the sitting rooms.

The men in her band as well as the tech crew that traveled with her were staying in the rooms on the floor below. The rest of Donnell's immediate team of Marcus, William, and Tommy as well as Charm's bus driver, Max, and personal bodyguard, Geveon, were staying on that floor as well.

Charm felt immediately at home in the hotel. She and Sandy were openly impressed with the huge, crystal chandelier in the lobby.

"Just look at this marble," said Sandy, running a hand along the top of a rich, walnut sofa table with an inlaid rectangle of red-hued marble.

Charm stopped to smell the delicate scent of the pink-tinged white roses in the bronze, globe-shaped vase. "I like the gold panels on the elevator doors," she said. "They remind me of Florence somehow."

A well-groomed man in linen slacks and an immaculate white shirt appeared by her side, introducing himself as Orlando. "I would be pleased to take your luggage," he said, bowing his dark head deeply. But when he attempted to take Charm's small hand bag and satchel, she demurred.

"A beautiful lady such as yourself should carry nothing," he tried to insist, but Charm, more annoyed than pleased with his persistence, shrugged his hand away.

Orlando continued his attentions, walking the girls up to their room. He watched as they surveyed the large sitting area of the suite and the smaller kitchen area until Sandy tipped him just to get rid of him.

When he was gone, the girls looked at each other and laughed. "Welcome to America," said Sandy with a fake accent, rolling her eyes. The girls dissolved into giggles.

They were still chuckling over Orlando's fatuous attitude when Guy and Geveon arrived with their luggage. Orlando once again followed the men into the room.

This time, Tiffany stepped forward and asked Orlando to see that they received extra towels as well as ice-cold bottled water from downstairs.

When he had left, she shrugged and told the girls, "Might as well put him to work," causing Charm and Sandy to laugh again.

Charm and Sandy explored the rooms, and then Sandy saw the bedroom with the lavish, antique Italian furniture and the bath with marble floors and counters and a huge jetted tub. "This is ours!" she declared.

Charm kicked off her shoes and fell back onto the huge sleigh bed. "Wow! This bounces," she said.

So Sandy had to try it too. Before long, the girls were jumping on the bed, laughing like loons.

Jonette, Megan, and Tiffany came to the doorway to discover what was so funny. Megan and Jonette also began to laugh, but Tiffany just shook her head. When a few minutes later Donnell and Natalie arrived, she motioned them toward the bedroom, and Donnell was treated to the sight.

The look on Charm's face when she saw him watching her made him begin to chuckle. Natalie laughed too, and soon, everyone was laughing except for Charm.

"It was just so…bouncy," Charm tried to explain, making the others laugh harder, so she gave up trying to defend herself and laughed with them.

Orlando arrived with the towels and water bottles. Donnell saw him first and immediately took a dislike to him when he tried to look in the bedroom to see why everyone was laughing.

Donnell firmly closed the door to the bedroom and sent Orlando on his way. The girls settled down although Jonette and Megan had to drag Charm and Sandy to their room to show them the special touches that had been added there, and then they all trooped into Tiffany and Natalie's room to inspect it more closely.

Eventually, however, jet lag caught the girls, and they slept soundly Tuesday night. As was their wont on tour, they did not awaken until after noon. After swallowing a protein shake and taking her turn using the marble tub, Charm went downstairs and used the workout facilities. Her vocal crew, Sandy, Jonette, and security detail joined her, and soon the rooms were buzzing with their light banter.

Following a late lunch in the hotel's restaurant, Kelly and Michael joined Charm and Megan for a four-hour practice session on the top floor. Charm wanted to work on the song Regina and Anne-Marie had written as well as two others.

"Why don't you change this chord to a d minor seventh?" asked Kelly who sang bass and played bass guitar. They were working on a new ballad Charm had tentatively titled "Dawn Breaking." He played the chord progression for the line on his guitar.

Michael replayed it on his small practice keyboard, adding the d minor seventh while Charm listened with closed eyes, humming the melody line.

"That will work, and I like the pensive air it adds to the words," she said, giving her approval. She scribbled the change on the music sheet where she had written the notes and chords.

They played and sang it again from the top with Megan adding her alto, and Michael picking out a tenor on the chorus.

"It still needs a bridge, but maybe we can add that at our next session," said Charm.

They were interrupted by the entrance of Donnell, Natalie, Gregor, and Marcus. Charm's eyes flew to Donnell. She wanted to fling herself into his arms, but she wasn't quite sure of their new status, and she guessed, correctly, that Donnell would not welcome a display of affection while he was "on duty," especially with the watching eyes of her team as well as his.

"Do you break soon for dinner?" asked Gregor. "We're all starved and the restaurant closes soon."

"Let's order room service," suggested Jonette, putting down the latest Fern Michael's book she had been reading. Sandy looked up from the fashion magazine she'd been perusing, and Tiffany nodded her agreement.

Donnell liked the idea. It would keep them out of the public eye, and maybe give him some relatively private time with Charm.

The menu was passed around, and Natalie, always practical, wrote down the orders. She called Seamus, but he, Geveon, and Max had been assisting the tech crew all afternoon, and they had already eaten. William and Tommy, however, would join them.

The band put away their instruments and music while Sandy and Jonette pulled chilled water bottles from the refrigerator for everyone. They discovered that the table had a hidden leaf, so they found enough chairs to seat all twelve of them at the table.

Orlando and another waiter brought their food. Bowing low over Charm's hand, he offered to stay and serve everyone "anything else required to make your meal a delightful one."

Annoyed, Donnell stepped forward. "That won't be necessary, thank you," he said, controlling his petulance and giving the man a pleasant smile.

Orlando eyed him. A hint of ironic amusement danced in his eyes for only a moment, but Donnell caught it. So did Natalie. She stepped into the bathroom and made a quiet phone call to Tommy and William who were on their way to the suite.

Orlando bowed deeply again and smoothly exited the room.

Natalie reentered the room and made a low comment to Donnell when he stepped forward to seat her after seating Charm.

During dinner, Donnell sat so that his arm bumped Charm's often. Charm retaliated by occasionally placing her left hand on his thigh. They pretended oblivion to the physical contact and enjoyment of the cheerful chatter taking place around the table. But the tension arced between them, keeping them tantalizingly on edge.

Donnell finally had Charm to himself when she stepped onto the balcony with a small glass of wine after dinner. He knew by now not to interrupt her moments of reverie, so he enjoyed the music of the honking horns and tapping feet from far below, the tantalizing smells of various foods and the not so pleasant scents of horse dung and other offal, the sight of the myriad twinkling lights splayed against the deep blue velvet of the sky.

Then he stepped directly behind her, and his enjoyment of the evening narrowed to the three cubic feet of space surrounding the two of them. He couldn't help himself; he had to lean in and nuzzle the side of her face.

Deliberately, Charm set her nearly empty wine glass on the table beside them. Then she turned and slid her arms up and around his neck, her lips searching hungrily for his.

Donnell groaned inwardly. They had to find the terrorists and lock them away for good, soon. He wouldn't declare his love for her until this case was finished. But just breathing in her scent made him long for the time when all was open between them with no unspoken feelings. What was it Mother McKinnon had said?

"Your lady needs to know she's most important with ye with no secrets between the two. ... She needs the man who captures her heart to see past the strength to the vulnerability and the longing."

Maybe he couldn't speak the words, but he could show her through his actions. He changed the angle of the kiss, deepening it until he felt his blood and body were sizzling.

Tiffany, seeing the tableau on the balcony, closed the blinds to give them some privacy. She also saved their lives as she effectively blocked the backlit view of someone with a trigger finger because at the same time, Donnell sat on a patio chair, pulling Charm down on his lap, and they disappeared from the observer's view.

*****

Charm slept late again the next day, but following her protein shake, she wanted to do some sightseeing of New York City. Natalie took Tiffany's place on security. Tiffany still wasn't totally healed, and Donnell didn't want her returning to full duties too soon in case they encountered trouble. Geveon and Max accompanied the five girls as well as Michael and Kelly.

They joined the joggers at Central Park, visited the Empire State Building, took the ferry to Liberty Island, and relished the taste of some famous New York franks from a street vendor. Charm enjoyed the carefree afternoon tremendously even though Donnell wasn't present. She and Sandy were cheerfully arguing the merits of shopping versus taking in a Broadway show that evening as they rode the elevator to the top floor.

Charm's first inkling that something was wrong occurred when she opened the door to see Tiffany lying back against the sofa with an ice bag over one eye. Tommy was hovering over her and William was sweeping up some glass in the kitchen.

"What happened?" Charm asked.

Tiffany sat up. "It was that bounder, Orlando, and some of his pals. You were right to suspect him, Natalie, and get Tommy and William to tail him."

"What did he do?" asked Natalie.

"I went downstairs to exercise for about forty-five minutes since I was stiff and sore when I awoke. When I returned, Tommy and William stopped me from entering the room, fortunately. We entered the service door and found them rifling through the luggage in the bedrooms. Two were in Sandy and Charm's room and one was in Jonette and Megan's room."

Tommy continued the story as Tiffany paused for breath. "The guy Tiffany took down saw her just before we attacked, and he gave her a hard time of it, but my guy and William's guy went down without a fight." He grinned.

"Don't worry," he added when he saw Natalie's expression as she assessed Tiffany's injuries. "Tiffany gave him more to think about than he gave her."

Natalie turned to William. "Your conclusions?" she asked.

"They did not complete their training if they're al-Qaeda operatives," he said with his precise English accent and a twinkle in his eye. "But they are probably part of a cell. We followed Orlando last night and located him with several others at a lower east end apartment. We saw Orlando send a few messages on his cell phone while he was on the sub. And the man Tiffany subdued was forwarding pictures. That's why he caught a glimpse of her out of the corner of his eye."

"So where are they now?" Natalie wanted to know.

"We turned them over to the Manhattan PD along with the info we had on the crooks so the PD can get the glory and leave us out of the picture." Tommy grinned.

"Good," was Natalie's succinct response.

"I wonder that they don't know we already have their list," Donnell said thoughtfully that evening when he heard of the incident. "I'll have to discuss this with Frank and Jasper and get their opinion."

Chapter Twenty-Nine

Charm's first concert was an incredible success. Word traveled, and within forty-eight hours, all of her East Coast concerts were sold out. Houston, Dallas, Los Angeles, Seattle, and San Francisco had followed, and the other venues were filling fast.

"Superb vocal technique!" read one critique. "Exploding with energy and enthusiasm!" another reporter penned. Charm handled the accolades following her first concert with aplomb. She felt as if she was riding the crest of a long wave of hard-earned success, and not just for her, but for her whole team. She was relaxed and confident.

Donnell, on the other hand, was not relaxed and confident. One concert with absolutely no sign of the terrorists or their work put him on edge for the next one, especially since the President would be attending this "debut" concert.

Donnell kept security small but tight for Charm's flurry of television appearances, except for the outside, three-song concert in Times Square on Friday morning. Frank, working with the police department, established a team of sharp-shooters at the top of every building. In addition, live video feeds of the crowds and the streets were watched and analyzed by another task force of experts.

They thought they had detected someone lurking in one of the doorways who was a possible link to a terrorist cell. He had continually adjusted his glasses as he looked at Charm. Was he taking pictures, memorizing her features, or just casually observing, an innocent bystander?

While the national alert system had not yet been upgraded, Tillot Thomason had quietly talked to the head of the CIA. As a result, their team of experts was examining the lists trying to identify events, venues, facilities, or areas as possible hit sites, and others were combing the internet and looking for terrorist cell chatter.

Meanwhile, homeland security department heads all over the country were on standby, and for once, the feebs or FBI were not squabbling over jurisdiction but were doing their part, looking for links and trying to break the code, as well.

No one had cracked the code yet. Donnell, his team from Interpol, and the team assigned to him by Tillot Thomason had scoured the entire Madison Square Garden facility. Donnell had personally talked to every single person assigned to work the night of Charm's concert. He knew them both by sight and by name as did Natalie.

Marcus had enthusiastically set to work with the video and internet task crew, sharing his knowledge of the case and winning the respect of every single man and woman on the American team. They had established video surveillance in the most obscure places, and they were monitoring terrorist chatter on all known frequencies and sites. Donnell was glad to leave these duties in Marcus's capable and energetic hands.

A team of sharpshooters had been stationed around the perimeter, and more guards were stationed blocks away. Normally calm, Donnell was going through a pack of Tums a day although he knew security was better than normal. For every task force he had working, Thomason had more. They had coordinated information, and Donnell was grateful that his father's friendship with Thomason had smoothed any territorial squabbles.

Frank had assigned Jasper to work more closely with Donnell than any other member of the team. He helped Donnell identify Secret Service personnel and acted as liaison between the Secret Service and Interpol. Years of observing his mother organize people and things for large events now served Jasper well.

Two different seats had been "advertised" for the President, but actually a third and then a fourth were established. Secret Service operatives in civilian clothing would be seated around the President and First Lady, and a team in the standard suit would also be used. In addition, Donnell and Tillot had established that Secret Service decoy teams be situated at strategic points. Anyone seeing these "teams" would think they were close in vicinity to the President.

He wondered aloud if they could find men who looked enough like the President to act as decoys as well, causing all within hearing to chuckle. The humor was a much-needed release of tension.

*****

"I like that lavender silk blouse on you," Pammy told Chelsea the afternoon of the concert. "You look really great in pastel colors."

Chelsea looked at her reflection in the mirror. Once again, they had raided Pammy's old closet and found several blouses with the discount tags still on them. Obviously, Nell had been shopping and had found some irresistible bargains.

"It's a shame Jasper has to work tonight, but at least he gets to come home with us afterwards," Pammy continued.

"He's been working late this entire week," complained Chelsea.

"I hear you've been working hard, too," countered Pammy. "Every time I've called, Mom has told me about how much you've been helping her with her plans for the Midsummer's Eve Charity Ball."

"I'm really enjoying it," said Chelsea with some wonderment in her voice. "I mean, I'm glad to help although I didn't think I'd enjoy the work so much. But I actually do."

"Won't you be looking for a new job soon?"

"Yes. That's an unfortunate result when the President chooses not to run again for office. But having worked for him certainly will add clout to my resume."

"Helping Mom with one of her charities will look good on your resume, too," said Pammy.

"I hadn't thought of that," said Chelsea, "but you're right."

"We'd better get downstairs," Pammy said with one final look in the mirror to check her lipstick. "I'm starting to get hungry, and I can't wait to meet Corey's new girl. They're meeting us at the restaurant when we get into Manhattan."

"What's Corey like?" asked Chelsea.

"He's the best and the worst of us," said Pammy somewhat ruefully. "Don't get me wrong. I love my brother, and he can be charming, fun, energetic, and passionate. But he has been burned one time too many by girls who want to date him for his social prestige or his money. So he has become cynical and somewhat cruel in his relationships with women."

Chelsea pondered for a moment. "What prevented you and Jasper from becoming that way?"

"I know I learned a lot from watching him, especially during high school. He cried over the first few girls, but he's put up walls since then. Jasper was younger, but I think he watched and learned, too."

"Perhaps your personalities differ from Corey's personality," suggested Chelsea as they descended the stairs to the kitchen.

"Oh my, yes!" exclaimed Pammy. "Corey is so much more driven than the rest of us, Mom and Dad included. Even when he was taking business classes in college, he was helping Dad develop his real estate holdings. In fact, with Corey's drive and ambition, he's been able to help Dad develop real estate in Montreal, Stuttgart, and Lisbon, to name a few of the places I've heard him and Jon discuss."

As Pammy had predicted, Corey was very charming. After they had placed their orders, Nell wanted to know of his latest travels to Europe, where he had been, what sights he had seen. Carter and Jon added their own stories and opinions. Chelsea enjoyed listening to the bright chatter as well as watching the family dynamics.

Corey's date was a pretty, dark-haired girl from Paris. Musette was the daughter of one of Corey's business associates overseas, and that she had dated Corey before became apparent. She smiled politely, but Chelsea soon realized that although Musette spoke faultless English, she had a difficult time following it.

Feeling sorry for her, Chelsea proffered several conversational gambits that were either ignored entirely or met with lukewarm interest. She glanced across the table at Pammy who made a small face in sympathy.

As they rose to leave, Musette made clear to everyone present that she considered Corey hers by clinging possessively to his arm and steering him away from the others.

They had decided to walk the several blocks from the restaurant to Madison Square Gardens.

"Well that's not going to last very long," said Pammy to Chelsea, indicating Musette's hold on Corey's arm. "Anyone wanting Corey's attention should give him a very long leash."

"At first I thought she wasn't talking because we were speaking too fast for her. But then I realized that she sees the rest of us as boring, old fogies who are in the way of her having a good time with him," Chelsea said.

"Yes, we are so old and boring," Pammy said in a prudish voice, causing Chelsea to giggle.

"Speak for yourself, Babe," said Jonathan who had, like a gentleman, taken the street side of the two girls. They were followed by Carter and Nell.

"I already know I'm considered old-fashioned," said Chelsea. "Just being from the South makes people think of me that way."

"Oh, please," Pammy retorted. "When you start wearing granny glasses and tidy whities, then I'll call you old-fashioned."

The entire group, including Nell and Carter who had caught up to them in time to hear the last of the conversation, broke into infectious laughter, causing others around them to smile as they joined the long queue to enter the arena.

Musette, who stood with Corey in the next line over, merely lifted an eyebrow and turned Corey away by pointing to something in the distance.

"They'll have to come over here," Pammy said confidingly to Chelsea. "Mom has the tickets." But as it happened, Musette sent Corey back to them for the tickets.

Their group was seated in Chelsea's favorite spot for a concert: five rows above the floor and to the left of the stage. Chelsea looked around for Jasper and was disappointed to see him nowhere. He had, however, promised to join them sometime during the second half of the concert. She had to content herself with that promise.

Jon pointed out the President's supposed box, equipped with bullet-proof glass. Later, they would learn that all of the boxes had bullet-proof glass.

The concert began with Charm's usual energetic numbers, and both Chelsea and Pammy agreed that she was as sensational as the media had portrayed. When they heard the second set of numbers, they realized, as often happens, that Charm had surrounded herself with musicians who were equally as talented. Corey and his problematic date were forgotten.

By the end of the third set of music, members of the security detail were congratulating each other on a safe concert. Jasper had been allowed to sit with Chelsea and his family although he'd have to leave before the concluding song.

Meanwhile, Charm had agreed to forego the dancing couples for her American concerts. The security risk was too high, and she didn't want to endanger her fans. She had, however, been working on a surprise ever since she had discovered that the President of the United States would be attending this concert.

Charm sprang her surprise at the beginning of her fourth set. The lights dimmed and the center curtains were pulled back to reveal her sitting on a low stool, dressed in the midnight blue dress shot through with silver thread, her guitar resting on her knees. She waited for the crowd to quiet.

"Tonight is a very special night for me," she began. "I understand that the President is attending my concert tonight, and I'm very appreciative of his interest in music."

She waited for the applause to fade. "But even more than that, I'm appreciative of the many men and women who courageously face death every day, from the security at this concert tonight to the men and women fighting in the military. And although I am not an American citizen, I will always appreciate the ideals of freedom and democracy that Americans cherish and guard so jealously. I wrote this song for all of you."

She strummed her guitar and sang

> May God keep America strong and true;
> Long wave the red, white, and blue.
> May God keep America strong and free
> And the ideal of liberty.

More of the curtain was pulled back to reveal the drummer who began a pulsing beat.

> More than two hundred years have come and
> gone
> Since America began freedom's song.
> She's proved that productivity
> Flourishes best under liberty.

To other countries such as mine
She's paved the way for freedom's time
And now in countries far and wide
Freedom stems evil's tide.

May God keep America strong and true;
Long wave the red, white, and blue.
May God keep America strong and free
And the ideal of liberty.

By the time Charm reached the second verse, Megan had joined her on the fiddle. She repeated the chorus softly one last time without any instrumentation.

Donnell stood in the wings listening with pride and amazement that Charm could still pull off a surprise like this in spite of heightened security and the stress she must certainly feel, knowing that her concerts were targeted.

He had wondered about the change in costume for the third set, but he also knew that Sandy was working on two new costumes for Charm.

The crowd erupted in wild applause, and Donnell knew that if they had not loved her before, they truly loved her now.

He was waiting for the curtain to rise on the rest of her band before he made a final sweep of Charm's dressing room when he received a call from Natalie.

"Donnell, I'm in Charm's dressing room; you're going to want to see this."

Once he was clear of the front area, he raced to the dressing room. Natalie stood near the dressing table with an envelope in her gloved hands. Sandy stood next to her.

"Don't get too close," Natalie warned before he could read the card. "I opened this, given the situation we're in, and the writing is bad enough, but a fine powder is present on this piece of notebook paper. I think it might be ricin. I'm going to send it to the lab for testing, but I thought you'd want to see the writing and the accompanying picture first."

The note read, "We get you, whore," and the picture was of a woman with her hands tied above her head, blindfolded and spread eagle with graphic sexual images of her being raped. Below the woman were a long knife, a tank, and a burning building.

Donnell fought the urge to kick something. "Okay, I've seen it. Bag it and send it off, and make sure no traces of powder fell to the floor here before Charm returns" he said grimly.

He turned to Sandy. "No costume change tonight for the final number. How did it get in here?"

"I don't know. It was sitting here on the makeup counter after the meet and greet, but I don't know who put it here," Sandy said.

He turned to Natalie. "Search the video tape. You work that angle, but we can't let this distract us from the concert."

"I'm on it," Natalie said.

Donnell returned to his station to hear Charm's final two numbers. He caught her before she went backstage to change into the filmy white dress she usually wore for her final number.

"We've had another mishap in your dressing room, Darling," he said.

"Not again," Charm said, groaning. "Is everyone alright?"

"Yes. Natalie caught it and is dealing with it."

"Don't even tell me what 'it' is. I don't want to know right now. I need to stay focused on my music."

They listened in silence as Megan and Michael performed their number.

Donnell cleared his throat. "You're singing 'To Love You,' right?

Charm nodded.

"I could give you something to help you focus on the meaning of the words," said Donnell.

Charm didn't like the glint in his eyes. "You wouldn't dare."

"Oh, wouldn't I? It is our song, you know."

"Yes, I know..... Donnell," said Charm with a warning in her voice as he lowered his mouth toward hers.

But he kissed her anyway, hard and fast, a shocking assault on her senses. "Now, Darling, think of me as you sing. I'll be standing in the wings here, imagining myself having my very wicked way with you," he said with a mockingly lecherous leer.

Her song was achingly, faultlessly lovely, just as Donnell had known it would be. He wanted to follow through on his words, but all of a sudden, Thomason's crew went on high alert. A woman with a gun was trying to enter the President's box. She had already taken down at least one of them.

Quickly, Donnell radioed Thomason that he would prolong the concert while they apprehended the woman. Then he signaled Gregor who was stationed by the sound and light technicians to tell them to keep the lights low while Secret Service apprehended their suspect.

But foiled at the entrance to the box, the woman wound her way to the seats below the box, firing shots at the glass. "He's mine," she screamed. "He should have dated me, not you. He's mine!"

Those in the crowd who weren't ducking for cover sat in stunned silence at her rampage but began scattering as the Secret Service wrestled the woman prostrate on the steps, handcuffing her and confiscating her gun.

Donnell strode forward and grabbed Charm's mike. "SIT DOWN!" he commanded in an authoritative voice. "Those in sections forty-nine through fifty-six exit immediately. Everyone else stay seated until they are clear. He paused, glaring at some on the floor who were moving toward the exits.

Once the woman was led, sobbing, from the area, Donnell directed the upper levels to exit first and then the lower levels. By then, the ushers and police were at their stations, firmly enforcing crowd control.

Charm was standing just off-stage, waiting for Donnell. Natalie met them in the back hall, indicating that the dressing room was available once again.

Just as Donnell was breathing a sigh of relief, Marcus contacted him, saying, "You need to know: there's been a fire at the Raphael, and William is in critical condition in the hospital."

Manhattan, NY and Chantilly, VA USA
June 2nd

Chapter Thirty

The fire had gutted the entire top floor. William, left on guard, had been shot with a stun gun and then left lying on the floor to inhale the noxious fumes. His life was ebbing fast; he wasn't expected to survive the night.

Quickly Donnell called for a meeting with Natalie, Tiffany, Gregor, Seamus, Tommy, and Geveon. He told them the news, and immediately asked Tommy and Tiffany to accompany him to the hospital; Natalie, Gregor, Seamus, and Geveon were to stay at Charm's side at all times, escorting her, Sandy, Jonette, and Megan to the hotel to see what, if anything, could be salvaged.

"This may be used to get us to drop our guard over Charm. Be doubly alert. I'll make alternate arrangements for a hotel for tonight, and we'll all meet there in ninety minutes."

"There's no need for that, Sir," said Jasper who had just come with news of the woman who had been escorted away. "My parents would be honored to have your entire crew as well as the band stay with them tonight."

As Donnell paused, he added, "They have the room as well as the security clearance. Mom loves company and is always prepared. She'll want to feed everyone, as well."

"Very good," said Donnell, making a snap decision. "Gregor, get directions from Jasper and upload them to my phone. Your group can head there after you visit the hotel; we'll be there as soon as we can. And make sure that the tech crew knows the change of plans as well. In fact, wait for the bus and the semis to be loaded, and all of you go together. I want that bus secured, too."

Jasper and Gregor moved toward the stage to alert the tech crew. Donnell had stood where he could see the doors of the dressing rooms down the back hall where the band members were still removing makeup and changing into street clothes. Now he moved toward Charm's door.

Charm opened the door just as he was about to knock. She was still radiating adrenalin-charged energy.

"Well, hello, Handsome. I was just coming to find you."

Her saccharin-sweet tone had him lifting an eyebrow and realizing she was still angry over his provocative kiss. He wondered how she would handle the news of the fire.

"I need to talk to all of your band members," he said. Just then Michael and Kelly opened their door.

Charm raised her hand to knock on Megan's door, but it opened. "I heard. What's up?" asked Megan.

"I have good news and bad news," said Donnell. The bad news is that the top floor of the Raphael was torched." Jonette and Sandy gasped, and Charm's eyes went wide.

"In the process, William was severely injured. I'm on my way to the hospital now with Tiffany and Tommy. I need to know that you'll be safe, Charm. This may be a diversionary tactic—divide and conquer." He locked eyes with her.

"I want you to stay with at least two of my crew at all times. In fact, I want the bus and tractor trailers packed and everyone traveling together."

"What's the good news?" asked Megan in disbelief. "I brought most of my stuff with me since Guy was renting and loading the bus tonight, but oh my."

The rest of the band nodded. "We left very little there; just overnight clothes, basically," added Michael.

"The good news is that we'll all be staying at the Peters-Templeton home tonight. I've actually heard of their estate called Rosemont. I'm sure we'll be pampered and treated like royalty," Donnell said dryly.

At the hospital, they found William unconscious and hooked up to machines. His condition had stabilized somewhat, but the next twenty-four hours would be critical. In fact, his parents were on their way from London.

Tiffany squeezed and patted his hand, imploring him to get well. Tommy added, "Get well, Man. We need you on the team."

Donnell stood on the other side of the bed looking down on one of the newest members of his team. His team rarely had injuries, but when they did, he felt so responsible, so guilty. He knew it was a risk they all took to do their job, but it still clenched his gut every time.

He identified himself to the head nurse at the nurses' station and asked that he be called immediately should any change occur and also when William's parents arrived. Then he called Frank and asked for a guard to be placed on duty at the door. Frank promised a guard would be there within fifteen minutes.

Donnell wasn't taking any chances. They waited, talking quietly about the case. When the guard showed in twelve minutes, Donnell was impressed. He told the guard precisely what to do, even down to making sure that hospital personnel would be watched while in the room, and then they headed for Rosemont.

Donnell asked Tommy to take the wheel of their borrowed undercover vehicle. He wanted to stretch his tired muscles and read the directions from his phone without having to pay attention to traffic, too.

They arrived at Rosemont over an hour later. The bus and trailers had just arrived. Donnell heard later that Natalie had kept the hotel visit to a minimum, accepting the profuse apologies of the owner while shepherding everyone in and out in less than twenty minutes.

They had retrieved anything that was retrievable, and that was limited mostly to the satchels of the security men on the lower floor although Natalie had found Tiffany's overnight bag relatively unscathed. It had fallen to the floor below and had never caught fire. Gregor had secured Donnell's satchel.

Meantime, Geveon and the bus driver were unloading the suitcases deemed necessary for the band members while the rest of the entourage were making the acquaintance of Mo, Liz, and Bert, and being shown to their rooms, girls upstairs and guys on the lower level. Eventually everyone reconvened in the kitchen where Nell had Panini sandwiches, chips, three kinds of salads, cookies, and gallons of tea and coke ready for their post-performance snack.

Chelsea helped Nell play hostess, but when appetites were sated, she had time to speak to Charm.

"I heard you met my family at The McKinnon's funeral," she began.

"Yes, of course," Charm replied, shaking her head as comprehension dawned. "I thought you looked familiar. You and your sisters look remarkably similar."

"My mom called and told me about everything that happened there," said Chelsea.

Charm sincerely hoped the song she had sung with Donnell had not been mentioned, but guessed that it probably had been discussed.

"You know that the attacks on you and your band and the attacks on me are all related, right?" asked Chelsea.

"Yes, I've heard speculation about that," Charm replied somewhat cooly.

"Oh, they definitely are," Chelsea assured her. "Do you have time for me to show you something?"

"Sure," said Charm. She looked around. The tech crew as well as Michael and Kelly were going to play a game of pool and then relax with a short swim before retiring as they had no concert the next day. Sandy and Jonette were already heading up the stairs to the room they were sharing, and Megan, who usually bunked with Charm, was staring moodily into a cup of hot chocolate.

"Let me take care of her first," she said softly to Chelsea, nodding toward Megan. "I think she's bummed about the fire."

"Of course," said Chelsea. "I'll just help Nell put the kitchen to rights."

Thirty minutes later Chelsea led Charm to the library. The dark green drapes were closed and the embers of a log still glowed in the fireplace, giving the room a warm, cozy feeling that was welcome against the chill of knowledge that someone was targeting their lives.

Taking down a book from one of the shelves on her right, Chelsea placed it on the table and opened it, pulling out two sheets of paper.

As she sat in one of the cushy leather chairs, Charm gasped suddenly, realizing that on one of the sheets of paper, she was seeing a copy of the list of terrorist hit sites Donnell had found.

"Tillot Thomason, Jasper's boss with the Secret Service, gave me permission to show these to you since you've already seen one and since the other one was supposed to come to me," Chelsea was saying. "As far as we can tell, these words in Arabic are a list of sites terrorists will be targeting soon here in the United States."

"But why target me? I didn't pick up their stupid list on purpose," said Charm. But then she thought of her Aunt Olivia and realized that perhaps Aunt Olivia was somehow involved.

"No, I'm sure you didn't, but you know how their society disregards, disrespects, denigrates, and depersonalizes women. I think that would be enough for them to see you as a threat. After all, you are in the entertainment industry which jihadists abhor as being extremely evil. You are also a self-confident, female entrepreneur, equally repellent to them."

"I never thought of it that way, but you are right," said Charm, her respect for Chelsea rising.

"So here are the lists, and the Secret Service as well as the FBI and CIA are all trying to 'crack the code' so to speak to discover what the hit sites are. But I've got some theories of my own. I just think it would be more fun to figure out the meanings with someone else, and if we work together, maybe we can discover the meanings before they do." Chelsea's eyes shone with excitement at the thought.

"And you can't discuss it with anyone not involved directly, right?" asked Charm. She was beginning to catch Chelsea's enthusiasm. "So what are your theories?"

To answer, Chelsea returned again to the bookshelf, talking as she went. "I grew up in the South, very traditional, you understand, and my family goes to church every Sunday. So naturally when I saw this list, I made the connection between the Arabic words and their translation as the twelve sons of Jacob."

"Both the Jews and the Muslims claim Abraham as their father," she continued, "but the Jews trace their lineage through Isaac and then Jacob and his twelve sons whereas the Muslims trace their lineage through Ishmael. Whoever made up this list is educated and, I would guess, highly religious. It's sort of a family feud between the two sons and their progeny."

"Wow! That's very interesting," said Charm.

"Oh, it gets better," said Chelsea. "When you look up the descriptions of the twelve sons of Jacob in the Bible, it gives information about each son and in what area they and their descendents excelled. For instance, Genesis chapter 49, verse 16 says 'Dan shall judge his people,' meaning that he was a judge. Wouldn't you think that translates to bombing the Supreme Court building or creating havoc there in some way?"

"Yes! I would!" said Charm. Her coolness had faded and had been replaced with an enthusiasm that nearly rivaled Chelsea's. "What else have you connected?"

"Verse thirteen talks about Zebulun being a 'haven of ships.' Couldn't that be one of the ports? So I looked up all the port cities in the United States. The top five are Los Angeles, San Francisco, Charleston, Portsmouth, and New York. I'm thinking a ship-launched bomb for one of those."

Charm looked at Chelsea in admiration. "I think you're absolutely right!" Anything else?"

"I'm still working out the rest. That's why I need your help. I don't want to bring Jasper into this yet because then he'll have to tell Tillot, and I want to flesh it out some more before I hand it all over to Secret Service."

"I'm in," said Charm with enthusiasm. "Let me sleep on all of this, and tomorrow we'll get our calendars together. I've got a few days off when I begin doing concerts in the South," she said as Chelsea closed the books with the lists enclosed and placed them back on the bookshelf.

"Awesome! I'm so glad you're willing to help. I thought maybe you'd be too caught up in yours-, your concerts to really care about it."

"What you mean is you thought I'd be a demanding diva or an air-headed bimbo," said Charm with a laugh.

Chelsea began to demur but sheepishly joined Charm's laughter.

"I can pull both acts if I need or want to, but my parents and the rest of my family keep me rather grounded," said Charm.

"So this is where you two are hiding," a voice spoke from the doorway. It was Jasper with Donnell close behind.

"I wanted to show Charm the house, but this room is so inviting, we just curled up for a girl talk," said Chelsea. She stood on tiptoe and gave Jasper a quick kiss.

Charm followed Chelsea's example but, not knowing what Donnell wanted Jasper and Chelsea to know about their relationship, merely gave his hand a good squeeze. Besides, she didn't know if she had forgiven him that kiss yet.

But Donnell was not to be denied. The day had been long and grueling, and he had been upset when Natalie reported that she couldn't locate Charm. He gathered her in his arms and just held her, breathing in her refreshing fragrance. She couldn't argue with his actions even if she hadn't yet forgiven him for his audacious kiss.

Chapter Thirty-One

A televised conference call with Frank and Tillot Thomason the next morning in the library assured Donnell that his decision to stay at Rosemont was a wise one. Jasper, also present, asked where Charm's concerts would take place for the next two weeks.

Looking at the list Donnell handed him, he said thoughtfully, "These are public knowledge, but Charm's hotels are not. The bus hired for transportation and the trailers are easily spotted. We could use the 'public information' card to hide her real location, and we could easily hire several buses that look the same to serve as decoys."

"Now you're thinking like a real agent," approved Tillot via telecom.

"For that matter, why use the buses at all except as decoys? Why not rent various vans to haul equipment and transport the band members in unmarked cars?"

"You're absolutely right, Man," said Donnell, slapping Jasper on the shoulder.

"Then you'd better hide that bus," said Tillot.

"Dad already had Max, the bus driver, park it in the large storage shed beside the stables."

"Good man," said Tillot. "Let's keep Charm and her entourage there at Rosemont as long as possible. As your mother pointed out, Jasper, Rosemont is about as safe as the White House with fewer visitors. What are the locations of Charm's next several concerts?"

"Her next eight concerts are in this general locale until the eighteenth when she goes south and then out to Texas and the West Coast," said Donnell.

"And we're fairly certain that terrorist activity on a grand scale will happen before the end of June," added Frank.

"Has anyone solved the puzzle yet?" asked Jasper.

"Not yet." Tillot ran his fingers wearily over his face. "We've all been working on it until we're bug-eyed."

"I think Chelsea has talked Charm into working on it, too," said Donnell with some amusement in his voice. "Jasper and I found them in the library last night with their heads together. If that keeps the ladies safe, I'm definitely in favor of them using their acumen to solve it."

"Chelsea is one sharp girl, and I think Charm is of the same caliber," said Frank. "Don't underestimate them, men."

"I agree," said Tillot. "Chelsea actually called me to get permission to include Charm in her puzzle-solving endeavor. Should she do so, she'll have several agencies willing to look at her resume."

"Let's refocus, here," said Frank. "Jasper, can you create a task force to arrange alternate modes of transportation for Charm and her entourage? Use Gary, Kyle, and Trinity, and let Martha head it up, reporting to you. You will keep both Donnell and me appraised. That will free Donnell and his crew to work on security."

"I appreciate that," said Donnell. "Your agents' knowledge of this locale is a tremendous asset. By the way, what happened with the woman who tried to accost the President last night?"

"I thought that might be of interest to you," said Tillot with a twinkle in his eyes. "That was Michelle Hinton Felder, Washington socialite. Apparently, she is somewhat unstable. Her twin sister, Maureen Hinton Feniway used to date the President, and Mrs. Felder believes it was she who the President should have dated and she who should share a spot in the Big White House."

They all laughed incredulously.

"By the way, she is the one who nearly drove you off the road down in Charleston. She thought she was tailing the President. And more records reveal that she has been stalking the President for some time now."

"What will become of her?" asked Jasper.

"Her husband, Harry, has agreed to get her professional help on a 'permanent basis,' meaning that she will be kept at a posh rehabilitation center in exchange for our quiet and our hushing of the media."

"Is that all for now?" asked Frank. Jasper looked at Donnell.

"I'm fine," said Donnell.

"Keep in contact, men," said Tillot, and the connection was severed. The screen Carter had shown them receded, portraying only a portrait of a Peters-Templeton ancestor.

Donnell pointed to the list of concerts still in Jasper's hand. "The tech crew needs to set up the equipment for Tuesday evening's concert and my crew needs to do a security sweep. Can we get vehicles and decoys for this afternoon? My crew usually works two to three concerts in advance, so we'll need transportation from the New Hampshire concert on Tuesday to the one in Connecticut on Thursday and then over to Pennsylvania for Friday and Saturday."

"I'm on it," said Jasper. "Meet me back here at one o'clock, and I'll relate the details. By the way, do you think we should let the girls know that we know that they're working on the puzzle?"

"No," said Donnell with a grin. "Let them enjoy thinking that we are dumb, ignorant men. Besides, we'll know where they are and what they're doing—easier for all of us."

*****

Relegated to the house for safety's sake, Chelsea missed going to church. But Nell and Carter had found a great service on TV, so following Jasper's teleconference, they cuddled on the sofa in the family room, watching the service.

Chelsea helped Nell prepare dinner, employing the use of the double convection ovens to cook four roasts with the attendant potatoes, carrots, celery, and onion. Mo, Bert, and Liz hung about waiting for food to fall or to be slipped to them by Nell or Rose, who also helped serve at the huge table in the meeting room.

Chelsea enjoyed watching the dynamics in the various groups represented: Charm's band, her tech crew, Donnell's security personnel, Jasper's family, and even their hired help, for Nell often had Rose's husband, John, and their two boys eat with them when Rose was kind enough to help serve.

Following the meal, the tech crew left to prep for Charm's concert the next day with Donnell following in another vehicle with his group. He left Natalie, Tommy, and Geveon behind to guard the girls. Sandy and Jonette opted for a nap, and Megan wanted to play pool downstairs with the guys who were taking full advantage of the myriad recreational activities available, from the pool table and Wii games to the inside squash court and the indoor pool.

This gave Chelsea and Charm the opportunity they wanted to spend some time in the library. Chelsea had just pulled out the lists and the Bible when Natalie entered.

"Do you mind if I join you?" she asked. She looked at the lists Chelsea had in her hand. "I see you're working on the puzzle. I wouldn't mind trying my hand at solving these riddles myself. Where do we start?"

Chelsea and Charm looked at each other and Chelsea gave a slight shrug. "I thought maybe we could make a chart," said Chelsea, walking to the cabinet where Nell kept paper supplies. She decided to do her own color coordinating and pulled out sheets of yellow, salmon, lavender, and blue.

Laying them on the table where they were seating themselves, she said, "I thought we could make a list of everything the Bible says about the twelve sons of Jacob on blue, then make a list of links to hit sites on lavender, put possibilities of methods used on yellow and probable dates on salmon."

"The dates are going to be the hardest," said Charm.

"I agree," said Chelsea. "However, I'm willing to bet that 'Rahab' refers to you, and that the date will be one of your concerts. But let's start with the easy part, the Bible." She moved around the room and pulled another Bible from the shelf, giving it to Natalie. Then picking up her own Bible, she had them turn to Genesis chapter 49.

For the next thirty minutes, they called out and wrote down information on each of the twelve sons of Jacob, or Israel, as he was sometimes called.

"This is so fascinating," said Charm. "I never knew the Bible had so much historical information in it." She started to pull a lavender sheet toward her, but Chelsea stopped her.

"We need to also check Deuteronomy thirty-three. It has some additional information on the twelve sons of Jacob. By this time, they were known as the twelve tribes of Israel since they were so large, and each would settle in a specific area of Palestine."

When they had finished adding to the list by consulting the thirty-third chapter of Deuteronomy, Chelsea said, "Now we're ready to try to link the information to suspected sites."

"Let's start at the top and work down," suggested Natalie.

Reuben is called 'unstable as water,' but that doesn't tell us much," said Charm with a disappointed look.

"Yes, but he's the one who slept with his father's wife," said Chelsea. "So how do we link that to a bomb site?"

"That's where knowledge of the Muslim mindset is helpful," said Natalie. "Many of the imams speak against the excessive evils of Hollywood to the point that they have a tremendous hatred for Hollywood. And not to be stereotypical, but inhabitants of Hollywood tend to sleep around. Couldn't we link Reuben to Hollywood?"

"Great!" said Chelsea with enthusiasm. "I think that's a connection. It's a start, anyway. We can revise and fine tune later, but right now, I think we should just put down the first thoughts that come to us. Simeon is next. What did we find about him?"

"All we have is that he was cruel, angry, and self-willed. I don't know how we can link him to anything," said Charm.

"Well then, let's skip him and go to Judah. Judah carried the Messianic line. I know that from Sunday School," said Chelsea. "It says here that he is a lawgiver, but I don't know what that means."

"Could it mean the President? Isn't he the lawgiver in your country?" asked Charm.

"He does sign into law the bills Congress passes, and wouldn't killing the head be good military strategy?" said Natalie. "What do you think, Chelsea?"

"Let's put it down. Just write the White House. We can always go back and change it if we want. Who's next?"

"Levi is next. He was cruel like Simeon," answered Natalie.

"That doesn't tell us much," said Charm.

"But the Levites were the religious leaders of Israel, so that could be linked to preachers who are outspoken against al-Qaeda," said Natalie.

"Who are the top three most outspoken?" asked Charm.

"One is in Texas. Of all the preachers I've heard, I think radical jihadists would be most angered by him," said Chelsea.

I'll write 'Texas preacher' by Levi then," said Natalie.

"Zebulun is the shipbuilder," said Charm, looking down the list. "Didn't you say something about the top five ports in the United States, Chelsea?"

"Yes. Since we already have Hollywood written down, I think we can cross Los Angeles off the list. Maybe San Francisco?" she asked doubtfully.

"I'll just write 'S.F. or some other port,'" said Natalie.

"That works for now. Dan was the judge, so I'm thinking the Supreme Court Building," said Chelsea, and Natalie wrote it on the list.

"Gad was a lawgiver. He 'tears the arm with the crown of the head.' Do you think that could be a financial thing?" asked Charm. "A head of state is nothing without financial backing."

"That's very good," said Natalie. "They've already bombed the towers; maybe some meddling in online banking with the largest bank. We'll have to check into that."

"Naphtali was said to be victorious in war and use 'beautiful words,'" said Chelsea. "I keep thinking that could have something to do with phone service, especially cellular service. Can you imagine what life would be like if no one had cellular service for just one day let alone two or three or four?"

"That would be awful. I can't live without my phone," said Charm.

"You and about two million other people," said Natalie, laughing at her melodramatic air.

"Okay. Four more other than Simeon. Asher was into oil, and another version says he made 'royal dainties.' In other words, he was a chef. But I keep wondering about oil refineries. Take away America's gas, and terrorists would decimate the trucking industry. What do you all think?" asked Chelsea.

"Very true," said Natalie, writing it on the sheet of paper.

"Issachar was a farmer. How could you destroy farmers?" asked Charm.

They all sat lost in thought. "I know," said Natalie suddenly. "Much of America's food comes from California, and California has several major dams. I was just talking to a marine buddy online the other day. His job is to scan the dam in his area for a special type of bomb that would cause the dam to implode rather than explode, creating a huge torrent of water and damaging crops as well as killing many people."

"Either that or crop dusting with a chemical that kills any living thing," said Chelsea.

"Write them both down," ordered Charm. "Then there's Joseph. What do we have on him?"

"Not very much, I'm afraid," said Chelsea. "But remember that he protected his brothers. We have this large plant in South Carolina that produces security vehicles for the military. Maybe other states have larger facilities, and we can check on that."

"Benjamin is called a 'wolf,' said Charm. "What can we get from that?"

They sat in silence, totally stumped.

"The sites we have listed are all over the country," said Natalie. "Obviously these terrorists are going for a massive attack, and even if half of them were diverted, they could still do serious damage. I think we should put the sites we have on a map of the United States and find the areas of the country where nothing is happening, then fill in the gaps with what we know about Benjamin and Simeon."

"I'm tired anyway," said Charm. "I need to do something active. How about a race in the pool?"

"You're on," said Chelsea. "You have a concert tomorrow, but maybe on Wednesday after lunch we can work on this again."

"Since time is of the essence, we really should get all of this info to Frank and Donnell as soon as possible," said Natalie.

Both Chelsea and Charm looked at her with alarm and protest clearly on their faces.

"Okay, okay!" said Natalie, throwing up her hands. "But after Wednesday, we really should turn this over to the experts. Too many lives are at stake."

"That's true," said Chelsea. "I don't want to have anyone's death on my hands. But won't our men be surprised at what we have?"

She finished putting the papers in the books and returning the books to the shelves. "Last one in the pool is a rotten egg."

Charm and Chelsea ran squealing from the room. Natalie followed more sedately. Surprised, indeed. She wouldn't be surprised if the girls each received medals for their work. If the experts at CIA, FBI, and Secret Service headquarters hadn't figured out the puzzle by Wednesday, she would make sure Charm and Chelsea received due recognition.

Chapter Thirty-Two

After dinner, Charm called the band together in the basement for practice. She was still working on "Dawn Breaking," and she wanted to get it just right. The song began in a minor key, but moved to the harmonic major with a steady, energetic, pulsing rock beat. Trying to fit the music to the words was particularly trying, but she had a feeling this was going to be one of her best numbers yet.

The night has been long, void of a song,
With no telling right from wrong,
I desperately need to be freed from
Misdeeds and cruel, crushing misery.

But dawn is breaking, splitting the night,
Bringing the light, permitting sight
Of what I can truly be.
Yes, dawn is breaking, damning the dark,
Stripping the stark, allowing a spark of
Creativity.
Oh, dawn is breaking, bringing me hope,
Letting me cope, dreaming of
Possibilities.

The night has been long, void of a song,
With no telling right from wrong,
I desperately need to be freed from the seeds
Of doubt, insecurity.

But dawn is breaking, splitting the night,
Bringing the light, permitting sight
Of what I can truly be.
Yes, dawn is breaking, damning the dark,
Stripping the stark, allowing a spark of great
Creativity.
Oh, dawn is breaking, bringing me hope,
Letting me cope, dreaming of
Possibilities.

They played the song over and over for more than two hours until Charm felt that it was just right. Megan added a beautiful harmony line. Then Michael put down his guitar and, retrieving his fiddle, wove a countermelody in and around both the harmony and the melody that was truly genius.

When they finally stopped, everyone was tired and hot, but the band's amped energy validated Charm's belief that this song would, indeed, far exceed anything in both musical creativity and crowd response that Charm had ever written.

Nell appeared with a tray of tall glasses of lemonade, each with frosted rims, a cherry, and a sprig of mint. When Charm received hers, she put the cold glass to her forehead and flushed cheeks, first on one side of her face and then the other. The maraschino cherry flavor added a tangy bite to the taste, but Charm couldn't identify the other flavors tickling her tongue.

"It's a special recipe handed down from my grandmother," explained Nell.

"You'll have to meet my mom when she comes," said Charm. "She's the producer of a televised cooking show in France, and she enjoys obtaining new recipes from all over the world."

Nell's eyes sparkled. "I could introduce her to some of the best cooks in Virginia as well as give her some history of our local cuisine." She clapped her hands together with glee. "Oh, this could be so fun!"

"I'll have to make sure that you two meet," said Charm.

Two filled glasses were left on the tray. "Now where is that son of mine and his girl?" asked Nell.

"They were headed for the gardens last time I heard. I think they wanted some alone time," said Charm with sympathetic understanding.

"I'll just put the glasses in the fridge down here, and you can give them the lemonade when they come inside," said Nell.

Nell left the basement, but she hurried upstairs to the master suite which overlooked both the east gardens in the back and the north garden on the side that was more sheltered and secluded. She was willing to bet that Jasper had taken Chelsea to the north garden.

She crossed the plush taupe carpeting and stood at the tall French windows draped in a fabric of roses against a deep green background. Sure enough, she was relieved to see Jasper and Chelsea sitting on one of her favorite wrought-iron benches that faced the house as well as a small goldfish pond. But they weren't looking at the goldfish. They were totally absorbed in each other, and even as she watched, Jasper bent his head to kiss Chelsea.

Nell knew she shouldn't be watching, so she backed away from the window. Her mother's heart, however, was glad. She worried over all of her children, but Jasper was the second to last of her children and sometimes overlooked. He had been so despondent after losing Allison. Angry, too, and Nell understood. Trust was a key ingredient in a good marriage, but you had to know that the person you were trusting was worthy of that trust.

Chelsea would be great for Jasper. She was so bright and intelligent, but more, she listened before she spoke, and although she exuded a calm gentleness, she was no die-away southern belle. She had enough grit in her to keep others from taking advantage of her sweet nature.

Nell was still backing away when she bumped into someone. She whirled away and automatically took a karate stance before she realized it was her husband.

"Easy, easy," said Carter.

"You scared me. I didn't hear you coming," said Nell as Carter pulled her into a hug to soothe away the fright.

"Spying on the lovebirds were we?" Carter enquired, lifting one eyebrow.

"I just wanted to make sure they were safe," said Nell. "And now he's kissing her, so I stopped watching. I'm so glad he's found someone, Carter," she said, her palms affectionately rubbing the five o'clock grizzle on the sides of his face.

"Me, too, but I'm thinking of hiring more security while everyone is here."

"I was hoping you would do that, Honey."

"I want extra guards around the perimeter and especially at the entrance in case anyone tries to ram their way through, and I'm going to talk to Jasper about placing a guard or two in each vehicle that the band actually uses."

"Are you going to tell the group about the extra security?" asked Nell.

"Yes. They'll feel better, and you know what can happen when more people are involved."

Nell's face grew taut in remembrance. One of her best friends, also a member of their freedom fighting group, had lost her life when one of the 'security' personnel hired had actually been an enemy infiltrator.

"Give them a password to use if they see one of the extra guards," suggested Nell.

"And what should that password be?" asked Carter, anxious to give his Nell something proactive about which to think.

"Roses," said Nell with satisfaction.

"Roses?"

"Yes. It's a girly word, it represents the two girls who need guarding, and our enemies won't think of that as a password."

"Roses it is, then. I'm going to make some calls and handpick the operatives I want here as security." He gave Nell a hug and a quick kiss.

Meanwhile, Jasper and Chelsea had helped clean the kitchen after a scrumptious dinner of marinated, grilled chicken, mashed potatoes and gravy, and green beans right out of the garden. Brownies and ice cream concluded the meal, and Chelsea appreciated the fact that Nell had included some comfort food for the displaced band members.

She and Charm had decided to wait for Natalie's return before working on the puzzle, and besides, Chelsea could sense that Jasper needed some down time from the case. Unwilling to go far from the house, they decided to walk in the gardens, fragrant with opening four o'clocks, roses, and gardenias.

They walked together in silence for some time, holding hands as they enjoyed the quiet of a Virginia evening, the song of birds, and the slight breeze that stirred the warm air, relieving it of oppressive mugginess and spreading the scent of the flowers.

Beside her, Chelsea could sense the calm that filled Jasper's soul. He had been working the case non-stop for nearly a week, about the same time they had been dating, if she could actually call it that. She was amazed at how she intuitively knew that he needed to get away from the case, focus on something else.

Chelsea was the first to speak, commenting on the beauty of Nell's gardens.

"The north side doesn't get as much sun, so Mom has worked hard to bring in plants that tolerate the shadiness of these oaks, maples and evergreens," said Jasper, indicating the branches of trees above them as well as the row of cedars that lined the fence like sentinels some fifty feet away.

"Oh, how lovely," said Chelsea as they rounded a corner, and she spied the light of the setting sun glinting off the surface of the goldfish pond. White water lilies and purple irises rose above the quiet surface. Below, Chelsea could just discern the orange of the goldfish as they swam silently, gliding with a lazy flick of the tail.

By mutual unspoken consent, they sat on the black wrought-iron bench, made somewhat private by the jasmine-covered lattice behind and above it.

Jasper's arms went around Chelsea, and he hungrily laid his lips on hers. This time, the kiss was not a gentle exploration but a hot searing assault that plumbed a new depth of passion for them both.

He broke contact for mere seconds to scoop Chelsea from her seat beside him and place her on his lap. This time, he angled the kiss differently so he could plunge deeper, tasting the sweetness of her mouth and mating his tongue with hers.

When he finally felt sated enough, he gentled the kiss, breaking lip contact, but keeping his forehead against Chelsea's.

Chelsea opened her eyes slowly.

"You're not mad at me are you?" he asked with his forehead still against hers.

"No, I think I needed that as much as you did." As their eyes met so close, she giggled and pulled her face away a few inches.

"We probably look like a couple of owls with our eyes that close together."

"Or some bug-eyed characters in an Animaniac cartoon," said Jasper.

He kissed her again, gently lingeringly. But passion was mounting, and he didn't know if he could trust himself to be a gentleman, especially with her sitting on his lap.

"Let me show you the rest of Mom's gardens on this side of the house before the sun sets," said Jasper. They walked through an arbor over which fragrant, pink rose blossoms climbed. A variety of hostas lined the path closer to the house, and Nell was training some ivy to grow up the wall by the fireplace.

Closer to the front of the house was a gazebo. It was very big, large enough to hold more than fifty people, and along the back was the door to a small utility room and a storage room. Beyond those rooms on the outside of the gazebo loomed a huge rock formation.

Chelsea and Jasper ascended the two stairs and stood watching the colors in the sunset. Chelsea sat on the low bench built into the wall while Jasper leaned against the railing.

"How are the plans for the Midsummer's Eve ball?" he asked.

"Your mother has everything under control, from the catering to the decorations. I'm nearly finished adding information about each guest on her guest list. I feel as if I actually know some of these people, crazy as it sounds."

"You do. And if we go, you'll be able to link a name with a face."

"I don't know if that's possible. Charm wants me to accompany her down south. Her family is going to join her, and they'll be staying at their bungalow in Hampton near Beaufort. If it's where I think it is, they are only a hop, skip, and jump away from my grandparents' farm in Walterboro."

Jasper's nerves began tingling again, and he didn't know why. "I wonder if our enemy is planning something for her Charleston concert," he stated suddenly, breaking their unspoken vow to refrain from discussing the case.

Chelsea searched his face as if she could discover the answer there. "If they don't try anything before then, they just might. Wait. What's the date of her Charleston concert?"

"I'm not sure off the top of my head, but I have a list of all of her concerts."

"Can I get that from you when we go inside? Do you have it here?"

"Sure. Her concerts are common knowledge. You could even get her concert dates off the internet. Why?"

"Don't ask yet. But I've got some links in the back of my mind, and I want to check them against the list of twelve hit sites that we have."

"Okay, but if you discover something, you need to let me or Donnell know immediately. So many lives are at stake right now, it's very sobering."

They were about to retrace their steps through the garden when Jasper said, "Wait. Let me show you something." He led the way to the back of the gazebo where the storage and wash room had been installed. The wash room had a high window that let in the waning light, a sink area and a row of shelves at one end. Making sure the door was closed, Jasper hit a small button hidden under the third row of shelves, and the shelves opened to reveal a small staircase.

"What in the world?"

"Sshh. Just follow me." He hit another button on his left and the shelves above them swung back into place. When they had shut completely, a light came on displaying the steps down. Wooden planks lined the walkway that led under the garden and up into the house. Halfway along the tunnel were alcoves, one on each side, with stashes of food on the left and on the right blankets, candles, matches, a gun, and were those things hand grenades?

"My dad likes to be prepared for anything," said Jasper. "How do you know about hand grenades?"

"We found some on Grandpa's farm, so he showed me how they worked. Your dad is something else."

They ascended another set of steps until they stood facing a wall. Once again, Jasper hit a button, this time on his right, and the light went out. He hit another button directly below it, and a panel slid open to reveal a room with dressing alcoves, two showers and a row of towels hanging on pegs. Chelsea saw the towel she had used the day before after swimming in the pool and recognition of where they were dawned.

"We're in one of the dressing areas beside the pool."

"Right. Dad loves this kind of cloak and dagger stuff. The tunnel itself was here when they bought the property. Mom discovered the entrance while she was gardening, and Dad had it fixed up and connected to the house. Actually, an old pump house used to sit here, but it was demolished and the tunnel entrance was covered before our house was even built."

"Have you ever used it before?"

Jasper's right eyebrow went up. "Of course. How do think Corey and I got out of boring social obligations?"

He looked down the hall. No one was using the pool, but they could hear the solid thump of billiard balls being hit periodically.

"Since no one is around, let me show you something else. This isn't exactly hidden, but it isn't advertised either."

He opened what looked like a closet door but was instead a narrow stairwell. "This goes all the way up to the second floor. I have often taken a midnight swim when I couldn't sleep and then sneaked back upstairs to my room. Of course my parents' room is above this, so I think they always knew. They just didn't say anything about it."

"That was after Allison's death wasn't it?" asked Chelsea softly as they headed past the pool and toward the game room.

"Yes. I couldn't sleep for many nights after that. The questions kept going around and around in my head."

He stopped and looked at the pool. "I don't know if you'll understand this, but I was so angry with her for not letting me know what was happening. The only way I could churn off the anger was to swim until I was exhausted."

"She underestimated your depth of feeling for her, and she went back to the comfort of her family. It's understandable but sad for you when you could have helped her."

Jasper gave her a hug, glad that Chelsea understood. The hug would have gone much further, but Charm flung open the door.

"There you two are. The tech crew and security have returned, and your Dad has called a meeting down here in the game room."

She turned to give them a few more moments of privacy then turned back. "Oh, and your mom left lemonade in the fridge for you as well."

They entered the game room. Others were still coming down the stairs. Carter had just cleared his throat to begin when Donnell's phone vibrated.

Everyone seemed to quiet at once so that when the expression in Donnell's face went blank, Natalie and Charm immediately moved forward.

"Yes. Thank you for letting me know," Donnell said before he snapped his phone off.

He turned and addressed everyone.

"William just passed away," he said soberly.

Sunday evening, June 3rd

Chapter Thirty-Three

If the threats from the terrorists had not seemed real before, they did now. William's death dampened everyone's spirits.

Carter cleared his throat once more, apologizing lest he seem insensitive to the anguish they were clearly suffering. "This is all the more reason for me to take the steps I've initiated.
I've hired additional guards for the perimeter of our property during your stay, and Nell and I hope you will stay" here he addressed Charm, "until you have to move closer to your southern concerts."

"We wouldn't want to incur any added expense..." began Charm, but Carter waved his hand.

"But you see, we are not just protecting you and your band, Charm. We are also protecting Chelsea and our son who are just as involved in this case as you are. In addition, I think we are fighting for the ideals of liberty and freedom from a tyrannical mindset. Nell and I are honored to do what we must to combat the forces of evil that would denigrate our system of government and laugh at our ideals of a democratic republic and a free enterprise system."

Here, Nell interrupted. "Don't let him get started or he'll give you an entire history lesson."

"You're right, Dear. I'm rabbit tracking. The guards we've hired have been handpicked by me, and since they are guarding the perimeter, you will probably never see them. They dress in black and are trained to make themselves invisible."

"However, should you see one of them," here Nell picked up the thread, "they need to give you the password. If you ask for the password and they don't give it to you, don't assume they are one of the guards we've hired. In fact, they are probably an imposter."

At this point, Donnell spoke. "I probably don't need to tell any of you this, but please don't go outside the fence."

Nell added, "Even if they say that Gram or Gramps or one of the dogs is in need of help, come back and get one of us first."

"Until these thugs are imprisoned, hundreds if not thousands of lives are at stake," said Carter. "And the life that you save may be that of the person standing or sitting next to you. Will you all promise to abide by these ground rules?"

Everyone present nodded their agreement, William's death in their minds.

"What's the password?" asked Chelsea.

"'Roses,'" said Nell.

Chelsea's eyes flew to Charm's and then to Natalie's. She nodded imperceptibly to both, and they nodded back. There would be a library meeting tonight.

Charm's first concern was Donnell, but he brushed off the comfort she offered. His Irish temper had been aroused, and, as Natalie predicted when she pulled Charm aside to explain, it would be a fierce and awesome sight to see.

"So far, we've been playing cat and mouse," Donnell explained to Charm when they were alone, wandering around the huge meeting room between the family room and the library. "But now it's war. For every man of mine they take out, I'm going to take out five of theirs, mark my words," he said in a harsh, rage-filled voice.

"You do whatever you have to do, Donnell," Charm said encouragingly. She wandered to the piano and played a few chords. Donnell sat on the narrow bench beside her.

"Just promise me you'll stay on the grounds unless you're doing a concert," he said. "I can't worry about you and defeat these terrorists at the same time. I need to know you're safe."

"You have my word that I won't leave the grounds unless I have a concert. At least, not on my own steam," said Charm.

"If they so much as harm any part of you..." Donnell threatened, his eyes black and deadly. He lowered his mouth and took hers in stormy passion.

His words and violent attitude sent a black thrill through Charm. She hadn't known she could arouse such dark passion in anyone. Nor had anyone ever cared for her like this before. The knowledge that she had the power to elicit such a response filled her with energy and excited nerves.

The palms by the piano provided a screen of privacy as Donnell ravished first her mouth, and then the rest of her face, nipping at her earlobe, trailing kisses down her neck to the pulse point in the little hollow at the base. Charm's gasps of pleasure only fueled his desire more.

His hands twined themselves in her hair, mussing it thoroughly. Stroking his hands down the side of her lithe body, he was about to cup her breasts when a warning voice shouted somewhere in the back of his brain. He couldn't become so besotted with her that he lost his edge and endangered her further.

He tried to ignore the voice, but reason won over passion, this time. The case had better be over by next time. He couldn't hold back much longer.

Swearing, he held her until his muscles eased their tension and his ragged breath was more controlled. Charm, however, had become utterly still. Oh dear, did she misunderstand?

"We've got to catch those terrorists soon. I'll be damned if they keep interfering with my relationship with you," he said, hoping she'd understand.

She did, at least he thought she did. Drawing apart slightly, she put her forefinger to his lips. "Good night, Donnell," she said standing. Placing a chaste kiss on his forehead, she fled, going upstairs to her room to regain her composure.

He still wouldn't express his love. Not yet. It hurt, but she would assume the best: that he would tell her after the terrorists had been caught. Meantime, she had concerts to perform and friends waiting for her in the library.

Chelsea was fairly vibrating with excitement when Charm joined her in the library. Natalie entered within seconds after Charm. Chelsea swung away from the computer where Charm could see a list of her concert dates on the screen.

"I think I've found a link in dates," she said, her eyes turning nearly green.

Natalie retrieved the papers and a pen as she and Charm quickly joined Chelsea in front of the computer.

"See the date for Charm's concert in Charleston? Does it seem familiar? I can't believe I didn't see this before!"

"My Charleston concert is the twenty-first of June. What of it?"

"That's the date of the Midsummer's Eve Charity Ball Nell has been planning! What if the ball is one of the targets? And what if your concert is also targeted? That would mean that the other acts of espionage are planned for the same evening."

"It's a big 'what-if,' but we' have nothing better," said Natalie. "I put all of the suggested sites on a map," here she opened a map she held in her hands, "and as you can see, they form a perimeter around the United States. Very few sites are actually in the interior; most are close to the coast. However, if even half of these sites were hit, especially the electrical grid and online banking, the interior infrastructure such as the trucking industry, would collapse within days."

Charm had been looking at their list again. "None of these sites have any dates attached to them except for the ball and my concert. Unless, of course, some sort of meeting is scheduled at any of these places on the twenty-first. We really need to check for meetings on the twenty-first."

"Great point, Charm!" Chelsea said, her excitement apparent again. She whirled her chair around and quickly typed some words onto the internet screen. In seconds, the home page of a website popped up, and Chelsea began scrolling down the screen.

"Here it is!" she nearly shouted. Lowering her voice she read, "Conference on 'Understanding Current Events and the Islamic Timetable' expected to draw thousands….June twentieth through twenty-fourth. That will be happening in Texas."

"Does the White House advertise upcoming meetings? And how about the Supreme Court? Are they slated to come down with any decisions around the twenty-first?" Chelsea asked Natalie.

"I don't know, but I'll find out," said Natalie. "Chelsea, I really think we need to give this information to Donnell and Jasper so they can pass it to Frank and Tillot. The twenty-first is only a week and a half away. So much needs to be done before then."

"You're right," admitted Chelsea. She looked at her watch. It showed the time was eleven thirty. "Should we wake them?"

"Of course," said Natalie. She pressed a button on her phone. "I need you and Jasper in the library."

The men arrived in less than five minutes. Donnell had never been asleep as he was still fully dressed. Jasper had hastily donned a T-shirt and basketball shorts.

Since Charm and Chelsea were ogling their respective men, Natalie took charge. "Chelsea and Charm have been working the puzzle, and I think they've made some important links. Come look at this."

She showed them the sheets of paper with the clues, the suspected sites, the locations on the map and the dates all pointing to the twenty-first. "The only things we haven't discussed much yet are the methods of sabotage."

Donnell was visibly impressed with the work the girls had done.

"We need to call Frank and Tillot right now," said Jasper.

"I agree," said Donnell.

When they reached Tillot, he wanted to see what the girls had done in person but was unwilling to risk revealing Charm's new location any sooner than necessary although they knew their enemy would discover it soon enough.

"Ask your father to turn on the teleconference screen, Jasper. Then call me back. I'll get Frank. He'll want to see this, too."

When the girls saw the ancestral portrait of a Templeton fade slowly to be replaced by a screen, they were duly impressed.

"Technology is just incredible," said Charm.

Tillot and Frank appeared on the screen, and Tillot asked Chelsea to relate her process for uncovering the suspected sites of sabotage.

"Charm made the link between meeting or conference dates and the date we think these attacks will occur, and Natalie put the sites on a map and made many valuable suggestions," said Chelsea in conclusion, eager to share the credit with others.

"Jasper, hold the papers up to the screen so we can scan them," said Tillot. Jasper did so.

"You've done some awesome work, ladies," said Tillot. "Get some rest now, and stay alert. The terrorists don't know how much we know, and they're getting desperate to prevent us from learning any more. Mark my words, they're going to try something else. Be very careful."

"We will, Boss," said Jasper, and the others murmured agreement.

When the screen faded, Carter wanted to look at the charts the girls had made, so another hour passed before anyone made a move to follow Tillot's advice to get some rest.

"I think we should work on this together tomorrow morning after breakfast," said Natalie, trying to stifle a yawn. "Six brains are better than three, and with some rest, we'll all be sharper. What do you think, Donnell?"

"We could. The facilities for the next two concerts are secured, and we worked a full day today. For us, an after-breakfast meeting would give me and my crew extra sleep. But I'm not sure about Sleeping Beauty here." He pulled one of Charm's curls. "She's not used to waking before noon, are you, Darling?"

"I'm sure I can do my part toward America's war on terror and the safety of her citizens," said Charm. Her voice was mocking, but her heart was racing. Donnell had openly called her 'Darling' before others. Once again, her heart began to hope.

I'll let Nell know we need a brain-food breakfast with plenty of protein and carbs," said Carter.

But the meeting did not take place. An early-morning four-car accident abruptly cut the power, interrupting several alarm clocks before the emergency generators started. The entire group, with the exception of Nell and Carter, slept late, worn with emotions over William's death and the shock of the fire.

Chapter Thirty-Four

Chelsea was the first to awaken and make her way to the sunny kitchen where a huge breakfast was waiting. When told of the accident and Nell and Carter's decision to let everyone sleep, she was philosophical about the matter.

"Now that Tillot's agents are working with the answers we provided for the puzzle, I don't feel such a burning desire to solve more of it," she confessed. "I think I'd rather finish your guest list for the Midsummer's Eve Ball."

"By the way, if the Ball is being targeted, what do you plan to do?"

"Carter and I were just discussing that," said Nell. We could cancel it, but it would be so much lovelier to lay a trap for these bullies. Since you seem to have answers, let us know if you think of anything."

"Oh no. I can solve puzzles, but taking down terrorists? That is in your department," protested Chelsea before she headed for the library.

Donnell was the next to enter. Nell noticed the circles under his eyes and wished he had slept longer, but she supposed, rightly, that between his internal alarm clock and his nerves, he wouldn't be able to sleep well until the case was finished.

Natalie and Tiffany arrived with Seamus, Gregor, Max, Tommy, and Geveon close behind. Nell noticed that although they were calm, they were a rather subdued group, still mourning the loss of a comrade.

Jasper entered, yawning hugely. After doing knuckle bumps and slaps with the men, he buttered a piece of toast to swallow with his coffee. Learning that Chelsea was already awake and working in the library, he decided to pester her into ditching the work and doing something with him.

The band members, used to sleeping late after concerts, entered the kitchen, greeting Nell affectionately.

"We've decided to make you the band mom," Megan said cheerfully to Nell. She seemed to have recovered from the impact of the fire, especially after discussing it with Nell the day before.

With Megan, Sandy and Jonette looking expectantly at her, Nell laughingly agreed. "But I have no idea what a band mom does," she said.

"You are already doing a terrific job," said Jonette. "Keeping this group well-fed is a major feat."

"Listening to our troubles is another part of the job description," said Megan. "You're already doing that, too." She was thinking of the helpful discussion she'd had with Nell.

"I think feeling free to keep us all in line should round out your duties nicely," said Sandy. "We have four concerts in the next five days, so it shouldn't be too difficult."

"I'm sure I won't have any difficulties at all," said Nell. "You young people just keep me from getting old and set in my ways. I enjoy being part of the action!"

The tech crew entered along with Charm, groaning for coffee, and for awhile, seeming pandemonium prevailed. Eventually, however, when Nell learned that everyone had the day free, she suggested some activities: gardening and help with dinner preparation, watching a movie on the large screen TV downstairs, swimming, horseback riding to Gram and Gramps house, and a squash tournament.

Listening carefully, Carter vetoed the horseback riding. He thought they should stay as close to home as possible given the circumstances. Also the temperature was predicted to soar to a sweltering 106 degrees.

Chelsea, who had given up on finishing the Ball list, had returned to the kitchen in time to hear Nell's suggestions. She told Jasper that if she wasn't going to work on Nell's list, then they could at least help with the gardening. Fifteen minutes later, they joined Charm, Megan, Sandy, and Nell in the garden.

For awhile, the group contentedly pulled weeds, their cheerful chatter breaking the monotony of the chore. But then Chelsea decided to pull off her sandals.

"Ooh, this feels great on my feet," she said.

All the other girls had to try squishing their toes in the mud.

Jasper muttered something about insanity pleas.

"I know," said Megan suddenly. "Let's do mud facials after we finish the weeding!"

"We can do our nails, too," said Charm, joining her enthusiasm.

"Too bad we don't have a masseuse here," said Chelsea. She looked provocatively at Jasper.

Jasper stood slowly as if not wanting to disturb a precarious balance. "You girls have lost it. I think I'm going to do some manly, he-man stuff like hunting or playing squash."

"That reminds me," said Nell. "I have a lovely pumpkin defoliation masque, if anyone is interested in that rather than the mud."

Jasper shook his head and left, muttering about "too much estrogen around here."

The girls giggled and continued discussing facials and pedicures.

When they had finished weeding their rows, Nell showed them how to pick the beans they would later eat for dinner that evening.

"This is so relaxing," said Charm to Sandy. "We should get Mom and Dad to let us start a garden next spring and summer since I won't be on tour then."

"My grandparents have a rather large farm in Walterboro," said Chelsea.

"Isn't Walterboro close to Hampton?" asked Charm. "My parents have a bungalow in Hampton."

"Hampton is just a hop, skip, and jump from Walterboro," responded Chelsea enthusiastically. "When you go down South for your concerts, I'll have to take you to the farm. You'll love it."

"And you'll love the bungalow," said Charm. "Maybe we can take some time off and do some shopping in Beaufort. My sister, CeCe, is the consummate shopper, and I know she'd love to come, too. You can bring your sisters. My goodness! That will be eight of us if Jonette comes, too. But we'll have so much fun!"

"Is this enough for dinner tonight?" Megan asked Nell, showing her the large bowl full of beans.

"That will do it," declared Nell. "Thanks for all your help, girls, especially with all of the weeding."

"It's been fun!" said Sandy cheerfully.

"That's probably because it's not something you have to do every week," said Nell wryly.

"Let's do the mud masks and let them dry while we're outside," suggested Megan.

Charm passed around hair bands that she wore on her wrist, a habit she had adopted when bike riding with her dad. The predicted heat of the day had seemed to indicate a revival of the habit.

They began smearing mud on their faces. Since they had no mirrors, Charm smeared mud on the places Megan had missed on her face, Chelsea helped Sandy, and soon the pale ovals of their faces were covered.

After rinsing their hands at the garden hose, the girls wandered to the side of the house where Chelsea and Jasper had been the evening before. The temperature had risen, but beneath the shade of the trees was relative cool.

Charm and Sandy were enraptured by the fish pond, so they all sat for several minutes trying to count the number of fish they saw.

They were up to eight when Chelsea saw a flicker of movement in her peripheral vision. She turned and saw a man dressed totally in black with even a black mask over his face standing by the cedars that lined the northern perimeter of the property and watching them intently.

"Do NOT raise your heads, girls, but we have someone watching us. And there's another," she said as she saw another man emerge from the shadows of the cedars.

"They may be the men Carter hired, but I don't like the way they're acting, and I've got an idea. Are you all with me so far?"

Everyone nodded. "Okay, pretend to watch the fish. Megan you point to another one. Now let's pretend that we get bored with the fish and we're going to race to the gazebo over there. When we get there, everyone crowd into the washroom at the back. If they follow us, running, Charm, you close and lock the door to the washroom, but do it quietly so they don't know where we went. Ready?"

They nodded solemnly. Chelsea smiled thinly. "Try to act like we're still having fun, girls!"

Chelsea flicked a quick glance at the men. They had moved further from the shadows of the cypress trees and toward the girls.

"I'll race you," Chelsea yelled and started running toward the gazebo. She arrived at the gazebo a few steps before Megan and Sandy. Charm was only seconds behind them. When they were all safely in the washroom and the door was closed and locked, she pushed the button and the door slid open revealing the stairs.

Behind her, Charm could hear the steps of the men as they entered the gazebo.

"Go down and keep going," she said in a quiet whisper, indicating that Sandy should go first. Sandy obeyed immediately, reaching back to grab Megan's hand. Charm went next. Chelsea waited only long enough to press the other button, and the door swung noiselessly closed behind her.

When the light didn't come on, she blessed the heavens although she knew walking in the pitch black would be terrifying for the other girls who did not know where they were going. Chelsea caught up to the others, but she ran her right hand along the wall. When she came to the alcove, she dropped back and grabbed a grenade.

Somewhere above her and at the end of the tunnel she could hear the door splintering and the crash of flowerpots in the washroom they had just vacated. She waited a few minutes, listening.

Low, guttural voices speaking in a foreign language suggested that her suspicion this was the enemy was right, but how could she convince Jasper and his parents? A daring plan entered her head. She actually hoped they would discover the button that opened the hidden tunnel.

Racing to the pool end of the tunnel where the other girls were huddled with nowhere to go, she found the button and pressed it.

"Don't wait for me. Find Donnell and Jasper," she said softly before she whirled around and ran back along the tunnel. Coming to the alcove again, she grabbed another grenade, then stopped to listen, trying to breathe quietly. She heard a grating noise, and realizing the men had, indeed, discovered the tunnel, she waited a few beats until she was fairly certain they were at the bottom of the steps.

Then pulling the pin of the first grenade, she hurled it, reaching down to pull the pin of the second grenade in the same motion. She hurled that one also, and then raced back along the tunnel.

The blast of the first explosion propelled her forward and dirt began to fall through the cracks of the wooden slats along the wall. The second blast literally brought down the roof, filling the tunnel with wooden debris, rocks, dirt, and dust. She was just placing her foot on the bottom step when a piece of wood hit her head, knocking her out cold.

When she came to, she was lying on a pool lounger, and Nell was bending over her, bathing her face with the wet corner of a towel.

"Where's Jasper?" Chelsea asked. She winced as her head reminded her of the knot from the piece of wood that had hit her and foretold the monstrous headache she would soon have.

"He and Donnell are searching the premises for the men who were after you."

"They should be trapped in the tunnel. That's why I detonated the grenades when I knew they had found the door and were coming after us. I'm so sorry for messing it up. I hope it can be repaired," she said apologetically to Nell.

Tiffany stepped aside to report Chelsea's information to Donnell via her watch/radio. When she returned she told the group gathered around Chelsea's lounger that three of the men Carter had hired were dead and that Carter was now superintending removal of debris from the tunnel so they could uncover the men who had chased the girls.

They were taking precautions lest the men were still alive, and Natalie was making sure that the perimeter of the property was doubly secured.

"The enemy is getting more daring and more deadly," said Charm sadly.

"I'm just thankful you are all safe," said Nell. Her face had paled with the news of the three deaths. "Now let's get you upstairs, Chelsea, and put you to bed with a good dose of painkillers.

"Before you go," Tiffany interrupted, "Donnell wants everyone who is not on security detail to be in lockdown mode in the house."

"I think we'll all be upstairs resting or else helping Nell with dinner," said Sandy. She looked at Megan and began to giggle. "Actually, I think we girls need to get the mud off our faces before our faces crack like eggshells."

Charm put her hands anxiously to her face; she had a concert the next evening, but eventually she and Megan began to laugh, too. It was the comic relief they desperately needed.

Chapter Thirty-Five

Youssef was taken alive from the tunnel. His brother was not. Youssef would have mourned his brother's death but for the fact that he believed his brother was now in Paradise having his way with the virgins Allah had prepared for him.

The smirk on his face told Donnell that the battle against al-Qaeda jihadists on American soil had only begun.

Tillot was ecstatic about the capture of Youssef. He had been near the top of the CIA's list for several years. Carter, who had handpicked the men who had been killed, was in mourning. He vowed that each cell would be brought down one by one.

Tillot also had news. The twenty-first of June appeared to be the date of attack. Several other attack sites had major events scheduled for that day. He asked that Chelsea and Charm review the list one more time. He wanted their ideas on modes of attack. Jasper agreed to relay the message.

Meanwhile, the girls, with the exception of Chelsea who was sleeping, congregated together in Charm's room to remove the mud from their faces, apply moisturizers, and give each other pedicures.

"I can't wait until this is all over," said Charm gloomily.

"Your face looks beautiful, Darling," said Jonette. She was older than the rest of the group and much preferred reading books to athletic activities.

"No, I mean the terrorist attacks," said Charm, giggling and throwing a pillow at Jonette.

"Gotcha!" said Jonette.

"I feel sorry for Nell," said Megan. "She's not saying much, but she and Carter have lost three close friends. I caught her crying over a bowl of potato salad she was fixing for our lunch and told her that she had fixed such a wonderful breakfast that we would probably not eat again until dinner time. She said she'd leave sandwich makings on the counter should anyone want a bite between now and then."

"That's what I'm talking about," said Jonette. "I made Charm smile, increasing her face value, lol, and Nell feels better when she can keep busy, I'm sure. We can't let these idiots 'terrorize' our emotions or we let them win on the psychological and emotional levels as well as on the physical level."

"I agree," said Sandy. "We need to be proactive; we need a plan of action."

"How is your karate?" asked Charm.

"I made it to brown belt before your first tour, but I haven't done much since then," said Sandy.

"Well, teach us some moves," demanded Megan.

Sandy stood and began demonstrating.

"This place isn't big enough," complained Megan.

"Let's move then," said Charm. So they moved to the upstairs sitting room that overlooked the fountain at the front of the house with three large windows. Sandy demonstrated basic moves and countermoves in case of an attack from front, from behind, with a gun, with a knife. She was a good teacher, thought Charm.

"We should have done this several concerts ago," said Megan, wiping the perspiration from her forehead.

"You're absolutely right," responded Charm. "I think we need to make a list of other things we can do to be proactive and on our guard, especially for the concert in Charleston that seems to be targeted. We can't just rely on Donnell and his crew."

"Let's do that tonight after dinner. Right now, I think we need to shower and then go help Nell with dinner," said Jonette.

Everyone agreed.

The group descended *en mobbe* to the kitchen less than forty-five minutes later. They told jokes and teased each other, keeping Nell laughing as well as each other.

When Chelsea joined them, they made her sit in a place of honor, giving her small, mundane jobs to do.

When the men from the band appeared following their squash competition—Kelly was declared the band league champion, to be pitted against the winner of the security league at a later date—Nell put them to work grilling some catfish and swordfish Gramps brought. Fresh corn on the cob, a green bean mushroom sauté, baked potatoes, and a huge spinach salad were added. When Nell produced two blackberry cobblers with vanilla bean ice cream, everyone groaned but still ate with enthusiasm.

As they ate their dessert, Jasper finally asked Chelsea the question everyone had been wondering.

"What made you suspicious of the men? You never even asked for the password, did you?"

Everyone paused to listen to her answer.

"No, I never did ask the password," she said slowly. "I think it was the way they were moving toward us. It seemed somehow very intimidating. And we didn't just 'happen' to see them. They were very obviously coming after us. Carter said they were to stay hidden as much as possible. I decided to run and ask questions later."

"Thank God you did," said Nell fervently.

"My first concern was to hide until they left even though they might get away. My plan was to get into the house the fastest way possible and alert Donnell. But then they found the tunnel, and when I heard them talking, I was sure by their language and accent they were from the Middle East. That's when I realized I'd have to do something drastic."

"What made you think of using the grenades?" asked Carter.

"We discovered some on my Grandpa's farm one summer, so he showed me how to use them. We blew up some rotten pumpkins with them. Grandma thought we were crazy, but it was fun!" Everyone laughed at this.

"Well, you're certainly to be commended for your quick thinking and trapping a wanted al-Qaeda operative. You are making quite an impression with some senior members of intelligence organizations," said Carter.

"I was really just trying to save myself and my friends, not make an impression with anyone," said Chelsea.

"Tell us more about the tunnel," said Donnell, noticing Chelsea's discomfiture.

"This property has been in my family for over two hundred years," said Carter. "When Nell and I decided to build a house, we discovered the tunnel, and after reading some old diaries of my ancestors, we discovered that it had been used by the Underground

Railroad, helping to free slaves before and during the War Between the States."

Nell continued the story. "Carter, here, has a love of the dramatic and mysterious, so he decided to use it as an underground bunker, so to speak, complete with supplies and munitions."

"It certainly proved useful today," said Donnell. "The enemy must be rather desperate to try to attack the girls when we were all here," he added thoughtfully.

"They must have missing links in their security," said Jasper. "First, I don't think they realized we were all here or they would have just tried to bomb the house. What is it with al-Qaeda and bombs, anyway? Secondly, I don't think they know what we know, or else they have realized it and they are as angry as a nest of hornets."

As everyone headed to the kitchen with their used plates and utensils, Jasper relayed Tillot's message to Charm and Chelsea.

Charm, in turn, told the girls in the band to start brainstorming without her as she needed to talk to Chelsea. Then she joined Chelsea and Natalie in the library. They reviewed the lists they had made, discussing each name, what site it could be, what would wreak the most havoc. Finally, as their frustration built, Natalie called a halt to the mind-numbing process.

"We need to ask ourselves what the terrorists want most and how they'll go about getting it," she said.

"I would say from studying their history, that what they want most is world domination with Islam as the main mode of law, but America stands in the way and has become a symbol of the power they crave and a way of life they despise," said Chelsea.

"They want to bring America to her knees, especially economically. They proved that when they bombed the Towers in 2001," said Charm.

"Exactly," said Natalie. "So what is the fastest way to devastate America economically?"

"Oil and shipping." "Internet and banking," said Charm and Chelsea simultaneously.

"Very good. And what are the best ways to kill thousands of people at one time?"

"The sub and dams." "Concerts, football, and NASCAR."

"Three things! Bravo, Charm!" said Natalie. "Actually, it's not football season, so we can rule out that one. But I'd never thought of NASCAR. Good work!"

"Let's see the list again," said Charm.

"This list is messy," said Chelsea. "Let's rewrite it with just the code name, the suspected site, and then add the method we think they might use. But we have to try to think like terrorists when we do it," she said with a smile for Natalie who had started them on this approach already.

Reuben	Hollywood
Simeon	Midsummer's Eve Ball
Judah	White House
Levi	Church Attack-TX/Jewish Synagogue
Benjamin	Military Base?
Joseph	Armored Car Facility?
Zebulun	SF or NY Port
Gad	Online banking
Dan	Supreme Court Building
Naphtali	Cell phones; electric grid
Asher	Oil refinery
Issachar	Farming—a dam?
Rahab	Charm's concert in Charleston, SC

"Since they are so bomb-happy, which sites do you think they'll bomb?" asked Charm.

"I'm guessing Hollywood, the White House, the ports, an oil refinery, a dam and your concert," said Natalie, running her finger down the list.

"The oil refinery will probably be an explosion of some sort," said Chelsea.

"The ball and the church/synagogue attack are more personal, so to make a definitive statement, I think they will do suicide bombers or random shootings," said Natalie.

"My concert is personal," said Charm rather heatedly.

"I agree," said Natalie, "but it also will be filled with people. Maybe they will try to eliminate you and then bomb the entire place."

"How will they interrupt phone service?" asked Chelsea. "They can't just bomb cell phone towers. Too many exist."

"I would guess they will use some of their computer experts to put viruses or bugs in the computers of the major cell phone carriers and/or use cell phone scramblers. They will probably try to do the same with online banking. Even if they only infected the two largest banks, it would prevent so many transactions from being completed that it would collapse the entire banking industry at least for a while," said Natalie.

"That certainly would negatively impact the economy," said Chelsea. "And if they create an explosion at the right oil refinery, it could cripple the trucking industry and travel within a week, further impacting the economy," she added.

"What about a dam being bombed?" asked Charm. "Usually a dam is above a large population or a large farming area. A detonated bomb would affect the food supply and, therefore, the economy."

"Good thinking, girls!" said Natalie. "When we have disasters of a large magnitude, the military is often called in to handle the crisis and keep order. What would effectively disable the military?"

"Since I try to listen to the news every day," said Chelsea slowly, "I've been intrigued by these new vaccines from China, and that they are required for all military and medical personnel. How difficult would it be to tamper with those while they are still over in China? Or even when they've arrived in the United States?"

"I don't know, but I'll certainly find the answer to that question," said Natalie, her hazel eyes sparkling with suppressed excitement.

Chelsea pointed to the words 'Supreme Court Building' listed beside Dan. "I'm not comfortable with this one. Not enough people would be impacted, and won't the Justices be on vacation? I'm thinking maybe a lower court that is deciding a case that will affect the Muslim population or maybe a law that Congress is working on that will impact 'religious freedoms.'"

"I don't know much about American law and policymaking, but doesn't your Congress pass the laws that are then interpreted and enforced by the courts? Instead of the Supreme Court Building being a bomb target, what about the building where Congress meets?" asked Charm. "Wouldn't that kill more people?"

"It certainly would," said Natalie.

"We still don't have NASCAR anywhere on the list," said Charm. "I know those races attract huge crowds because some of my friends at Universite in Paris follow NASCAR."

"I'll have someone check race dates," said Natalie, writing NASCAR in bold letters at the bottom of the list and adding it to a small notepad on which she had been writing notes.

"The New York subway isn't on the list either," said Chelsea. "Maybe some of the CIA or FBI operatives will have some ideas of whether or not it's a viable hit site."

Natalie added the subway to her notepad and Charm wrote it on their list.

Chelsea yawned, and the other two observed that she was still rather pale.

Natalie closed her notepad. "Thanks, girls," she said. "I'll make sure Donnell and Tillot get this info, and you two get some rest."

"Let us know if they discover anything else," said Chelsea. "We both have a rather personal interest in this since they keep trying to kill us," she added dryly.

Natalie promised to do so.

Chapter Thirty-Six

Charm's next four concerts on Tuesday, Thursday, Friday, and Saturday cemented her popularity in the American music culture. The farthest away was Tuesday evening at the Verizon Arena in Manchester, New Hampshire.

The exhausted band and security crews did not arrive back at Rosemont until six o'clock on Wednesday morning. Fortunately, they had no concert Wednesday evening.

Thursday's concert was in Connecticut, and the Friday and Saturday concerts were in Pennsylvania, much closer to Rosemont or 'home' as the crews were beginning to consider it. The lack of any terrorist threats both relieved and bothered Donnell, Frank, Tillot, and Jasper.

Following a quiet two-day weekend at Rosemont—Chelsea and Nell realized that Monday was considered part of the weekend for musicians—the round of concerts began again, but this time, the Albany, New York concert at Times Union Center was the farthest from Rosemont.

Meanwhile, Chelsea was working on the Midsummer's Eve Ball with Nell, defusing last-minute problems. They spent an enjoyable day on Wednesday with the caterers. Nell was smart enough to engage two different companies that had often worked compatibly with each other at some of Nell's other charity fundraisers.

They taste-tested some new items the caterers had developed, including a roasted, red pepper, sesame oil, cream cheese dip; some macadamia/coconut crunch flounder croquettes; and a blueberry, pomegranate based drink.

Chelsea didn't care for the blueberry, pomegranate drink, and although it matched the color scheme of blues, purples, silver and white, Nell wanted a lighter drink to accompany the exquisite berry and lemon petit fours.

Their next stop was the ice carvers. Since the ball occurred on Midsummer's Eve, Nell had chosen a whimsical theme of elves, sprites, and fairies. Both were impressed with the intricate detail Ramon and his crew included in the ice carvings.

"If you were going to come to the ball, we'd stop at this little store where Pammy and I often shop for clothes," said Nell regretfully.

Chelsea was being forced to use her saved vacation time before her job was officially terminated, so she had agreed to accompany Charm to the Dumotte family bungalow when Charm's concerts moved south.

"I wish you could come to the ball, but under the circumstances, I won't have terrorists trying to gun you down in such a public spot. Why they're still trying to kill you is beyond my understanding."

Her words, said so matter-of-factly, sent a chill down Chelsea's spine. "Have you and Carter developed a plan yet?" she asked.

"We have. Actually, we have three plans since we don't know exactly how the terrorists will try to attack, if they really do plan to attack us at all."

"Jasper said the CIA has uncovered some internet 'chatter,' and they have rated the probability that your ball is a hit site at eighty percent."

"Well then, I'm glad for the measures we've taken, the first being that no other family members are allowed to come!" said Nell firmly. "Pammy is disappointed, but we need her and Jon to carry on should anything happen to us, and you and Jasper will probably be in the thick of things down South as it is."

"You really think Jasper will be coming south, too?" asked Chelsea. "Since the President won't be there, Jasper and I thought he would be kept here in the D.C. area."

"True, and the FBI is handling more of the details in connection with Donnell and his group, but since you are still officially part of the Presidential staff, Tillot will probably allow

Frank's special task force to continue operating. They already know the finer details of the case, and the twenty-first is only a week away."

"I hate waiting for all of this to happen," said Chelsea.

"I totally understand. I've always found that the most difficult part, too," said Nell. "But that's why it's important to have projects to work on, tasks to accomplish, and things to do. When I keep busy, I don't obsess over what could happen, and very often, while I'm thinking about the task at hand, my subconscious will analyze the larger picture, and when I stop for a few minutes, I have some new insight or solution."

"My mind works that way, too!" said Chelsea.

As they neared the exit to Rosemont, Nell's mind turned to the more practical matter of dinner for whoever would be home. "Let's stop at Henry's Farmer's Market and see what they have. I like to get their fresh eggs as well as additional fruits and vegetables. I've a yen for quiche tonight. Rose is baking some carrot cake while we're gone."

They spent an enjoyable half hour perusing Henry's wares, Nell finally settling on some local honey, some pecans for pies later, and fresh lettuce, spinach, and carrots to go with the eggs she was purchasing in three dozen flats.

"I can add some tomatoes, onion, and cucumbers from my own garden for a great salad to go with the quiche."

"That sounds delicious," said Chelsea.

Later, enveloped in a huge apron, Chelsea helped Nell by rolling pie crusts while Nell chopped and combined ingredients for the quiches.

Jasper, who had again hitched a ride to work with Carter, entered the kitchen about an hour and a half later to find his mother and Chelsea poring over Nell's collection of family recipes. Nell had taken Charm's offer to introduce Nell to her mother to heart, and she wanted Chelsea's input into which recipes to showcase.

"Oh my. I didn't realize how late it was," said Nell, jumping up to clear away the recipes and set the table.

"I'll do it, Mom," volunteered Jasper.

Just then they heard voices at the back door. Pammy and Jon had given Gram and Gramps a ride. Corey's black Jag was right behind them.

With the security and tech crews at Charm's concert, dinner would be a smaller group tonight although Nell and Chelsea had prepared a total of eight quiches, six for the crews and band when they returned at two a.m. "I can always freeze them up to a week if they don't get eaten," Nell confided to Chelsea.

"Oh, they'll get eaten," Chelsea prophesied.

And they did. Corey, Jasper, and Chelsea sat up late watching a movie, and they heard Charm and her entourage arrive. Nell had thoughtfully placed the utensils and food downstairs so they could eat sitting informally on the couches, chairs, and even the floor. The bacon, spinach, and crabmeat quiches were a big hit along with the salad and carrot cake.

Not much was left when everyone, sated and satisfied, began discussing the move from Rosemont to the bungalow which would occur Saturday evening or rather Sunday morning following the Raleigh/Durham concert in North Carolina.

Charm's parents were already there, stocking foods and ensuring fresh linens for the beds. CeCe, who had come with them along with Charlie, was impatiently counting the days until Charm's arrival. She wanted some girl time, especially the kind that involved shopping.

Before Donnell had left the Dumotte's home in Samois sur Seine, he had made sure Catherine and Christian had secure phones. They had been instructed to reveal their travel plans to no one, not even their respective secretaries and associates. He had especially cautioned them against divulging their plans over the internet.

Since Donnell could not, Frank had met them at the exit where Highway 78 met I-95. The Dumottes had flown to Charleston from Cancun, a likely vacation spot since the Dumottes were fond of the Caribbean. After Frank met them, they had traveled on to Hampton where the bungalow was located. Frank had swept the bungalow for bugs and then left Forrest and Sam as guards before traveling back to Virginia.

The attacks were still a week out if their calculations were correct, and already, several of the code names had been used in terrorist chatter. And while the band members were grateful for the protection Donnell's crew provided, they were becoming worried.

"It's all very well and good for you to guard us, Donnell," began Michael, "but what can we as the band do to protect ourselves? I feel like a duck sitting at the end of a gun barrel."

"The first thing you can do is to be especially observant," said Donnell. "If you see anything out of the ordinary, let one of us know immediately. Thirdly, it wouldn't hurt to know some of the basic hand signals such as your index finger pointed out, your thumb up and the other three fingers curled in to represent a gun. Even if you do that with your hand at your side, it can be a signal to another band member that someone has a gun."

They all took a few moments to practice the gesture.

"Another gesture is to hold up the number of fingers that indicate the number of suspects you've seen. You can do it casually as if you are just stretching, but it will help us to determine what kind of manpower to use."

"What if we're all performing onstage, and we see a suicide bomber about to detonate themselves and everyone else?" asked Charm.

"Oh come, Charm!" said Kelly. "Just change the lyrics of your song to indicate in which section the bomber is. Your fans will hardly notice. You will alert security and save the day!"

"Right," said Charm with an inflective drawl to show sarcasm.

After those remarks, they suggested scenario after scenario, some with plausibility but others with a minimum of credibility. Following the one with Charm shooting a gun right out of a terrorist's hand, she announced she was going to bed.

"Wait, wait," said Megan finally serious. "I think we should use the next several concerts to practice our powers of observation, trying to notice details that could mean trouble."

"Just don't cry wolf or use the signs unless it's for real," warned Natalie. "And try to never be anywhere by yourself. Stay in groups of two or more. That goes for the tech people, too," she said, looking at Sean who did lighting and George who ran the sound board as well as Max, the bus driver, and Geveon.

When everyone had headed for their respective sleeping quarters and Jasper had given Chelsea a lingering goodnight kiss at the top of the stairs, Corey made his way to Jasper's room.

"Boy, you are in it deep, aren't you?" he asked.

"In what deep?" retorted Jasper, thinking he was referring to his relationship with Chelsea.

"This terrorism stuff. It's the real thing, isn't it?" Corey asked soberly.

"Yes, it is," said Jasper.

"If there's anything I can do to help, let me know."

"I will," said Jasper.

"And by the way, I like Chelsea even better than I liked Allison. She's more down-to-earth, and she and Mom get along really well, too."

"Yes, I'd noticed that," said Jasper. "So what happened to the French chick?"

"Musette? Too clingy for me. You know I hate that stuff. She came here with Daddy who gives her a credit card and tells her to go shopping. She was bored and practically threw herself in my arms when she realized I was here. Great kisser though," he said and grinned in remembrance.

"How much longer will you be in town?" asked Jasper.

"Dad has asked me to stay until after the twenty-first. They don't want me at the ball, but if I think of a way to bring down a few terrorists, I may crash it anyway." Corey grinned unrepentantly. "Where will you be?"

"I've been asked to go south to help guard the girls, not a particularly unpleasant task," said Jasper with a grin. "Actually, I'm supposed to help Donnell, especially by facilitating travel arrangements, including decoys. Should be fun!"

"Well, stay safe, Bro, and try to get the bad guys before they get you," said Corey, giving Jasper an awkward man hug with the backslaps to go with it.

"Haven't you heard? The good guys always win!" quipped Jasper.

"Not always," said Corey soberly. "But let's go with that."

Chapter Thirty-Seven

Jasper looked at the message on the computer screen over Frank's shoulder. With the help of the automatic translator, the Pashto dialect, now in English, was clearly a directive to proceed with plans for Benjamin, Issachar, and Asher.

It was a Saturday afternoon, and the message had been intercepted a mere four hours prior. Frank and Tillot had been alerted immediately, and since Jasper was already in the office with Frank discussing last minute details of the move south, he had joined the others in the situation room.

They knew that Asher meant oil. Not only were oil refineries being placed on the highest alert level, but workers on the Alaskan pipeline were being warned as well.

Tillot had thought Chelsea's wry comments about the H1N1 vaccine were meritorious. Some investigation had revealed that a shipment of the vaccines was due to be unloaded following their trip from China and sent to various military bases, with the largest orders due to arrive in Fort Benning on Tuesday and Fort Hood on Tuesday or Wednesday. Vaccinations were set to begin on Thursday, June twenty-first.

Then one of his men had linked Benjamin, known as the wolf in Jewish literature, to the Third "Greywolf" Battle Team stationed at Fort Hood. The "coincidences" continued to grow. However, what they didn't know was if the vaccines had already been contaminated or if they would be tampered with in transit.

Either way, the Commanding Generals had been notified and no military personnel would receive vaccines although, in an effort to catch the perpetrators, no one other than the CGs knew of the change in plans yet.

Issachar was the farmer son of Jacob, the Jewish patriarch. Although Tillot respected the idea that a dam above a large farming area could be the target, he also wondered about crop dusters dumping large amounts of poison from the planes instead of simply pesticides. These conjectures left too many avenues of terrorism open.

The state of California, however, produced over fifty percent of the nation's fruits and vegetables. Ironically, it also had the largest number of dams. In Colorado, as well, was the well-known Hoover Dam, another possibility. But on the East Coast was the Tennessee Valley Authority with large agricultural areas, dams that produced electricity, and several nuclear power plants.

All dams were inspected daily by specially trained military personnel. Placing an implosive bomb on one of the dams would not take long, however. At least the time frame had been narrowed considerably. That one thing could give them the edge with 24-hour surveillance over a three-day period. They would take no chances.

"We've got another one," said another man to Jasper's left, excitement lacing his voice. "Problems with Naphtali," read the cryptic message.

"What's Naphtali?" asked Tillot, looking up at the flow chart on the wall.

"Cell phones," several voices chorused in response.

"Isn't Verizon the largest carrier?"

"Yes," came the answer.

"We're already on that, Boss," said one of the operatives in the room. "We've been in contact with Verizon, T Mobile, and Sprint. All three companies believe they are invincible to attack. But indications lead us to believe that the terrorists have stolen information from Israel's foremost computer experts on using cell phone blocking techniques on a massive scale."

"We'll quickly discover just how good al-Qaeda's computer geeks are," said Jasper.

"Let's finish our plans," said Frank. "Some of us have to work in the field."

"Carry on," Tillot directed the ops in the room.

Frank led the way back to the small cubbyhole of his newly commandeered office.

"What were we discussing?" asked Tillot.

"Sleeping arrangements at the Dumotte's bungalow," answered Frank. "They have sleeping porches, one upstairs and one downstairs, as well as four bedrooms, so everyone has a place."

"Aren't the Merrills expecting Charm to stay with them at least one evening?"

"It's two evenings, and since Jasper and I are already familiar with the setup of their home, that won't be difficult either and could very well throw off the terrorists."

"Great! Do we need any more men down there?"

"No, I don't think so," responded Frank slowly. "We have Donnell's crew, and two of our own are already at the bungalow, Sam and Forrest. And, of course, we'll be working with the Charleston Police Department as well as the Homeland Security Office down there. How heavy is FBI involvement?"

"Amazingly, they're letting me handle it. Chelsea's contract isn't being terminated until the end of the month; so technically, her welfare is under our jurisdiction still."

"Okay. Anything else we need to discuss, Boss?"

"I don't think so," responded Tillot. "Just try to stay safe down there, men."

*****

Jasper spent the rest of the afternoon and early evening trouble-shooting small situations and answering questions about the move to the bungalow which would occur immediately following Charm's concert. Martha Miller and Kyle Callaway, members of Frank's team, had arranged the transport, and this time another bus would be used although they would take a round-about way to board it.

Everyone seemed to sense that this was it. So far, only Charm had been threatened, but now, each band and tech crew member felt personally threatened. Nerves were beginning to fray. If they were this taut now, Jasper wondered how everyone would be feeling by Wednesday and even Thursday morning. Keeping everyone calm seemed to be a major part of his job description.

After a final meal at Rosemont, and with many thanks to Nell and Carter, the group began dispersing. Martha thought that bringing the bus to Rosemont would be dangerous, so it had been parked several miles away within a grove of trees at Jasper's grandparent's house. Members of the group were transported via golf cart along the track Chelsea and Jasper had followed the day of the helicopter bombing. Kyle had stayed with the bus along with Max, the driver.

When everyone, including Chelsea, had boarded, Max started the engine, and they rolled from the copse of trees and onto the road. At the freeway, Donnell's team and Frank's team fell into line, traveling sometimes beside, but most oftentimes behind the bus.

The night spent traveling passed uneventfully. The sun was tingeing the eastern sky with bands of peach and pink when the vehicles left Interstate 95 and headed for the bungalow. The trailers full of equipment were going directly to the concert venue.

Jasper noticed that the trees grew much closer together, great cover for evildoers. Many of the roads were unmarked, and, other than the small town through which they passed, neighbors seemed to enjoy a mile or two of elbow distance.

At last they turned from the small two lane road onto a dirt road that wound beneath tall pines and towering, majestic oaks with their mantles of Spanish moss. The bungalow, framed in weathered, gray cedar, blended with the sylvan setting.

But the lamps on either side of the wide veranda porch gleamed in welcome, and the sun touched the tops of tallest trees with warm beams. It looked magical in the first light of dawn.

The welcome from both Catherine and Christian was no less magical.

"Come in, come in," said Christian heartily.

"I imagine you all want to make acquaintance with a bed," said Catherine. She led the girls to an upstairs sleeping porch, screened on two sides. The glass windows had been swung open to invite the breeze. Eight single beds stood on either side of a central aisle, inviting in crisp, white linens and plump, white comforters.

To the right, a short hall with closets on either side led to a large bathroom with huge mirrors over four sinks on one side of the room, and four showers and four toilet stalls on the other side. The décor was done in the palest of peach and gold with plush white rugs scattered wherever they would provide comfort for bare feet.

Sam was already staying in one of the downstairs bedrooms that contained four single beds, so Martha and Trinity joined her there. CeCe had her own bedroom downstairs, but Charm chose to stay with her band, at least for now. She loved the sleeping porch with the sweet breezes wafting in and the golden sunlight sending shining beams through the trees.

The men had the same type of sleeping porch downstairs, done in mint green and gold and white. An extra bedroom held four single beds, and Charlie was more than willing to sleep in a sleeping bag on the floor in his bedroom to be near Donnell, whom he idolized.

Sam and Forrest, Catherine and Christian kept guard while everyone else slept. Even Charlie, newly imbued with visions of Bond-like action, prowled the perimeter of the property.

Donnell, as was his wont, awoke first. He joined Christian, Catherine, and Charlie in the kitchen for lunch. The rest of his team as well as Jasper and Frank soon joined him. They began making a dent in the huge bowl of shrimp salad, fresh fruit, coffee for the northerners and peach-infused, sweet tea that Southerners so enjoy.

The rest of the security members made their way to the large eat-in kitchen, and soon the kitchen hummed with conversation.

Christian sat beside Donnell, waiting for him to swallow some of the black coffee that kept his nerves keenly on edge.

"I need to discuss an invitation we've received with you," began Christian.

"I'm listening," said Donnell.

"We've all been invited to Mr. and Mrs. Dan Lowther's place tomorrow for horseback riding and a barbecue. Mr. D.P. owns the largest herd of Marsh Tackies, horses left by the Spaniards that are now considered a native species. We've known D.P. and Mrs. Dan, as she likes to be called, for many years, but I don't want to put you under undue stress."

"Actually, this is a rather easy week. Charm has only three concerts this week, Charlotte, Charleston, and Greenville, and we've already done preliminary work at the Ovens Auditorium in Charlotte. A day of relaxation, provided we were not followed here, might give everyone some calm and objectivity."

"That's what I thought, too."

"Can my team visit the Lowther's and their place before you commit?"

"Absolutely. I hope you don't mind, but the Lowther's are Charm's American godparents, and I've already told them some of the situation. D.P. and his men are primed for action. They've had to defend their herd against rustlers, and they're not afraid to use, hm, less than legal means if necessary."

"Much like our enemy," said Donnell wryly. "Let me talk to Frank. Could we leave in about thirty minutes?"

"That would be fine. I'll just call D.P."

Donnell talked to Frank, and soon all of Donnell's crew and half of Frank's detail were on their way to the Lowther's ranch.

Mrs. Dan was gracious—Donnell could see why Southern Americans were known for their hospitality—and D.P. drove them all around his ranch on golf carts. He and Frank formulated a plan, and D.P. vowed to supplement their personnel with three of his most trusted men.

"You all call on us anytime you need anything, men. Mrs. Dan and I have known Charm and her family since Charm was a bitty girl. Christian and Catherine are fine folk, and we'll do anything we need to protect their girls. Charlie, too, for that matter!" D.P. said with a grin and a wink.

As they returned to the bungalow, Donnell kept hearing a roaring noise. He began to worry until they entered the drive and saw that the racket was being made by four-wheelers. The band members had enjoyed their lunch and were now working it off.

Donnell was treated to the sight of Charm coolly popping a wheelie on her four-wheeler as she drew up with a flourish to the garage where they were housed and hopped off to let Sandy take a turn. Wisps of red hair curled around her shining face, and her green eyes glowed with fun and mischief.

Meanwhile, Chelsea was patiently showing Jonette how to ride, and even Megan was enjoying herself, blond hair flying and a super-sized grin on her face. Max and Geveon continued to stand guard along with Forrest and Sam, but the roar of the other four-wheelers could be heard in a crescendo as the male band members made their way back to the bungalow, a cloud of dust following them.

Donnell made sure that each of his team members had a chance to ride the four-wheelers; he noticed that Frank did the same. A little relaxation would go a long way to keeping them all primed for action on Wednesday and Thursday.

Frank claimed old age in declining a ride. But Martha, who was older than Frank, was the biggest surprise. She and Jonette put-putted at a leisurely speed in a wide perimeter around the house.

After showers and the evening meal of grilled fish and steaks, Charm called a practice, and the rest who weren't on guard duty played the board games Christian and Catherine produced.

Jasper challenged Chelsea to a game of Chinese checkers, but when she beat him three times in a row, she realized his mind was nowhere close to what he was doing.

She pulled him to his feet and led him to the large front porch, replete with eight natural wood rocking chairs grouped around covered tables. Lamps and citronella candles on either side of the doorway kept most of the evening bugs at bay although Chelsea chose two rocking chairs at the far end of the porch.

"Now tell me what's bothering you," she said softly.

"I'm just keyed up, I guess," said Jasper. "Normally, I'm the guy who is calm, cool, and collected, but the closer we get to the Charleston concert, the more I wonder if anyone will be gone when it's all over. I look around the group and just pray that it won't be anyone I'm seeing."

Chelsea was silent, not really knowing what to say but also realizing that the words she did say should be chosen with care.

"Sorry. I don't mean to dump my negative thoughts on you."

"No, no. I'm just thinking of what I want to say," said Chelsea, pulling her chair close and placing her hand comfortingly on his arm.

"I'll start," said Jasper. "If any of those terrorists lay a finger on you, I'll hunt them down and kill them with my bare hands if it's the last thing I do."

Chelsea stared. His passion was so out of character for someone who was usually so laid back. The fact that it was for her gave her a thrill, exciting her even more as she realized in awe that she could elicit that kind of emotion from him.

This time when Jasper pulled her from the rocking chair and to his lap, he did not even think about being a gentleman. He only knew he could never get enough of this woman as long as he lived. He ravaged her lips, her neck, even daring to tease with his lips where the cleavage between her breasts began at the vee of the t-shirt she wore.

Drawing in a ragged breath, he stopped his perusal of her enticingly aroused body and counted to ten, willing his blood to stop pounding. He had vowed after Allison to save sex for marriage, and he was certain that Chelsea, with her upbringing, felt the same way.

"Thank you for stopping," said Chelsea, confirming his thoughts. "I mean, I'd love to have you continue. You're wonderful, Jasper, but I want to remain a virgin until I'm married. I hope you don't mind."

"Of course not. I've made the same decision. I just can't bear to think…" his voice broke.

"It's okay, Jasper. Just like our forefathers before us and even your parents, we'll fight this battle for democracy and freedom because it's our turn to fight. And we won't look back and second-guess our decisions no matter what the fallout is. You already know how my family feels about that." She laughed, thinking back to the political discussion he had heard at the first family dinner he'd attended.

Jasper laughed, too, feeling strangely comforted yet energized and encouraged, as well.

"I don't speak much about my faith because it is so criticized in Washington culture, but I believe that God controls everything that happens in our lives, and I can't help feeling that, like Esther, we've been brought to this time and this place for a purpose higher than our own. Does that sound too hokey?"

"Oh, no," said Jasper. "I've always felt a sense of destiny on my life. I've just never linked it to my faith although it certainly makes even more sense that way."

The sharing of their inmost thoughts on faith and duty linked them in an even tighter bond than physical intimacy could do. Jasper and Chelsea both sensed it and were glad the other was willing to save a physical culmination of their relationship for later.

Donnell watched the couple from the cover of darkness where he stood guard. They had old-fashioned values that many others did not share, yet working so closely with Jasper since his arrival in America, he had come to regard him as a brother. He would do anything to protect them, and he knew Jasper would do the same for him and Charm.

He did not know what Chelsea had said to Jasper, but he seemed less tense as they re-entered the bungalow.

The day had been relaxing. Donnell just wondered what the next day would bring. He hoped they could have another terror-free day. They would have to stay on their guard.

Chapter Thirty-Eight

Monday dawned as beautifully as the previous day had. Charm stretched like a cat, marvelously relaxed from the fun of the previous day. She had not sought to be alone with Donnell, instinctively knowing that after the fireworks of their previous time together, their relationship would never be simple.

He wasn't ready to commit, so, okay, she could live with that. But she could still enjoy herself, sending him occasional provocative looks. Maybe she would get burned, or just maybe he would declare his love after the brouhaha with the terrorists was resolved. And if he didn't, maybe she would just take matters into her own hands.

With that delicious thought curving her lips into a smile, Charm opened her eyes, stretching again. No one else was up except for Natalie and Tiffany who were probably on patrol duty.

She wandered down to the kitchen in her blue silk pajama bottoms and matching kimono wrapper. Southern would be her style today. She would enjoy her tea hot with a piece of buttered toast and a fresh sliced nectarine, as she sat in one of the rocking chairs on the front porch with the sun blessing her face.

After thirty minutes of contented rocking, she was ready to dress for the day, but a small pebble landed on her plate, and a voice in Irish brogue said, "And sure, that's a pretty sight for poor eyes!"

"Donnell! Where did you come from?"

"From the creek over yonder," he replied with a very poorly affected Southern drawl. He bowed in front of her and produced a wild rose from behind his back.

"A rose for a rose?" he asked.

"It's beautiful, Donnell," said Charm. She was confused. He didn't look like a man pining for love.

"Ah, but not as beautiful as the rose sitting in this chair," said Donnell. "Walk with me to the creek?"

"I need to change first," said Charm, sitting up very straight in her chair.

"I had noticed that," said Donnell with a knowing glint in his eye, "but I'm trying to avoid licentious thoughts on this pure morning."

Charm couldn't believe it; she actually blushed. "I'll be right back," she said breathlessly.

Whatever could Donnell be up to she wondered as she quickly changed to white shorts, a pink tee and comfortable tennis shoes and socks. Looking in the mirror, she gave a few quick brushes to her hair, and then tucked the rose behind her ear.

She was back on the porch in less than five minutes, finding that Donnell had taken her vacated chair.

"Ready?" she asked, half breathlessly, half challengingly.

"Ready," he said, standing and taking her hand.

They walked companionably without speaking toward the back of the property where a creek gurgled cheerfully. Her father had been clearing the brush a little at a time along the creek bed, but when he had found the wild roses, he had painstakingly created a natural arbor for them to grow over and around.

They stood under the arbor, absorbing the peace of the place.

"I talked to your father last night," said Donnell.

"You did? About what?"

"About something my grandmother said."

"And what did your grandmother say?" asked Charm. She was even more confused.

"When I went to Ireland for Granda's funeral, she told me not to be too cautious."

"But isn't that part of your job description?"

"Yes, but I'm not talking about my job description any longer." He searched her face. She still wasn't tracking with him.

"I'm talking now about my feelings for you, Charm. I love you Charmaine Marie Dumotte, and I'm asking you to marry me…whenever it fits into your schedule," he added somewhat wryly. "Will you?"

Charm looked at him in amazement.

"Come, Darling. Don't tell me you are just having your fun."

That loosened her tongue. "No, I mean yes." She stopped and took a deep breath. "No, I'm not just having fun, and yes, a thousand times yes!" She flung her arms around his neck; then stopping, her face inches from his, she said, "I love you, too, Donnell McKinnon. I just thought you were going to wait until after this terrorist activity was over."

"I was," said Donnell with a sigh. "But Mother McKinnon's words kept ringing through my head, and I wanted to make sure you knew how I felt just in case something happens."

"God bless Mother McKinnon," said Charm fervently. "What exactly did she say anyway?"

"She said, 'Don't be too cautious in following your heart's desire. Your lady needs to know she's most important with ye with no secrets between the two.'"

"No secrets, huh? I like that part even better," said Charm.

Donnell could see where her mind was headed. Swiftly he bent his head to kiss her and change the direction of her thoughts. He sipped, he savored until she pressed her body fully against his. The unspoken invitation sent his control spinning, but he grabbed savagely at it, easing out of the kiss, leaning his forehead against hers and feeling for a small box in his pocket.

He opened his eyes, pulling slightly away from her and saying huskily, "There's still the matter of a ring."

When he opened the box, Charm gasped with surprise. "How did you...where did you... when did you have time to get that?"

"My mother gave it to me before I left Ireland. It belonged to her mother, and she knew I would have need of it. I'm going to put it on," he said, kissing each finger of her left hand and leaving the fourth finger for last. "But I want you to know that if you don't want to wear it until the terrorists are caught and even after that while you're performing, I will understand. Some things don't need to be shared with the general public."

He slid the beautiful square cut diamond on her ring finger. Three smaller diamonds in gradually smaller sizes were embedded in the band on each side of the one in the middle. They caught the sparkle of the morning sun as Charm wriggled her fingers.

"It's beautiful, Donnell, and perfect," said Charm.

He bent his head, kissing her slowly, deeply, tenderly.

"When do you want to announce our engagement?" he asked huskily when at last they parted. "I don't want to make you even more of a target, and I don't want to lose my job, so I would rather wait until after the Charleston concert, but maybe we can make it a bit of a party after this case is resolved. If we all get out of this alive."

"Hush. Don't even think that way."

"I have to, Charm. It's a very real part of my job. That's why I wanted to make my intentions known now. If they kill either one of us, we may have to deal with the 'what ifs,' but not with the 'what.'"

Charm listened to Donnell with her head lowered. She would not let terrorists take her joy, her heart, her love. So when she raised her head, although tears trembled on her lashes, her voice was firm and resolute.

"I will always love you, Donnell. And we will not let these bastards steal our joy or our love," she said firmly. "And yes, we will make a party of it when this is over. May I tell Sandy and my parents?"

"Oh, yes, absolutely. Just swear them to secrecy. I'll not have you made an even higher prized target."

"I'll wear the ring on a chain until then."

*****

Charm smiled all through the morning and all through the afternoon horseback riding except when she wasn't concentrating on putting her horse through his paces.

In addition to the herd of Marsh Tackies, D.P. had several show horses. Charm, CeCe, and Charlie had all been taught the Eastern style of riding, and Sandy and Chelsea knew a fair amount about it as well. Now that D.P.'s children were grown and had moved away, his two grooms, who doubled as jockeys, were not loathe to let the girls work the horses.

The rest of the group with the exception of those on guard duty saddled some of the Tackies for a trail ride.

Even the sweat trickling between Charm's breasts and down her back as she worked on her diagonals couldn't remove the smile of pure happiness from her face. Sandy knew something was up, but she kept her own counsel.

Charm had decided to wait telling anyone except her mother and father. She had shared the news with them in the privacy of their bedroom following Donnell's proposal. Her father had been content to say that Donnell was a very lucky man, but her mother had pulled her into a warm hug and had shed a few tears.

After quick showers, the girls raided CeCe's closet for sundresses, and then they headed back to the Lowther's house. The pork had been roasted and pulled the day before. Now it simmered in Mrs. Dan's special sauce, ready to be served with baked beans, a creamy dill/basil potato salad, sliced tomatoes, green beans and okra sautéed in sesame oil, with Mrs. Dan's famous coconut cake and churned peach ice cream for dessert.

Charm alternated between being nervous about the upcoming concert and the tension surrounding it and being deliriously happy. She decided the latter won because she still had a hearty appetite for Mrs. Dan's delicious food.

Meantime, Jasper and Chelsea enjoyed the new peace they had found that was keenly edged with sexual tension. They altered the original twenty questions game to five questions, including others in the game. Questions and answers raced merrily around the loose circle as they discussed favorite foods, childhood memories, and music.

Even Mrs. Dan was caught off guard when asked who her favorite rock star was. "Elvis," came the answer, and bright discussion of music from another era made her feel quite young again when she discovered that some of them liked Elvis's music, too!

As for Charm, her bubble of happiness lasted the entire next day even when everyone was separated and driven in "taxicabs" to Charlotte. The bus remained parked in the large barn on Christian's property.

The Charlotte concert was a huge hit, and although security was high, no sign was seen of any terrorists. Donnell wondered if they saw no terrorists because of high security or if the terrorists were lying low, waiting for Thursday.

Martha, not wanting to take any chances of the band being followed under cover of darkness, had arranged for a bus to transport the crew to the airport where they boarded a private plane and flew to the air station in Beaufort. A change in mode of transportation was just the thing to confuse observers and keep their final destination secret.

The military had balked at the use of a private plane, wanting them to use a military plane instead, but Martha knew that use of a military plane might eventually lead any clear-thinking terrorist to consider the MCAS in Beaufort when no such plane arrived in Charleston. She wanted the bungalow to remain secret for as long as possible.

Wednesday was to bring severe afternoon thunderstorms to the area, so Martha once again proved her organizational skills by arranging for the tech crew and supporting security to travel to the Charleston Coliseum via I-95 and I-26 on the bus with their personal equipment.

The band and the rest of the security personnel as well as Charlie and CeCe were split amongst three vans. One met the bus during a break at a gas station where Highway 78 and I-95 met, another group was taken to the Lowther's to board their van, and still another group met their van in a vacant church parking lot.

All except the tech crew would meet at the Merrill residence in Summerville where Chelsea's family was expecting them.

The transfers went smoothly, and Donnell, who had traveled with the tech crew along with Natalie, Tiffany, Jasper, Sam, and Gregor, was both impressed and relieved. Each white van arrived at ten minute intervals at the Merrill residence with Frank and Davey Merrill getting the vans quickly into the garage and everyone sent to their respective rooms.

Extra cots and mattresses had been procured for the bedrooms in both the bunkhouse for the men and the upstairs bedrooms in the house. Galeah thoughtfully made sure each of the performers had real beds, but even the cots had thick mattresses and fine linens so no one complained.

A fine Southern feast of fried chicken; potato, macaroni, and green salads; black-eyed peas with bell pepper, onion, and okra; and sliced tomatoes was followed with blackberry cobbler and vanilla ice cream.

The day was hot, and even at five p.m. the humidity was stifling, so the group confined themselves to the large screened porch, the dining room, and the living room.

When most everyone was sated, Galeah commandeered Chelsea and her other two girls to help with cleanup. Charm, Sandy, and Jonette volunteered to help. Meanwhile, Frank dragged Donnell and Natalie to the library with its low lamplight and cool interior to show them Mr. Merrill's exceptional security system installed behind innocuous bookcases. Tiffany followed.

"I wish Marcus was here," commented Donnell. "He would enjoy seeing this. But he needed to confer with head of security for the North Charleston Coliseum and set up his own equipment."

"He will be back soon," promised Natalie. "He, Gregor, and Jasper wanted to talk to Andy North who is head of security at the North Charleston Coliseum, and Gregor wanted to find a good site to set up his equipment."

Just then, Donnell's phone vibrated. The message stunned him.

"Boss, you're never going to believe this but we just saw an al-Qaeda member in the lobby of this budget hotel around the corner from the Coliseum!" reported Marcus.

Chapter Thirty-Nine

A massive thunderstorm with plenty of pyrotechnics had removed some of the humidity from the air, making the jasmine- and honeysuckle-covered porch off the library tolerable. Chelsea, Charm, and Sandy sat on the large cushion-laden swing. An occasional toe on the cool, painted concrete floor kept the swing in motion.

Jonette was reading another novel as she sat in one of the three high-backed wicker chairs. Trinity, who had been assigned on-site guard duty when the others had rushed to meet Marcus at the Coliseum, sat in another, and Megan occupied the other.

CeCe along with Kielah and Lindy, Chelsea's sisters, sat cross-legged on large, jewel-toned pillows of ruby, topaz, and sapphire. Gina, Chelsea's twenty-one-year old cousin, and Lanie, Lawton's girlfriend joined them.

"Have you and Harry set a date yet?" Chelsea asked Gina, eager to catch up on the news.

"I wanted something before school begins in August, but we're probably going to have to wait until December at the end of the semester."

"What happened to the April wedding you always dreamed of?" asked Chelsea.

"Harry doesn't want to wait that long, and, I confess, neither do I," Gina said with a rueful smile. "And Caden is so excited about getting a new daddy. How could I make my son wait any longer?"

Chelsea chuckled, and Charm smiled in sympathy, thinking of the ring hanging on a chain under her blouse.

"What about you, Chelsea? I hear you and that Secret Service man have been spending many hours together," said Gina, teasingly.

"Jasper loves me, I'm sure of it, and I, I love him," Chelsea confessed slowly. She held up her hand as the others exclaimed and murmured in approval. "He probably won't say anything until the danger we're facing is over," she said.

Noting the look on her sisters faces, she added, "Not a word of this to Mom and Dad. Or else."

"Of course not," protested Lindy. "We would never say a word," added Kielah. "Besides, you know too many things about us," said Lindy with mock demureness.

"That's true," said Chelsea, laughing.

"I'm nearly in the same boat," said Charm. She hesitated, mindful of her promise to Donnell for secrecy. She would not endanger Donnell's job for anything, so she changed the subject. "I think we should make some plans for my concert. We girls are not helpless and we can do our part. I wouldn't mind some extra eyes and ears backstage tomorrow."

"We've been practicing self-defense nearly every day," complained Megan. "Isn't that enough?"

"Oh, I don't know," said Lanie, speaking for the first time. "We girls have more than one way of defending ourselves. Do you still carry 'Lil' Gator'?" she asked Chelsea.

"Sure do," answered Chelsea. "Grandpa Merrill is a proud NRA member, and he taught me how to shoot as well as any of the boys."

"And I have 'Rebel.' No one is going to take away my privilege as a citizen to carry a gun. I know my Second Amendment rights," said Lanie with asperity.

"I don't have a handgun, but I still have that phone that Natalie gave me," said Sandy, pulling it out of her pocket. "It's on a private frequency."

Charm stared at Sandy. "When did she give you the phone? I don't even have special phone."

"While we were in the hospital. You were out of things, and since my injuries weren't as serious, they wanted me to call if anything untoward happened."

"I have one that Tillot gave me," said Chelsea.

"Will the phones work if the terrorists take down cell phone access?" asked Lanie.

"I think so. They're on a private frequency, too" said Sandy.

"Do you have any other phones like that?" asked Lanie. "Because if you do, we could form some kind of phone chain."

"My mother and father were given phones by Donnell," said Charm. "Maybe I can get them to let us borrow them."

"When are they coming?" asked Sandy.

"Tonight," responded Charm. "Then maybe we'll have four phones."

"Great," said Chelsea. "If we're going to be a presence backstage, we really should plan to work in groups of two."

Sandy put down the novel she was reading. "That's a good idea," she said.

But Trinity objected. "The men are not going to like this," she said. "They won't want interference from 'civilians.'"

"We're not civilians," Lanie said firmly. "We're Charm's friends. Right, Charm?"

"Absolutely," said Charm.

"What time will you be going over to the Coliseum?" asked Lindy.

"I'll do a sound check at about eleven, break at two for lunch, take a nap or rest in the bus until five, and then we start the makeup, hair, and costuming in time to do the 'Charmed Circle Fan Club' meet and greet at six."

Lindy sighed with disappointment. "Well, that leaves Kielah and me out. We have cheerleading camp tomorrow until five."

"What do you and Jonette do while Charm is doing her sound check?" Chelsea asked Sandy.

"I usually make sure her costumes are ready in the dressing area, and Jonette places her makeup and hair products on the dressing room table in a certain order so everything is right at our fingertips when we're getting Charm ready. We do the same with Megan's makeup and costumes."

"The bus is already there?" asked Lanie.

"Yes. It's usually parked in the back," replied Sandy.

"Does anyone watch it?" Lanie asked again.

"Yes. Geveon or Max are usually in the front area, reading a newspaper or getting online to catch up on news from home," said Charm.

"Sandy and I are usually finished before Charm is," said Jonette, "so we usually go back to the bus to order or prepare lunch."

"Mom will be glad to pack a lunch tonight for all of us," said Chelsea, "and we'll help. I think we should put two of us in the dressing area, two of us in the bus, and two of us with Charm at all times. That is, if you and Gina want to help," she said, turning to Lanie.

"You couldn't keep me away," said Lanie with a grin.

"My whole day is free," said Gina. "If Mom is willing to have some 'grandma time' with Caden, you can count me in."

Trinity looked troubled, but she was wise enough not to voice her concerns again.

"We'll only need three phones in that case," said Lanie. "Let's program them tonight to speed dial and speed text auto messages."

"Why don't we just text numbers," said Chelsea. "Two can mean come at once, three can mean come but proceed with caution, four can mean converge to Charm's location, et cetera. That way, if a situation occurs, we can press a number with the phone still in our pockets, and, hopefully, no one will be the wiser."

"Such as a terrorist," said Gina.

"Exactly," responded Chelsea.

"Never come between a girl and her phone," said Lanie, and they all laughed.

Trinity added a word of caution. "Just be careful girls. If a suicide bomber is threatening to blow up himself or herself, sometimes a cell phone can act as a detonator, depending on how sophisticated their system is."

"Oh. I hadn't thought of that," said Gina.

Galeah entered with tall glasses of her special limeade. "Your parents just phoned," she said to Charm. "They will be here in about thirty minutes, and they're bringing a surprise."

"I wonder what they've got up their sleeves now," said Charm.

"You look tired, Mom," said Chelsea. "Come sit down with us; we'll scrunch over."

"I would like to rest a bit, and the storm left a nice little breeze for us," said Galeah.

The talk drifted to general topics as the girls enjoyed the refreshing beverages and waited for Charm's parents to arrive. Galeah had just returned the empty glasses to the kitchen when she saw the Dumottes exit their vehicle. She hurried outside to greet them.

"Welcome," she said, holding out both hands.

First Christian, then Catherine kissed her on both cheeks. Behind them, another woman rose gracefully from the back seat of the car. The emerald green of her silk suit accentuated the sheen of her glossy, black hair, turned her eyes a brilliant shade of emerald green. She was quite the most stunning woman Galeah had ever seen.

"This is Charm's aunt, Olivia Valentino, the fashion designer," said Catherine in introduction.

"Welcome to Charleston, South Carolina," said Galeah.

"I am very happy to be here," said Olivia. "The South has an ambience I wish to incorporate into my designs."

"Then you will especially enjoy the evenings when Charleston becomes a sensuous, sultry siren," said Galeah with a laugh as she led them through library and to the porch where the girls were still sitting.

As soon as Charm saw her parents, she jumped up to greet them, kissing and hugging them both even though she had seen them only that morning. She was not unaware that, in reality, harming her family would be a much worse retribution for her supposed theft than any personal form of punishment.

"We brought a surprise," said Catherine, tugging at the arm of someone in the shadows.

When Charm saw her aunt, her hesitation was barely perceptible, but both Chelsea and Trinity caught it. "Aunt Olivia," she exclaimed, giving her aunt a resounding smack on each cheek.

"And I brought gifts with me, as well," said Aunt Olivia, beaming at the group of girls. "My personal scent has been bottled for its first wave of production. I believe I have enough half-ounce samples for everyone!"

She pushed the oversized sunglasses studded with real diamonds to the top of her head and began digging in her oversized, leather bag. The scent, titled *Dreams*, was bottled in star-shaped glass in pastel colors.

Charm was nervous for a few seconds that she and the other girls wouldn't like the scent, that it would be too flamboyant. But everyone agreed that the delicate yet powerful scent was wonderful.

"So what brings you to Charleston, Aunt Olivia?" asked Charm.

"Your concert, of course. I've not been to one in the United States yet, and I will combine business with pleasure by finding fabrics and designs that reflect the Charleston culture: a mixture of the Caribbean, African American, and English cultures—what a rich palette with which to work. Even this humidity and heat play a part, but don't let me run my tongue." She stopped her exuberant explanation abruptly.

"I have special seats reserved for Mom, Dad, CeCe, Charlie, and Chelsea's family. You are welcome to join them, Aunt Olivia," said Charm.

"I shall, I shall," said Olivia.

The group was too large to sit on the front porch, so Galeah suggested they adjourn to the living room where she would serve a choice of blackberry watermelon sorbet, blackberry cobbler baked by her sister-in-law, Aunt Clara, or homemade cookies and coffee, iced if they wanted it that way.

"Sandy, you're going to have to let out all my outfits," declared Charm. She wanted to try the sorbet and the decaf iced coffee.

Before she had time to do more than get some coffee, Chelsea pulled her to the empty library with Trinity right behind. Trinity made sure no one followed and that no one else was in the room.

"I haven't even had time to get some sorbet," Charm complained.

"Why did you hesitate when you saw your aunt?" asked Chelsea.

"Do you have reason to suspect your aunt is involved in any way?" asked Trinity.

Charm held up her hand for quiet and sank onto one of the sofas with her coffee balanced on her knees.

"I love Aunt Olivia," she said slowly. "But I just find it odd that she said she couldn't get close to me at the concert in Rome when she has my private cell phone number. And, in addition to that, it was at that little bistro in Rome after the concert where I 'stole' the portion of the list the terrorists have been trying to retrieve from me."

"Do you think she planted it?" asked Trinity, her mind clicking and reorganizing facts into logical order.

"I don't know," said Charm, clearly agonized over the fact that her aunt could be a part of the torment she was amidst. "If she is a part of this and she did plant it, to what purpose? And which side is she on?"

Instantly sympathetic, Chelsea, mindful of the coffee, gave Charm a quick hug. "I don't know the answers, but truth is always better to hear than lies. Whatever the truth is, you will be able to live with it."

"Does Donnell know of your aunt's suspected involvement?" asked Trinity.

"Oh, yes. He knows."

They heard a commotion from the kitchen area. "Speaking of the Devil, I'll bet he has arrived," said Charm with a shaky chuckle.

The entire crew from the Coliseum had arrived although some who had been there longer were showering.

"Mom's going to need some help in the kitchen, and I'll make sure you get your sorbet," Chelsea said.

Ninety minutes later, Donnell and Frank had announced a brief meeting of their combined forces in the bunkhouse when Davey pulled Frank aside.

"Chelsea's Uncle Craig just called," he said quietly. "He wants you and your crew to watch the news tonight. The mayhem appears to be starting, and his entire force has been put on the highest alert.

Chapter Forty

Tillot ran his hand over his tired face and through his hair. The last twenty-four hours had been grueling, and the night and day to come, he was sure, would prove even more so. The President and Vice-President, along with their families, had been spirited to private and well-guarded locations.

The information about Marcus seeing a member of al-Qaeda, followed by the news that a man at the Coliseum had been observed filming video on the outer balcony of planes taking off and landing at the nearby airport, placed Charleston on the map in a big way. He was willing to bet it was either two members of a cell or the same man.

In addition, a single individual, male, had fallen to his death when his bungee cord had failed at the top of the Hoover Dam. It may have been a replay of a Bond movie, but the results still could have been disastrous. A bomb had not been found, but a detonator had. Divers and other security personnel were searching for a bomb.

Furthermore, in an effort to avoid media scrutiny, only the top ports had been put on the highest security alert, yet somehow Tillot had a feeling a leak of this news would occur within only a few hours.

Some of his men were watching the news to assess any damage control needed, many others were watching screens of major buildings and venues around the country, the team that monitored internet chatter was intercepting new messages every single minute, and something kept niggling at the back of his mind. NASCAR, that was it.

The one thing those drivers needed the most was gasoline, and instead of looking for a bomb near an oil refinery, certainly deadly enough, what if a race was planned and the terrorists intended to bomb it? He wasn't particularly a fan, but he would become one or assign someone to become one.

After that, he would take a short nap before the next day began. He would need all the stamina he could muster.

****

The bunkhouse was crowded, but everyone was unusually quiet as they watched the news, listening for items that could be linked to terrorism. When the information about the Hoover Dam was reported, they realized that the next twenty-four hours would be busy, indeed.

Frank and Donnell were on their phones, gathering news from headquarters. With the contaminated vaccinations quarantined, two known catastrophes had been averted. Eleven more to contain, if possible.

****

The girls had already made their plans, so they slept well that evening. Charm awoke first with her usual ebullient spirits. She determined she would not allow mere terrorists to spoil her day. Dressing casually in shorts and a tee shirt, her hair pulled into a ponytail, she decided to go for a quick jog around the neighborhood.

She didn't see the need to alert anyone as she planned to be gone less than twenty minutes; however, she was sure she would have company. Sure enough, Natalie, who was monitoring the security video feeds, saw her as she was stretching. She quickly ran upstairs to ask Tiffany, who would probably be the most rested, to cover the monitors for her. Tiffany could do that without shoes, and Natalie was already dressed. Besides, Donnell needed his rest.

Quietly Charm opened the back door and went to the opening beside the gate. Natalie, following behind, waved to Gregor to stay in the shadows of the bunkhouse. She gave Charm a lead, knowing from past conversations with Donnell that she liked to welcome the sun without interruption.

The morning was still gray, but a slight breeze stirred the humid air and a mockingbird was imitating the cardinal's short peep from the mimosa tree next door. Charm jogged slowly down

Charleston Street, mindful of her steps by the huge oak trees whose roots made the asphalt uneven.

She turned right, looking for the sun. Turning right again, she found a small park with winding paths, bronze statuary, and silent pools of water lilies. She slowed to a walk and caught the first ray of the sun as it gilded the leaves of an oak and a crepe myrtle.

The day would be a good one, she promised herself. She had a lot for which to live, and she would not let those terrorists rob her of any of her family members, crew or Donnell. Her chin lifted, and anyone who knew her well would know to steer well-clear of her ire today.

Hearing a pebble clink against asphalt, she turned, half expecting to see Donnell behind her. When she saw Natalie instead, she motioned for her to walk beside her.

"All ready for the big day?" asked Natalie.

"Now I am," said Charm.

They walked around the park, stopping to admire the bronze statue of a small, red fox, the white gazebo that was perfect for an intimate wedding, and the turtles that came to the surface of the pond as they passed, hoping for food.

As they neared Sumter Avenue, they heard a single shot. Instinctively, Natalie pushed Charm to the ground, drew her weapon, and turning, took a fighting stance before they both realized it had been the backfire of a car.

Charm sat on the ground, brushing the gravel and detritus from her knees. She looked up into Natalie's chagrined face and burst out laughing.

"I'm glad you think it's funny," said Natalie, reluctantly joining Charm's with her own weak laughter.

When she had calmed herself, Charm said, "I think I'm just relieved that it wasn't what we thought. Let's jog the rest of the way back, okay?"

They arrived in the driveway panting. Donnell was waiting for them near the door of the bunkhouse. When he saw Charm, he shoved his coffee mug into Gregor's hand, pulled Charm close to him, and gave her a hard kiss full of pent anger and frustration. Then grabbing the coffee mug once again, he disappeared into the bunkhouse.

Charm's mouth was agape, and she didn't know if she felt angry with Donnell or sympathetic with his frustration.

"The backfire woke him, and he was out here like a shot, no pun intended," said Gregor.

"He wasn't very happy that you chose to go jogging."

"Indeed," said Charm. "I had to do something to get rid of the angst and mentally prepare for the day."

"Can we adjourn to the kitchen? I need some coffee," said Natalie. She also wanted to get them inside in case of prying eyes.

"Yes. Of course," said Charm.

Inside, they found Chelsea, her sisters, and Lanie, who had spent the night, helping Galeah as she created a huge southern breakfast. She was deftly flipping pancakes on a griddle when they entered. Lindy was stirring a pot of grits and keeping an eye on the spicy sausage gravy to accompany it while Kielah stirred the scrambled eggs and turned bacon. Chelsea was slicing kiwi and strawberries, and Lanie was beheading a juicy pineapple.

"Oh my," was all Charm could think to say.

Galeah showed her where the plates, utensils, and cups were located. Turning to Natalie, she asked her to put the juice on a tray on the buffet table beside the coffee service. Natalie was not loathe to do this job since the need for caffeine was now urgent.

Galeah pressed a button near the back door and announced breakfast to the awakening group in the bunkhouse as Lindy and Kielah dished up the foods they had been preparing. Soon the room was filled with people, and the sounds of spoons clinking against serving dishes, juice and coffee being poured, and the low hum of talk were heard.

Most of the girls were sitting on the sun porch, enjoying the light morning breeze and the trills of birds welcoming the sun.

Lawton had worked late again, but he had taken the time to dress since Lanie was present. He gave her a quick kiss and made her scoot over so he could share the large Adirondack chair in which she was sitting.

"Really?" Chelsea heard Lanie ask Lawton several minutes later. "Really?" she asked again, clutching his arm in excitement.

"What?" Chelsea asked.

Lanie turned to Chelsea, but then turned back to Lawton. "You tell everyone," she said to him.

"Okay." He stood, clinking his spoon against his coffee mug. "I have an announcement to make."

Everyone looked at him expectantly, and Mr. Merrill put down the newspaper he had been reading at the patio table.

"I interviewed with TSM yesterday right before I went to work at the print shop, and they have hired me as a computer programmer, effective the first of July." Before the congratulations began, he added, "Now Lanie and I can set a date."

The acknowledged lovers received the congratulations of the rest although the girls seemed more excited about a coming wedding, and the men were more congratulatory of Lawton's new job.

The unacknowledged lovers held hands briefly under cover of the other table where they had been sitting. Donnell was reluctant to let go of Charm's hand, so she rested it lightly, tantalizingly on his leg right above his knee. His eyes flew to hers.

She looked back at him, all innocence.

"You're killing me," he said in a low voice. "I'm going to get some more coffee." He rose and congratulated Lawton and Lanie, too, on his way to the kitchen.

Meantime, Chelsea couldn't resist a glance at Jasper. His gaze was locked on her, and she could detect that certain look in his eyes that meant...well, she didn't want to think about it, especially with two sisters, her mother and her father in proximity. Lawton, would be too far gone over the moon for Lanie to notice anything amiss with a mere sister.

Well, maybe not. Those in love had an uncanny sense of it in others. She looked at Lawton to find him looking at Jasper knowingly.

Oh dear. This would never do. She rose to take her dishes to the kitchen. She was just rinsing her plate and placing it and a few others in the dishwasher when she sensed Jasper standing behind her. He put his long arms around her and hugged her close. Fortunately, no one else was in the room for the moment.

Jasper's phone vibrated.

"Hello, Mom," he said.

"Just a minute. Yes, she's here. I love you, too. Of course. I'm always careful. Here's Chelsea." He handed her his phone.

"Hello?"

"Hi, Chelsea. Do you remember how many ice sculptures we agreed on with Ramon? He is saying we wanted seven, but I thought we had agreed on six."

"Actually, you agreed on eight. Right before we left, you said something about putting two in the foyer to greet the guests."

"That's right! I'm so glad I had you to help me with this even if only for a week or so. I sure wish you and Jasper could come."

"I'd love to be there, too, but I think we're needed here. Are you ready for any 'unplanned activities'?"

"Oh yes. You have no idea. I'd say more, but just suffice it to say we've hired extra help. Once this is over, we'll have a party at the house to discuss all the finer, *hidden* details."

"That sounds great," said Chelsea. She had not lost the emphasis on the word, "hidden," and that gave her some ideas.

She passed Jasper's phone back to him and was ready to go upstairs when Donnell began to speak.

"Just a minute everyone." Donnell stood in the kitchen doorway. He moved so those in the kitchen could rejoin those in the sun porch. Looking around, Chelsea realized that Charm and her entire crew, Frank and Jasper's security detail as well as Donnell's entire crew were present with the exception of Natalie and Tiffany. They still had guard duty.

Frank joined Donnell as he began to speak. "Today is the day we believe the terrorists will attack, but we are prepared. I want everyone going into this to feel confident that we have done everything in our power to stop these perpetrators."

"My team has made preparations, Frank's team is prepared, Andy, head of security at the Coliseum, is working with us, the police are on standby, and even the girls are ready."

The girls looked at each other, then at Trinity. Donnell interpreted the looks.

"Yes, Trinity told me, and I have no problem with what you have planned."

The girls looked at each other in relief. But Donnell continued.

"However, if anyone on my team or Frank's team tells you to do something, you are to do so immediately. Your life as well as the lives of others may be dependent on your immediate compliance." He glanced around at the group, making sure everyone understood.

"We've got eyes and ears everywhere, so let's stay calm, confident and focused on catching these bloody varmints today."

An hour later, they were all on their way to the Coliseum with the exception of Chelsea's sisters, parents, and brother.

Andy met Frank and Donnell at the back entrance. Looking at them and their teams, Chelsea saw by the clenched jaws and the coldness in their eyes that many of them had assumed a calculated detachment. They were all business now. Grimly serious, they took their pre-arranged places.

Chelsea stood on one side of the stage, her hand in her pocket, ready to pull her pistol. She could see Lanie on the other side, watching as Charm and Megan and the rest of the band plugged in their mikes and their instruments and prepared for the sound check.

Gina had elected to help Jonette and Sandy with the costumes and makeup. Chelsea knew she wasn't as thrilled about putting herself in danger as Lanie was. She had little Caden to think of. Lanie, on the other hand, thrived on excitement.

Each microphone, each amped instrument, and each of the electrical cords were checked. Charm and Megan started and stopped singing the same song five times. Each time, some small, technical glitch had to be eliminated. Watching, Chelsea realized how boring a sound check was.

In addition to checking the electric instruments and microphones and making adjustments on the sound board, the lighting was also discussed, especially for the first set of songs when effective lighting added to the dynamic tour de force of energy Charm wanted to create.

At last it was over, and the band retired to the bus to enjoy the picnic lunch Chelsea's mom had provided. Most of the band members either took short naps or loaded themselves with caffeine for the coming concert. Charm elected the former although she knew she probably wouldn't really sleep. But it was better than wasting her energy waiting for an unknown assailant or trying to second-guess what would happen next.

She consciously forced herself to relax every muscle in her body. She usually listened to music to block unwanted noise, but today she wanted to keep one ear open to hear what the rest of the girls were discussing.

Natalie stood guard while Gina, Megan, Lanie, and Chelsea played a card game, Sandy stretched out beside her, and Jonette, bless her, had decided to give Charm a massage. Sighing with pleasurable expectancy, Charm turned over on the makeshift sofa seat. She could still listen to the soothing Celtic melodies in her earpiece and enjoy the massage. Later she would listen to pulse-pounding rock to get her ready for the concert.

She must have dozed, for the next thing she knew, she was awakened by a huge boom.

Chapter Forty-One

Immediately, everyone except Sandy and Charm was on their feet, peering out the windows of the bus. Sandy sat up and jiggled Charm, who was sound asleep with the Celtic music still playing dreamily in her ears.

Inside the Coliseum, Donnell was talking on two blackberries and his walkie-talkie watch simultaneously.

"Hold your posts, everyone," he said.

Andy North appeared beside him. "It's a car in the parking lot of the hotel next door," he said. "It exploded and caught fire. We should hear a few more booms from other cars beside it," he said just as a gas tank from a nearby car exploded, sending another sonic sound into the air.

Donnell reported the situation to his group as well as to headquarters, again repeating his orders for everyone to stay at their posts. "This seems like a diversionary tactic to me," he said in explanation.

Natalie reported that the girls were fine and that Charm had slept through the initial explosion. The three ops who had the bus in their sights reported nothing amiss there.

In less than eight minutes, the police had arrived and had closed the road in front of the hotel and the Coliseum. Several people had been injured from parts flying off of the first car to explode, and two people who had been three cars down had been burned rather severely.

EMTs who had been lunching a few doors down were already on the scene treating injuries and preparing the more severely wounded for transportation to the hospital at MUSC.

After some consultation, authorities decided the concert would occur as scheduled although Charm's stage manager and Donnell had agreed to an unadvertised fifteen-minute delay on the start time. Alternate routes to the Coliseum were being broadcast on all major radio and television stations. Traffic would be snarled for a while.

"Are the dressing rooms clear?" came Natalie's voice. "Charm and the rest of the band need access to the dressing rooms soon to prepare for the concert."

Donnell ran his fingers through his hair. "Let me check and clear them just as a precaution before they move from the bus," he said.

Taking their "jobs" as Charm's new bodyguards seriously, Gina stood in the hall close to the back door, watching the comings and goings of the Coliseum staff. Lanie stood at the entrance to the stage just down the hall in the other direction from Gina while Chelsea stood right inside the doorway of Charm's dressing room.

She kept the door ajar slightly, blocking the view of Charm sitting in front of the mirrors in hot curlers and her undergarments while Jonette and Sandy worked on her hair and makeup. CeCe and Megan sat in the corner discussing two new makeup lines that had recently hit the market. CeCe liked the Astorian line and was trying to convince Megan to try it.

Charm tilted her head back and kept her eyes half closed while Jonette rubbed a thin layer of foundation on her shoulders and neck for the new off-shoulder costume with the daring décolletage Sandy had recently finished sewing. Count on CeCe to let nothing distract her from her favorite subjects of makeup and fashion, Charm thought.

Then she considered the latest events. "I'm not going to let them ruin this concert," she said half under her breath.

"That's the spirit!" said Sandy.

While Jonette was finishing Charm's makeup, Sandy busied herself with the three large wardrobe cases that stood in the corner opposite CeCe and Megan, making sure the costumes were in order and removing the first one from its hanger.

When Jonette had finished the makeup and was ready to start on Charm's hair, Sandy placed the first costume carefully over

Charm's shoulders and had her stand for the fasteners and zipper. Once she was satisfied with the costume, she signaled Megan.

"Ready, Sugar?" she asked, practicing some new, southern endearments and eliciting smiles from everyone. "Let's go to the next room and get you started," she said.

CeCe went with Megan and Sandy, leaving Charm alone with Jonette to finish her hair. Charm fiddled with her ipod, finding some hot rock and roll to rev her up for the concert.

Jonette had just unrolled the fourth curler and Chelsea had just entered the room when a grating noise caused all of them to look toward the wardrobe cases. A small figure dropped down from the air vent in front of them, brandishing a gun.

He was a slight, thin man with three days of dark stubble on his chin and a fanatical gleam in his eyes.

"Now I get both bitches at one time!" he said gloatingly as he shoved the door closed.

He motioned them to move to the back of the room where CeCe and Megan had been sitting.

A thousand thoughts whirled through Charm's mind. She could not, would not die at the hands of this crazy man. But what could she do? She noticed Chelsea still had her hands in the pockets of the windbreaker she wore with the gun concealed inside.

Don't use it, she tried to communicate. If Chelsea drew her gun, the man would take down at least one of them. None of them deserved to die.

She saw Chelsea's fingers in the left pocket move slightly. Wait! That was the pocket where she kept her phone. Had she hit the number and the button that would alert the others? It was their only hope.

"Even if I get killed, whole Coliseum will blow!" said the man, motioning them to get down on the floor. He fingered a small device that almost looked like a ballpoint pen. Belatedly, Charm realized it was a detonator. Apparently, the vest he wore was loaded with explosives.

He held the device high and began chanting words in what sounded like Arabic to Charm. She caught the word "Allah" and then with horror, she realized he was counting down.

At that precise moment, two things happened simultaneously: the door flew open, and a woman appeared from behind the wardrobe cases with a gun in her hands. A silk scarf covered most of her face.

As the man pivoted toward the door, firing his gun, a single shot from the gun of the woman took the man down before Chelsea had time to fire a shot from her drawn gun.

Gina, Natalie, and Lanie stood in the doorway, looking in amazement at the man's crumpled body on the floor and at the woman who was still in gun stance. She slowly lowered her gun and began to unwind the long, floral silk scarf from around her head and face.

"Aunt Olivia?" Charm exclaimed incredulously.

Aunt Olivia shook out the silk scarf, her hands shaking slightly. Then she crossed to Chelsea. "You are too young, child, to kill someone. I wouldn't want it on your conscience, but it will be on your record." She shoved her gun into Chelsea's hand and plucked Chelsea's gun from her hand. "Just a loan for now," she said.

Then she addressed Charm. "We will talk later tonight, Darling." She turned to include the girls at the door. "For now, I have never been here. Natalie, I must give you a message for your boss." She drew Natalie aside.

"You tell your boss, for his ears only, that Madame Orr was here. He will know what to tell authorities." She disappeared behind the costume cases again.

"Wait," called Charm. But when she went to look behind the wardrobe cases, her aunt was nowhere to be found.

Donnell was the first on the scene. When Natalie whispered the name Aunt Olivia had given, he immediately closed the door to the room. Lanie and especially Gina looked ashen. Quickly he moved so that they were facing him with their backs to the corpse. Then he asked to be told exactly what had happened.

When he was confident that he had the story correct, he told them, "I shouldn't have to say this, but I don't want you discussing what happened in this room with anyone, not even amongst yourselves."

"But what about Aunt Olivia?" asked Charm.

Her face was too pale for Donnell's liking, but he resolutely put away any personal observations and kept strictly to business.

"Your aunt obviously doesn't want her name involved in this in any way, so for now, Chelsea shot the terrorist when he was distracted by Natalie opening the door. Everyone got that?"

They all nodded mutely.

If anyone tries to talk to you about it, even the police, tell them you can't discuss it yet. If they insist, tell them I have to be present. Any questions?"

"When will we be allowed to talk about it? Ever?" asked Chelsea.

"We'll debrief after the concert," replied Donnell. "Now I want everyone to move to the next dressing room. We'll get the costume cases moved over there. Don't take anything else until the police take their pictures. Megan should have enough hairspray or whatever you need in her dressing room, right?"

Jonette nodded, and the girls filed out of the room trying to avert their eyes from the body of the man who had tried to kill them. Everything had happened so quickly. Now that it was over, they were all somewhat shaky.

Andy North was waiting for Donnell on the other side of the door. But Natalie motioned for him to give her a minute.

"What about the terrorist's claim that the whole Coliseum will blow? Do you think he was bluffing?"

"I think not," answered Donnell grimly.

"The terrorist said something to the girls that make us think more havoc is planned," said Donnell.

Andy nodded sagely.

"I'm going to let you and your crew work with the police while we look for other suspicious activity."

"Before you do," said Andy "we've had our eye on someone for about two weeks now, and I think it may be related."

Donnell lifted an eyebrow and waited for him to continue.

"One of the ushers spotted a man taking pictures of incoming and outgoing planes several weeks ago. The police put a tail on him, and apparently, he is also interested in flying. He has taken a plane up several times and seemed content to fly around the Charleston area. The police are over at the municipal airport right now because he is due to fly again tonight."

The pieces of the puzzle began to click into place in Donnell's mind. "Do you think he's going to try to bomb the concert tonight or maybe fly the plane into the Coliseum?"

"I'm thinking that's exactly what he has in mind."

"When will the police know?"

"Not until after the concert begins, I'm afraid. Where did the terrorist" Andy pointed to the room, "come from?"

"From the air conditioning vent," answered Donnell. "From the stubble on his chin, my guess is that he's been up there several days, maybe even up to a week."

"Probably went up during the concert last weekend," agreed Andy. "We did notice a loose vent grate in the men's restroom. It's such a shame we didn't catch that, but I'm glad the girls are safe."

"For now," said Donnell. He was still somewhat grim, the last two hours etching lines of weariness on his face. He gave a half salute and strode away to check in with each group. He wanted to stop by Megan's dressing room, but he knew Natalie had everything under control there.

Back in Megan's dressing room, nerves were stretched. Jonette, Megan, and CeCe knew an attempt by a terrorist had been made.

"How can you stay so calm?" CeCe asked her sister.

"Because I have to perform for several thousand fans in about an hour, and they deserve their money's worth," Charm said. Unknowingly, she set the tone for the whole team.

Colin came by to give Charm the ten-minute warning for the Charmed Circle Fan Club meet and greet.

"Let one of us come with you," suggested CeCe. "That way, the focus won't be totally on you, and besides aren't shared burdens lighter? Maybe I'll get a little glory as your little sister, you know."

Charm gave her a hug. "Thank you, Little Sis. Megan you come too. We'll be the three musketeers."

"Group hug," said Megan.

Charm opened her arms, and all the girls joined for a big hug. When the circle broke, they all had tears in their eyes.

"No tears, no tears," said Jonette. "I don't want to redo all that makeup." She fanned Charm's face and then Megan's with a sheet of music Megan had been studying.

Donnell appeared to escort the girls to the meet and greet. He had taken the time to put on a suit jacket over the black t-shirt he was wearing for the job. Charm was, once again, impressed that he would take the time to dress up for her.

Charm was amused with how her fans flocked to talk to CeCe. They probably found her more approachable. She overheard one girl gushingly ask what it was like to be sister to someone famous. CeCe handled the questions with aplomb, never taking any of it seriously.

"That was fun," she said when it was all over. She joined the fans to be escorted to her reserved seat with the rest of her family, still chattering with several of them.

Donnell watched carefully as Megan joined the rest of band onstage. Charm stood quietly beside him. He pulled her into a quick hug, taking care of her dress and her makeup.

"I love you, Darling. Go knock it out!" he said encouragingly.

And Charm did. As soon as she was on stage, thoughts of anything but the music and communicating with her audience flew out of her head.

Thirty minutes into the concert, Donnell got the call for which he had been waiting. Their man had been apprehended. With him he had been carrying two huge duffel bags loaded with enough explosives to take out the Coliseum and everything else within a half mile radius. That would have included Tanger outlet mall, the airport, and part of Charleston Air Force Base.

Many lives had been spared.

Chapter Forty-Two

The news trickled to the crew, mostly via text messages. The relief was palpable. However, they still had to answer the questions of the police and run the gauntlet of the media.

Since Donnell and Jasper both had previous experience in these respective areas, following the concert, Donnell made short work of the routine police questioning, and Jasper handled the media.

Chelsea became the heroine of the hour, and the media quickly capitalized on her connection to Summerville. The rest of the family was able to leave without much fuss or fanfare, but Jasper finally had to commandeer a ride in a police car for Chelsea. Since he was no longer needed at the Coliseum, Frank told him to enjoy the ride back to the Merrill residence. With a grin, he suggested they both ride in the back of the car, just for the novelty of it.

His arm securely tucked around Chelsea, the first thing Jasper did was to call his parents.

Everyone was concerned about the possibility that the Midsummer's Eve Ball had been a target.

Even though the time was long past midnight, his mother answered on the first ring.

"Jasper, Honey? Are you and Chelsea and the band okay? We've been so worried about you. We've been hearing bits and pieces all evening."

"We're all fine, Mom. We have two terrorists, one dead and one in custody. It just took forever to get through the media. We're on our way back to the Merrill's now. What about the ball? Any activity there?"

At this point, Chelsea made Jasper turn his phone to speaker.

"Oh, Honey, you have no idea. They disguised themselves as caterers and tried to rob everyone first before blowing up the place. But we had sharpshooters stationed above the ceiling tiles, some of our own men and women. Each one was assigned a certain area, so on your dad's signal, they fired simultaneously."

"Wow! That must have caused quite a response from those being robbed."

"It sure did! After they recovered from their fright at hearing six guns fire at the same time, they gave those men and women a five-minute ovation! Too bad they all disappeared before the police descended." She chuckled.

Your dad had to do some fast talking to keep their names from the press. The police are taking credit for exemplary work, but that's the way we like it. We just left the place. Here, let me turn this thing on speaker so your Dad can talk too."

"Good job, Dad," said Jasper. "Did Corey show? He wanted to join the action."

"He was one of the sharpshooters."

Jasper could hear his mother voicing her disapproval.

"Now, Nell, don't get upset. He was determined to be in on the action, and he's had plenty of target practice."

"I'm just glad everyone is safe. I feel as if I could sleep a week after this. But I'm sure we'll be hearing more. Aren't nine other hit sites unaccounted for yet?"

"We'll probably only get snatches of sleep tonight," said Jasper "between messages on our phones and whatever is released to the news."

"Tomorrow's another day, Son. Snatch whatever sleep you can," his father advised.

"I will, Dad. Love you and Mom."

"Love you, too, Son. Chelsea, too."

"Thanks," said Chelsea. "Love you two, too!"

The connection was terminated, and Chelsea snuggled against Jasper's shoulder. She knew exactly what Nell meant about sleeping for a week.

But the media attention was not over. Some reporter had discovered her home address and snapped a few pictures as she stepped from the police car. She ran to the back door, away from prying eyes.

Inside, Galeah was setting up a buffet for the hungry crews to eat as they arrived. Sub sandwiches, chips, and platters of melon, berries and apple slices along with gallons of iced tea and coffee made a simple but nourishing meal.

Thirty minutes later, everyone was squeezed into the living room with the curtains securely drawn against over-eager reporters, watching the news. Lawson had conjured three other TVs so they could watch several channels.

Listening to the conversation, Chelsea realized that Uncle Craig's Homeland Security team still hadn't reported an all-clear. When Donnell and Natalie arrived, Chelsea expected to have all her questions answered about Charm's aunt, but she soon realized that although Charm's family was present, Aunt Olivia was not. And neither Donnell nor Natalie seemed inclined to discuss it.

When Chelsea's picture appeared on the screen and her apparent heroism was reported, everyone cheered. Chelsea looked to Donnell and then Natalie to set straight the record, but Natalie caught her eye and nodded her head, "No."

Charm looked at her with a knowing gleam, but she, too, kept silent as well as Jonette. Natalie crossed to Lanie and Lawton; Gina had gone upstairs to check on her sleeping son.

So. Apparently she would forever claim the glory with only six others the wiser. No, make that eight with Aunt Olivia, herself, knowing the truth; moreover, she refused to hold back the truth from Jasper.

But then everyone's attention was claimed when news of a security guard inside the Supreme Court Building sacrificing his life to tackle a suicide bomber was reported. The decision on *Hassan vs. the United States* had been given by the judges, and did the parties involved not like their decision or was this a terrorist attack asked the newscaster.

"It's a terrorist attack," everyone chorused in answer.

"Which of those Jewish brothers was that one, Chelsea?" asked Charm.

"'Dan' was the lawgiver. You were the 'Rahab' on the list. 'Benjamin' was the contaminated vaccines to Fort Hood, I'm sure of it. The dam dude would be 'Issachar.'"

That story was interrupted by a newsflash about a plane exploding at an LAX terminal; the extent of the damage and the toll on lives was yet unknown.

"That might be the Hollywood guy," said Jasper doubtfully.

"Could be if maybe they were planning to attack or suicide bomb Hollywood," said Chelsea. "And that would account for 'Rueben.'"

In other news, some cell phone disruption was reported. It was sporadic but widespread enough to cause some consternation. In addition, Bank of America patrons were reporting denial of access to their accounts. Aha, thought Jasper. The al-Qaeda geeks had scored some major points in those areas.

"That would be 'Naphtali' and 'Gad,'" said Chelsea. "Seven of the thirteen accounted."

The news flashed to the averted robbery at the Midsummer's Eve Ball. No channel seemed to make the connection between the events although some reporters were mentioning terrorist activity in connection with cell phone usage and banking problems.

"Who was the cruel brother?" asked Charm suddenly. "Maybe he fits the Midsummer's Eve Ball. To try to rob the people before killing them all is very cruel, and many important people were at that event."

"The cruel brother was 'Simeon,'" responded Chelsea. "It certainly seems to fit."

CNN was now covering the unfolding story of the LAX airport explosion. But other stations were reporting a religious conference in Texas being attacked in a Columbine-type raid, and two Texas oil refineries were on fire. Another station was reporting the bombing of an armored car production plant in Michigan with large contracts from the military.

"There's 'Levi' and 'Asher,'" said Natalie. "And I'm willing to bet the armored car plant is 'Joseph.' Isn't he the brother who 'protected' his brothers?" She crooked her fingers in quotation mark symbols with her last words.

"Only two more to go," said Lanie. "I sure hope more civilians won't be injured."

Just then all three stations went to local news, carrying the same story. Another man had been arrested at the small municipal airport located beside Charleston International Airport and the Air

Force Base. He had been about to take off in another small, rented plane loaded with explosives. No one was sure of the target, but the crater left by the detonation would have made the Oklahoma bombing seem small.

Some site in the southeast had dodged a major hit. Conjecture about the intended hit site was rampant, but many believed it had been the nuclear site on the Georgia/South Carolina border while others were sure it was either the Charleston Port Authority or Charleston Air Force Base.

"No wonder we haven't heard from Uncle Craig. He's going to be up all night with this," said Kielah. "Poor Aunt Clara."

They watched a few more minutes, but no other pieces of relevant information were available yet. Lanie yawned hugely. "I have to go home. I have to go in to work tomorrow at ten," she said, making a face.

Gradually, the room emptied. Galeah hurried to clean the kitchen. Jonette and Sandy helped before they retired. When no more news appeared to be coming, Frank's group headed to the bunk house, and Donnell's group, after a final check with headquarters, did the same. Chelsea gave Jasper a quick kiss goodnight, not even considering any watchful eyes. She found Gina asleep beside her son on the roll-away bed placed in her room. She barely had time to kick off her shoes before she snuggled into the inviting comforter and fell soundly asleep.

Charm and Donnell were soon the only ones left. Donnell was taking the first watch. Frank and some of his men would take over around four.

"Is it really over?" asked Charm tremulously.

"I haven't received final instructions from my boss, but I believe it is," said Donnell, brushing a strand of hair from Charm's pale face. "I'm going to be busy with huge amounts of paperwork for the next week and so will Frank's team, but can we keep the group together long enough to make our announcement?"

"Let's have a party at the bungalow tomorrow," said Charm as she swayed toward him.

Donnell bent slightly and turned off the last TV. Then he cupped Charm's face in his hands, leaning his forehead against hers.

"I wanted so much to be in that dressing room with you this evening, propriety be shamed. Do you mind that I wasn't?"

"Aunt Olivia surely surprised me," said Charm pulling away from him and frowning. "Why couldn't we talk about her?"

"She's a double agent. Didn't you guess that?"

Charm shook her head.

"She came to see me when she arrived stateside. She confessed to knowing that you had the paper. She had followed the men who were planning these attacks to Italy. She saw them at that little bistro in Rome, realized they had left one of their sheets on the table, and was ready to retrieve it when you and your crew entered. She was so flustered when she realized you were at the table."

"Why didn't she come and talk to me? It would have been a great cover."

"She saw Ms. Gamarov and knew to reveal herself would not be wise. She watched you tear the sheet of paper in half and take part of it with you, and she feared for your life. Sure enough, you began to receive threats."

"Did I tear it in half? I don't remember that," said Charm.

"Actually," continued Donnell, "she had determined the date of the attacks long before we did. She's been to Charleston several times on reconnaissance so she could help you when you would need it most."

"She took Andy North into her confidence, and he had a small, cleverly concealed door built into your dressing room. They even planned where to put your wardrobe cases. I didn't even think to do more than a casual check behind those. Fortunately, the enemy didn't either."

"When Andy had a tail put on the man videotaping planes, he realized Olivia's concerns were deadly accurate. He was so glad to have us here even though he didn't reveal anything to me about your aunt. I don't think he trusted too many people at that point."

"I wonder what made him trust her? He didn't even know her well."

Donnell looked at her in amusement. "Your entire family, including you, Darling, carries themselves with such confidence and authority. A man would have to be made of iron to resist any of you." He bent forward to kiss her, but Charm wanted more of her questions answered.

"What about the name she used?" asked Charm who had been standing close enough to Natalie to hear the whispered name. She couldn't bring herself to say it: "Madame Orr."

"That is the name by which your aunt is known internationally. I knew immediately with whom we were working although I didn't realize until I talked to Andy that she is your aunt. You must never reveal that you know the real woman behind that name."

"We'll have to caution the rest of the girls once again," said Charm.

Natalie already talked to Gina and Lanie. We just need to talk to Jonette and Chelsea, but I'm rather confident Chelsea won't be saying much to anyone except, of course, Jasper."

"I wonder why she chose to reveal her name now?"

"She would best answer that question, but I think your aunt wants to retire from the spy business. It does get wearing, concealing yourself, sometimes from those you love most. Any more questions?" he asked testily.

Charm tilted her head to the side and thought for a moment. "No, I can't think of any. But I do want to get you back for those kisses."

"Oh? And how do you propose to do that?"

Her eyes lighted mischievously. "Let me show you." And she did, driving him to the very edge of his self-control.

In the lonely watches of the night, a vessel neared San Francisco harbor. From the fog, a small craft fired a missile which nearly turned the vessel into a floating funeral pyre for thousands of military men and women.

But in split second timing, the captain had seen a blip on the radar, and to avoid missing a motorboat piloted by besottedly drunk idiots, the vessel stilled its motors, and the missile hit the bottom of the sea without detonating.

The small craft simply disappeared from radar. Later, the captain realized the enemy's error in calculating altitude for detonation had spared the West Coast from an underwater blast and the resulting tidal wave. Some Clemson engineering students finally determined how the small craft had disappeared, but the captain loved a good fog the rest of his life.

On the East Coast, a small plane had been trying to enter the no-fly zone above the White House all evening. On the third attempt, it suddenly erupted into flames and went down. Pilots of security forces for the President were cleared of firing on the small plane, but the mystery remained although some people reported seeing a ground to air flash seconds before the plane was engulfed in flames.

Morning, which didn't arrive until after eleven for most of them, brought a slew of reporters to the Merrill residence. Galeah finally turned off their home phone.

Martha had already solved the problem of getting them to the bungalow for the party Charm insisted everyone attend. They were driven to Charleston Air Force Base and flown down to Beaufort where several cars were waiting to take them to their destination.

That destination had been changed at the last minute to the Lowther's home when Charm's dad spotted someone in the woods. It was only a lost hiker, but he was taking no chances.

Chapter Forty-Three

"And you use a shot of bourbon to add a unique flavor?" asked Catherine. She was in a deep conversation with Mrs. Dan and Nell as they discussed regional recipes. Catherine was already planning on doing a week of shows on cuisine from the South.

Nell, Carter, Preston and Corey had flown down for this very special occasion, and the Merrills had been invited as well.

Most of the crew was seated outside on the wide porch. The ceiling fans wafted lazy currents of air, stirring the huge baskets of ferns that had been hung at intervals. Observing everyone, Donnell was impressed with how relaxed everyone was, so different from just two days before.

Mrs. Dan came to the door and announced dessert being served. "But before we do that, we have a special announcement, so we want everyone to come inside."

As soon as everyone was in, Mr. Lowther turned to Donnell who was standing with Charm beside him in the center of the large, open area between the kitchen and the family room.

"Two days ago, I broke some rules of Interpol," he began with a very serious expression on his face. "I did not know how this assignment would end. It could have ended with terrorists on the loose and any of us dead. So after a discussion with Christian, and without consulting my superiors at Interpol, I came to a decision." At this point, Donnell looked at Christian, who began to speak.

"Donnell did a very wise thing; he discussed some things with Charm, and with great pleasure, my wife and I would like to announce the engagement of our daughter, Charm Marie Dumotte to Donnell McKinnon."

The room erupted in applause and congratulations. Charm pulled the ring from its chain around her neck, and with great ceremony, Donnell placed it in the appropriate place on the third finger of her left hand.

When the decibels diminished, Carter stepped forward. "I want to thank the Dumottes for inviting us and the Lowthers for allowing us to stay in their home. The hospitality of the deep South is definitely underrated. But my son asked us to bring something special with us, and after consulting with several other people, I've brought it here tonight."

Carter handed Jasper a small box. Jasper, who was holding tightly to Chelsea's hand, went down on one knee, looked up into her blushing face, and said, "I've talked to your mother and father and told them how much I love you. Will you do me the honor, Chelsea Merrill, of marrying me?"

"Yes," Chelsea managed to say faintly, and once again the cheers and congratulations raced merrily from all corners of the room.

Jasper had just managed to put his great-grandmother's ring on Chelsea's finger when Mr. Dan hit the side of a wine goblet with a knife. As everyone quieted, he held up his phone and hit the speaker button.

"Good evening, everyone," said a voice that they all knew well. "I want to congratulate each one of you on your exceptional service not only to this great country, the United States of America, but also for your loyalty and passion for the great cause of freedom and liberty around the world. Each one of you has contributed to this cause, sometimes at great personal sacrifice."

They all thought of William, and Nell and Carter thought of their fallen comrades.

"I understand that my aide is present. Is that true?"

"Yes, sir," answered Chelsea.

"I would tell you that you are fired," he said, and everyone laughed. "But I think I must commend you for your bravery and commitment, and if I fired you, I'm sure millions of Americans would call for my impeachment. So instead, I hear congratulations are in order on your upcoming nuptials."

Chelsea and Jasper looked dumbfounded, but Nell simply looked smug.

Mr. Dan said something, and the President spoke again: "Donnell McKinnon of Interpol and Charm Dumotte are engaged, too? Well, congratulations, to you as well."

"Thank you, sir," said Donnell.

"God bless all of you. When you finish your paperwork, tell your bosses that I said to give you all a week of vacation with pay."

Everyone cheered except Charlie who had his eye on a large slice of pecan pie.

The End

Nell's Incredible Quiche Recipe

1 9-inch pie shell	1 ½ cups of milk/light cream
4 eggs, beaten	½ teaspoon parsley
1 cup/4 oz. shredded cheese	½ teaspoon minced onion
1 cup of crabmeat, imitation crabmeat, chicken or other desired meat (may also use vegetables)	½ teaspoon salt

Prick inside of the pie shell on bottom and sides with a fork. Bake shell at 450° for 5 minutes or until light golden brown. Remove from oven and allow to cool while preparing filling.

Put cheese and meat or vegetable in pie shell. To the beaten eggs add milk, herbs, onion and salt. Beat until well blended; pour over mixture in pie shell. Bake at 375° 30 to 35 minutes or until knife inserted near center comes out clean. Let stand 5 minutes before serving.

Note: Nell likes to add herbs that she grows in her garden such as rosemary, basil or dill to her quiches.

Nell's Quick Pie Crust Recipe

2 cups all-purpose flour
¼ teaspoon salt
¾ cup of shortening
5 Tablespoons of ice-cold water; more if desired

Sift together flour and salt into a 2-quart bowl. Add shortening and chop it in with pastry blender or fork until mixture looks mealy. Add 2 T. of the cold water; mix in lightly with fork; add more water until dough sticks together and forms a ball. Use as little water as possible, especially in the South where humidity is high. Roll out on lightly floured surface; use as desired. Makes two 9-inch pie shells.

Tasty leftover: Roll out leftover dough; dot with butter, sprinkle with sugar, cinnamon, and nuts (if desired). Roll up like cinnamon roll dough, lengthwise, pinching dough together where it ends at the top. Bake at 350° until light golden brown.

Nell's Best Ever Pumpkin Bread

3 cup sugar
1 cup of oil
1 teaspoon cinnamon
1 ¼ teaspoons salt
4 eggs

⅔ cup water
3 teaspoons soda
3 ½ cups of flour
2 cups pumpkin
1 cup nuts, if desired
(add last)

Combine all ingredients in a large bowl and mix well with electric beater at low speed. Grease 3 bread pans and divide batter evenly between the pans. Bake 1 hour at 350°; let cool before removing from pans.

Nectar of the South Fruit-Syrup for Infused Teas

This is more of a suggested, try-it until-you-get-it-how-you-like-it recipe.

Combine 1 cup of sugar with one cup of any desired fruit in a saucepan. Add enough water to cover. Slowly bring mixture to a boil, then immediately reduce to lowest possible heat. Allow to reduce, checking frequently. For pulpy fruits, strain before adding to tea.

I have used this recipe (which was given to me by a Southern chef word of mouth) with limes, peaches, and strawberries (individually, of course!). I purchased small spouted containers in which to put the syrups for storage in the refrigerator and also for serving. Guests can use as much as they want to flavor their tea.

Don't miss the next book in the *Secrets* series, *Secret Agendas*, or the prequel, *Secrets of Two Sisters*, coming soon!

Here's a sneak peak of *Secret Agendas*!

Chapter One

As soon as she saw the dark blue car drive slowly by the house, she knew. Was it just pure luck that she happened to be standing by the baby grand piano in the front room, gazing through the sheer curtains at the street, but really at nothing at all?

She had been remembering something. Yes, she had seen a picture on the stand beside the piano, one of her and Bob when they had first met in college. They had been madly in love, were still, in fact.

And for that reason, when his attorney practice had grown and he had started to try bigger and bigger cases, they had put together a safety plan.

She walked purposefully toward the kitchen and the small alcove where she kept her pocketbook, emergency fanny pack, and cell phone, sweeping them all into her arms just as she had practiced so many times.

Flipping open the cell phone, she speed dialed a message to Brian's and Brant's teachers at the small private school they attended. She did the same for Brianna's pre-school. She sent Bob a coded message as well.

He was in court this morning giving opening statements for the Merrill property rights case. Was this situation connected to the case? Bob and his team had been researching, preparing for this day for slightly more than six months now.

The opposition was very powerful with the backing of many members of the United Nations. As his fame grew as a Constitutional attorney, so did the danger for his family. The sound of a car door opening sent her scurrying up the stairs.

In less than two minutes she was in the small hiding place Bob had created in the third floor attic. Finishing the large room, they had bought furniture and empty trunks to "store" there; their truly private belongings were safely stored in another state.

But Bob had built a three-foot walkway that ran along the front and sides of the house. Carpeting had made it a quiet place to walk, and a fake wall made of taut and painted fabric at the back of the closet leading to this walkway would fool anyone who gave it a casual glance.

She heard the motor of their car idling. It sounded like it was on the other side of the street. Good. The two men she had seen would either have to bring their car closer, or they would have to get out.

Closing her eyes since she couldn't see them anyway, she willed her ears to hear every detail of their movements. The other car door opened.

Now they were ringing the doorbell, once, twice. Shouldering the door didn't work. Of course it wouldn't. Bob had done everything possible to keep his family safe, including a specialized door and frame. Pop, pop, pop. They were using a gun.

She heard their steps as they moved through the house. The kitchen, dining room, living room, den, screened porch. Please don't hurt the kittens, Bianca and Butterball, she thought.

They were coming up the stairs to the second floor and the bedrooms. Four bedrooms, three baths, five closet doors opened and closed.

Now they were on the stairs leading to the attic.

She barely breathed as she heard the door to the "closet" where she was hiding open and then shut.

"...not here," she heard one man say to the other.

The attic door shut. A creak sounded on the stair landing. Would they finally leave? Now they were on the first floor again.

The door to the garage opened and shut. Her car was safely parked there, a dead giveaway that she was not far away.

Silence for three long minutes—she knew, for she was counting the seconds. What were they doing? A faint metallic sound. Then she heard footsteps striding confidently down the steps and across the street.

Two car doors shut. The motor revved, and the car moved down the road.

She counted to sixty and then left her hiding place. She ran to the bedroom. Nothing had been touched.

Picking up a packed backpack from the back of the closet, a small case with her jewelry, and a manila envelope with all their important papers, she headed down the stairs toward the kitchen and nearly opened the garage door when she caught the barest whiff of gas and a faint ticking sound.

Oh no. She was certain the house was going to explode any minute.

Now she raced through the screen porch, kicking the jamb to keep it open. Hopefully the kittens would think it was a game and follow her, but she had no time to check.

Out the back door, down the hillside, and through the woods in back she ran. Heading to the right, she crossed a creek and up the next hill.

When the explosion hit, she didn't even look back even though like Lot's wife she wanted to. A wave of nausea hit her, but she clamped her mouth closed. She would not give in to it.

She cut across Mrs. Crosby's backyard while fishing in the fanny pack for another set of keys. She had them.

She unlocked Bob's old car that Mrs. Crosby allowed them to park in her drive and drove as sedately as possible to the parking lot where she was to meet the children. Would they be there?

They were. She thanked the teachers from each school, and then they were off. The children were, mercifully, quiet. She had practiced this with them several times in the past year; she could see in the rearview mirror that Brian, thirteen and the oldest, had questions. But he would wait quietly. Poor boy. He was most aware of the danger that they faced.

Brant, at ten was more exuberant, but he idolized his older brother and would do exactly as Brian did sans the concern and worry Brian kept to himself.

Brianna wanted her blanket. Brian retrieved it for her, and she settled down in her booster seat with her thumb in her mouth.

All at once, Belinda Worthington began to shake all over. The stress of the last fifteen minutes was catching up with her. She just couldn't fall apart now. She had to put some distance between her children and those who wanted to hurt them.

Chapter Two

Corey Peters-Templeton was the most pompous, arrogant man Gina Galbraith had ever met. But she couldn't stop thinking about him. He had piloted the plane that her cousin, Chelsea, had sent to pick up her and her sister, Gwen; her cousins, Kielah and Lindy; her mom; and Aunt Galeah for a gala weekend in Virginia to plan the wedding.

He had audaciously and impudently kissed her before she had disembarked from the plane. He had gently, but insistently poked fun at her cautious, carefully constructed plan for life which was so opposite his gung-ho, no-holds-allowed, caution-to-the-winds approach to life.

He had splashed water in her face when they were standing by the fountain on the waterfront in downtown Charleston, he had listened to her seriously when she was describing the multitude of problems she was encountering in the teaching profession, and he had captured her heart with his sensitivity to Caden, the little son she was raising on her own.

Chelsea and Jasper's wedding was six days away, and since the Virginia trip five months ago, as the maid of honor not only had she been thrown into his company on many more occasions, but she found herself thinking of him when she should be concentrating on the circle of children listening to the next chapter in the *Magic Tree House* book she was reading aloud in class or on what the principal was saying during the teachers' meeting.

Now, Harry Morrison, her fiancé, would be arriving tomorrow for the wedding. What was she going to do?

Her cousin, Chelsea Merrill, had announced her engagement in June to Secret Service agent, Jasper Peters-Templeton. Gina had been glad to be part of the events that led to their engagement, but she had finally finished her teacher's training at Charleston Southern University, and she was in the middle of her first year of teaching. She wanted to concentrate on her own life goals and dreams for a while, thank you very much.

Myers Elementary School had granted her a position teaching third grade, and she was thrilled that she finally had the financial means to care for three-year-old Caden the way she wanted.

The phone rang. It would be her mother calling to check on her and Caden. Her mother, Gloria Galbraith, had just taken a new job as a nurse at TriCounty Hospital, third floor coronary unit. Mom would just be going on duty to care for her heart surgery patients. Gina smiled to herself, remembering how her mother had cared for her dolls' "heart ailments" with a stethoscope and Band-Aids. If only life were that simple now.

"Miss me, Honey?" asked a male voice, startling Gina out of the fond memory.

"N-n-no," she stuttered, caught totally off guard. Darn. Corey's calls, infrequent as they were, always seemed to come when she was thinking of him, making her aware of her jittery response. Had he guessed her reaction and enjoyed teasing her, or was this just his way of talking to girls?

"Here I am, pining away for a kind word from you, and you can't even lie and say you've missed me," he said teasingly.

"I've been hectically busy," retorted Gina. "The wedding is Saturday, but I'm still teaching until Thursday. Where are you, anyway? Shouldn't you be here already to support your brother, Jasper, as he marries?"

"Who says I'm not here?"

Gina's heart skipped a beat, and she looked around her tiny apartment, expecting to see him pop from behind the loveseat or the sofa. Silly, she chided herself. Still, she moved to the window and peered out cautiously.

"You just checked out your front window to see, didn't you?"

Gina drew her hand from the curtains guiltily. She straightened and threw her shoulders back. She would not let him disturb her.

"Where are you, Corey?" she asked in her best 'teacher' voice.

"Right now I'm standing at the window of one of the bedrooms of Flowertown Bed and Breakfast looking at the seminary across the street."

"Really?" She couldn't quite squelch the eagerness in her voice.

"Really. I just flew down with Jasper. Since he's going to be mooning around Chelsea all night at the Merrill's, I thought maybe you and I could go out to eat, catch a movie, walk around town or the park or whatever you'd like."

Gina's spirits lifted then sank. She had so much to do to prepare for the substitute teacher coming in for her on Friday. And could she possibly get one of her cousins or her sister to babysit on such short notice?

And she really should consider the fact that people were beginning to pair them together when she was engaged to Harry. But she so wanted to go.

Corey sensed her hesitation. "We don't have to stay out all night if you have some things to do for school. Maybe I can help you," he suggested using all his persuasive powers.

"I still need to get a babysitter, and Harry's coming home tomorrow," she began, weakening.

"Harry isn't my brother's best man, I am. Isn't entertaining me part of your job description as maid of honor?" he said in a wheedling tone. "How about if I call you back in thirty minutes?"

"Okay. That will give me enough time to make some calls."

"Just don't think your way out of it," Corey advised before he hung up. "I need a relaxing evening. I've been flying all day, and now I need to unwind. You really are relaxing to be around, Gina." Then he hung up.

Gina stared at the phone. As usual, it was all about him with a backhanded compliment so she couldn't really get mad at him. His arrogance was still very annoying even though she knew he took his flying seriously.

What had she let herself in for now? Well, she had to talk to Corey sometime. Harry would be arriving tomorrow, and while Corey knew about her fiancé, Harry, Harry knew nothing about the way she and Corey had been thrown together time after time since July.

He had even flown down more than a few times in the past months on his own, taking time to visit Grandpa and Grandma Merrill on the farm. Poor dears. They needed all the encouragement they could get right now with the County trying to take away their property rights.

They brightened every time they saw him. He was brilliant, really, and often argued the case back and forth with their attorney. He should have become an attorney himself. But he had told her he couldn't stand the pressure of a trial. He'd rather throw his dad's money around, wheeling and dealing in real estate.

It was all about property. She sighed, but then she chided herself for wool-gathering. She needed to make some phone calls and procure a babysitter.

Ten minutes later, her sister, Gwen, had agreed to come to her small apartment off of Main Street. Gina knew that in another ten minutes all the cousins would know she was going out with Corey that evening.

She couldn't, wouldn't consider it a date. How could she when she was engaged to another man? It was her duty, she decided, as maid of honor. Oh, how Corey would hate being considered a duty!